"Joseph shouldn't be s̶ ̶ ̶ ̶ ̶ ̶ ̶ ̶ ̶ ̶ ̶
She managed a wobbly sm̶ ̶ ̶ ̶ ̶ ̶ ̶ ̶ ̶ nor should you. You've been
incredibly kind, Mr. Kendrick, but I do not hold you to any
obligations you feel you may have—"

He moved so quickly she barely had time to gasp. A
moment later, she was sprawled inelegantly on his lap,
staring up into his glittering gaze.

"What are you doing, sir?" Her voice came out more like
a squeak than a demand.

"You *are* daft if you think I give a damn about any of
that," he said. "And Joseph loves you, silly girl. He'd kill me
if I let you leave."

She tried to steady herself by bracing her hands on his
massive shoulders. "That's . . . that's very kind of you. And
I know you believe you made a commitment to me, but you
didn't. And . . . and it's silly to think you or any man should
wish to marry me. Or want to. I'm not the marrying kind,
you see. I'm . . ."

She trailed off when his gaze narrowed to ice-blue slits.

"Are you quite finished?" he asked with heavy sarcasm.

She felt the first stirrings of irritation. "I'm not sure."

"I am."

"I don't see how."

"Because of this."

He swooped down and captured her mouth in a soul-
searing kiss that blasted every thought and every reservation
straight to oblivion.

Books by Vanessa Kelly

MASTERING THE MARQUESS

SEX AND THE SINGLE EARL

MY FAVORITE COUNTESS

HIS MISTLETOE BRIDE

The Renegade Royals

SECRETS FOR SEDUCING A ROYAL BODYGUARD

CONFESSIONS OF A ROYAL BRIDEGROOM

HOW TO PLAN A WEDDING FOR A ROYAL SPY

HOW TO MARRY A ROYAL HIGHLANDER

The Improper Princesses

MY FAIR PRINCESS

THREE WEEKS WITH A PRINCESS

THE HIGHLANDER'S PRINCESS BRIDE

Clan Kendrick

THE HIGHLANDER WHO PROTECTED ME

THE HIGHLANDER'S CHRISTMAS BRIDE

Anthologies

AN INVITATION TO SIN
(with Jo Beverley, Sally MacKenzie, and Kaitlin O'Riley)

Published by Kensington Publishing Corporation

THE
Highlander's
Christmas
Bride

VANESSA KELLY

ZEBRA BOOKS
KENSINGTON PUBLISHING CORP.
www.kensingtonbooks.com

ZEBRA BOOKS are published by

Kensington Publishing Corp.
119 West 40th Street
New York, NY 10018

All Kensington titles, imprints, and distributed lines are available at special quantity discounts for bulk purchases for sales promotion, premiums, fund-raising, educational, or institutional use.

Special book excerpts or customized printings can also be created to fit specific needs. For details, write or phone the office of the Kensington Sales Manager: Attn.: Sales Department. Kensington Publishing Corp., 119 West 40th Street, New York, NY 10018. Phone: 1-800-221-2647.

Zebra and the Z logo Reg. U.S. Pat. & TM Off.

First Printing: November 2019
ISBN-13: 978-1-4201-4703-2
ISBN-10: 1-4201-4703-X

ISBN-13: 978-1-4201-4704-9 (eBook)
ISBN-10: 1-4201-4704-8 (eBook)

10 9 8 7 6 5 4 3 2 1

Printed in the United States of America

*This one is for Trish, my amazing big sister,
and Beryl, the sister of my heart.
You are two of the best people on Planet Earth.*

ACKNOWLEDGMENTS

Publishing is a crazy business, so I'm particularly grateful to my agent and editor for their skill, kindness, and sanity. I'm also thankful for the wonderful staff at Kensington, and for their help in bringing my books to the world. And the art department—good Lord, you folks are terrific!

Finally, to my dear husband—I WOULD lose my marbles without you!

Chapter One

The edict was delivered in a tone of mild regret, completely at odds with the appalling effect it would have on her life.

"But . . . but you cannot just kick me out," Donella Haddon stammered. "What the devil would I do with myself?"

A spasm crossed Reverend Mother's dignified features. "Remember where you are, my child."

Donella would have been able to describe the prioress's study in the Convent of the Sacred Heart even if blindfolded. After all, she'd received a fair share of gentle but guilt-inducing scolds in this very room.

"That is precisely my point," Sister Bernard intoned. "Our dear sister never remembers where she is."

As Novice Mistress, Sister Bernard was Donella's immediate superior and the bane of her existence. She stood behind Reverend Mother's chair, her spare features obscured by her cowl and the sun shining through the window at her back. Donella could easily imagine Sister's disapproving frown, because she'd seen that on a regular basis, too.

"My final vows are only a few months away." Donella

waved her arms, her wide sleeves flapping like a sparrow's wings. "It would be an utter disaster to turn me away now. I've given up *everything* to be here."

When Mother's iron-gray eyebrows arched up, Donella winced. The prioress was a truly saintly woman, but no one could argue with those eyebrows. They conveyed volumes, and the message was that Donella's goose was indeed cooked.

"My dear, such dramatics are unnecessary. I've discussed your progress with Sister Bernard and Sister Agnes—"

"Oh, drat," muttered Donella.

Sister Agnes was the Mistress of Liturgical Music and even more exacting than Sister Bernard. If those two had lined up against her, Donella's goose was scorched beyond recognition.

"And we're all in agreement," Mother firmly continued. "We believe that life in an enclosed order may not be the correct path for you. Some time in the outside world would be helpful in ascertaining your true vocation."

"Or if you even have one," Sister Bernard said. "In my opinion, that remains to be seen."

Donella clamped her lips tight against the impulse to stick her tongue out at the old . . . the good woman. Sister Bernard had never trusted Donella's vocation.

In truth, it was hard to argue with their assessment. For months, she'd had the growing sense that she'd once again made a fatal mistake. Ghastly little twinges of guilt and anxiety had kept her awake at night and distracted her during the day.

Something was very wrong. She knew it, and so did Mother and the rest of the sisters.

Her scalp prickled with perspiration under the close-fitting cowl. What in God's name *would* she do if they shoved her out into the world? Over three years ago, she'd run from that world as fast as she could, carrying no doubt that she'd made the right decision.

"Sister Bernard, you've always worried about me because I was not raised within the Catholic Church," Donella said, trying to sound calm. "But I can assure you that my conversion was entirely sincere."

"Hmm," replied the nun.

Really, the woman was *such* a snob. The aristocratic granddaughter of a French émigré family in the Bourbon line, it was no wonder she sniffed down her long nose at Donella.

Still, Donella's great-uncle was the Earl of Riddick, a descendant of Scottish kings. She'd stack her relatives up against snooty Sister Bernard's any day.

She supposed that made her a bigger snob than Sister.

Face it, old girl. You'd probably make a terrible nun.

"It's not your faith we worry about, my dear," Mother said. "It's your . . ."

"Complete inability to follow the rules," Sister Bernard finished.

Donella shook her head. "But I'm very good at following the rules. Everyone knows that."

So good, in fact, that everyone also believed her to be a total bore. Certainly Alec Gilbride, her cousin *and* former fiancé, had thought so. He'd found her so boring he'd run away from home at the age of sixteen and refused to come back for ten years.

Sister Bernard snorted. "You fall asleep in chapel on a regular basis, you have trouble memorizing the liturgy, you deliberately sing off-key—"

"I do not." She sometimes just lost her place because her mind wandered.

"You frequently break the Great Silence," Sister Bernard ruthlessly continued, "and you have a fatal tendency to interrupt your elders. That is most surprising, since we were assured by your family that you were an obedient, biddable girl."

"That's exactly what I am," Donella countered. "Obedient and biddable."

"If you were, you lost the knack of it." Sister's tone was as dry as a communion wafer.

That was probably true. But if they kicked her out now, it would prove to her family that they'd been right about what her great-uncle had called her *mad scheme* to run away from life.

Reverend Mother finally intervened. "My child, why do you wish to become a nun?"

Donella blinked. For several dreadful seconds, her mind went blank.

Think, you idiot.

"Because it's so peaceful and quiet," she finally blurted out. "And because I love God."

When Mother grimaced, Donella couldn't blame her.

"And I do like the music," she lamely added.

Never before had Mother or any of the other sisters asked that simple but fateful question. Becoming a Catholic nun in Scotland was not for the faint of heart, so it had probably never occurred to them to question her vocation. Besides, her uncle had given the Carmelites an exceedingly generous dowry as payment for Donella's entrance. No abbess in her right mind would have looked askance at the support of a powerful Scottish earl, even a non-Papist one.

"One does not enter a convent seeking to hide from problems," Mother said. "It has been our experience that unresolved issues can loom even larger inside these walls, as I think you're finding out."

Donella pressed her hands onto Mother's scarred oak desk and leaned forward to meet the older woman's wise gaze. "I'll try harder. I swear I will. Just give me another chance, please."

Mother shook her head. "No, dear child. You have done as well as you can, but this is not the life for everyone."

"Perhaps she could try the Franciscans," Sister Bernard suggested. "They're not as exacting as we are."

In other words, that order might be inclined to overlook her many failings, especially if she brought along her substantial dowry.

Donella sank into the creaky chair in front of Mother's desk. Since she was clearly going to get the boot, there was little point in standing on her best behavior.

"And of course we'll be returning your dowry," Mother said.

Since that would leave the convent in something of a bind, Donella would see to it that either Uncle Riddick or Alec made a generous donation to the convent to offset the financial blow.

At the thought of her cousin—the man who'd rejected her to marry another woman—Donella felt sick. More than anyone, Alec had supported her wish to enter the convent. He'd done it because he truly cared about her. He'd brought everyone else in the family around too, and now she'd failed them all yet again. Her family loved her, but they hadn't a clue what to do with her.

And now, neither did she.

"I suppose I could try the Franciscans," she said. "Are there branches of the order in Scotland?"

"There's a convent house in Galway, Ireland," replied Sister Bernard.

And wouldn't that go down like a treat with her great-uncle? Scotland was one thing, but Ireland?

"Whether the Franciscans would accept you is beside the point," Mother said. "As I said, you need to ascertain if you have a true vocation. The best way to do so is by returning to the outside world."

Panic flared inside her body. Donella didn't know if she'd ever be ready for the outside world, where she'd again face all the troubles she'd so gratefully left behind.

"Mother, I beg of you—"

The prioress rose to her feet. "My child, what is the fundamental principle of life within a religious order?"

Donella came to her feet as well. "Obedience, Mother. First to God, and then to you."

"Correct, and I am requiring this final act of obedience from you. Accept my decision with good grace and take this time to search your heart for what you truly desire. If you do this in good faith, you will find the answers you need."

"Yes, Mother."

Mother. The word echoed through her memory. Her real mother had also demanded obedience, until she'd made it utterly impossible for Donella to comply. They'd almost lost everything then, and only by the grace of God—and her great-uncle—had disaster been averted.

"I'll have to go into the village and arrange for a carriage," Donella said. "I could do that tomorrow, if you like."

Now that the departure had been forced on her, she had no wish to linger. Knowing how thoroughly she'd failed made her hot with shame.

"That won't be necessary," the prioress said. "I wrote to Lord Riddick this morning and informed him of my decision. I'm sure he will want to make his own arrangements for your return to Blairgal Castle."

Donella had to struggle to hold back a most irreverent curse. She'd hoped to at least be able to explain this wretched state of affairs to her family in person. Now, even that small measure of control and dignity had been taken away from her.

"We likely won't hear back from my uncle for several days if he has to make all the arrangements. He's very busy, you know."

"I'm sure he can spare a carriage and escort," Mother said dryly. "We'll wait to hear back from him. For as long as it takes."

Hanging about would simply prolong the agony. "I'm sure I could easily hire a post-chaise down at the inn. I could pack in a trice and be on my way."

Sister Bernard looked scandalized. "Your uncle would not wish you to travel alone, my dear girl. It would appear exceedingly slipshod and indecorous."

"It's only a two-day journey. I'm sure I'd be perfectly fine." At this point, she scarcely cared if she ended up murdered by bandits.

"You will stay in the convent's guesthouse until we hear from your uncle," Mother said firmly. "You can spend that time getting used to the world again and thinking about your future."

What future? As far as Donella could tell, she had none.

"Of course, Mother," she replied, trying to sound like she meant it.

The prioress rewarded her acquiescence with a smile. "You might even enjoy it after your years of enclosure. You can walk about the village, do a little shopping, and have a good chat with Father Thomas at the church. I have every confidence he can help you make peace with this decision."

"If only it had been my decision to make, Mother."

The elderly nun let out a gentle sigh. "My dear, I know this is a blow to your spirit—and to your pride. But you do have a choice as to how you will respond to this challenge. You can either see it as a failure or as an opportunity. I hope you will choose the latter."

Since there was no response to that eminently practical

if irritating advice, Donella simply crossed herself when Mother blessed her.

Sister Bernard went to open the door to the main hallway. "Go to your cell and begin packing. I'll join you shortly."

"Yes, Sister."

Donella walked out with as much dignity as she could muster, resisting the urge to slam the door. She never slammed doors or stormed off. In fact, she rarely made a fuss about *anything*.

The reward for all that good behavior had usually been a big, fat, kick in the backside. And now it had happened again.

Maybe it was time to start kicking up a fuss.

Chapter Two

Logan Kendrick eyed the tiny but implacable force blocking him like Cerberus at the gates of the underworld. Carmelite nuns weren't exactly his forte, but he'd give it a try.

"Sister Margaret," he said, smiling, "you understand that Miss Haddon should depart as soon as possible. We must reach Perth by nightfall."

The nun tucked her hands into the wide sleeves of her brown habit. She seemed to be returning his smile, but it was hard to tell given how wrinkly she was. The old gal, at least eighty, carried herself with ramrod dignity and looked capable of hauling him out back and paddling him for bad behavior.

"As I explained, Miss Haddon is at chapel with our sisters, who are praying for her safe travels. When the service is concluded, she will join you."

Logan gazed pointedly at the plain bracket clock above the small and decidedly empty fireplace. It was bloody freezing in the old-fashioned parlor, although the old nun seemed immune to the cold.

"And do ye ken when that might be, Sister?"

He could practically see her scoring another black mark on his soul. Cheeky behavior was clearly not welcome in the Convent of the Sacred Heart.

"When Reverend Mother deems it over."

He gave her an apologetic smile, which he thought showed remarkable forbearance on his part. The last thing he wished to do was play nursemaid to Donella Haddon, an almost-nun who'd failed to make the grade.

Logan was currently negotiating a series of critical financial arrangements with Lord Riddick, the girl's uncle. If he were successful, it would greatly benefit his company, Kendrick Shipping and Trade, by substantially increasing its size. So, when he had happened to mention to Riddick that he was travelling to Perth on business, the old fellow had asked for help in dealing with a *wee family matter*.

His lordship had been as closemouthed as a bear trap when it came to details, however. He'd simply said that his great-niece would be returning home, hopefully for good, and that he'd consider it a great, grand favor if Logan would make a slight detour to Dundee and escort the lass to Blairgal Castle.

"Well, Sister, I will simply have to possess my soul of a little patience," Logan said.

"A challenge for you, no doubt," she tartly responded.

"Perhaps I can ask the good Lord for help." Unable to resist the temptation, Logan gave her a wink. "Will you pray with me, Sister, and ask God to take pity on a poor sinner like me?"

She snorted. "I think our Lord has enough on His hands. But perhaps I can offer you a cup of tea while you wait."

It was clear that the nuns were richer in spiritual than temporal possessions, so he'd not have them wasting their precious tea and sugar on him. What he truly wanted was a dram.

"Thank you, but I'll just step out to speak with my groom and make a few arrangements for our journey. Miss Haddon can signal when she's ready, and we'll be on our way."

Sister Margaret nodded her approval, leaving him to duck out the low front door and into the courtyard.

Gazing up at the ironwork cross atop the old building, Logan wondered at the courage it must have taken Miss Haddon to defy her family. She'd chosen to become not only a Papist but had entered a bloody convent to boot. Catholics were a rarity in Scotland, mostly tucked away in remote corners of the Highlands. It was no wonder, given the level of bigotry and suspicion they often encountered. Now Miss Haddon would be reentering a world hostile to the likes of her and would have little to look forward to but a quiet spinsterhood on her uncle's country estate.

The woman would never be accepted back into polite society, especially not in hidebound, staunchly Protestant Glasgow.

And neither would Joseph.

Logan scowled at his boots, shoving his hands deep into his coat pockets. His son would have no chance of a good life in Scotland. As much as he missed his boy, best that Joseph stay in Canada, where he was safe, cared for, and loved.

With an effort, he forced away the pain that gripped him whenever he thought of his son. Instead, he focused on the opportunities before him, now that he was back in Scotland. Whatever their faults, Glaswegians were good at business and so was he. His success in the Colonies had opened a fair number of doors since his return, ones that would have otherwise remained closed to a reprobate like him.

It didn't hurt that he now had the backing of his brother, Nick, Earl of Arnprior. Soon, he hoped, he'd have Lord Riddick's, too. With Nick's influence and Riddick's investments, Logan had little doubt his company would soon dominate the timber and fur trades in Scotland and a good chunk of England as well.

That was the plan anyway, if he could ever get out of this bloody village in the middle of nowhere and back to Glasgow where he belonged.

He turned at the sound of a quick footfall from the road. Davey hurried through the convent's iron gates to join him.

"Sorry to bother ye, Mr. Logan," the young man said. "Foster sent me up to see how much longer ye might be."

Foster was Riddick's coachman and Davey was one of Blairgal's grooms. Logan had offered to hire a post-chaise, but Riddick had insisted that his niece would be more comfortable with Blairgal servants she'd known her entire life.

Having already waited over an hour, Logan sighed. "God is apparently working in mysterious ways today, so we'll have to wait and see."

Davey looked dubious. "Whatever ye say, sir."

"Has Foster been able to secure a suitable team at that laughable excuse for a local inn?"

"Just job horses, sir. He ain't well pleased, ye ken, but he said the inn don't see much in the way of traffic."

"I'm shocked to hear that."

Davey smiled. "Aye. It's that hard to imagine our Miss Donella holed up in a dreary place like this, although I suppose I shouldna be sayin' such a thing."

Logan propped a shoulder against one of the stone porch columns. "I've been wondering the same thing. You were working for Lord Riddick when Miss Haddon joined the convent, weren't you?"

"That I was, sir."

"That decision must have put the cat amongst the pigeons."

"Aye, the family was fashed, I can tell ye. And then puir Miss Donella up and got—"

Davey suddenly caught himself, wincing a bit.

Logan had found everyone to be tight-lipped about the lass. There was obviously a bit of a mystery when it came to Miss Donella.

"You were saying?" he prompted.

"Nothin', sir."

They both turned at the sound of thumps from inside the guesthouse. It would appear the lady of the hour was finally about to make an appearance.

"Ah, at last. Have Foster bring the carriage around, Davey."

"Aye, sir."

The young man hightailed it out of the courtyard, as if relieved to escape further questioning.

Not that it had been much of an interrogation. Mostly it was just idle curiosity on Logan's part. He'd every expectation that the next two days in the company of a spinsterish, pious lady would be utterly flat.

When the door to the guesthouse opened, Logan adopted a smile, ready to be as sympathetic as the situation demanded. The poor girl would be sadly pulled, no doubt. He could only hope she wouldn't spend the entire trip weeping into her handkerchief and bemoaning her fate. If she did, he'd have to retrieve the flask of very fine whisky he'd stowed in his travel kit for a necessary fortification.

A tall young woman wearing a stunningly ugly bonnet stalked out to the porch and stopped short when she saw him. Her gaze scanned him from head to toe, and then her tight-lipped expression transformed into one of outright disapproval.

For his part, he could do nothing but stare back at her like a chucklehead.

Good God.

Miss Donella Haddon looked neither pale nor morose, and not particularly nunlike. In fact, she was the most beautiful girl Logan had seen in a long time.

"Excuse me," she said. "Are you going to stand there gaping at me all afternoon? Will I have to go down to the inn and fetch the carriage myself?"

She had a bonny voice, as clear and musical as a rippling Highland stream. At the moment, it was as chilly as one, too.

Sister Margaret appeared from inside. "Gracious, Donella. Remember what Mother told you about intemperate language."

"As if I could ever bloody forget," Miss Haddon muttered.

When Logan choked back a laugh, she shot him a lethal stare, as if daring him to say a word.

"I'm sorry, my child," Sister Margaret said in a long-suffering voice. "I do not believe I heard you correctly."

Miss Haddon closed her spectacular green eyes and sucked in a deep breath. Naturally, that pulled Logan's attention to her bosom, which seemed a little too large for her ill-fitting, drab pelisse.

Why was she so poorly dressed? As Riddick's niece, she needn't go into the world looking like a charity case.

Even with the deplorable outfit and her irate glower, Donella Haddon was a true Scottish beauty, with pale, perfect features, an enchanting spray of freckles across her nose, and bright auburn hair peeking out from under her bonnet. Her tall, elegant figure also possessed enough curves to satisfy the most exacting of men.

Why the hell hadn't anyone told him the girl was so bloody gorgeous? He'd been expecting a dreary little miss, and instead he'd been saddled with a beauty, something he surely didn't need.

Logan had sworn off women for some time now. He was too busy for one thing. For another, he had no intention of getting married again. Taken together, they meant avoiding any eligible lasses that wandered into his orbit.

Ineligible lasses were off-limits, too. Nick would murder him if he engaged in that sort of nonsense, especially in a city as small and gossipy as Glasgow.

Unfortunately, he was not immune to the lure of a pretty girl—far from it, in fact, given his monklike state. He could only hope that her chaperone for the trip was the most dour and suspicious of nuns.

He pulled himself together. "Sister Margaret, I'd imagine the poor girl is distressed to be saying good-bye to you and the others. It's no wonder she's fashed."

When Donella opened her eyes, her frustrated expression suggested she'd like to cosh him over the head.

Sister Margaret obviously read the same message and laid a gentle hand on Donella's arm. "I'm sure you're upset, my child. But Mother gave you excellent advice that will help you to face this particular challenge with a lighter heart. Is that not so?"

The girl visibly collected herself before giving the elderly nun a sweet smile. "Yes. Thank you for the reminder, Sister."

"You must do more than remember, my child," Sister chided. "You must act on it, too."

Donella's expression changed again, and for a long moment she looked like a sad, lost little girl. Logan had to resist the insane urge to pull her into his arms for a comforting cuddle.

"I will do my best to take Mother's advice to heart," she said.

Sister Margaret nodded her approval. "We all have our crosses to bear, my dear. Try to bear yours with a glad heart, and never forget that our heavenly Father will provide."

Lord Riddick certainly would, anyway. Logan hoped the old fellow would do it without piling on the lectures. That would be adding insult to injury at this point.

"Can't blame her for being a wee bit snippy, Sister," he said. "I'd probably feel the same if I found myself tossed out on my—"

Logan caught himself just in time. While the nun regarded him with mild horror, Donella's gaze was cold enough to send his balls into full retreat.

"There's no need to linger, Mr. Kendrick," Sister Margaret said. "We sent Miss Haddon's trunk down to the inn this morning so it will already be in the carriage." She glanced up at the sky. "Dusk will come soon enough."

"I do believe I made that point an hour ago," Logan replied with polite sarcasm.

When the ladies stared at him again, he mentally winced. Taking potshots at nuns was hardly sporting, even if one of them was now an ex-nun. What the hell was wrong with him?

"Not that I minded waiting," he added.

Donella turned her back on him, bending gracefully to hug the old woman. "I'll miss you, Sister. Thank you for everything you've done for me."

Sister Margaret sketched a blessing over her. "Write and tell us how you get on, my dear. And God bless you."

With a stern nod to Logan, the nun disappeared into the guesthouse.

"Is the carriage waiting outside the gates," Donella asked, "or down at the inn?"

"It should be here soon. And we're still waiting for your chaperone, are we not?"

Donella looked blank. "I don't have a chaperone."

Oh, hell. "Isn't one of the sisters coming as an escort?"

"That seems rather redundant. I've got you to escort me and, presumably, my uncle's coachman and grooms."

"We'll be on the road for two days. You need a chaperone." He waved a hand. "You know, to prevent gossip."

She rolled her eyes. "No one is going to gossip about me, sir. Aside from my immediate family and the servants, no one even knows I'm leaving the convent."

Logan's irritation broke free. "I bloody well know, and I have no intention of spending two days on the road with a gently bred spinster."

Donella regarded him with patent disbelief. "Your virtue is quite safe with me, sir. I just spent the last three years in a convent. Until last week, I was *actually* a nun."

She turned on her heel and marched out the convent gates. Logan yanked off his hat, rubbed the back of his head where a headache was gathering, then jammed it back on and started after her.

"I don't care if yer the Blessed Mother herself," he said when he'd caught up with her. "Ye canna travel without a proper chaperone."

When he was annoyed, his brogue tended to surface. And right now he was very annoyed.

Donella flicked a dismissive hand, not breaking stride as they headed down the dusty road toward the inn. The wind kicked up dirt devils and tossed his hat from his head.

Repressing a curse, Logan swiped it up. The lassie, naturally, didn't wait for him, and he got an excellent if brief view of her pretty ankles when the wind off the nearby firth whipped her dress up around her shins.

Where the hell was the carriage? Foster should have picked them up by now, but he was nowhere in sight. That fit in with every other blasted thing gone wrong today.

He quickly caught up to Donella. "Don't you even have a maid to accompany you?"

She stopped dead in her tracks, forcing him to skid to a halt.

"What?" he asked in response to her glower.

"*I* repeat. Until last week I was a nun. Nuns do not have maids."

"No servants at all?" While he knew little about convents, she *was* the bloody niece of a rich, influential earl.

"I realize there are many silly myths about Catholics, but nuns do not have servants. And there are no mad monks, wailing ghosts, lurid orgies, or any other of the nonsense you might have heard."

He swallowed the temptation to joke about orgies. "Och, lass, I have nothing against Papists. In fact, my—"

"I don't care."

When she stomped off, Logan couldn't blame her. He'd sounded like a complete moron. But he was still debating what to do with her. They would spend two nights on the road without a chaperone. He couldn't believe Lord Riddick hadn't anticipated this rather pressing need. Did the old fellow really think the girl's former status would protect her from the way gossip flew about the Highlands? Not likely. Not when she was travelling with a Kendrick male— especially this Kendrick male.

Donella glanced over her shoulder. "Are you coming? Because as you so aptly pointed out, the less time we are together, the better."

Once again, he easily caught up with her, despite her long stride that ate up the ground. No mincing about for her. She was all business and as tart as a lemon ice.

Logan was quite fond of lemon ice.

"You are a snippy lass, aren't you? Is that why the nuns kicked you out?"

Her glare aimed to turn him to stone, but she kept her mouth—it was a very pretty mouth, rosebud pink—firmly shut.

"I'm Logan Kendrick, by the way. In case Sister Margaret didn't tell you."

"I know exactly who you are," she said with a disapproving sniff.

"Ah, so you've heard of the Kendricks."

"Of course. With the exception of Lord Arnprior, you are generally considered a bad lot."

"You're behind the times, lass. We're all reformed now."

"Huzzah for you." She tilted her chin to peer up the road from under the brim of her oversized bonnet. "And where *is* the carriage, for heaven's sake? At this rate, we'll hardly get out of here by nightfall."

Since they were almost at the inn and no carriage was in sight, Logan could only assume some mishap had occurred.

He couldn't resist the impulse to tease her. "Aye, it's late. Maybe we can have a nice, friendly chat to pass the time. Doesn't that sound like fun?"

"The only thing I intend to do on this benighted trip is pray, Mr. Kendrick."

"Then I do hope you'll say a few prayers for me, Miss Haddon."

"I will pray that you keep your blasted mouth shut." She quickened her pace, all but scurrying away from him.

The entire day had descended into a staggering farce. It was bound to be an interesting trip back to Blairgal, if Donella Haddon didn't murder him before the day was out.

Chapter Three

Donella eyed the man sitting across from her in the carriage. With his hat tipped over his eyes, arms crossed over his chest, and long legs stretched out, he looked ridiculously comfortable. She, however, was crowded against the side of the coach as she tried to avoid jostling into him.

She couldn't really blame him for taking up room. Logan Kendrick was a veritable giant. But she *could* blame him for being cavalier, high-handed, and incredibly annoying. In fact, Donella was fairly certain she already hated the man.

Thankfully, at least he'd stopped talking. She fully understood the awkwardness of their situation, but she had no intention of offering an apology for any inconvenience. It wasn't her fault that neither Reverend Mother nor her uncle had thought to provide a chaperone. Unfortunately, it had never occurred to her to ask about such a pertinent detail, either.

In fact, she'd had no control over the travel arrangements whatsoever. She'd told Mr. High and Mighty Kendrick exactly that after yet another delay in setting out. After all, how could she be blamed for one of the horses throwing a shoe just as Foster was pulling out from the inn to come fetch them?

As for the lack of a chaperone, well, what did it truly

matter? As far as Donella was concerned, her life was as good as over. She'd failed at being a nun, and after working so hard at it, too. Just like she'd worked so hard at everything else in her life before joining the convent.

It was perplexing, because she used to be good at things, whether it was managing a large household, helping the local vicar in his charitable work, or excelling at her studies and music. These days she seemed to be stumbling about in the dark without a clue what to do next.

The carriage jolted through a large rut, forcing Donella to grab for the strap. Her companion stirred not a jot.

Mr. Kendrick was big, bold, and swaggering, with a self-confidence that set her teeth on edge. He was also quite handsome, with thick black hair, strong features, and eyes the blue of a mountain loch—deep, clear, and so penetrating they stole one's breath.

When Donella had first emerged from the guesthouse, those eyes had swept over her in frank appraisal, no doubt because she looked like a perfect dowd in her ridiculous bonnet and gown. The sisters had done their best, but her old clothes had long since been given to the poor or ripped apart and refashioned for other purposes. She hadn't cared one whit about her appearance during the week she'd wandered about the village and surrounding countryside, worrying about her future and waiting for her escort to Blairgal.

But she *had* cared when Logan Kendrick fastened his sardonic gaze on her, sizing her up and obviously finding her lacking. The notion that he would think her attractive was ridiculous, which rendered the need for a chaperone entirely moot. He'd probably shoot himself before engaging in a flirtation with her, much less putting her in a situation that would necessitate he do the honorable thing by offering marriage.

She scowled at his sleeping form. "I'd boil myself in oil

before I married the likes of you," she muttered. "Just like one of the early martyrs."

When Kendrick tipped up his hat to look at her, Donella almost slid off her seat.

"Careful, lass, or you'll end up arse over teakettle," he said, after thrusting out a hand to stop her slide. "Now, what were you saying? Something about marriage and martyrdom?"

Donella righted herself with as much dignity as she could. "You misheard me. I was praying to Saint Valentine."

Oh, God. She'd pulled the first martyred saint she could think of out of her frazzled brain. The fact that Valentine was also the patron saint of romantic love was incredibly embarrassing.

"That makes perfect sense," Kendrick said. "No lass in her right mind would ever think to equate marriage and martyrdom."

"Really? Why do you think there were so many convents in the first place?"

"Maybe those poor ladies just didn't meet the right man."

He was clearly twitting her. She had the urge to stick her tongue out at him.

To avoid the temptation, she made a point of lifting the shade and squinting out against the setting sun. Would they never arrive at their inn? She wanted to crawl under a pile of covers and sleep, desperate to forget for a few hours what a mess her life had become.

"It's not much longer," Kendrick said in a more sympathetic tone. "The Perth Bridge should be only a few minutes ahead."

"We're stopping in Tibbermore, correct?" A small village, Tibbermore was a more secluded and private stop than the bustling market town of Perth.

Kendrick rolled his broad shoulders, trying to stretch in the tight quarters. "Yes, and not a moment too soon. I've had enough of carriages for one day."

"We'll have a long day tomorrow, I'm afraid."

"Aye, but then we'll reach Blairgal fairly early the day after." He smiled. "I'm sure you'll be glad to get home."

Home.

She wondered if Blairgal or Haddon House, her brother's small estate, would even feel like home anymore. She'd never expected to see either place again.

She forced a smile. "Yes, of course."

"And happy to see your family, no doubt."

"Why would you assume otherwise?" She tried not to bristle, but why did he even care?

His eyebrows ticked up. "I'm simply trying to make conversation to pass the tedium of the journey."

She winced. Clearly, her nerves were getting the best of her. "I apologize, sir. I suppose I've fallen out of the habit of polite conversation."

He regarded her with a softer eye. "Carmelites observe the Great Silence, do they not?"

Donella was surprised he would know such an arcane detail. "Outside of chapel or meals, we observed silence. Only in the most pressing of circumstances did we break it."

"Did you like it, all that quiet?"

She thought about it for a few moments. "I grew up in a noisy family, and there was a great deal of clan business taking place and visitors coming and going at the castle. The quiet was something of a relief."

In particular, Donella's mother had dragged chaos in her wake, making life a trial. But family history was certainly not something to share with a stranger—or anyone.

"Right," Kendrick said. "Your uncle is a clan chieftain, I believe. The Haddons are one of the larger Sept families in Clan Graham."

She'd almost forgotten how nice it was to talk to a true Highlander. Few people understood the complicated and sometimes-frustrating tangle of relationships and clan ties.

"Malcolm Haddon, one of my father's brothers, is the current chief. And Lord Riddick, my great-uncle, is heavily involved in clan business. Gatherings were held at least once a year when I was growing up, and there were always celebrations around holidays and marriages. It was quite . . . lively."

"That's one way to describe the gathering of the clan," he replied. "Barely controlled mayhem would be more accurate."

"It sounds like you didn't much care for them, either."

He gave a small shrug, a shifting of those impressive shoulders. "I did when I was young. What lad wouldn't be fond of drinking, feasting, and dancing with pretty Highland lasses?"

She didn't think she imagined the hint of self-mockery in his tone. "What changed for you, then?"

His sudden smile was charming—and insincere. "Nothing changed. I simply grew older and wiser. So, you enjoyed your peaceful life in the convent, did you? Coming from a large and noisy family myself, I can almost envy such a thing."

Donella recognized the polite dodge. "I didn't always enjoy it. The silence, I mean."

"Why not?"

"It was too quiet sometimes. You could practically hear a fly crawling across a windowpane or the stones of the building settling into the ground. At night, you might think you were entirely alone, with not another soul in the world." The memories of her cloistered life rose before her, poignant, complicated, and as painful as one's first love.

"Sometimes I imagined I could hear voices from the graveyard, calling to me from under the earth," she murmured, almost to herself.

Then she actually registered those words and heat flooded her face. "And now I *do* sound like a character from one of those lurid tales." She gave an embarrassed chuckle. "How silly of me."

In fact, she sounded mentally unhinged like her—

Donella slammed the door on that thought.

Kendrick simply raised an eyebrow. "Ah, so there *were* mad monks and shrieking apparitions wandering about the place. You've been holding out on me, Miss Haddon."

"It was a convent, Mr. Kendrick, not a monastery. No monks of any sort. Or apparitions. Reverend Mother wouldn't allow it."

He grinned. "I do hope the cemetery was at least appropriately gothic, with morose angels leaning sideways over crumbling gravestones."

His smile was so likable it was hard not to return it. Logan Kendrick could exude charm as easily as whisky flowed from a bottle. Fortunately, she was immune to that sort of thing.

"Nothing of the sort, I'm afraid. The previous owner kindly donated the manor house and grounds to the church when he built a new mansion near Edinburgh. Many generations of his family are buried on the grounds, so he stipulated that the sisters must maintain the graves as long as we remained in residence. My room overlooked the oldest part of the cemetery." She flashed a wry smile. "When the wind blew through the trees on a stormy night, it felt like the dead were whispering to each other, moaning from beyond the grave."

"Can't say that I blame the poor devils. Must get rather boring down there in a moldy old box."

"You do realize that the souls of the dead are long departed. It's only dust and bones in the ground."

"I'm a Highlander, lass," he said. "Ye ken we believe in ghoulies and the fae folk. It's our birthright."

"Yes, I've heard that," she dryly replied.

He studied her with a slight frown, as if trying to puzzle something out.

"And what about all that praying? Nuns and people like you pray all the time, especially for blighters like me. That's why you're all so holy. Someone has to do it to make up for the rest of us."

She blinked at his sudden change in demeanor. "I never said I was holy, Mr. Kendrick. And nuns are people, as good or as flawed as anyone else. There's nothing extraordinary about us."

He waggled a hand. "Of course nuns are different. Not like regular women at all."

Was he deliberately trying to annoy her? If so, it was working. "That's ridiculous. Nuns are no different from other women, not in the essentials."

"Except for one thing. They don't like—" He caught himself, as if suddenly rethinking the nature of their conversation.

"Yes?"

He looked out the window. "Sorry. Forgot what I was going to say."

Now he wanted to call a retreat? *I don't think so.*

"We don't like men, you mean? Believe me, you wouldn't be the first to say it. Men generally think we're dried-up old spinsters, hiding away from the world."

Of course, in her case it just might be true. Not the dried-up part, but the hiding away part. It was probably why she found his remarks so annoying.

"That was not what I was going to say," he said defensively.

"It doesn't matter."

She made a show of pulling back the shade and peering out the window. "I do believe we're about to cross the Perth Bridge. Did you know it's quite the landmark in this part of Scotland?"

"Miss Haddon—"

"It has eight arches, from what I understand. Quite the engineering marvel."

"Miss Haddon," he started again through clenched teeth. He was cut off when they came to a jolting halt.

"Now what?" she exclaimed. "This is getting to be ridiculous."

"I'll find out. You just stay put."

She glared at him. "Sir, if I wish to step out of the carriage for a breath of fresh air, I will do exactly that."

He muttered something that sounded like *bloody woman* before reaching for the door handle. He was halfway out the door, ducking low under the frame, when he froze.

"Goddammit," he cursed.

"Sir, taking the Lord's name in vain will not help the situation, whatever it is."

He looked over his shoulder, his expression so grim that any further reprimand died on her lips.

"Unfortunately, Miss Haddon, my language wasn't strong enough."

Chapter Four

Until they'd started arguing again, Logan had been enjoying their conversation. But then the lass had started talking about the murmurs of the dead. He'd heard those voices too, and he needed no reminders.

Now, on top of everything else, it looked like some blasted morons were going to try to rob them.

He stepped down and peered ahead into the gathering gloom. Foster had stopped the carriage at the east end of the bridge because four riders had blocked the opposite end. One gave a signal, and the men nudged their animals forward, taking up the width of the bridge as they advanced.

"Is this what I think it is?" Logan asked.

"They raised my hackles," the coachman replied. "That's why I stopped so sudden-like. But if they're thinkin' of robbin' us, they're takin' their sweet time."

"They're nae actin' like highwaymen," Davey opined from his perch at the back.

Logan threw an ironic glance over his shoulder. "Ever been held up before, Davey?"

The young man winced and shook his head.

"I think you'd best retrieve the pistols," Logan said.

"Aye, sir."

"Daft to be tryin' something so close to Perth," Foster said. "Anyone could come along."

"There's been hardly any traffic in either direction for over an hour," Logan replied. "Sensible folk are already indoors."

The mysterious strangers' actions raised Logan's hackles, too. He'd developed finely honed instincts during his time in the Canadian wilderness, dodging predators with claws and sharp teeth, as well as those that walked upright and carried guns.

After a quick rummage through the boot, Davey handed over a pistol.

"Do you have another one?" Logan asked.

"Nae, sir. Mr. Foster has one under his seat, but that's it. It's rare to have trouble on the roads, these days."

Logan had another pistol in his travelling kit somewhere at the bottom of the boot, underneath Donella's luggage.

Idiot.

He'd grown complacent these last few years. In Canada, he'd never travelled without a brace of pistols strapped over his body and usually an extra one shoved in the back of his breeches.

Donella popped her head out the door. "What's going on? And why do you have a pistol?"

"I'm just being cautious. Please get back inside."

Instead, she leaned out over the step and peered ahead. "Are those men a problem?"

"Possibly."

"I suppose they're going to hold us up," she said, clearly exasperated. "Mr. Kendrick, I suggest you inform the nitwits that I am the niece of the Laird of Riddick, and that he'll not be best pleased with any nonsense."

"I'll be sure to make that point," Logan said, priming his pistol.

"There's no need to be sarcastic. And I'd like a weapon too, please."

"We'd *all* like more weapons, lass. Now, for the love of God, get back in the bloody carriage and stay down."

Her plump lips thinned into a silent scold, but thankfully she complied with his order. While high-handed she might be, Donella was smart enough to know when to listen.

Logan moved a few steps onto the bridge, narrowing his gaze on the slow advance of the horsemen.

"What the devil are they about?" he muttered.

"They've got pistols," Foster said. "I can see them in their laps."

Logan shielded his eyes against the last rays of the setting sun. "They're masked, too."

All wore caps pulled low and dark neck stocks over their mouths and noses. All except one, who'd tied on an incongruously cheery red scarf.

"Bandits," Davey said. "The laird will nae be happy."

Logan glanced up at the coachman. "Foster, can you turn the coach or back the horses off the bridge?"

"It's tight, sir, but I think I can do it."

There was an inn a short ways back. With luck—and a few warning shots from the rear—they might make it to safety.

Logan strode toward the back of the carriage. "Davey, you ride with Miss Donella. I'll—"

"Hold up, Mr. Foster," Davey yelped. "We've got trouble behind us, too."

Three more masked horsemen now occupied the stretch of road they'd just travelled, something Logan hadn't anticipated.

What the hell was going on?

"Foster, set the brake and retrieve your pistol," he ordered. "We've got to make a stand."

"Aye, sir."

Logan clapped a hand on Davey's shoulder. "I've got another pistol in my kit. I don't care if you have to throw every bit of luggage into the road; find the bloody thing and guard our rear. Don't hesitate to shoot."

Davey looked pale. "A . . . aye, Mr. Kendrick."

He raced back to the boot while Logan went to the carriage window.

"We're in trouble," he said to Donella.

"I heard." She reached behind her head and began to fuss with her bonnet.

It was odd to worry about her appearance at a time like this.

"I want you to get down on the floor and stay there," he enunciated, as if talking to a child.

Donella scowled. "I'm not a moron, Mr. Kendrick. I know what to—ah, finally."

She extracted a quite lethal-looking hatpin, then yanked off her bonnet and tossed it onto the opposite seat.

"Perhaps we should give them what we've got and have done with it," she said. "It might be safer."

The shiny russet curls that tumbled around her jawline momentarily distracted him. Aye, she was bonny, and that scared the hell out of him. Especially considering what could happen next.

"They're not acting like your average highwaymen," he said.

He leaned back to flick a glance in both directions. The horsemen on the bridge were still advancing at a walk. The men behind had stopped about a hundred yards away, blocking any chance of exit.

Something about this was very off.

"How many of them are there?" Donella asked.

"Seven. Three behind and four ahead, all masked and armed."

"Oh, dear. That sounds rather well planned, doesn't it?"

"Which is why I want you down on the floor."

She grimaced but gave him a nod and slid down to the floor, gripping the hatpin.

While he admired her courage, her feeble weapon could do more harm than good. A good jab in the right place might give an attacker pause, but would just as likely infuriate him.

Donella obviously read his mind. "I'm a Scotswoman, sir. I will defend myself, no matter what."

He quirked a brief smile. "Let's hope it doesn't come to that. Just sit tight until I come back and get you."

"They're almost here, sir," Foster barked.

After glancing behind to make sure Davey was covering their rear, Logan strode to the head of the carriage and leveled his pistol. When one of the horsemen raised a hand, the riders halted some yards from the carriage.

For long seconds, Logan and the masked riders exchanged stares. On the other end of the bridge stood Perth. He could see the lights in the windows of houses and shops, and smoke curling up from chimneys. Even though civilization loomed close by in the shape of a tidy, prosperous town, they were isolated. Possibly no one would even hear if shots were fired. The sounds of water rushing below the bridge and the rising wind in the trees conspired against them.

Logan raised his voice. "I happen to be an excellent shot, so I suggest you let us pass."

"There be seven of us and three of ye," said the one who'd held up his hand. "We mean ye no harm. But ye *will* follow our orders, or we'll do what needs must."

"If it's money you want, one of you louts can come get it," Logan replied. "But if we keep standing about, someone's bound to come along and raise the alarm, which will put rather a crimp in your plans."

"We dinna want yer money. It's the lass we've come for. Hand her over and we'll be on our way, and no harm done."

What in hell . . .

How did they know who was in the coach? The scenario

was becoming increasingly bizarre, since few people knew Donella was returning to Blairgal Castle.

"Foster," he said quietly, "did you notice anything suspicious back at the inn while we were waiting for Miss Donella?"

"Nae, sir. There were only a few locals hangin' aboot, havin' a pint or two."

"There must be some confusion," Logan said, again raising his voice. "I'm a businessman from Glasgow, and the woman in the coach is my wife. Be assured that she will not be going anywhere with you."

The gang's leader waved his pistol. "Och, the flower's nothin' of the sort. Just hand her over and we'll be on our way."

The flower? Now what the hell was the idiot talking about?

"Och, that's nae good," muttered Foster.

Logan shot him a quick frown before cocking his pistol.

"Have it your way," he said to the masked leader.

Three pistols were lifted and cocked in return.

"Hold, ye daft idiots," barked the leader before turning back to Logan. "We'll nae be hurtin' the lass. Word of a Highlander. But we will be takin' her. It's up to ye how hard or easy ye want to make it."

"They dinna seem that keen on a fight," Foster said to Logan. "And I'm thinkin' this is Clan Graham business, what with the flower and all."

"I have no idea what any of you are talking about," Logan replied, "but I agree this is some sort of ridiculous clan situation." Clan issues, especially ones that involved matters of honor, could be a royal pain in the arse.

"Why do you want her?" Logan called out.

"None of yer business."

"You've made it my business. And that means it is now Kendrick business, since I'm the brother of the Laird of Arnprior. Run afoul of me, and you run afoul of Arnprior and Clan Kendrick."

That set off a round of uneasy muttering. The group's leader silenced his compatriots with a few sharp words.

"We have nae quarrel with the Kendricks. And if ye want to keep it that way, ye'll hand the lass over."

"That's not going—"

The sound of the carriage door flying open interrupted him. Logan turned to see Donella leaning out, looking immensely irritated.

"Will you please cease this endless palavering?" she loudly said. "I am freezing in this stupid carriage, and I would prefer to reach our destination by nightfall."

"You are not helping," Logan gritted out.

"And you are not getting the job done." She jumped down and marched up to him. "I feel like I'm in the middle of some idiotic parlay instead of a kidnapping."

"I'm trying to prevent a blasted kidnapping *through* a blasted parlay."

She cast a haughty look down the road at their erstwhile abductors, who were now muttering excitedly to each other.

"Since you know who I am," she called out, "you must also know Lord Riddick will be most displeased by this insult. If you do not move aside, there will be extremely deleterious consequences to your regrettable behavior."

"Them's a lot of breaketeeth words from such a slip of a lass," one of the horsemen said.

"Aye," replied the one wearing the red scarf. "Hard to imagine that she and—"

Their leader smacked Red Scarf in the shoulder. "Shut it, ye boobies."

His action startled Red Scarf's horse, which shied into the one next to it. For a few moments, a great deal of cursing and maneuvering ensued while the men brought their animals under control. It would have been a farce but for the fact that the idiots were armed. Logan hauled Donella behind him to shield her, in case one of them accidentally discharged his pistol.

"There's no need to manhandle me," she huffed.

"I don't trust those morons not to shoot someone."

"No one is shooting anyone. I will handle this."

He glared at her. "Do you have any idea who they are?"

"No, but they know who I am." She made a disgusted noise. "*The Flower*. I always hated that name."

"Come along now, Miss Donella," the leader said in a wheedling tone. "We willna hurt ye, but ye have no choice."

"Absolutely not," she shouted back, leaning to see around Logan. "My uncle will hunt you down for even attempting such a thing."

"Yer uncle is a tired old man. And this is Riddick's fault in the first place. We're only takin' what's been ours all along, from years ago."

Donella sucked in a breath.

The horses surged forward.

Logan shoved his pistol into his waistband and swept Donella into his arms. He tossed her into the coach and slammed the door, ignoring her protests.

"Do *not* come out," he said.

She glared at him. "I'm not an—"

A boom from the top of the carriage cut her off.

Foster had gotten off a shot, and it looked like he'd winged one of the bastards. Red Scarf was reeling in his saddle, trying to maintain his seat.

Logan yanked his pistol from his waistband and fired at the leader. The man shrieked as his hat flew from his head and he tumbled from his horse.

The two unhurt scoundrels yelled out curses, as they tried to bring their startled horses under control.

When a pistol discharged behind him, Logan wheeled around. Davey had fired but missed the riders to the rear, who were now charging forward. Two of them dismounted and launched themselves at the groom, while the other remained in the saddle to cover his companions. Davey fought like a wildcat, but the bastards knocked him to the ground.

With a few quick strides, Logan reached them, plucking an attacker from the writhing pile of bodies and heaving him over the side of the bridge. With a snarl, the mounted man leveled his pistol. Logan pulled a blade from his boot and threw just as the man fired his weapon. Shards of stone exploded from the wall behind him. The ball missed Logan only by inches.

His assailant screeched and clutched at the knife buried in his shoulder. He jerked halfway out of his saddle, accidentally pulling his horse around in the opposite direction. The animal bolted down the road, with his rider flopping like a fish on a riverbank. One of the other horses, spooked by the commotion, bolted and raced off down the road as well.

Trusting Davey to handle his remaining assailant, Logan turned back toward the front of the carriage. Foster was lashing his whip at one of the remaining riders, keeping the man well occupied in trying to prevent his mount from rearing out of control.

The fourth rider, however, was off his horse and at the carriage door. A brute of a man, he'd clamped a hand around Donella's calf and was dragging her toward him. The lass put up a mighty struggle. Her skirts were rucked up as she tried to kick him off, all while desperately grabbing on to the doorframe.

A pulse of fury shimmered through Logan, a white-hot bolt that seemed to light up the sky. He charged forward, hell-bent on throttling the bastard for daring to lay hands on her.

As he clamped a hand on the brute's shoulder, Donella lashed out with her other foot, connecting solidly with her attacker's groin. The man jerked upright with a strangled shriek. Logan yanked him off the carriage step and threw him down to the roadbed. He hit the paving stones and curled into a ball, hands clapped between his legs as he loudly moaned.

Logan reached for Donella and helped her sit up. "Are ye all right, lass?"

"I . . . I'm fine."

With shaking hands, she struggled to rearrange her clothing. One of her stockings had come undone, exposing her pale skin and fine-boned ankle. Logan pulled down her skirts and then helped her climb back onto the seat of the carriage.

"That was a grand hit, Donella," he said gruffly. "Well done."

Her lips trembled into an uncertain smile. "I was trying to stab him, but I dropped my hatpin."

Logan glanced at the man in the road, still a whimpering ball. "Trust me, that was considerably more effective."

"You were very impressive, too," she earnestly said. "You tossed that man over the side of the bridge like a sack of potatoes." Then she frowned. "I do hope you didn't kill him."

"I doubt it, but I'm not wasting any tears over the idiot."

Her gaze slid away as she reached for her bonnet. "I'm fairly certain they didn't wish to hurt me, despite their rough handling."

At the sound of clattering hooves, Logan glanced forward. The man who'd attacked Foster had retreated, and Red Scarf had obviously helped the leader back onto his horse. Without a backward glance, the three riders took off in the direction of Perth, leaving their injured compatriots behind.

"And I'm fairly certain they *did* wish to hurt Davey and Foster, and me," he said.

She flashed him a troubled glance. "Yes, that was very bad."

There was something she wasn't telling him, but now was not the time for an interrogation.

Donella put on her bonnet. "What next, sir?"

"We get out of here before the bastards have a chance to regroup."

"Although I don't approve of your language, Mr. Kendrick, I do approve of that course of action."

"I'm glad to hear it," he said dryly.

He stepped down and closed the door of the carriage. The man in the road was starting to show signs of rousing himself, so Logan grabbed him by the collar, dragged him to the side of the bridge, and dumped him over. A yell and a loud splash followed.

Donella opened her window and leaned out with a scowl. "Was that really necessary?"

"Yes." He glanced at Davey, still rolling about on the ground with his attacker. "Davey, stop larking about and put an end to it."

"I'm trying, sir," the groom exclaimed in a strangled tone. "But he ain't fightin' fair."

Logan plucked the man off Davey and tossed him head-first into the stone guardrail of the bridge. The fellow collapsed into a sad heap on the cobblestones.

Davey clambered to his feet, glancing first at his opponent and then at Logan.

"I reckon he won't be gettin' up for a while," the groom said, sounding a bit awestruck.

"That's the plan. Reload your pistol, lad. Take some ammunition from my kit if you don't have any."

"Aye, Mr. Kendrick."

When Logan headed toward the front of the carriage to speak to Foster, he caught Donella staring at him with her mouth slightly ajar.

"Yes, Miss Haddon?"

She pointed to the unconscious man crumpled against the bridge. "I'm just wondering why you didn't toss him over, too."

He shrugged. "Och, that would just be showing off."

"Mr. Kendrick, I'm not sure all this mayhem was truly necessary, under the circumstances."

"Under the circumstances?" he echoed with disbelief. "It was truly necessary to save your pretty little arse, Miss Haddon."

"Sir, that language is entirely—"

"What aren't you telling me?" he interrupted.

For several moments, only silence greeted him.

"I have no more insight into this matter than you do," she finally said.

"Then I suppose we'll have to roust the local magistrate in Perth, or find the constable—"

"No!"

Logan frowned at her panicked tone. "Again, what aren't you telling me?"

"Nothing. But my uncle Riddick wouldn't like us to make a public fuss over this."

"He'll not like anyone trying to kidnap his niece, either."

"There is clearly more here than meets the eye," Donella said firmly. "I insist that you let my uncle handle this. Besides, you've tossed half these men into the river, and with the exception of that unconscious person, everyone else has fled."

"Happens she's right, sir," said Foster from the coachman's seat. "I canna see them ahead at all."

"But they'll likely return for their friends," Donella said. "We should go."

Logan debated with himself. He loathed mysteries, and there was definitely a mystery here. The lass was the key, but she wasn't sharing.

"This is quite probably a clan issue, which means my uncle will wish to maintain control over the situation," the girl added. "Not turn it over to a magistrate."

He mentally grimaced. Although a good man, the earl was notoriously traditional and high-handed. And given the delicate state of Logan's business negotiations with the old fellow, he couldn't afford to offend him or his favored niece.

Davey turned and peered down the road. "I hear somethin', sir. Several horses, maybe."

Logan heard it too, and that tipped the scales.

"I'm going to ride up with Foster," he said to Donella. "Pull the shade down and bloody well keep out of sight."

"Yes, sir," she said in a sarcastic tone.

"And don't think this is the end of it, lass. We *will* be having a discussion once I get you to safety."

"I assure you, there is nothing to discuss." She slammed the window glass shut and pulled the shade closed.

Chapter Five

Less than an hour after the attempted abduction, the carriage turned into the yard of a small coaching establishment in the village of Tibbermore.

Donella breathed out a shaky sigh of relief. Although still distinctly unnerved, she was convinced her life had never truly been in danger. Revenge against her uncle seemed a large part of the mysterious plan.

That it was a clan matter was beyond doubt, and those affairs were usually messy and occasionally violent. The risk to her innocent escorts had frightened her more than any threat to herself.

That her would-be abductors were willing to injure her uncle's men *and* a Kendrick placed it on the level of a full-blown clan feud. Uncle Riddick had certainly made enemies in his time. But he was a powerful and respected laird, and the attack was a grave insult to him, with potentially dire consequences.

Thankfully, Mr. Kendrick had saved the day. He'd dealt with the villains with a casual disregard for his own safety, dodging bullets and tossing assailants off the Perth Bridge like skittle pins. She'd not seen such easy, awe-inspiring strength since the clan gatherings of her youth, when handsome and braw Roddy Murray had always cheerfully bested his many rivals. Back then, all the lasses had swooned over Roddy.

Donella, regretfully, had swooned right along with them.

But Logan Kendrick was quite different than the good-natured but dim Roddy. Beneath Kendrick's roguish charm lurked something grim, even dangerous. And although he'd tried not to kill any of the attackers, she had no doubt he'd have done so if necessary. The man had shown himself to be quick thinking, decisive, and ruthless.

Donella was used to strong, fiercely protective men. Her brother and cousin certainly fit that bill. But Kendrick rattled her in a way no man ever had, even though they'd just met. It was not a feeling she enjoyed.

He was also clearly intent on getting to the bottom of the incident. Donella had some suspicions regarding their attackers, although she prayed she was overreacting. But whether her suspicions were valid or not, whatever was afoot was private family business. For the sake of her reputation, not to mention her family's good name, she intended to keep her secrets to herself.

When Donella entered the convent, a number of barely repressed scandals had been hidden away with her. Now that she was out in the world again, she would do whatever it took to keep those scandals safely buried.

The carriage door opened, and Donella squinted against the glare of torches lighting up the coaching yard.

Kendrick appeared in the doorway. "It's safe to come out. I've had a quick look around and all seems as quiet as the grave."

She took his hand and stepped down to the cobblestones. "That's rather unfortunate phrasing, given our circumstances."

He flashed a sardonic smile. "Nay, lass. Not with me here to protect you."

Kendrick loomed over her, a powerful giant of a man. The

fact that his assessment was likely correct didn't make it any less irritating.

"Are you always this self-confident? It's annoying."

Her voice was sharp, more for her own sake than his. Because if Donella were entirely honest, she had to admit she found him attractive. It was utter nonsense, of course, given that she'd just been released from a convent. Not to mention the sort of man he was. She shouldn't even be *thinking* of him that way.

His eyes gleamed with mischief in the flickering torchlight. "I try never to lie, Miss Haddon. As an almost-nun, you should appreciate my honesty."

"I am not an . . . oh, never mind."

Kendrick was clearly a tease, and she had no intention of responding to his nonsense.

"May we please go inside?" she asked. "I'm rather chilled."

"In just . . . ah, here's Davey now," Logan said when the groom hurried over. "I wanted him to do another check of the building. Everything all right, lad?"

"Aye, sir. The innkeep's wife is waitin' to show Miss Haddon up to her room."

Kendrick dismissed Davey with a nod and led Donella toward the two-storied, whitewashed building. The inn looked small and old, but also trim and homey. Tubs of late-blooming mums flanked the entrance and the windows gleamed bright from the lamplight within.

"You're not expecting more trouble, are you?" Donella asked. "No one followed us, did they?"

"Apparently not, but I won't take risks with your safety."

"Thank you, but—"

Donella stumbled to a halt, gazing up at the gently swaying sign over the front door. She hadn't been able to read it when she stepped down from the carriage. Now, in the light pouring out through the open door, she could see bold, black letters painted on the white background.

THE OLD MURRAY INN

Her vague suspicions—which she'd tried to ignore for the last hour—broke over her like a cresting wave. She pressed a hand to her waist, as if to hold her pitching stomach in place.

Kendrick dipped his head to study her, then glanced up at the sign over their heads. "Is there a problem, Miss Haddon?"

His words barely penetrated the roaring in her head.

He rested a gentle hand on her shoulder. "Lass, tell me what's wrong."

"N . . . nothing."

Kendrick made a frustrated sound. "I can't help if you won't tell me the truth."

"It's none of your business." Then she mentally grimaced, irritated by her sharp reply. "Besides, there's nothing to tell."

His gaze narrowed. "Donella—"

"Sir, I don't believe I gave you permission to make free with my name." She swept past him and through the door.

Kendrick muttered something about *daft lasses* and followed her inside.

The timbered-roof entrance hall contained a small desk, a chair, and a few wooden settles tucked into the corners. A long hall stretched toward the back of the inn, and a door on the right opened into a cozy taproom where an elderly gentleman dozed into his ale and a scrawny young fellow was behind the bar, polishing glasses.

A middle-aged woman garbed in a round gown and starched apron bustled out from the hall to greet them. She had salt-and-pepper hair topped by a neat mobcap, and looked a trifle harassed.

"Beggin' yer pardon. I was roustin' my husband to look

after yer carriage and cattle," she said. "It's a pleasure to have ye under our roof, Miss Haddon. I can show ye to yer room now, if ye like."

"Thank you, ma'am." Donella stripped off her gloves. "And you are . . . ?"

"Mrs. Murray. The family has owned this inn for nigh on two hundred years. We've served many a traveller to these parts, and we pride ourselves on our hospitality. Ye'll be havin' a foine supper and a good night's sleep tonight, Miss Haddon."

The woman's chattiness was both useful and horrifying. For a moment, Donella debated whether to ask Kendrick to pole up the horses and take to the road again.

The innkeeper peered at her with concern. "Are ye needin' a cup of tea straightaway, miss? Or a wee dram to chase away the chill?"

"The cat appears to have seized possession of Miss Haddon's tongue," Kendrick said. "We've had a bit of a difficult journey."

Donella shot Logan a warning glare before mustering a smile for the confused-looking Mrs. Murray. "I'm simply fatigued."

"Then we'll fix ye up with a nice wash and a spot of tea while yer waitin' for supper. If ye'll step up with me, Miss Haddon, I'll show ye the room."

Donella's anxiety eased under the warmth of the woman's kind manner. The Murrays were a large, diverse clan, with many branches. It was silly to think that these simple innkeepers would have knowledge of the troubles between Mungo Murray's branch of the clan and the Haddon family.

"Do you have a private room where Miss Haddon can take her supper?" Logan asked before Donella could reply.

"Nae, sir, we've just the taproom. There's one other gent stayin' with us who'll be havin' his supper down there, but he won't be botherin' ye or the lady. He seems a quiet and polite sort of fellow."

"I think it best—"

A balding little man in breeches and a leather jerkin darted through the front door, interrupting them. Eyes wide, he skidded to a halt in front of Donella. Wisps of sandy-colored hair stood straight up from his skull, as if they'd somehow taken fright.

"Mr. Murray, why are ye runnin' in like a looney?" Mrs. Murray scolded. She gave Donella an apologetic smile. "This is my husband, miss. He's forgotten his manners, I'm sorry to say."

The innkeeper swiped a hand across his perspiring forehead and collected himself. "Yer Miss Haddon, I take it. I beg yer pardon."

His wife regarded him with disbelief. "Ye cannae have forgotten that Mr. Kendrick would be returnin' this way with the lady. He told ye that himself only two days ago."

"Of . . . of course not," he babbled. "I . . . I just was thinkin' they were comin' tomorrow night, is all."

Kendrick frowned. "Is that a problem? I'd hate to have to pole up and try to find another inn if you cannot accommodate the horses."

"We have plenty of room, sir," Mrs. Murray assured him before rounding on her husband. "Were ye not just in the stables, seein' to Mr. Kendrick's carriage and team? Where have ye been if not doin' that?"

Murray bristled at his wife, but it was clear he was extremely unsettled.

Donella found that extremely unsettling.

"I was out back, ye ken. I didna see them arrive," the innkeeper said.

His wife snorted with barely concealed disgust. "Be off

with ye to check on Mr. Kendrick's men and his cattle, or ye'll get the sharp side of my tongue."

Although clearly resenting his wife's order, the innkeeper gave Kendrick a deferential bob and scurried out the door with a backward, worried glance at Donella.

Kendrick raised his eyebrows at her. "That was a bit . . ."

"Odd," she finished.

"Och, there's nae need to worry, miss," said Mrs. Murray. "My husband can be a bit scattered at times, is all. I'll pop out to the stables in a wee bit to make sure yer men and the horses are settled for the night. Then I'll see to yer supper."

"I think it best for Miss Haddon to eat supper in her room," Kendrick said. "She's had a tiring day, and she needs her privacy."

"I don't mind eating in the taproom," Donella said, reluctant to cause additional trouble. "Mrs. Murray has enough to do."

"Sorry, but I'll have to insist." Kendrick's gaze held a clear warning. "You'll be undisturbed in your room and better able to rest."

It was clear her protector still harbored concerns, as did she, and Mr. Murray's behavior had done nothing to allay them. It might be best to pole up the horses and leave. It was a gruesome thought, though, given how cold, tired, and famished she was.

Kendrick suddenly flashed a smile as he pressed a hand to her shoulder, stroking a thumb along the slight protrusion of her collarbone. "Not to worry, lass. I'm just being a wee bit careful."

Donella froze, startled by the warmth of his hand cupping her shoulder. She gazed up into his steely blue eyes, and something instinctive urged her to sidle closer, seeking his strength and protection.

An expression that looked remarkably like interest sparked

in his gaze—the sort of interest a man took in a woman who'd caught his fancy. It had been years since she'd been a woman in that position. For Donella, dreams of romance were part of a distant past.

Despite that blunt truth, a most disconcerting tingle started behind her knees and travelled upward. She forced herself to slip away from his touch.

She was *not* that kind of woman and never would be again.

"Of course, Mr. Kendrick," she said. "Whatever you think is best."

His smile transformed into one of sardonic amusement. Blushing, Donella silently cursed the man for making her feel so awkward and self-conscious.

For a moment, she thought he would tease her. Thankfully, he switched his focus to Mrs. Murray.

"So, you'll see to it that Miss Haddon gets supper in her room?"

"Aye, sir. Whatever ye want shall be."

"Good. I'll eat in the taproom with my men."

Mrs. Murray nodded toward a staircase at the end of the long hall. "I'll take ye up, miss."

Donella started to follow but paused to glance back at Logan. "Is this good night, or will I see you later?"

When his smile flashed roguish, she couldn't hold back a glower.

"I merely wish to discuss the plans for tomorrow," she said with as much dignity as she could muster.

"Of course. You can count on it, lass." Then he winked at her.

She turned on her heel and stalked off. He was a terrible flirt, which is exactly what one should expect from a man like him. While he was undeniably brave, and she could only be grateful for his protection, it seemed clear he'd earned his reputation as one of the infamous Kendricks. Those men had cut a swathe through a hefty portion of the Scottish female population.

Well, she had no interest in flirting with him *or* being the butt of his jests.

Mrs. Murray led her up the narrow staircase to a room at the end of the hall. "I'll be putting ye in our best room, miss. It's farthest away from the public rooms, and nice and quiet. Warm too, since it's right over the kitchen."

Donella gratefully took off her bonnet and shook out her curls as she scanned the small room, comfortably furnished with a four-poster bed with a floral quilt and pillows covered in starched linen. A handsome leather wing chair stood before the fireplace, and a round table with two high-backed chairs was tucked under the eaves. Compared to her cell in the convent, the simple room seemed almost extravagant.

The innkeeper closed the window curtains before expertly building up the peat fire that had already been smoldering on the hearth.

"It's a lovely room, Mrs. Murray. Thank you."

"It's nae what ye'll be used to at Blairgal Castle, but ye'll find it a bit more cozy than any convent. Now that's plain livin', I ken. Yer well shot of it, if ye don't mind me sayin,' miss. No life for such a foine lady as yerself."

Donella blinked. "How did you know I'd been in a convent?"

Now that the fire was burning nicely, Mrs. Murray stood and wiped her hands on her apron.

"Och, Miss Haddon, there weren't a body within fifty miles that didn't know ye were meant to be the future Lady of Riddick." She shook her head. "And to be thrown over by a *Sassenach,* no less. No wonder ye ran off to join a nunnery."

Apparently, three years hadn't been long enough to kill the chatter that had surrounded her broken engagement to Alasdair.

"I appreciate your kind words, Mrs. Murray, but your

sympathy is unnecessary. I never wished to marry my cousin, and I'm very fond of his wife. We're *all* very fond of Mrs. Gilbride."

Mrs. Murray made a skeptical sound. "Then why did ye run off and hide in a convent?"

"I wasn't hiding. It was my choice, and one I was happy to make." She hoped her firm tone would put an end to the embarrassing conversation.

The innkeeper looked skeptical for a moment, then visibly brightened. "Still, ye found a grand, braw man in Mr. Kendrick. A lass couldna do any better, and I give ye both my hearty congratulations."

Good God.

"Mr. Kendrick is simply a friend, Mrs. Murray. Nothing more. He's . . . he's escorting me home at my uncle's request."

Under the woman's penetrating stare, Donella felt the blood rise to her cheeks. Of course the situation would look dodgy to the average stranger—a single man and woman, travelling together with no chaperone in sight.

"Mrs. Murray, do you think I could have a wash and a cup of tea before dinner?" she asked rather desperately. "I'm quite parched from all the dust on the road."

The innkeeper nodded. "And me natterin' on while all ye want is a little rest. I'll send up a nice pot of tea and some hot water. Then I'll see what my man's done with your luggage."

"Thank you."

Mrs. Murray trotted to the door but paused to look back. "I still say ye could do worse than Mr. Kendrick. And if ye don't mind me sayin' so, he seems fair taken with ye."

Donella did mind but kept those rather rude thoughts to herself.

Chapter Six

Donella came blearily awake. Where was she? Not in her convent cell, waiting for the great bell to call her to early morning prayers. Why didn't she know where she was?

A spurt of panic jerked her upright. Her heart pounded as her gaze darted around the unfamiliar, shadow-drenched room. It took several slow, steadying breaths for her mind to settle, but the fog finally lifted and her memory dredged up the gruesome events of the last few days.

"Drat," she muttered as she flopped back onto her pillow.

As tired as she was, she longed for daybreak. One more night on the road and she'd be home to Blairgal and her family. Although it would be an awkward reunion, with a host of uncomfortable questions, she'd be safe in her uncle's stronghold. Even more importantly, she could share with him the fears that had seemed ridiculous one moment but all too real the next.

Mungo Murray.

The name conjured up painful, humiliating memories. She'd spent the last ten years trying to erase them. Now, her past had come back to haunt her, and at the worst possible time.

Over a solitary dinner in her room—Kendrick had eaten downstairs with Foster and Davey—she'd almost managed to convince herself that it was just her imagination spinning out of control. Mungo and the Murray Clan had surely long forgotten her. The likeliest explanation for the abduction attempt was that word had somehow gone round that she'd left the convent, and some enterprising group of bandits had tried to take advantage of her situation. She wouldn't be the first wealthy young lady to be abducted and held for a ransom or used as a bargaining chip in marriage negotiations.

That last bit was the troubling part. Ten years ago, Uncle Riddick had stood fast against the demands of Mungo Murray, and the vile man's threats to ruin her reputation. While her uncle had prevailed, as he always did, Mungo had vowed to extract revenge for the insult to his family, and especially to his son's honor.

Donella feared that day of reckoning had finally arrived.

After her unnerving conversation with Mrs. Murray, Donella had considered telling Kendrick of her suspicions. He obviously knew she was withholding information, and it would almost be a relief to tell him the truth. She'd kept silent for ten years, hiding the whopping, great secret that rattled behind her like a rusty chain. But now she no longer had the convenient shield of the convent to protect her.

Uncle Riddick had made Donella swear on the good name of Clan Graham to hold her tongue on what they referred to as *the incident*. That wasn't quite as serious as swearing on the Bible, but it was enough to inspire caution and the resolve to keep her suspicions to herself until she was safely home.

As for any further dangers on the road, she'd simply have to trust Kendrick to keep her safe. He'd done a splendid job so far, and she had little doubt he'd continue to do so even if she *did* keep refusing to answer his nosy inquiries. Fortunately, after brusquely reminding her to bolt her door, he'd taken himself off for the remainder of the evening.

Shivering a bit, Donella wriggled down under the quilt. As she tried to decide between saying a rosary or counting sheep, the quiet shuffle of footsteps outside her door made her freeze like a startled rabbit.

A key turned in her lock. A moment later, footsteps retreated down the hall.

Why would anyone lock a door that was already bolted? Had she misheard?

Rising, she grabbed her woolen shawl, flung it around her shoulders, and strode to the door. She pulled back the bolt and cautiously tried to open the door. Her heart jolted because someone had indeed locked her in.

Kendrick? He was irritating, but she doubted he would lock her in without telling her.

Ignoring a spiraling sense of dread, she cudgeled her brain for ideas. She had only one option—to pound on the door and, if necessary, start yelling. She could only hope that Kendrick would hear her first, and not the likely nefarious person who'd locked her in.

"Mr. Kendrick, can you hear me?" she called out after banging on the solid oak panel.

She waited several seconds before banging again. "Mr. Kendrick. Please wake up."

Silence met her straining ears.

Donella was winding herself up to start yelling when she heard the quick tread of boot steps.

"I'm here, lass," Kendrick said. "Are you all right?"

She sagged against the door in relief. "Yes, but someone's locked me in."

He rattled the lock. "What the devil?" he muttered.

"Can you please get me out of here?"

"I'll have to roust the Murrays out of bed. Although I suspect one of them is the prime suspect."

"Yes. I admit I find the notion disturbing."

"We'll get it sorted. In the meantime, bolt your door."

She shot the bolt.

"Good girl," he said. "If anything happens before I'm back, start screaming and I'll come running."

Donella devoutly hoped she would not be forced to resort to screaming—or fighting off more kidnappers.

Racing to her bag, she quickly dressed, thanking the saints for front-lacing stays and a dress that buttoned up the front. She wound a bandeau around her hair, and then retrieved the fireplace poker and went to stand by the door.

It seemed to take Kendrick forever to return. Donella quietly tapped her fingertips against the door, counting the long seconds as they passed. Had he been attacked and was lying unconscious? She felt woozy at the idea, so she rested her forehead against the door and said a few prayers to try to calm her unsettled nerves.

Finally, she heard footsteps, and then a key was inserted into the lock.

"It's me, lass," Kendrick said. "Open up."

Donella pulled back the bolt and opened the door. She blinked at the sight of him, clad in breeches and boots with only a leather vest over his naked chest. Since her eyes were but a few inches away from his torso, she was able to instantly deduce that his chest muscles were *quite* impressive.

He grimaced. "Sorry. When I heard you yell, I just grabbed what was close at hand."

Donella got *herself* in hand. "It's perfectly fine, sir."

Then she narrowed her gaze at Mrs. Murray behind him, dressed in a nightcap and wrapper and holding a lamp. "Ma'am, did your husband lock me in?"

"He did, I'm sorry to say," the innkeeper grimly replied.

"And where is he now?"

"Locked away in our bedroom. He'll nae worry ye, miss. For the moment, anyway."

Donella threw a startled glance at Kendrick.

"Aye, we're in trouble." He sounded more irritated than anything else.

She sighed. "Of course we are." She stepped aside to let them in.

When Kendrick threw the door bolt again, her stomach sank. Not just trouble—danger.

Mrs. Murray set the lamp down and cast Donella an unhappy look. "Mr. Kendrick told me of yer troubles, miss, and I was fair shocked. I'm right sorry to say that my fool of a husband was part of the plot to abduct ye."

Donella pressed a hand against her stomach. "That's why he was so surprised when he saw me. He expected the kidnapping to be successful."

The landlady nodded. "I would have locked him in the cellar myself, if I'd had a clue what he was up to with those hulver-headed cousins of his."

"So, it *was* someone from the Murray Clan," Donella said.

Mrs. Murray gave a morose nod.

"Do you know why?"

"I asked Mr. Murray that very same question," Kendrick said. "He refused to give me a straight answer but seemed to think you would know why."

Donella's stomach, which had been attempting to sink to her feet, promptly jumped into her throat. "I . . . I have no idea why the Murrays would wish to abduct me."

Kendrick's hard gaze flickered from her to Mrs. Murray, who pointedly looked at the ceiling.

"Try again, Miss Haddon," he said.

Donella scrambled to come up with something that sounded halfway sensible. "Most likely it has something to do with an old dispute between my uncle and one of the smaller branches of the Murray clan. I'm not entirely sure which family, or what the original problem was."

Kendrick crossed his arms over his chest, which caused various parts of his anatomy to bulge with muscle. "You are stating the obvious. What I want to know is what part you play in this farce. Whichever group of idiots this is, they seem to be going through a lot of trouble to get at you."

She crossed her fingers behind her back. "I truly don't know. You'll have to ask my uncle when you see him."

"And you have nothing else to add, madam?" he asked Mrs. Murray in a lethal tone.

The innkeeper was not to be intimidated, even by Logan Kendrick. "I'll nae betray my husband or my clan, sir. Ye'll have to speak to the laird to get yer answers."

Donella breathed a mental sigh of relief. "Of course you can't betray your clan, Mrs. Murray. And I appreciate your help, even though I'm sure it's put you in an awkward position."

"I willna allow my husband to be part of foul deeds against the Flower of Clan Graham or the Laird of Riddick," the woman stoutly said. "I may be a Murray by marriage, but my mam was a Graham on her da's side. I owe it to her memory to keep ye as safe as I can."

"Bloody clan nonsense," Kendrick muttered.

Donella pointedly ignored him. "The question is, what's to be done now?" she asked Mrs. Murray. "I assume your husband locked me in so another attempt could be made to abduct me."

"Aye, sometime before dawn."

"In the next two or three hours," Kendrick said.

"I'm thinkin' we'll be havin' company sooner rather than later," Mrs. Murray replied with a grimace.

"All right. You help Miss Haddon get ready, and I'll go to the stables and get my men to pole up the horses." Kendrick started for the door.

Donella held up a hand. "No, wait."

He paused in the doorway, impatient. "Yes?"

"If we rush off, they'll just come after us, like they did at the Perth Bridge. They know where we're going, after all. They're bound to catch up with us at some point."

He rubbed a hand over his head in clear frustration, pulling open the edges of his vest and exposing more muscle, liberally dusted with black hair. Donella had grown up in a family of brawny men, but Kendrick was even more formidably masculine than they were.

"We don't have all night, Miss Haddon," he growled. "If you have another suggestion, let's hear it."

She peeled her gaze from his chest. "We split up. Send Foster and Davey south to Dunblane, on the regular route to Blairgal. Our pursuers will follow the carriage. We take another route, away from Blairgal. There are less travelled ways to get to my uncle's castle. Once we throw them off our scent, we can take one of those."

Donella already had a very good idea of which way to go, but she had no intention of sharing it with Mrs. Murray.

Kendrick's gaze flicked to the innkeeper for a moment. Then he crossed his arms over his chest, frowning at the floor as he thought it through.

Donella quelled her impatience. He was a typically stubborn and overly protective Highland male. She could practically see him sifting through the objections in his mind, concerned not for himself but for those in his care.

"What happens when the blackguards catch up with the carriage?" he said. "Your grandfather won't be best pleased if they're hurt."

Mrs. Murray shook her head. "They'll no be hurtin' them if the lass isn't with them. I'm certain of it. She's the one they want."

Kendrick's suspicious gaze shifted between the two women. "Yes, and I wish like hell I knew why."

Blast. Why couldn't he let it go?

"As Mrs. Murray points out," Donella said firmly, "Davey and Foster have a better chance of getting back to Blairgal unharmed without us. Once they do, Uncle Riddick can send help."

"This is ridiculous," he exclaimed. "I'm tempted to stay here and confront the bastards myself. It's the Nineteenth Century, for God's sake. One simply cannot go around abducting women."

Argh.

"Mr. Kendrick, there is *very* bad blood between some of the Murray clan and my family. Surely you haven't forgotten how deeply resentment can run between clans, even nowadays."

"She's right, sir," Mrs. Murray said. "They won't hurt yer servants, but they will hurt ye, if ye stand in their way."

He waved a dismissive hand at that notion.

"I could get hurt if there's a fight," Donella pointed out.

His eyes narrowed to wintery-blue slits. "I don't like being manipulated, lass."

When she simply gave him a smile in reply, he cracked a grudging laugh. "All right, we'll try it your way." He glanced at Mrs. Murray. "I'm assuming you can provide Miss Haddon and me with horses?"

The woman shook her head. "I've just one, sir. The others are jobbed out."

"Is it a sturdy animal?" Donella asked. "Could it carry both of us?"

"Aye, miss. It's a draft horse, and strong enough to carry ye both. Ye can hire a second horse once ye reach another inn, I ken."

"Goddammit," Kendrick muttered, as if he'd just remembered something.

Donella frowned. "Sir, that language is—"

"Do you know how bad this will look if we're recognized?" he interrupted. "Before, we at least had Davey and Foster to lend us a measure of respectability. Now we'll be travelling alone, on the same horse no less."

"Oh, dear," she weakly said.

He was right. That would be extremely bad for both of them. Her reputation, already hanging by a thread, would be in tatters.

"Perhaps ye could pretend to be husband and wife," Mrs. Murray suggested.

Kendrick looked appalled. Donella certainly understood his reaction, although she couldn't help feeling a tiny bit insulted.

"That is not an option, Mrs. Murray," she said.

"*Indeed* it is not," he said.

"Feel free to make a constructive suggestion. For once," Donella couldn't help saying in a snippy tone.

Kendrick ignored her jibe, regarding her with a thoughtful expression.

Donella waved her arms. "What?"

"Miss Haddon's hair is very short," he said to Mrs. Murray. "And she's quite tall for a woman."

The innkeeper looked blank for a moment, then snapped her fingers. "Aye, that she is, sir."

"What are you talking about?" Donella asked.

"You have what she'll need?" Kendrick asked.

"Our stable boy's things should do the trick," Mrs. Murray replied.

"Perfect. Then get Miss Haddon ready. I've got to give Foster and Davey instructions and get this blasted plan in motion."

The wretched man thought she could pose as a boy? How charming. Donella gritted her teeth as Kendrick opened the door and disappeared without a backward glance.

The innkeeper turned to her with a smile. "Now, miss. Let's get ye out of those clothes."

Chapter Seven

A pat to the knee dragged Donella out of an uneasy doze.

"We're here," Kendrick said. "Let's get you into a proper bed, so you can have a proper sleep."

An unlikely image flashed through her sleep-deprived brain—Kendrick's arms wrapped securely around her as they snuggled under a quilt. It made her jerk away from him, hard enough that she nearly tumbled off the rear of the horse.

Kendrick grabbed her wrist and pulled her forward. Without thinking, Donella wrapped an arm around his waist and flattened herself to his back to keep from falling.

Her breasts were unsecured by stays and covered only by a thin shirt and a sturdy woolen jerkin. It made her aware of her body in a way she'd never noticed before—especially when pressed against *him*. She felt curiously unfettered, as if some part of her had been let free after a long and dreary confinement.

Still, her boy's attire was scandalous, and the sooner she donned proper clothing—and put some distance between herself and Logan Kendrick—the better.

She braced her other hand on his broad back. "Sorry, I didn't mean to startle the horse."

The poor animal, a large, sturdy fellow, had been forced to carry them for several hours, much to her backside's discomfort. Kendrick had done his best for her, draping a thick woolen blanket behind his saddle, but no amount of padding could eliminate the misery of bouncing around on a horse's rump.

"Och, you've done well under less than optimal circumstances. Hang on for a moment longer and I'll get you down from there."

Donella peered around the cobblestoned yard of the coaching inn, boxed in on three sides by a two-storied building and lit by a single lantern set by the front door. A small chaise and an old-fashioned travelling coach were tucked into one corner of the yard. The hushed atmosphere suggested a small inn that did not see much traffic from the main road.

"Where are we?" she asked.

"About a mile off the highway. I thought it best to avoid the larger inns."

Given the hastily assembled nature of her disguise, that made sense. It was doubtful that Donella's new identity would stand up to much scrutiny.

Kendrick impatiently looked about. "Where's the bloody . . . ah, finally."

A door swung open, spilling light in an angled ray across the stones of the courtyard. A stoop-shouldered man with a lantern hurried out to greet them. "Sorry, sir. I was in the back of the house when ye rode in."

"You have rooms available?" Kendrick asked.

The fellow eyed them with curiosity. "Aye. Will ye be needin' one or two?"

"My brother and I will share one."

The porter hooked his lantern over a post and went to the horse's head. Kendrick swung his leg over for a sliding dismount, then turned to reach for Donella.

"Come along, laddie. I'll help you."

"I'm fine," she said, affecting the gruffest tone she could manage.

His massive hands encircled her waist.

"Your muscles must be cramped. Don't want you falling on your arse, now do we, lad?" he teased.

Donella swallowed an ill-considered retort and leaned into him, letting his strong arms guide her to the ground. She stumbled when her boots hit the cobblestones, but Kendrick held her steady and much too close. Her short wool coat had flared open, and her body pressed directly against him. If she'd thought his back was muscled, his front was more so. In fact . . .

Her mind skittered away from the thought as he spun her around and started her toward the inn. He held on to her arm, which was probably a good thing, since her legs were indeed tight and sore from the ride.

Her knees were a bit wobbly too, although she suspected another reason for that.

"You'll see to my horse?" Kendrick asked the porter.

"I'll wake a stable hand. If ye'll wait by the desk in the hall, I'll be with ye in a trice."

Kendrick steered Donella toward the open door, keeping a firm grip when she stumbled again. "Careful, lass," he murmured. "We don't need you cracking your skull."

"It's the boots. They're too big."

Since her convent shoes had not been suitable for riding, Mrs. Murray had unearthed a pair of old boots owned by a former groom. They'd been forced to stuff socks in the toes to make them wearable.

"I'm sorry about this." Kendrick ushered her into a small but tidy entrance hall. "I know it's all incredibly uncomfortable for you."

Donella sank into a chair at an old writing desk with numerous cubbyholes stuffed with papers. The chair was cane-backed and hard, yet it felt like heaven after the horse's bouncing rump.

She pulled off her knit gloves and wriggled the warmth back into her fingers. "Hah. Uncomfortable is kneeling for two hours on the stone floor of an unheated chapel."

Kendrick went to build up the small peat fire in the hearth. "And did that happen often?"

When she started to tug the itchy woolen cap from her head, he gave her a warning shake.

Sighing, she pulled the cap back down over her rumpled hair. "Sister Bernard thought it an appropriate punishment for my numerous transgressions."

He tossed her a sympathetic glance. "Were they really that numerous?"

"I'm here, aren't I?" she replied, trying to make a joke out of it.

Pity from him was the last thing she wanted. True, she'd been rejected once again, but she'd find another way to get where she needed to go, even if she wasn't yet sure of the destination.

Kendrick propped a shoulder against the stone mantelpiece. For a man who'd fought off a band of attackers, organized an escape, and ridden halfway through the night, he looked remarkably fresh. His boots had nary a scuffmark, and his doeskin breeches clung to his long legs with perfect tailoring.

He looked exactly what he was, a wealthy member of the landed gentry—not a respectable farmer of modest means, travelling with his little brother. While she might fit the part in her cobbled-together outfit, his appearance did not match their cover story.

Kendrick flashed her a roguish smile. "Do tell me more, Miss Haddon. And don't leave out the good bits."

Refusing to be charmed, Donella ignored his teasing. "I don't know if we're going to pull off this little charade. You look nothing like a Country Harry, although I expect I could pass for your scruffy little brother."

He waggled a hand. "I think you're more the problem than I am."

"Really? This outfit is shapeless, and I look perfectly grubby."

"Not entirely shapeless. And then there's your face."

"Which is no doubt as grubby as the rest of me." She wrinkled her nose. "And this outfit does smell like it belonged to a stable boy."

"True, but you *are* the Flower of Clan Graham. A little dirt can't conceal your charms."

Donella repressed a stab of irritation. "It's a foolish name that I was glad to leave behind. I would be grateful if you didn't refer to it again."

His smile turned rueful. "I was only teasing, lass."

"I'm not one for teasing, as I'm sure you've noticed."

"I have noticed. It's commendably nunlike of you."

She tried not to clench her teeth. "I'm no longer a nun, in case you failed to notice that, too."

Something considerably warmer than amusement gleamed in his eyes. "Oh, I've noticed."

After three years in the convent, Donella had forgotten how irritating men could be, and how easily they could wind her up.

She scowled at the floor, trying to keep her temper under control. "Where *is* that blasted porter?"

At the sound of footsteps from outside, Kendrick straightened up. "I believe salvation is finally at hand, Miss Haddon."

"Thank goodness. I'm so tired I can barely think."

"Just a few more minutes, then you can sleep," he said in a soothing tone.

Lovely. Now he was treating her like a fractious toddler. Donella supposed she couldn't entirely blame him.

The porter entered the hall, a blast of cold air and

dead leaves whirling in behind him. He slammed the door shut, shaking his head and muttering imprecations about *old Brumby*.

"Is there a problem?" Kendrick asked.

"Nay, sir. Just a little trouble roustin' the stable hand out of his bed." He grimaced an apology. "We dinna usually have travellers callin' this late."

Donella started to apologize, but Kendrick shook his head. He'd warned her to speak as little as possible, something that was proving to be a bit of a challenge.

"We're sorry to put you out," he said. "Were you able to make appropriate arrangements for my horse?"

"Aye, sir. Got him rubbed down and bedded for the night. Ye'll not be needin' to worry about him."

"Splendid, Mr. . . ."

"Just Hamish, sir." The porter rummaged in the old desk. "We don't stand on ceremony 'ere at the Crown and Thistle."

"Excellent. Then I'd be grateful if you could show us to a room, preferably one at the back of the inn. My little brother is dead on his feet, and I've got to get him into bed."

Donella felt her face heat up. When Kendrick flashed her an amused look, she cursed her fair skin and russet hair. She rarely blushed, but when she did there was no hiding it. Her blasted escort had an uncanny ability to make her color up like a schoolgirl.

Hamish glanced up from his inspection of ratty-looking quills and finally gave Donella a good look. She slouched down in her chair, trying her best to imitate a rumpled boy.

The porter studied her with a puzzled expression. "Yer brother, eh? Not much of a family resemblance."

"Half brother," Kendrick said in a bored voice. "And far more trouble than he's worth. Just got expelled from school, in fact. The good sisters didn't know what to do with him."

Donella glared daggers at him.

"He looks the type to give no end of trouble," Hamish

said. "Best give him a wee paddlin'. Spare the rod and spoil the child, my mam used to say."

Kendrick's eyes gleamed with unholy mirth. Donella made a silent vow to murder him once she got to safety.

"I'll be sure to see to that later, Hamish. But our room, if you don't mind."

"Right, sir." Hamish pulled a bottle of ink from a cubbyhole. "If ye'll just sign here."

Kendrick signed the ledger.

The porter peered at the signature. "Mr. MacDonald, eh? Well, follow me up, sir."

Donella forced herself to her feet but then froze, as understanding *finally* blasted through the fog in her brain.

One room. They would be sharing *one room*.

Kendrick cocked an eyebrow, but she just shook her head. No sane person, especially a farmer of modest means, would book a separate room for his grubby little brother. As shocking and unnerving as it would be to sleep in the same bedroom with him, she'd simply have to manage it.

She trudged down a long hall to the back of the inn. Hamish fumbled with the key, then let them into the room. He quickly lit a fire in the small grate and pulled the chamber pot out from under the high bed. Donella was suddenly riveted by the entirely ordinary pot, which to her addled brain now took on a sinister aspect.

How would she attend to her personal needs with her *brother* sharing the room? While she'd experienced some humiliating and terrible things in her life, this was starting to rank fairly close to the top.

"Please bring a pitcher of hot water," Kendrick said. "We would both like a wash. Oh, and an extra blanket, if possible."

Again, Hamish regarded Donella with disapproval. "Best not to spoil the lad, if ye ask me. A night sleepin' on the floor would do him a world o' good."

"Why do you think I want the extra blanket?" Kendrick said with a wink.

Donella stuck her tongue out at him.

Hamish tsked and scuttled out, promising to return in a few minutes.

"Was that performance really necessary?" she asked. "You made me sound like a budding criminal."

Kendrick shrugged. "Hamish was on his way to believing you were *not* a boy. My little act was necessary to divert his suspicions."

She still couldn't help scowling at him. "Then I'll be sure to look as bratty as possible when he returns."

"Actually, I think you're quite a natural," he replied with annoying insouciance.

"Now, see here, Mr. Kendrick—"

A knock interrupted her. "Here's yer blanket, sir," said Hamish, handing it through the doorway.

"Excellent timing. This little scamp was about to deliver me a rousing scold."

"Dinna be takin' lip from the young'uns, sir," Hamish advised. "A spankin' is the cure when they get smart with ye."

"I will take that under advisement," Kendrick replied, barely repressing his amusement.

It was the dead of the night, they were on the run, and yet the blasted man was apparently enjoying himself. She, however, was tempted to smash the blasted chamber pot over his blasted head.

"The kitchen boy will be up with hot water soon." Hamish peered around the door at Donella. "And ye best behave yerself, lad, if ye hope to avoid a paddlin'."

She could only level a ferocious glare.

"Touched in the head, I reckon," Hamish muttered as he departed the room.

She mentally flinched. The old fellow's comment was much too close to home.

Kendrick, pulling off his greatcoat, paused to study her. "What's amiss, lass?"

Donella decided she truly did want to break Logan Kendrick's skull.

No wonder they kicked you out of the convent, with that temper of yours.

"What's amiss? I spent the last three hours clinging to the back end of a horse, someone is trying to abduct me, I'm in a smelly disguise, and you have just convinced a perfect stranger that I'm mentally defective. If anyone ever finds out about all this, I will be completely humiliated."

Kendrick tossed his coat onto the worn leather club chair in front of the hearth.

"If anyone finds out about this little escapade, embarrassment will be the least of your problems." Then he grinned. "Although even you must admit there are some rather hilarious elements to our situation."

"Really? Because no one is threatening to paddle you."

"Very true. Although the suggestion does have a certain appeal."

For a moment, her mind went blank. Then she took a hasty step back. "If you come near me, I will make you sorrier than you've ever been."

He blinked, startled by her reaction. "It was only a joke, lass. A bad one, obviously, and I beg your pardon."

She eyed him, unsure how to respond to his rapid change in demeanor.

"Miss Haddon, I would never harm you," he quietly said. "Never. And I am clearly a moron if I gave you that impression. In fact, my oldest brother reminds me on a regular basis that I am indeed a moron. I have a lamentable tendency to joke at the most inappropriate moments. Please forgive me."

Regret softened the hard angles of his masculine features. Donella tried to find the words to respond, but they tangled up on her tongue. She'd always been a disaster when it came to managing men—probably because she didn't understand them—and it would seem she was holding true to form.

Kendrick spread his hands wide. "Lass, yer killin' me over here."

It was the exaggerated brogue that did it. She had to smile.

"Of course I forgive you, sir. And I apologize if I overreacted."

"You'll not be apologizing to me. I had no business teasing you, especially after the day you've had. What you need is some sleep."

Donella cast a furtive glance at the bed.

Kendrick sighed. "I would truly love to be able to give you some privacy, but it would raise too many questions and not be safe."

"I know. I'm being silly."

"Not at all. But you will sleep on the bed, and I will take this tattered excuse for a blanket and sleep on the floor."

Now she began to feel guilty. "That's not very fair. After all, you're doing all the hard work."

"Och, I've slept in rougher conditions."

"I lived in a convent, remember? I slept in a small, cold room on a narrow cot. We were called to prayer during the night and then again at dawn."

"That sounds rather gruesome."

Suddenly, and in a great wave of loneliness, she missed the safety and peace of her old life so fiercely she almost burst into tears.

She plopped down on his coat in the creaky leather chair, finally overcome with the trials of the day. "I know," she whispered. "But it was my home."

He approached her as one would a skittish foal. Hunkering down, he took her hands and began chafing warmth back into them. Until he touched her, Donella hadn't realized how cold she was.

"I'm sorry you miss it."

She gave an awkward shrug. "It's for the best. I really wasn't a very good nun."

His eyes, normally the color of blue ice on a mountain lake, turned warm with sympathy. "Maybe it wasn't the right life for you. And you have another home to return to. Blairgal is a grand place, and your family is eager for your return."

Donella rarely cried, but his kindness brought the sting of tears to her eyes.

"I . . ." She had to stop and clear her throat.

"Lass, if you cry, I'll be forced to do something drastic," he said gruffly.

"Such as?" she managed.

"Run from the room, most likely. I'm *terrified* of crying women. And children? Even worse."

His silly comment made her laugh.

Kendrick grinned. "That's better. Now if we could only . . . ah." He rose and went to answer the tap on the door.

"Here be yer water, sir," said the sleepy-looking kitchen boy.

Kendrick handed over a shilling and took the water pitcher.

"I'll visit the necessary while you have a quick wash and get in bed," he said to Donella. "All right?"

She nodded, grateful for his tact.

By the time he returned, she'd stripped down to her stockings and shirt and crawled under the covers. The mattress was thin and the linens stiff and scratchy, but she was so happy to be finally lying down.

Kendrick tapped on the door before stepping into the room. He shot the bolt and then went to check the latch and close the shutters on the single window.

"I'm sorry you have to sleep on the floor," she said softly.

"I'll do fine. Just try to rest."

He snuffed the lamp and shadows fell over the room.

Donella turned on her side and gathered up the pillow,

trying to ignore the fact that he was but a few feet away as he tugged off his boots and stripped down to his breeches and shirt.

For a few moments, he stood in front of the hearth, his frame outlined by the flickering light of the fire. As he shook out the blanket, his brawny shoulders shifted under the fabric of his shirt. The man was built like a warrior, with long, hard lines and superbly controlled strength.

When Kendrick crouched down to arrange his blanket on the floor, his breeches stretched tight, outlining the tight muscles of his backside and thighs. Donella's mind seemed to go soft and fuzzy at the sight of him, and her body flushed with heat. Mortified, she quickly rolled onto her back, accidentally sending her pillow off the bed.

"All right over there?" came his low, rumbling voice.

Drat.

"I knocked my pillow off."

"I'll get it for you."

"No, I'll do it." She started to shoot upright before remembering she was barely clothed. She instantly slid back under the covers.

"It's no problem." Two long steps brought him to the bed, and he swiped up the pillow and held it out to her.

Clutching the covers to her neck, she snaked out a hand and grabbed the pillow. She awkwardly wedged it under her head.

Kendrick watched her maneuvers with amusement. "Miss Haddon, you do realize that your virtue is perfectly safe with me."

She scowled. "Of course. For one thing, my brother and my cousin would murder you, and then they'd make you marry me."

"In the reverse order, I hope, for your sake."

She glared up at the ceiling, hating that she'd sounded so foolish. What was wrong with her?

With a chuckle, he returned to his makeshift pallet. She listened to him settle in, then closed her eyes, determined to ignore the disconcerting circumstances as best she could.

Despite her exhaustion, however, her ruffled nerves prevented her from falling asleep. Rustling noises from near the hearth suggested Kendrick was chasing slumber, too.

Maybe if they talked a bit, she would soon drift off.

"Why MacDonald?" she asked.

"Sorry?"

"Why did you pick that particular name to sign the register?"

"It's my grandfather's name. Angus MacDonald."

"Ah, I had an uncle named Angus—Angus Graham. He was chieftain of our particular branch of the clan. He's dead, though. He died during my first year in the convent."

"I'm sorry."

"Thank you. He was a good man, if a bit stern. Is your grandfather still alive?"

"Very much so. I expect Grandda will outlive us all."

"Does he live in Glasgow, too?"

"At the moment, he lives in Canada. Halifax, to be exact."

She turned her head so she could see him. Lying under the blanket, his greatcoat rolled up under his head, he was a large, comforting presence between her and the dangers of the outside world.

"What's he doing there?"

"Stirring up trouble, I expect."

"What sort of trouble?"

"It's a long story, too long for tonight. You need your sleep."

"But—"

"Go to sleep, Donella," he said firmly. "We have a long day ahead, and I don't want to have to lug you about because you're half-dead on your feet."

She bristled. "I'll be fine. You needn't worry about me."

"Excellent, but I'll be half-dead if you don't let me sleep. And that *will* be something we have to worry about."

She realized she was being rather selfish. "Sorry, I didn't mean to—"

"Lass, just *go to sleep*."

Torn between irritation and guilt, she turned from him, resigning herself to a sleepless night.

Chapter Eight

Donella was half-sprawled on her stomach, her arms wrapped around her pillow. She seemed incredibly innocent in her abandoned slumber.

The fact that she'd kicked off most of her covers was something of a problem—a *big* problem. Her shirt had twisted around her body, riding high on her thighs and exposing the creamy white skin between the paltry hem of the garment and the tops of her stockings. The blasted thing was pulled tight around her rump, outlining unexpected and delightfully generous curves. Her russet hair, gleaming in the pale light of dawn, was a glorious mess that barely reached her shoulders—one of which was fully revealed by her sagging neckline.

All that delicious skin was so smooth and tempting that Logan's fingers itched to stroke it.

He briefly closed his eyes, fighting for control. While the lass was no longer a nun, she'd just spent three years holed up in a convent. Logan had committed his fair share of sins over the years, but he didn't need to add lusting after an almost-nun to the list.

Gingerly, he inched the quilt up over her gorgeous arse.

Then he leaned over the bed to gently tap her sleep-flushed cheek.

"Wake up, lass," he murmured. "We're in trouble."

She breathed out a weary little sigh and rolled over onto her back. Her lush lips parted and the tip of her tongue slipped out, wet and pink. Logan had to clamp down hard on the urge to take her mouth in a devouring kiss.

Get a hold of yourself, you randy bastard.

He tapped her cheek more firmly. "Donella, you need to wake up."

Her thick lashes fluttered up. Eyes as green and soft as moss, hazy with sleep, stared up at him. For a moment, Logan felt like he was falling into something so peaceful and sweet that nothing could ever disturb it.

A moment later, her gaze snapped into focus, turning as sharp as cut glass. "What did you say?"

"We're in trouble. Time to go."

She sighed. "Trouble. Of course." Then she eyed him for a few seconds. "You'd best let me get up."

"Oh, right." He stepped away from the bed, feeling like an idiot.

Donella sat up. Though she dragged the covers around her shoulders, he nonetheless got a peek of the tops of her pretty breasts, as round and creamy as the rest of her.

God, she really was going to kill him.

He turned his back and began shoving his gear into his kit.

"What's happening?" she asked.

"There are men in the yard asking questions about us. About you."

"How did they find us so quickly?"

He flashed a glance over his shoulder but jerked his gaze away when she threw back the covers and slid to the floor.

"Not Mr. MacDonald and his brother," he said. "They're looking for Logan Kendrick and Donella Haddon."

"I suppose our bait and switch wasn't that effective after all. I just hope they didn't hurt Uncle's men."

"I think it's unlikely. It's you they're after."

"Still, this is my fault. You're all in danger because—"

"Try not to worry, lass. Davey and Foster know how to take care of themselves."

"Oh, blast," she muttered.

Logan yanked on his vest, and then chanced looking over his shoulder. Donella had managed to wriggle into her breeches but was having trouble lacing up her woolen jerkin.

"Do you need help?"

"Apparently, I'm all thumbs when it comes to boy's clothing."

He crossed to help her, brushing her hands aside and quickly lacing her up. She stood quietly as he worked, although her cheeks turned a bright shade of pink.

"Thank you," she said in an adorably gruff tone when he finished.

"My pleasure."

It was an automatic response, but he couldn't fail to catch her wince.

"Hopefully not," she muttered when he turned back to his packing.

Logan didn't know whether to laugh or curse.

"Did you actually see our pursuers?" she asked.

"Yes, when I went out to use the necessary. I was about to cut across the yard when three men rode in, their horses lathered up. It seemed suspicious this early in the morning, so I lurked about to see what they were up to."

"You're rather large to be lurking. Are you sure they didn't see you?"

"Lass, I excel at lurking. No one saw me."

She grabbed her boots and socks. "And are you sure they actually referred to me by name?"

"Miss Haddon, I hear as well as I lurk."

She grimaced and went back to dragging on her boots. "What time is it?"

"Going on seven. Hamish is still on duty, and he'd just commenced a gabfest with our unwelcome visitors when I snuck back here."

"Oh, that's not good."

"Yes, the old boy doesn't strike me as discreet. He'll be happy to describe who arrived at the inn last night."

Donella stomped her foot down into her boot and straightened. "So, what do we do?"

"Since we can't go waltzing out the front door, I'm off to do a little more skulking to see if we can make it out through the back. If not, we'll have to use the window to make our escape."

She regarded his proposed exit with a dubious eye. "Are you sure you'll fit? You are rather large."

"I'm aware of that." It would appear that large men were not her type, which he found rather irritating.

She was a nun. She doesn't have a type.

"I'll manage it," he added, "but I would prefer the back door."

"How are we going to get to our horse?"

"We're not."

Her eyebrows shot up. "We're walking?"

"Yes. We're going up into the hills."

"But—"

"Donella, we can discuss the plan once we get out of here, all right?"

Her lips thinned, but then she gave a terse nod. "What do you want me to do?"

"I suggest you take the chance to use the chamber pot, since we'll be leaving as soon as I return."

She winced. "I must say this is turning out to be the most embarrassing episode of my entire life."

He flashed a smile as he headed to the door. "Chin up, lass. Just think of it as a grand adventure."

"I hate adventures," she muttered.

He slipped out into the hall. For a woman who hated adventures, she'd done well, displaying both strength and character. Most girls of her class would have succumbed to hysterics long ago. And though she had a tendency to argue, she'd followed his orders when it counted.

Logan had the impression from her family that Donella was a biddable, even shy woman who retreated into the background. Yet he'd found her quite the opposite, which probably accounted for her dismissal from the nunnery. Donella might not be the sort of girl to flirt or talk the ears off a man, but biddable or shy? Not a chance.

He'd only known her for a few days, but there seemed to be more to Donella than her family realized.

The inn was stirring. Dishes clattered in the taproom and footsteps thumped on the floor above. The entrance hall was empty, but that meant Hamish was likely still out gabbing with the mysterious riders. If those men had a particle of brains, they would soon deduce that something was off about Mr. MacDonald and his strange little brother.

Logan risked a careful look out the window. A stable boy washed down the cobblestones, but otherwise the yard appeared deserted. But that did them no good since they needed to head up into the hills, not back on the road.

Retreating, he paused to leave some coin on the desk, then quickly made his way back down the hall to the door at the end of the wing. He'd just cracked it open when he heard a shout from the direction of the stables. Feet pounded across the cobblestones, followed by more shouting and a call to search the inn.

Dammit to hell.

Under normal circumstances, he'd have no qualms about confronting the blighters but wouldn't take any chances with Donella's safety. He had to get her out of harm's way as quickly as possible.

Moments later, he was back in the room. Donella was fully dressed and folding up a small bundle into a makeshift sack.

"I thought we might be able to use the blanket and extra candles," she explained.

"Good thinking." He shot the bolt across the door.

"I see it's the window."

"Aye."

Donella followed him to the window. Logan slung his kit over his shoulder and yanked back the shutter, then pushed the latticed window open.

"I hope you made use of the chamber pot," he said as he hoisted her onto the sill.

She swung her legs over. "If you mention that one more time, I will clobber you."

The drop to the ground was a little high for his liking. "Careful, now. We don't want you—"

Donella kicked off the sill, landing in a neat crouch before looking up at him. "You were saying, sir?"

He snorted and dropped his kit and her bundle to the ground. When he started to climb through the opening, he discovered it was *quite* a tight fight.

"Don't get stuck," she warned.

As if he'd let that happen.

Logan pulled back and stripped off his greatcoat, tossing it down to her. Then he grabbed the top of the window frame and pulled himself up, then swung through in one go. He managed to tear a sleeve on the way down, but otherwise was unscathed.

Donella blinked at him. "That was quite impressive."

"I might say the same about you, lass."

Her smile was shy. "Thank you. I was rather athletic as a young girl." The smile faded. "For a while, anyway."

There was a story there, and he found himself wanting to hear it. For now, he had other things to worry about, like getting their arses out of harm's way.

He shrugged back into his greatcoat. "Athletic is good right now."

Donella had already slung her bundle over her shoulder, so he grabbed his kit and guided her toward a farmer's field behind the inn. They dodged through a kitchen garden, having to crouch at one point below a low hedge when they heard some more shouting, but they were able to skulk away without incident.

A few hedgerows and a field of oats later, they were safely away. Repeated glances over his shoulder told Logan that no one had yet thought to check behind the inn.

Miracle of miracles, they'd pulled it off. Now, all they had was a stiff day's climb up to a crofter's cottage. There he hoped they would find shelter and a hopefully not-too-long and not-too-cold wait for rescue. He trusted that Davey and Foster had gotten through with his message to Lord Riddick. If not, he would have to devise another plan to get Donella home.

They splashed through a little creek that separated the field from the first set of foothills. Logan glanced at Donella, who seemed unperturbed by their narrow escape.

"Ready for a climb, lass?"

She shot him a wry glance. "'I will lift up mine eyes unto the hills.'"

Then she set off briskly up the narrow track, leaving him to follow in her footsteps.

* * *

Logan glanced back, checking Donella's progress. She'd fallen considerably behind him now, grimly making her way up the narrow track. He'd offered several times to take her bundle, or even haul her up the steepest bits by the hand. Each time, she'd politely declined with the reminder that she too had grown up in the Highlands and was sturdier than she looked.

She didn't look particularly sturdy, though, with her willowy build and pale complexion. While he couldn't help but worry, Donella was both stubborn and proud, and he'd not insult her again by insisting she needed help.

Thankfully, they'd evaded their pursuers—more Murray clansmen, presumably. He suspected it might not occur to them that he would take a gently born lady into the mountains. The blighters had probably headed back out onto the highway or gone haring off down the blessedly large number of country lanes.

If their luck held out, Logan and Donella should reach the rendezvous point before nightfall.

Alec Gilbride probably wouldn't be there. Donella's cousin was resourceful, but it would still take him a full day to reach the remote crofter's cottage high in the hills above Loch Katrine. And that would only be if Foster and Davey had made it back to Blairgal Castle in good order. While Donella was right to feel anxious about the well-being of Riddick's men, Logan continued to downplay her concerns. For one thing, she didn't need the additional worry. For another, Foster and Davey would feel honor bound to protect their laird's niece by any means necessary, no matter the cost.

Logan reached a level stretch of trail with several large, flat rocks by the side of it. Thank God the weather had cooperated. Even though it was almost the end of November, the skies were sunny and the breezes fairly mild. But dusk would be upon them soon, and the temperature would plummet. Climbing these narrow, rocky paths after dark would be treacherous, and spending the night outdoors would be challenging. He'd done it hundreds of times over the years, both in Scotland and in Canada. He would survive just fine.

But Donella wasn't dressed to spend a night on a cold mountain, even with a fire and huddled under a ratty old blanket. For all that the convent had toughened her up, she was still unused to conditions like this.

She huffed as she trudged up the last bit to join him, starting to limp. They'd been climbing for hours, with only brief stops and yet the lass hadn't complained once. She'd even completed the first part of the climb with serene good cheer, but the last few hours, when they'd moved out of the foothills into proper mountains, she'd fallen silent, concentrating on putting one foot in front of the other.

Donella looked up as the path leveled out, stumbling to a halt as if surprised to see him there. "Why are we stopping?"

"I thought we could both use a rest. That last stretch was rather steep."

She rolled her eyes. "You mean you think *I* could use a rest. You'd be miles ahead by now, if not for me."

"Nonsense. You climb better than any woman I've ever known."

She sank down onto a nearby rock and dropped her makeshift pack on the ground beside her. "Do you actually know any women who climb?"

"A few."

She raised a skeptical eyebrow.

"Back in Canada," he clarified. "The trappers' wives often travel with them. They were as capable of surviving in the wilderness as their husbands."

"Uncle Riddick mentioned once that you had established a fur trading business in Canada. He said you'd done quite well."

"Furs and timber. My business is based in Halifax, but I'm in the process of expanding in Scotland, too."

She stretched out one of her legs and began absently rubbing her knee. Clad as she was in close-fitting breeches, it was impossible to avoid noting that her legs were long and shapely.

"My uncle also has interests in the timber trade." She flashed him a smile that looked more like a grimace as she worked down to the muscles of her calf. "You should talk to him about it sometime. Uncle is always looking for ways to improve his businesses, and I'm sure you'd have much in common."

Logan made a noncommittal noise. *Uncle,* in fact, had a reputation for being rather cutthroat when it came to business. And since he'd only just started talking to Riddick about possible joint ventures, he wouldn't mention it to her. Experience had taught him that displays of eagerness in the early stages of negotiations were never a good idea.

Besides, he made it a point not to discuss business with elegant Scottish ladies. They were rarely interested, for one thing, and some had an alarming tendency to gossip. Not that Donella seemed the gossiping sort, but she *was* a Haddon. Anything he told her would likely make its way back to her uncle.

He glanced across the valley at the rugged hills. The sun was rapidly setting and would soon fall behind Ben Venue on the opposite side of Loch Katrine. Best they get a move on, or they'd never reach the cottage by nightfall.

"It's grand, isn't it?" Donella said.

Logan followed her gaze to the vista of woodland pastures topped by the craggy hills of the Trossachs. Flashes of blue in the glens hinted at the small lochs and streams that dotted this part of Scotland. In the distance, the setting sun glinted off the watery shield of Katrine, which they might have to cross to reach the safety of Donella's ancestral home.

The loch was his back-up plan. If Alec failed to show by midafternoon tomorrow, he'd get Donella down to Katrine, find a boatman, and cross to Blairgal by water. It was risky, since it would involve going into one of the local villages, but it would also be the quickest way to get her home.

"Those years in the convent . . . I'd almost forgotten how beautiful it is here," Donella dreamily added.

He studied her face, with its high, elegant cheekbones and proud nose, both softened by a whimsical splash of freckles. The lines were splendid, befitting an ancient Celtic princess. With her long neck and straight-backed posture, one might think she'd just stepped off the dance floor instead of trudging up a mountain path. Even the tousled hair and rumpled cap couldn't detract from her natural beauty. In fact, he rather liked the effect. It made her seem almost raffish, like a tomboy, but one who, in an instant, could transform into a beautiful, graceful woman.

It was a silly thought that made his heart hurt like hell. Because in a way that made no sense at all, Donella had suddenly reminded him of his wife.

He stared out at the splendid view, forced to blink several times to clear his vision.

"Yes, it's quite grand," he said gruffly. "Nothing like the mountains around Loch Long, of course, but the Trossachs will do nicely."

Donella made a derisive sound. "The Trossachs are *miles* better than your part of Scotland. We have Loch Lomond, after all, and Rob Roy's cave, and Ben Venue, and Loch Katrine—"

He held up a hand to stop her, stifling a chuckle. Castle Kinglas and Blairgal Castle were only a day's ride from each other, and yet she displayed the bred-in-the-bone loyalty to hearth and home that typified the Scottish clansman or woman.

"You have them, but we have Loch Long," he said.

"What's so special about Loch Long?"

"It's long."

Donella laughed. It was the first, full-throated laugh he'd heard since meeting her, and it was warm and sweet and comforting, like a bowl of hot chocolate on a cold winter's morning. He and his brothers had drunk the stuff by the jugful when they were lads. In those days, when their family had been happy and whole, life had seemed like a wonderful adventure just waiting to happen.

The sound of her laugh was entirely unexpected, and it eased the ache to his soul when he thought of his wife and all he'd lost with her passing.

"On that ridiculous note," she said, rising and peering up the trail, "I suppose we'd best be on our way. How much longer, do you think?"

"Only about an hour to the top, and then a wee jog down to the crofter's cottage. We'll spend the night there and hopefully join up with Alec in the morning."

"Are you sure he'll be able to find us? Alasdair was away from home for over ten years. He might not be familiar with these parts."

Logan picked up her bundle and handed it over. "I gave Foster very specific instructions."

Donella nodded before starting up the trail, her limp more pronounced than before.

"Hold up, lass."

She looked over her shoulder. "Yes?"

"I'm worried about that limp."

She waved a dismissive hand. "It's just a blister. I'll be fine."

Blisters were anything but fine. They could quickly go raw, or even get infected. Then they'd be in trouble.

He dropped his pack. "Sit down and take off your boot."

"Don't be ridiculous. As you've already noted, darkness is fast approaching, and we need to reach that cottage before nightfall."

The prissy, almost-nun had returned. Bizarrely, he found her even more adorable when she was scolding him.

"You don't have to prove your mettle to me, Miss Haddon. But it's foolish for you to suffer if there's something I can do about it."

"My boots are too big, so they're rubbing. I'll soak my foot when we reach the cottage."

Logan adopted a glower that sometimes caused women to shriek and men to wobble at the knees. "Take your damn boot off. I will not have you suffering, nor will I allow your foot to become infected."

When she rolled her eyes, he could only deduce that he was losing his touch.

"I'm not exactly suffering the trials of Job," she retorted. "It's simply a blister. I will be fine."

She marched on, defiantly limping up the trail. Short of holding her down and wrestling her boot off, there was nothing he could do until they reached the cottage.

"Very well. It's your bloody foot."

"That it is," she responded, not looking back. "Now, get a move on, Mr. Kendrick. Night will be upon us soon enough."

She was full of grit, that one. Again, she reminded him of his wife. Deceptively fragile looking, Marguerite had embodied the resilience and strength of her people. And like Marguerite, Donella had the blood of warriors running through her veins.

Tragically, Marguerite's strength had been no match for the illness that had ruthlessly drained the life from her body. Foreigners like Logan had brought that disease to the colonies. In the end, it had killed the woman he'd loved, who'd given him life and hope after all the disasters that had befallen him and his family.

"Keep up, Mr. Kendrick."

The tart, feminine voice floated back, prodding him to move. Shaking his head, he followed in her limping, determined footsteps.

Chapter Nine

As darkness chased them up the mountain, Donella worried they'd missed their chance to reach the crofter's cottage, thanks to her. The blister on her foot had transformed into a burning brand, scorching its way down to the bone and slowing her limping gait to a crawl. If they didn't reach that blasted cottage soon, she had every intention of lying down in the middle of the path and quietly expiring.

At this point, she might have preferred to be kidnapped by the Murrays. At least her potential abductors would have probably fed her and let her sit down, instead of dragging her up a stupid mountain in the middle of the night.

When she walked into something big and rocklike, she bounced back hard enough to lose her balance. Fortunately, the boulderlike object snaked a hand around her waist before she tumbled to the dirt in an inelegant heap.

"Watch it, lass. Don't want you taking a fall," Kendrick said.

He had a talent for stating the obvious.

Donella shoved her cap out of her eyes and glared up at him. "Why did you stop without warning? It's a miracle you didn't knock me down the side of the mountain."

"Not to be overly precise, but I just *stopped* you from

tumbling down the mountain. Besides, it's not much of a mountain. More like a big hill."

"That is hardly the point."

"No, the point is that I told you that we were stopping, but you didn't hear me."

"You did?"

"Twice."

She winced. "Sorry. I suppose I was, um, thinking."

He smiled, his teeth a brief flash of white in the gloom. "Don't fash yourself. It's been a long day and a hard climb."

"Are we stopping to rest again?"

"No, we're stopping because we're finally here." He jerked his head. "There's the cottage."

It was now so dark she might have walked right past the small structure, tucked away as it was under a gloomy stand of pine trees.

"It doesn't look like anyone's home."

"Not to worry. I know where the key is." He steered her toward the front door. "Once I get a fire lit, we can get your boots off and assess the damage."

"It's just a blister," she automatically replied.

"Yes, and as I told you—"

"Can we please have this silly argument later. I'm freezing and just want to get inside."

His fingers briefly flexed on her arm, a clear sign he was struggling to hold on to his patience. She couldn't blame him. What had originally been a promise to a friend and only a moderate inconvenience had turned into a monumental disaster.

"You're right, of course. I apologize."

She sighed. "No, I should apologize. You've done nothing but protect me since this ridiculous business began. And I've been repaying your kindness by acting like a shrew."

"Lass, you apologize too much. What you've been through these last few days would try the patience of a saint."

He guided her to a rustic wooden bench by the front door. Donella almost groaned with relief as she sank down on the hard seat.

"Sister Bernard would assure you that I am far from being a saint," she said.

"Ah, the dreaded Mistress of Novices. I'll have to have a chat with the good sister, if I ever encounter her. She obviously doesn't know your true mettle." He rummaged behind a large, empty tub off to the side.

"She'd only lecture you to the point of boredom."

Kendrick straightened up. "Got it." He inserted a large key into the old-fashioned lock and opened the door.

Donella steeled herself to get up. She was beginning to think she would topple onto her face if she had to take another step.

Perhaps life in the convent had weakened her, not toughened her up as she'd thought. She'd joined to become a stronger, better version of herself, but she'd failed both herself and the sisters. She'd failed her family too, after they'd done so much to help her achieve what she'd thought was her dream. That sense of failure was overwhelming.

"Are you all right, Miss Haddon?" Kendrick quietly asked.

"Oh, yes. Just tired."

She began to stand but abruptly sat back down when her head started to swim. Staring down at her lap, she sternly told herself not to faint.

Kendrick hunkered down before her. "You're not going to keel over, are you?"

"Not if I can help it," she gritted out.

A blast of cold air whipped around the side of the cottage. She welcomed the bracing sensation against her clammy skin.

Kendrick tipped up her chin. "You're white as milk."

"Nonsense. It's too dark to tell." Now that her head had

stopped swimming, she felt embarrassed by her momentary weakness.

"That's exactly how I can tell. You look like a ghost in the dark."

He stripped off a glove and pressed a hand first to her forehead and then to her cheek. His palm was rough and warm, and she had a ridiculous impulse to snuggle closer to him.

"You're sweating," he said.

"How kind of you to point that out," she replied, embarrassed.

"You best not be falling ill, lass," he gently chided. "Your uncle will murder me if anything happens to you."

"I am not falling ill. And if you're worried about my uncle, I can write a last will and testament relieving you of any responsibility."

"Here's a better idea. Let's try to avoid that outcome."

Before she could reply, he hauled Donella up and swept her into his arms. He did it so quickly and easily that she barely had time to gape at him before he nudged open the door and carried her inside.

"Mr. . . . Mr. Kendrick," she sputtered. "Put me down this instant."

"If I did, you'd fall flat on your face and probably knock yourself out. And then your uncle would have my head, if your brother and your cousin didn't have it first. I can handle two of them, but not all three at once."

She found herself irritated that he seemed more worried about her family's possible wrath than he was about her condition. Her annoyance was irrational, since it mattered not one whit what Kendrick thought of her.

He certainly was keeping a good hold on her, though. Donella was clasped so firmly to his chest that it was nerve-wracking, embarrassing, and . . . surprisingly nice. It had been a very long time since anyone had held her so closely, especially not a strong, handsome man.

That she was enjoying it so much was wildly inappropriate.

"Stop being ridiculous and put me down," she ordered.

"Only when I can see well enough to do so without making things worse. I'd hate to drop you into the woodbox or end up poking your backside with something pointy."

"*Mr.* Kendrick," she began in freezing tones.

"Ah, there's a bed in the corner."

"Not the bed," she yelped.

She felt rather than saw him wince. "Christ, lass, you don't need to shriek in my ear."

Now it was her turn to wince. "I'm sorry. But please don't take the Lord's name in vain."

"I'll try to remember that for next time."

He carefully lowered her into a chair a moment later. She didn't know why she was being so squeamish, but she couldn't bear the notion of Kendrick easing her down onto the bed. It just seemed too . . . intimate.

Her eyes began to adjust as a small degree of light filtered through the open door. He'd placed her in a rush chair next to a sturdy but rough-hewn table. Kendrick was now at the back of the room, stacking squares of peat onto the grate of a large hearth. He rummaged in a basket off to the side, retrieved a tinderbox, and soon had a tidy fire burning.

"That's better." A sardonic smile lifted one corner of his mouth. "Are you still in a pucker, or is it safe to approach?"

"I am not in a pucker," she said firmly, trying to reassert her dignity.

He came to fetch the lamp from the table. "Lass, you screeched so loudly you practically made me deaf."

"Don't be—"

When he lifted an eyebrow, she sighed. "I suppose I did, didn't I? Sorry."

"You apologize too much," he said as he took the lamp over to the hearth.

"You make it sound like some sort of nasty habit."

She wearily pulled off her cap. It itched and was quite odiferous, and she sincerely hoped she'd not have to wear it again. The previous owner was well rid of it.

Kendrick lit the lamp and brought it back. "That's better, eh?"

His smile was warm and kind, and it wrapped around her like a soft blanket. Logan Kendrick might be too big and too blunt, but he was also surprisingly gentle when he wanted to be. Donella generally didn't like people taking care of her, but she might make an exception with him.

"Let me just shut the door," he said. "Then we'll get that boot off and take a look at your poor foot."

Donella was quite sure her foot looked gruesome. Still, the notion of exposing any part of her body made her shy—unaccountably so, given all they'd been through together these last few days.

She'd lived a life of modest seclusion for so long, her only companions other women. In the convent, the sisters had never seen each other in a state of undress. Although living was communal, privacy was strictly maintained, and overly personal relationships discouraged. The strictures that had guided her life for the past three years were now being tossed out the window with disorienting speed.

It was such a little thing, stripping off one's boots and socks. But not for her.

"I'm sure it's fine," she said.

"I'm sure it's not. You can barely walk."

When Kendrick found some candles and lit them off the lamp, it brought the shadowed room into focus. The crofter's cottage was typical, with an open space divided by furniture into various uses. A bed with a simple wooden frame and straw mattress was tucked under the eaves, and a washstand stood close at hand, along with a sturdy rocking chair. In the center of the room, where she sat, was an oak table flanked by matching benches. The opposite wall held an open cupboard with mismatched dishes and crockery. Next to the cupboard, a narrow opening led into what appeared to be a small pantry.

Given the lack of linens on the bed and the dust on the furniture, the cottage had probably been empty for weeks, if not months.

"How do you know about this place? It's not close to Kendrick lands."

Castle Kinglas, his family seat, was on the other side of Loch Long. A full day's ride, if not more.

Kendrick disappeared into the pantry. From the sounds of it, he was searching for supplies.

"When we were younger, my brother and I used to hike these parts on our school holidays," he said.

"Lord Arnprior?"

"Yes. It was before he inherited the title, of course." He poked his head out. "We used to climb the trails from Loch Achray to above Loch Katrine, so we got to know Tom Morris, the crofter who lived here. Tom said we were always welcome to stay, whether he was here or not."

She glanced around. "It would appear Mr. Morris no longer resides here."

He disappeared back into the pantry. "Tom lives down in Callander with his daughter. She insisted he move there when he turned eighty-nine." Donella heard him snort. "He wasn't much happy about it, I can tell you."

"It's quite lovely that you kept up with him. You were away in Canada for at least seven years, were you not?"

When he didn't reply, she assumed he hadn't heard her. Not a surprise, since he was making a great deal of clattering noise in the pantry.

A moment later, he emerged with a pitcher and a handful

of flannel cloths. "I'm going outside to pump some water, and then we're going to wash and bind up that blister."

"Can we not do it in the morning? I'd much rather have a bit to eat and then go to sleep."

That was the absolute truth, since this day couldn't end soon enough. And tomorrow would hopefully bring her cousin, Alasdair, to the rescue and get her safely home.

Kendrick's eyes narrowed to ice blue slits. "Miss Haddon—"

"I wish you would stop referring to me as *Miss Haddon* in that dreary tone. You really do sound like Sister Bernard."

"Would you prefer I call you Donella?" he sarcastically replied.

"Not in that tone of voice."

"Whatever tone of voice I use, that boot is coming off."

"*Mr.* Kendrick—"

"Now who sounds like Sister Bernard?"

He put the supplies on the table and sat on the bench, then carefully took her hand. She resisted the impulse to pull away—not that she had much of an impulse to do so.

"I know you're embarrassed," he said, "but you're not an empty-headed, spoiled miss. You know what could happen if we don't take care of this foot."

She sighed. "I'm afraid I'm acting rather foolish. It's just that . . ."

"It's just that you barely know me, and there's nothing comfortable about this situation."

Donella felt even more of a fool. "I'm sorry."

"Did we not agree that you apologize too much?"

She thought about it. "No, I don't think we did."

He shook his head. "I'm going out to fetch the water. Boot and sock off, please, before I get back."

"Yes, sir."

He tapped her nose with a gentle finger. "Cheeky lass."

Cheeky lass. No one had ever called her that before. She rather liked it.

By the time he returned, she'd wrestled off her boots. It had been painful, but not as bad as it could have been, since the boots were so large.

"Why are your socks still on?" he asked.

"Well . . . the one seems to be stuck."

He muttered under his breath, then poured some water into a tin basin and set it on the hearth to heat.

"All right," he said. "Let's have a look."

Any embarrassment she felt disappeared under a wave of pain as he began removing the sock. She squeezed her eyes shut, trying to hold back either tears or a string of very nasty oaths.

She felt him gingerly peel away the rough fabric, which seemed to have fused itself to her skin. When he had to tug a bit, she hissed out a choked exclamation.

"Sorry, lass. I know it must hurt like the devil, but I've almost got it off."

She cracked open an eyelid. Crouched before her, Kendrick's head was bowed, his focus on her foot. She saw the grim set to his shoulders and the fine sheen of sweat on his forehead.

As he coaxed away the last bit of fabric, she had to swallow against a sudden rush of nausea. Something popped, and warm liquid gushed down the side of her foot.

"You had a blood blister, too." He glanced up with a sympathetic grimace. "Your foot's a bit of a mess, I'm afraid. I'll have to wash it and then wrap it with some clean flannel. With a bit of luck, you won't get an infection."

Donella swallowed, forcing her stomach back into place. Now that the blasted sock was finally off, the pain was starting to recede. She leaned to the side, trying to get a look at her foot, cradled in his palm.

Oh, dear.

She hastily straightened up. One side of her foot was all chafed and bloody.

"It's not as bad as it looks," he assured her. "Once we get it cleaned up, it'll feel much better."

She mustered a weak smile. Without the boots and socks, she was exposed up to her calf. When one of his long, tanned fingers brushed over her ankle, she felt herself go light-headed again—but not from the pain.

Donella cleared her throat. "Thank you."

He adopted a stern expression. "I wish you had told me it was this bad. Any longer, and you might have ended up with a raging infection."

"We were on a mountain, with very few supplies. I'm sure your doctoring skills are quite impressive, but there really wasn't much to be done up there."

He wadded up the sock and propped her foot on it, then rose to fetch the water. "I could have done something."

"In case you've forgotten, we were escaping some very nasty men trying to kidnap me. My foot could wait."

"I have not forgotten them for a moment."

He returned with the basin and set it on the table next to the other supplies.

"I just hope my uncle got your message. But what do we do if Foster and Davey failed to get through?"

He shrugged, as if it didn't much matter. "Then we'll make our way down to Loch Katrine and secure a boat. That'll get us over to Riddick lands in good order."

It was entirely possible that their pursuers might be waiting for them in villages where one could hire a boat for the crossing. There were relatively few ways to reach Blairgal. Whether by road or boat, they risked exposure.

Kendrick stood and shucked off his greatcoat. He reached into an inner pocket and pulled out a fine silver flask.

"In need of fortification, are you?" she asked.

"No, but I think you are."

When he extended the flask, she shook her head. "I never drink spirits."

"You might want to take it up, since I'm going to start cleaning your foot by pouring some of this over the blisters."

She stared up at him, so tall and tough looking, but with an easy smile softening the lines of his chiseled jaw. The smile didn't fool her one bit.

He jiggled the flask, clearly determined that she drink.

Grimly, Donella took it and brought it to her lips.

"Careful, now," he warned. "Just a sip to start."

She ignored him, taking a generous swallow. It rocketed down her gullet like liquid fire.

"Good Christ," he exclaimed, yanking the flask away. "Donella, are you trying to kill yourself?"

She coughed, wiping her streaming eyes. "Best to get it over with," she wheezed.

"You're daft."

"You wouldn't be the first to say that," she muttered.

He shook his head again as he fetched the steaming water and returned to take a seat on the bench. He shifted sideways to face her and reached for her ankle.

"Could I have some more whisky?"

He studied her. "Are you sure?"

"Might as well make it as painless as possible."

Now that the burn in her throat had subsided, she longed for more of the whisky's heat. She'd been cold for so long that she'd almost forgotten what it felt like to be warm again.

Kendrick handed over the flask. "Try not to get cup-shot. I don't want you passing out on me."

She'd only been tipsy once in her life, and the results had been disastrous. But she was a mature woman now, and the current circumstances were decidedly unromantic.

After a cautious sip, Donella took a generous mouthful before handing back the flask.

"I'm ready," she said, trying for a stout demeanor.

Kendrick gently grasped her ankle and propped her foot

on a piece of toweling he'd draped over his muscled thigh. He then soaked a piece of flannel with whisky.

Already feeling a bit woozy from the strong spirits, Donella clasped the edge of her chair to brace herself.

"Feel free to yell," he said.

"I will do no such thing," she retorted, only slightly slurring her words.

When he pressed the cloth to her foot, she was sorry that she did, indeed, let out a very loud yell.

Chapter Ten

For all her delicacy, Donella Haddon had a shriek as loud as three cats brawling in the night.

"Sorry. I know it hurts like the devil." Logan winced in sympathy as he kept the cloth pressed to her lacerated foot.

"I didn't expect it to hurt so much," she gasped.

She'd bleached white as chalk. Perspiration beaded her hairline, plastering short curls to her forehead. Her hands were clamped like vises on the edge of the cane seat.

He feared she was about to faint. "Lean against my shoulder, lass."

Instead, she pulled upright and stared straight ahead, sucking in slow, measured breaths, as if silently counting them.

Logan wanted to whack himself over the head with the old frying pan he'd found in the pantry. If he'd known her foot was this damaged, he'd have dealt with it hours ago—by force, if necessary. While Donella had the courage of ten Highland warriors, she was insanely stubborn, just like her curmudgeon uncle.

She dredged up a sickly smile. "I'm not the swooning sort. I'm just woozy from the whisky, although I can't say I'm sorry I drank as much as I did."

"Most men would have keeled right over."

He lifted the cloth. One blister was the standard sort,

although as ugly as Hades and almost as big as a guinea coin. The other, right next to it, was an oozing blood blister. It was a miracle she hadn't gone into a dead faint when he'd touched it.

Aye, she was a stoic one. In temperament, she reminded him of his brother, Royal. He'd been grievously injured during the war but had never uttered a word of complaint. Also like Royal, Donella's stubborn pride skated a wee bit too close to martyrdom. Sometimes, demanding a bit of attention—fighting for what one needed—was exactly the right thing to do.

Donella, however, seemed to prefer to sacrifice comfort in order to do what she thought was necessary.

It was an admirable trait, but right now Logan couldn't help but worry about the state of her foot. During his years in Canada, spending months in backcountry, he'd seen more than one strong man and woman brought down by infection. Even a small scratch could go bad and with frightening speed. Once the poison got into the blood, it was usually impossible to stop without taking drastic measures.

Measures like cutting off a foot. He'd seen that happen to an Acadian trapper he'd had to help hold down during the amputation. It was a hard, vivid memory that Logan had never forgotten. The idea of that happening to this sweet, courageous girl—

A cool touch to his cheek yanked him out of the ugly memory.

"You're looking a little queasy yourself," Donella said.

For a moment, all he could do was stare back, arrested by the emerald glitter of her gaze and the smooth texture of her winsome features. With her full lips so close to his, he suddenly felt a powerful bolt of lust, one so appallingly inconvenient he almost choked.

Comic alarm transformed Donella's expression.

"You're not going to be ill, are you?" She snatched her hand away. "Do *not* be ill on me, sir."

Logan forced a quick recovery. "Don't be daft. It's just a wee blister or two, as you said yourself."

She leaned down to look again. "I don't believe I did say that. And it's disgusting." She sighed. "I suppose I should have listened to you, after all."

"What's done is done."

"I hope Alasdair brings horses along with him tomorrow. I cannot imagine how I'll put those dreadful boots back on."

"Don't worry about that now. Just let me clean and wrap this, and then we'll see if we can rustle up some tea and food."

She flashed him a grateful smile but fell quiet again when he carefully started to wash her foot with a fresh cloth and warm water. It took some time, since bits of wool from her sock were stuck to one of the blisters.

He glanced up from his grisly work to see her teeth grinding down on her lower lip. She clearly needed a distraction annoying enough to take her mind off the pain.

"So, the good sisters gave you the heave-ho for obvious reasons," he said. "But what I can't understand is why you'd want to join them in the first place."

She shot him a scowl. "Why wouldn't I?"

"Because it seems a waste. You being the Flower of Clan Graham and all."

"I believe I asked you not to use that ridiculous term. And there's nothing wrong with being religious—or Catholic, for that matter."

"Of course not, though I was raised to be a dutiful member of the Church of Scotland, myself."

"It apparently failed to take."

He bit back a laugh as he wrung out the cloth. "My wife was Catholic, as was her family."

She was silent for a long beat. "I didn't know you were married."

"I was, back in Canada. My wife died there."

She pressed a sympathetic hand to his arm. "Forgive me. I'm so sorry."

"It was a long time ago," he said brusquely.

"Yes, but—"

"You haven't answered my question. Why did you hike off and join a convent? That must not have gone down well with your family."

"You have a talent for understatement."

Logan waited her out.

She finally shrugged. "I suppose it doesn't really matter if I tell you. Most people know the story, anyway."

"I'm always lamentably behind when it comes to gossip."

"This old gossip goes back thirteen years, now."

"You decided to join a convent thirteen years ago? Good God."

"No, that's when Alasdair ran away from home rather than allow Uncle Riddick to announce our betrothal to the clan."

Logan's hand froze on her foot. "Alec Gilbride, heir to the Earldom of Riddick. Your cousin."

"Correct."

"You were supposed to marry him?"

"Correct."

He stared at her before bursting into laughter.

"It was anything but amusing," she said with offended dignity.

"Sorry for laughing, lass. It's just the idea of you and Alec Gilbride married." Alec was as brash and irreverent as she was dignified and modest.

"Alasdair felt the same, obviously, since he stayed away for ten years."

When she ducked her head, blushing, Logan mentally

winced. For some reason, the next words were hard to say. "Did you love him very much?"

She glanced up, clearly surprised. "I was only fifteen years old. We were mildly fond of each other in the way cousins are, but our families made the match. They were set on a formal betrothal and marriage a year later."

He reached for a length of clean flannel. "Clan business, I reckon."

"Isn't it always? My parents and the Haddon clan chieftain were greatly in favor of the match, as was Uncle Riddick. The strengthening of clan bonds . . . that sort of thing."

"I know it well. But why didn't the two of you simply refuse?"

"Ye were gone from Scotland too long, ye ken," she replied in a sarcastic brogue.

"I know very well that family and clan can be a royal pain, but no one can force you to marry. Not these days, anyway. And I refuse to believe that a man as forward-thinking as your uncle—despite his reverence for tradition— would pressure you to do such a thing."

He had trouble imagining how anyone could force Donella to do anything against her will, despite her quiet ways.

"I promised my father that I would marry Alasdair," she said, as if that explained everything. She hesitated for a few moments. "When Papa was on his deathbed, he asked me to promise that I would marry Alasdair when he returned to Scotland. The fact that it took him ten years to come home did not mitigate my obligation."

"And your family *knew* you didn't wish to marry Alec?"

She waggled a hand. "Well, I more or less went along with it."

It was hard to imagine her going along with something that insane. "That sounds positively medieval, if you ask me."

"Perhaps, but a deathbed vow is a very serious matter, you understand."

He understood that the whole thing was bloody ridiculous. "Didn't anyone take your side?"

"Alasdair did," she said dryly.

Logan chuckled as he adjusted her foot so he could get a better angle for wrapping it. She really did have a lovely foot, slender and finely arched, with dainty toes that just begged to be tickled and stroked.

In fact, he might even like to kiss them.

He began to wind the flannel around her ankle. "So, Alec rode off to war while you remained at Blairgal, patiently waiting."

"Not so patiently," she muttered.

"What's that?"

She flinched. "Nothing. Could you not wrap it so tightly?"

"Forgive me. I'm a blunt instrument, as I'm sure you've realized. But I need to make sure the bandage doesn't get loose and rub the skin."

"No, you've been incredibly kind. I'm just tired."

He carefully adjusted the wrapping. "Almost done, but you can't leave me hanging. What happened when Alec returned?"

"He didn't come home alone."

Understanding finally dawned. "He brought Edie home with him?"

Donella's smile was wry. "Indeed, he did."

The current Mrs. Gilbride was the former Eden Whitney, an Englishwoman who now ruled her husband's family with a firm but loving hand. She'd rolled up the entire clan as far as Logan could tell, a remarkable accomplishment for a pampered *Sassenach*.

"That must have gone down like a treat," he said.

"You cannot imagine. When I realized that Eden and

Alasdair were in love, I knew that to force him into marrying me for the sake of our families would be a great injustice to both of them."

"And to you, since he didn't love you."

"True, but—" A funny sort of grimace contorted her features.

"Did I hurt you?"

She shook her head. "In any event, Alasdair and I soon reached an understanding, and he was free to marry Eden."

"Why do I have the feeling that you're leaving out all the good bits?"

"Because I am," she firmly said. "Are you almost finished?"

He tied off the ends of the flannel strips. "Still, it must have been quite the ruckus."

Her quiet sigh was so weary it nearly broke Logan's heart.

"I will only say that I was grateful to depart for the convent immediately after the wedding."

"You stayed for the wedding? Why in Christ's name—"

"Mr. Kendrick!"

"Why in the name of all that's holy," he corrected, "would you put yourself through that sort of public humiliation?"

"It wasn't so bad."

"Really?"

She scrunched up her nose. "It seemed the right thing to do. Eden is an extremely nice person, and I wanted to show my support for her."

He rested a hand on her ankle. "You're a bonny lass, Donella Haddon. I hope you know that."

She blushed. "Thank you, but don't forget that I truly had no wish to marry Alasdair. I just didn't know how to get out of it."

"But why run off to a convent? Surely there were legions of other handsome fellows sniffing about."

"That is an exceedingly improper observation, and I did

not run off to a convent. I'd been thinking about it for a long time and was finally free to act on my wishes." She held out an imperious hand. "My sock, please."

He handed it over. "Shall I put it on for you?"

"Certainly not."

Her chippy tone suggested he'd been more than successful in distracting her.

"How about that cup of tea?"

"That would be lovely."

She gingerly rolled on her sock and then wriggled her foot. "It hardly hurts at all," she said in a pleased tone.

"It will hurt once you put that boot on."

She pulled a comically exaggerated face. With her mussed curls, boy's clothing, and dirt-smudged nose, she looked like an adorable urchin.

"But it should be much better by tomorrow, don't you think?" she hopefully asked.

Not if she had to walk on it. But with any luck, Alec would show up and their ordeal would be over.

As he prepared the tea, it dawned on him that he hadn't been bored once in the last two days or been fashed about the problems in his life. He'd always been the cheerful one in the Kendrick family, but a rain of punishing blows had knocked the joy out of him years ago. Oh, he put on a good show for the sake of his brothers and the family. Yet it had been a very long time since he'd had what anyone would call fun.

Despite the risk and danger, he'd found this little adventure tremendously interesting, if not downright entertaining. True, he always missed his son with an ever-present ache. But these last few days, on the road and back in the mountains again, he'd felt more like his old self. It would seem he'd needed a challenge and, in some improbable way, he'd needed Donella Haddon.

When he returned to her with the tea, she was not looking as well as she'd been only minutes ago.

He set the teapot on the table and tipped up her chin. "What's wrong?"

She forced an artificial smile. "Nothing that a cup of tea won't fix."

"Donella—"

"I'm a little cold, that's all."

In fact, she was shivering.

Logan wrapped her coat and then his own around her shoulders, before pouring a mug of hot tea for her.

"Do you think I could have a bit more whisky?" she asked. "It did seem to warm me up."

"You can have whatever you want."

"What I'd really like is a warm bath, but that will have to wait until I get to Blairgal."

Logan had another of those horrifically inconvenient flashes—Donella, wet, soapy, and naked in a bath. With him.

"How about a bit of bread and cheese?" he said. "You need to eat."

"I think I'm too tired to eat."

"Donella—"

"All right, I'll try."

"You'll do more than try." He started toward the pantry to fetch his pack.

"Yes, Sister Bernard," she muttered.

"None of your sauce, lass."

That won him a reluctant chuckle, but it was clear she'd reached the end of her tether. She needed food and sleep but, most importantly, needed to get warm.

She was nodding off when he returned but jerked awake when he set a plate in front of her.

"Just a few of those rolls and some rather nice cheddar I nipped from the inn's kitchen this morning," he said apologetically. "Didn't have time for much else."

"This is a normal meal for me. Grand banquets tend to be frowned upon in the convent."

"What, no ortolans in Armagnac or sweetbreads in butter sauce?"

She shuddered. "Are you trying to ruin my appetite?"

He shoved the plate closer. "Eat, lass."

She ate some cheese and a chunk of bread, washed down with the fortified tea. Logan also bolted down some tea and food, then headed to the door to fetch more water.

"There's a chamber pot under the bed," he said.

She sighed. "Why do we spend so much time discussing chamber pots?"

He flashed her a wry smile and went out. When he returned, she was standing in front of the fireplace in her stocking feet, wrapped in their coats but shivering. It was probably from fatigue and reaction as much as the cold, but he wouldn't take chances.

"Ready for bed?" he asked.

"I could probably fall asleep standing up. I suppose you didn't find any extra blankets," she added, eyeing the unadorned mattress.

"Unfortunately, no."

She mustered a smile. "You shouldn't have to sleep on the floor again. If you would drag the rocker over to the fireplace, and fetch me that blanket I took from the inn, I can sleep quite well sitting up."

"Lass, if you think I'm sleeping on the bed while you're in a chair, you've lost your mind."

"I'm sure you're just as tired as I am. You need your sleep, too."

"Donella, get on that bloody bed before I pick you up and dump you on it."

"There's no call to be rude," she said with offended dignity.

"Apparently there is."

She grumbled but handed over his coat and got on the

bed. The tick mattress crackled as she curled into a ball, wrapping the small, threadbare blanket around her upper body. Unfortunately, the blasted thing barely went past her hips, leaving her legs exposed to the cold.

Logan snuffed out the candles and lamp before layering more peat on the fire. Then he took his greatcoat and draped it over her.

She looked over her shoulder. "Mr. Kendrick, you'll freeze without your coat."

He sat down on the edge of the mattress and started pulling off his boots. "I won't, because we're going to share it."

She shot up as if she'd been blasted out of a cannon, almost knocking him off the bed. "What?"

Logan winced. "Lass, you really need to stop the screeching."

This time, she didn't bother to apologize. "We *cannot* share a bed."

"It's that or freeze to death. And if you freeze to death, your family will murder me."

"They would not."

"They would. And that would mean *my* family would have to murder someone in your family, and then we'd have a clan feud on our hands." He grinned at her. "Although we'd both be dead, so I suppose it wouldn't really matter to us."

Her lips reluctantly twitched. "Now you're just being silly."

"I am, but not about you freezing to death."

"I told you, I'm perfectly f—"

"This is not up for discussion."

She glared at him, mutinous and still shivering.

"I know you're embarrassed," he said gently, "and I'm truly sorry for that. But even with the fire, this cottage is going to get very cold. The only way to keep warm is for us to share the coat."

He could practically hear the anxious debate going on in her head. He hated pushing her, but it had to be done.

"Och, well," he said, "I can sleep in a chair, but you'll have to take my coat."

Her eyes went round. "But you'll freeze without it."

"Better me than you."

She threw him a sour look. "Very well, you win."

As he'd suspected, her concern for him rather than herself did the trick.

"I don't mind," he replied, trying to sound soulful. "If it makes you more comfortable."

"You may cease playing the martyr, Mr. Kendrick. It's a role for which you are very ill-suited."

He grinned and finished pulling off his boots as she scooted to the other side of the mattress. Logan crawled onto the bed and tried to arrange the greatcoat over their bodies. She was almost falling off the other side in her effort to keep some distance between them, which meant the coat couldn't fully cover them both.

"Comfortable, are we?" he asked.

"V . . . very."

"Unfortunately, this doesn't work with you way over there, Miss Haddon."

Without waiting for her reply, he pulled her against him, fitting her into the curve of his body. She let out a startled squeak but didn't resist as he shifted the greatcoat to cover them.

Still, she held herself rigid, muscles locked in frozen protest. The lass had a lovely body, but right now she felt as cuddly as a hitching post wrapped in a layer of wool.

"This wouldn't be the first time I've found myself in a situation like this," he said in a conversational voice.

It took her a moment to respond. "I find that hard to believe."

Her wild curls tickled his nose. She smelled like peat smoke and fresh mountain air, and her skin carried a faint, salty tang. A sudden yearning twisted through him, and he had to resist the impulse to lean down and kiss the soft skin at the nape of her neck.

"When I was in Canada, I was stupid enough to get caught in the middle of a blinding snowstorm."

She shivered, so he tucked her even closer. She didn't protest.

"That sounds dreadful," she murmured. "How did you survive?"

Logan vividly remembered Joseph Pisnet, his future partner and father-in-law, arguing against going out that day. But Logan had been foolish enough to think that growing up in the mountains of Scotland had prepared him for the wilds of Canada.

"I was lucky to have a partner who knew how to survive in such conditions. He showed me how to build a makeshift shelter and taught me the best way to keep warm."

"Like this?" she asked in a sleepy voice.

"Yes, though the best way is to strip naked, crawl under a pile of furs, and huddle together as close as you can."

"I'm *not* doing that with you, no matter how bloody cold it gets."

He stifled a laugh. "Not necessary, in our case. But when you're truly on the verge of freezing to death, needs must."

"If your partner was so smart, why did he let you get into such a fix?"

"I didn't really give him a choice. I was a hardheaded Scot, and he reckoned it was the only way I would learn."

She fell silent, and Logan began to think she was dozing off. He, however, was wide-awake, not surprising, given the lovely, round arse curved so sweetly against his groin. And of *course* his blasted cock wanted to do what came naturally in the vicinity of such an enticing female.

Even if the female was entirely off-bounds.

"Did you like living in Canada?" she asked softly.

He welcomed the distraction, although the question was too complicated for a simple answer.

"It was a good challenge. I needed that."

"So you left Scotland for the challenge?"

"Yes."

What other answer could he give? That he'd left because he'd all but destroyed his family? That he'd betrayed his brother—his laird—in the most profound and tragic of ways? It had been years ago and Nick had fully forgiven him, but it wasn't something Logan ever wanted to talk about.

Especially not while holding Donella in his arms. For some odd reason she made him feel . . . well, *vulnerable* was the best word.

"I've never been anywhere exciting like that, Mr. Kendrick. I wish you'd tell me about it."

"I will, after you get some sleep."

She gave a soft huff. "No, you won't. You're just like me. You don't like to talk about yourself."

He blinked, startled by her insight. He held himself still, mentally bracing against more questions, ones he would do his best to dodge.

When her quiet breaths evened out and she slumped against him, he exhaled a sigh of relief. Certain secrets were simply too ugly to share—especially his.

Chapter Eleven

Donella slowly began to surface. Something warm and hard surrounded her, cocooning her against the chill. She couldn't remember the last time she'd slept so deeply, and instinct urged her back into slumber.

Then a dazed sense of awareness bolted through her brain, and her eyes flew open. An arm was wrapped around her body, holding her against an obviously masculine chest.

Panic flooded her veins as she struggled to remember where she was, and with whom. If not for the heavy leg flung across her lower extremities, she would have shot up in an instant.

Get out of the bed, you idiot.

Donella was about to push the man away when a quiet snore sounded in her ear. She'd heard that sound before, although not in such close proximity. The arms that held her belonged to Logan Kendrick and she was snuggled under his coat, doing her best not to freeze to death. When she'd dropped off last night, too exhausted to fight the anxiety of sharing a bed with him, he'd held her with careful courtesy, trying to preserve her modesty.

Now, they were plastered together, and she could feel everything from stem to stern, including . . .

Good. God.

With that particular appendage nudging against her backside, freezing to death was no longer a problem. In fact, heat flamed across her skin like a raging fire, and she wondered if one could spontaneously combust from embarrassment.

Thankfully, Kendrick was deep in slumber, obviously exhausted from the events of the last few days. But with that heavy leg thrown over her legs, it would be almost impossible to extricate herself without waking him up.

And *that* would surely be as embarrassing for him as it was for her. For all his brash ways, he was a gentleman. God only knew how he would respond if he awoke and found himself in such a state with her cuddled against him. Donella had no idea if his current physical condition was natural to the situation, but she imagined it could lead to all sorts of problems, each more disastrous than the rest.

To think that only a few weeks ago she'd been preparing to take her vows. Now she found herself in the close embrace of a man who was almost a stranger. Even worse, her body was clearly enjoying the feeling of safety and shelter in his arms.

It was an appalling reaction, of course, and meant she needed to get up *right now*.

Gingerly, she freed an arm and folded back the coat. Then, she started to wriggle her hips toward the edge of the mattress. It wasn't easy, since he was a veritable giant and his leg was heavy. Still, in just a few inches she'd be able to slide free and roll to the floor, hopefully without waking him.

Before she made it, Kendrick snorted in his sleep and rolled onto his back, taking her with him. When she yelped in surprise he jerked, and then tightened his arms. Donella was now lying directly on top of him, back to front, with both his arms wrapped around her and their legs tangled together.

"Mr. Kendrick," she hissed, now beyond embarrassment. "Please wake up and let me go."

His breath huffed through her hair. Then he sighed, starting to finally come awake.

"Mmm, you feel good," he murmured in a sleepy, rumbling voice as he hugged her closer.

Donella could feel her eyes bugging out of her skull. Blast the man. Why wouldn't he *wake up* and realize their predicament?

She was about to stomp her heel against his shin when she heard a crunching sound from outside, and a thump near the front door. She froze, horrified.

"Donella, are you there?" called a voice she'd recognize anywhere.

"Alasdair," she squeaked. "Don't come—"

Kendrick suddenly shifted. "What the devil?"

The latch rattled and the door flew open. Standing in the doorway was Alasdair Gilbride, his commanding height and broad shoulders outlined by the pale light of dawn. His face was in shadow, but Donella had no trouble imagining that her cousin's eyes were bugging out just as much as hers no doubt were.

If she could have fainted to avoid what was coming next, she would have happily done so.

Alasdair shook himself free of his brief paralysis and charged into the room.

"What the hell is going on?" he thundered, his gray eyes blazing with fury.

He reached down and grabbed Donella by the arms, lifting her straight off the bed. He plunked her down at his side and wrapped an arm around her before turning to glare at Kendrick, who'd shot up into a sitting position but was clearly still trying to get his bearings.

Alasdair took a menacing step forward. "Kendrick, if you've hurt Donella, I swear I will end you."

She grabbed her cousin's coat sleeve and gave it a shake. "He didn't. We were just sleeping, for heaven's sake."

Alasdair's baleful gaze stayed on Logan. "That doesna look like sleeping to me, ye bastard."

When her cousin's brogue came out, bad things tended to happen. Alasdair was the kindest of men. But when he lost his temper, the results could be unpleasant.

Kendrick swung his legs off the mattress and glared right back. "Don't be an idiot, Gilbride. We're on a mountain, without proper supplies, in November. We were simply trying to stay warm."

"Bollocks. I know what I saw, ye bastard. Ye took advantage of Donella," Alasdair snapped.

Logan swiftly rose and dragged on his greatcoat.

"If ye call me a bastard again, Gilbride, I'll knock yer bloody teeth down yer throat."

Splendid. Now Kendrick's brogue was up, too.

"No one is punching anyone," she exclaimed. "There is *no* reason to do so."

"Ye were in bed together. Ye were under his coat, bloody plastered against each other like—"

Donella hauled off and smacked her cousin on the shoulder. "Cease that ridiculous brogue, Alasdair. And do not contradict me. When I say nothing happened, *nothing* happened."

"Told ye," Kendrick said with a smirk.

Donella pointed at him. "Stop talking right now."

He opened his mouth, then clearly thought better of it.

She turned back to her cousin. "Alasdair, I promise on my honor that nothing untoward happened between us."

"He's a Kendrick," her cousin scoffed. "Do you really expect me to believe that?"

"Yes, and Lord Arnprior and his brothers are your friends. You *know* them."

"Which is exactly why I don't trust them. Well, I trust Nick, but I don't trust him. I know exactly what kind of man Logan Kendrick is."

"It takes one to know one," Kendrick said with typical masculine idiocy.

Just as typically, Alasdair rose to the bait. "All right, Kendrick. We're taking this outside. Donella, you wait here until it's finished."

She rather wished she had a pistol, so she could shoot them both. Instead she limped over to the door and braced her hands on the doorframe.

"Be careful of your foot," Kendrick warned.

She ignored him. "There will be no fisticuffs or dueling," she said to her cousin.

Alasdair's gaze went even flintier. "Get out of the way, Donella."

"No."

"Best do as he says, lass," Kendrick said. "I won't have him insulting your virtue."

"My virtue is not insulted. Besides, Alasdair is *my* relative. He's allowed to be stupid."

Her cousin bristled. "I am not being stupid."

"Actually, insulted isn't quite right," Kendrick said, frowning. "Impugned is more accurate."

Donella wished the chamber pot was within throwing distance. "It's not up to you or Alasdair to decide if my virtue has been impugned. Or insulted. Or *anything*."

"No, it's up to Grandfather," Alasdair said. "And he'll not be best pleased to hear about this."

He waved an arm to take in their disheveled state, as if that explained everything.

"There is no reason for him to know about it," she said. "Unless you can't keep your bloody mouth shut."

Her cousin's eyebrows shot up. "Oh, that's a splendid way for a nun to talk."

"I am *not* a nun anymore!"

Her outburst shocked Alasdair into silence. Kendrick was beginning to look amused, but for once he had the sense to keep quiet.

She pressed her palms against her eyes, reaching deep inside for patience.

"Donella?" Alasdair asked in a cautious voice.

She dropped her hands. "Cousin, there is no reason for Uncle Riddick or anyone else to find out that Mr. Kendrick and I were forced to spend a night alone together."

"Two nights, actually," Kendrick added.

He was *very* lucky the chamber pot was beyond reach. "Only for a few hours the first night, and you slept on the floor."

"Two nights on the road, without a chaperone?" Alasdair sighed. "Who else saw you?"

"No one recognized me."

"How is that possible?"

"I was dressed as a boy, travelling as Mr. Kendrick's little brother."

Her cousin finally seemed to notice what she was wearing. Then he glared at Kendrick. "And no one saw through this incredibly inept excuse for a disguise?"

"It's not inept," she protested.

The men ignored her.

Kendrick waggled a hand. "It wasn't exactly foolproof. The men who were pursuing us certainly figured it out."

"Then Donella's reputation is on the brink of ruin," Alasdair said. "If this gets out—"

"It won't as long as we keep our mouths shut," she snapped. "And deny everything, if necessary."

Her cousin shot her an exasperated look. "I've got four of my men outside this cottage, keeping watch. They will certainly deduce that you and Kendrick were alone."

Kendrick sank down on the bed and scrubbed a weary hand over his head. It made his already-messy hair stand straight up. "Of course you brought men with you. I *asked* you to bring men with you."

"Four witnesses," Alasdair said.

Donella pressed her palms flat on the door, sudden panic making her dizzy. "Is Fergus out there?"

Her brother *would* kill Logan—or force him to marry her at the point of a pistol.

"No, I sent him north along the road to Perth, just in case you'd had to double back."

"You must never tell him about this, Alasdair. You know what he's like."

"Better than anyone," he dryly replied.

When Alasdair refused to marry her, Fergus had challenged him to a duel.

Kendrick muttered something under his breath before exchanging a fraught glance with Alasdair.

"Well?" her cousin said to him in a challenging tone.

Kendrick let out another sigh and rose to his feet.

"What just happened?" Donella warily asked.

"Alec wants to know if I'm going to do the right thing by you, which I am."

Donella gaped at him.

"Good," Alasdair said. "I'll leave it to you as to how to approach the issue with my grandfather."

"Very, very carefully," Kendrick replied.

Donella finally picked her jaw off the floor and pushed

back. "Absolutely not. I will not be forced into this situation again. Not with Mr. Kendrick, not with anyone."

"Lass, be reasonable," her cousin said. "You remember the storm of gossip after we decided to break our betrothal. This will be ten times as bad."

She limped up to him and jabbed him in the chest. "*We* decided to break our betrothal? My role in that decision, you'll recall, was to walk into the library the night of our engagement party to find you on the sofa with Eden, with your hand up her skirt."

Alasdair turned bright red. "It wasn't that bad."

"No, it was worse."

Kendrick perked up. "Really?"

"Yes, really. It was utterly mortifying for everyone involved, especially me."

Donella couldn't help but enjoy her cousin's well-earned discomfort just a wee bit. That incident, although providing the necessary excuse to break their engagement, had nevertheless been intensely humiliating. And now she was in yet another situation where an unwilling man was being pressured into marrying her.

With the exception of Roddy Murray, it would appear that unwilling men were the only sorts of suitors she could ever expect to find.

"Well, aren't you the hypocrite?" Kendrick sardonically said to Alasdair.

Her cousin glared at him. "Donella knows how sorry I am about everything. But she didn't want to marry me, either."

"That is exactly the point," she said. "I don't wish to marry Mr. Kendrick any more than I did you. And at least if I'd married you, I would have been Countess of Riddick one day."

"I'm not exactly a pauper or a muckworm," Kendrick protested. "There are plenty of girls who'd be thrilled to marry me."

"Excellent. Then by all means ask one of them."

He stalked over, looking intimidating despite his wrinkled clothing, two-day beard, and stocking feet. "You needn't make it sound like I'm the worst thing that could happen to you, Donella. I'm not an ogre."

"No, you're simply another pigheaded man who cannot hear what I'm saying."

When Alasdair chuckled, she shot him a dark look. "You're even worse."

"Now, hang on—"

"Please just be quiet, the both of you!" Kendrick snapped. "For just *one* bloody minute."

Donella had no desire to hold her tongue and was about to snap back at him when she looked into Kendrick's suddenly weary, frustrated features. Then she remembered all they'd been through the last few days and the many risks he'd taken to keep her safe.

When Alasdair opened his mouth to argue, Donella elbowed him. "Let Mr. Kendrick talk."

Kendrick took her hand, twining her fingers with his. "Lass, you know everyone will think I dishonored you, regardless of the truth. I cannot allow you to be hurt, which means we must face some hard truths."

His change in manner made her throat go tight. She shook her head.

"Come, my dear. We need to be sensible about this."

She had to clear her throat before answering. "Mr. Kendrick, if you had a true choice, free and clear, would you wish to marry me?"

He hesitated a moment too long before flashing a rueful smile. "I wasn't planning on marrying anyone, but I can think of much worse things. You're a splendid, brave lass, Donella."

"And too good for the likes of you," Alasdair said.

"Says the man who ran away to avoid marrying me," Donella retorted.

It was a churlish comment, but understandable given that she was struggling with an unexpected sense of disappointment at Kendrick's less than enthusiastic reply. What in God's name was wrong with her?

Alasdair winced. "Sorry, lass. I—"

"It doesn't matter," she interrupted. "I'm going to be joining another convent as soon as I can, anyway. So the issue is moot."

Her comment stunned the men into silence. It rather stunned her too, since she hadn't thought that far ahead, at least not so definitively.

"But you just got kicked out of the convent," Alasdair blurted out. "How can you go back?"

"I did not get *kicked* out," she said through clenched teeth. "And there are other orders besides the Carmelites."

"Clerical orders aren't like haberdashers," her cousin said. "You just can't shop around until you find one that suits you."

Kendrick sighed. "So now I'm pushing you back into the convent to avoid scandal. Splendid."

She laid a hand on his arm. "You've done nothing but protect me and care for me. And we both know that nothing happened."

Nothing, that is, other than that she'd finally found a man—a friend—who seemed to understand her. The *real* her.

When their gazes locked, she saw genuine warmth and regret in his eyes. At the fleeting sense of what might have been, her heart twisted into a knot.

"Aye, we do," he finally said.

She turned to her cousin. "You owe me, Alasdair. As a man who was caught in a truly scandalous position, you know exactly *why* it was scandalous. And as the woman who caught you in that position, I also know that what happened in this cottage is entirely different. Mr. Kendrick did not compromise me in any way."

Alasdair blew out an exasperated breath. "Dammit, you could always run rings around me. Very well, I'll do what I can to contain any blowback. And I'll explain the situation to my men."

Relief made her laugh a bit shaky. "You mean you'll threaten to knock their heads together if they say anything."

"Exactly. And I won't tell Fergus or anyone else in the family. But you'll have to explain it to Grandfather."

She nodded. "I'll take care of Uncle Riddick."

He studied her for a few moments, then flashed a grin and swept her into a huge embrace. "Since I've not had the chance to say it, welcome home, lass. It's grand to see you."

She hugged him back, surprised by the upwelling of her emotions. She and Alasdair had never been very close, but she realized now how much she'd missed him. How much she'd missed all her family.

"Thank you, dearest. I cannot tell you how ready I am to get home and out of these dreary clothes."

"I think we'd best try to sneak you in before Grandfather gets a look, or he'll pitch a fit. Of course, he's pitching a fit anyway over this business with the Murrays. Any idea what it's about? He went as tight as an oyster when I asked him, and Fergus wasn't much better."

"Just stupid clan business from years ago that the Murrays clearly have not forgotten," Donella said. "I have no idea how they heard I was leaving the convent, or why they would even care."

She hated lying, even when it was necessary. She'd make it up with some extra prayers.

"Stupid clan feuds," Alasdair said, disgusted.

"Aye, they are," Kendrick agreed. "Now we'd best get Donella back to Blairgal, then sort it out. I take it we'll be riding? Your cousin is in no condition to walk."

"My foot is rather a mess," Donella said at her cousin's concerned look.

"We have one extra mount," Alasdair replied. "Donella will ride with me."

Kendrick shook his head. "Better she ride with me. You take the lead, so you and your men can keep us out of trouble."

Alec glanced at Donella, who nodded her approval.

"All right," her cousin said, "let's be off."

Logan was already pulling on his boots. "Let's step outside and give the lass a minute of privacy. And I want to fill you in on exactly what happened."

When the door shut, Donella hurried through her ablutions and then stacked the dishes neatly in the pantry, wishing she'd had the time to wash them. Still, she was tidying up as best she could when Logan and Alasdair came back in.

"Leave it, Donella," Alasdair said. "I'll send someone to clean up."

She sat down to pull on her boots. Unfortunately, even carefully inserting her injured foot inside sparked a nasty jolt of pain.

"Och, that's not going to work," Kendrick said.

He retrieved a pair of socks from his pack.

"I still have to wear my boots to walk," she said, pulling on the socks over the ones she already wore.

"You won't be walking."

Kendrick helped her up from the bench and then hoisted her into his arms.

"Is this really necessary?" she asked, embarrassed.

"The less you walk, the better."

"This is silly—"

"Stow it, Donella. I'm not letting you damage that foot any more than you already have."

"Oh, very well," she grumbled, sliding her arms around his neck. "By now, I suppose I should be used to you ordering me about."

"You certainly should."

Then he glanced at Alasdair, who was watching them with an enigmatic expression.

"Well?" Kendrick said. "Are we ready?"

Alasdair stepped aside and swept a flourishing bow. "After you, Sir Galahad."

"Bugger you," Logan retorted as he stalked out.

"Language, Mr. Kendrick," Donella couldn't help saying.

His only reply was a sardonic snort as he carried her out to the horses.

Chapter Twelve

Logan had thought about stopping by his offices before returning to Kendrick House, but after three days with no shaving and little access to water he looked more like a brigand than a businessman. And if he smelled as bad as he looked, his employees wouldn't thank him for popping in to check on things.

As he turned his horse onto Queen Street, he spotted the wife of one of his bankers. He automatically moved to doff his hat, before realizing that he'd lost it somewhere. Instead, he offered the lady a smile and a friendly nod. She looked initially stunned and then horrified. He couldn't entirely blame her. How was she to know he'd spent the last three days protecting an innocent maiden from nefarious kidnappers, then deflecting a murder threat from the maiden's idiot cousin for the non-existent impugning of her virtue?

Well, almost non-existent impugning. There was no doubt he and Donella had crossed a line, however inadvertently. Waking up with her supple, enticing body snuggled up against his erection had not been part of the plan. If not for Donella's quick thinking—and even quicker temper, matched only by her stubbornness—Logan had little doubt he'd be asking Lord Riddick for her hand in marriage.

Or facing death from any male relative of Donella Haddon.

Oddly, he'd been more than a bit annoyed by her refusal to even consider the notion. For an entirely deranged moment, the idea of marrying Donella hadn't seemed awful. In fact, it had seemed rather interesting, which only proved he was in dire need of a good night's sleep.

Still, when they'd finally parted at the border of Riddick lands, where a carriage awaited them, Logan was reluctant to let her go. Donella had seemed to share that feeling, unexpectedly throwing herself into his arms and giving him a fierce hug.

"Thank you, Logan Kendrick," she'd whispered in his ear. "I'll never forget you."

Instinctively, he'd hugged her back, her short, silky hair brushing against his cheek.

Donella had then gently kissed Logan's cheek before hastily climbing into the waiting carriage. He'd been rather stunned by that kiss and had felt color rise to his cheeks.

Alec, naturally, had snorted out a sardonic laugh but then had sincerely thanked Logan. "We owe you a great deal, old man. You have our gratitude."

Logan wanted not gratitude but a business deal with Lord Riddick. That discussion, however, had nothing to do with Donella and was for another day.

He'd watched as the carriage and its armed guard swiftly departed, carrying Donella safely away. It left him oddly bereft. He would miss the lass and wished he could somehow see her again.

Then he'd remembered that he was done with women. Marguerite had been the love of his life, and she'd given him a beautiful son. It was more than he deserved.

Logan guided his horse past George Square and into the more residential parts of the city. Dusk fell rapidly, as it did this time of year, and lights glowed in the windows of the houses that lined the quiet streets. Within a few minutes, he was turning into an elegant garden square, fronted by mansions built by the wealthy Tobacco Lords of the last century.

Kendrick House, the largest on the square, was lit from top to bottom. With almost the entire family in residence, he doubted he could sneak in. The Countess of Arnprior would take one look at him and command him upstairs to take a bath, as if he were a naughty boy who'd fallen into a puddle. Victoria was a bit of a stickler, who ran the Kendrick household with a firm hand. She was also kind, funny, and brilliant, and the woman Nick had needed in his life.

Victoria had been what they'd *all* needed. She'd healed the fractured bonds of their family and forced Logan and Nick to confront and forgive the mistakes and tragedies of the past.

Dismounting, he tied the horse to the hitching post and climbed the steps to the portico. Before he could knock, the door opened and young Will, one of the footmen, greeted him with a look of concern.

"Are ye all right, sir?" Will eyed Logan's disreputable appearance. "We were expecting ye home over a day ago."

"I encountered some unexpected business on the road. Can you have one of the stable lads look after this fellow, Will? He's had a long day."

"Aye, sir."

When Logan stepped inside, he frowned at the chaos. Boxes and various pieces of luggage were piled in the middle of the hall floor, while two footmen struggled to wrestle a huge trunk up the stairs. Henderson, the butler, was conferring with the head chambermaid. And the blasted dogs were barking their fool heads off in the drawing room.

Henderson glanced at him, delivered a quick set of instructions to the maid, then hurried over.

"I apologize for the commotion, sir," he said as he took Logan's coat. "It's all been very sudden."

"What's going on, Henderson? Has the Prince Regent himself arrived for a visit?" Since Prinny was Victoria's natural father, it was an inside joke with the family and senior staff.

"No, sir." A rare grin split the butler's spare features. "It's Mr. Mac—"

The door to the drawing room opened and out tumbled two of the family's pack of exceedingly silly Skye Terriers. The man who followed in their wake froze Logan in his tracks.

Angus MacDonald, his grandfather, came barreling across the hall. Since the old fellow was supposed to be in Canada, his appearance was a stunner.

"Laddie, we've been waitin' for ye." Angus threw his skinny arms around Logan and hugged him. Since he barely came up to Logan's shoulder, he landed somewhere around the midsection.

"It's grand to see ye," Angus choked out.

Logan returned the embrace. "It's wonderful to see you too, Grandda. And surprising."

He had to raise his voice. The dogs, tumbling around their feet like gigantic dust balls, yapped their heads off.

Technically, Angus was Logan and Nick's stepgrandfather, since his daughter had been the old earl's second wife. But Angus loved all the Kendrick brothers with equal devotion. No grandfather could be more loyal—or more old-fashioned and pigheaded. Despite his stubborn ways, he had a kind and loving heart and would do anything for his family.

Anything included committing murder to save the life of Royal, Logan's younger half brother. That was why they'd shipped the old fellow off to Halifax. Royal and his wife, Ainsley, had been forced to flee as well after Ainsley shot the man who was going to kidnap her wee little daughter. Only recently had most of the legal complexities arising out of that unfortunate incident been resolved, lifting the cloud of prosecution from over their heads.

No one had expected the newly established Halifax branch of the family to return to Scotland anytime soon, since they'd all seemed happily settled in their new lives.

Angus stepped back. "Ye're lookin' as queer as Dick's hatband, lad, and ye're not smellin' the best, either. What have ye been up to?"

Since the old man normally knocked about wearing an old kilt and worn-out leather vest, his criticism was a bit comical. With his grizzled hair, shabby tam, and grubby clay pipe, Angus often resembled a caricature of an antique High-lander. Today, though, he was as neat as a pin in breeches and tailcoat, with boots that were presentable, at least for him.

"Just a little trouble on the road." Logan paused a moment. "Grandda, don't take this the wrong way, but why are you here?"

The old man looked hesitant. "Well, ye see . . ."

"Ah, Logan. There you are." Logan's sister-in-law hurried out of the drawing room. Victoria gave him a quick once-over, frowning. "Do I even want to know?"

"Probably not. Now, perhaps you'll tell me what's going on?"

She and Angus exchanged a glance. "You didn't tell him?"

"Didna have the chance."

Not *another* crisis. Logan hoped he would have time to splash water on his face and change his clothes before he had to start bashing heads together or breaking someone out of jail.

"Can someone please tell me what's going on?"

Victoria smiled. "Nothing awful, dear. It's just a surprise."

"I love surprises," he growled, "so bloody well tell me."

"Well, ye see," said Angus, "I've brought home—"

"Hello, Papa."

The little voice caused Logan to spin on his boot heels to

face the drawing room. His head spun too, because there stood Joseph. The boy's hands were folded neatly across his stomach as he regarded Logan with a wary gaze, as if unsure of his reception.

"I brought yer son home," Angus proudly said.

Logan fought to marshal his overwhelmed thoughts. He hadn't seen Joseph in over a year but had planned on sailing to Canada in March for an extended stay. To now have his son standing in the hall of Kendrick House, right before him . . .

"I told you it was a surprise," Victoria said with a twinkle.

Angus poked him on the arm. "Say hello to yer boy, ye jinglebrains."

Logan lunged across the hall, sweeping his child into his arms. He hugged him close, his heart pounding like a blacksmith's hammer. Joseph was the first thought in his head in the morning and the last at night. His absence was a wound that never fully healed, closing over when the boy was with him and ripping open when he said good-bye.

Joseph had been safe in Halifax with his grandparents and Royal and Ainsley. The thought of his son taking that six-week sea voyage, even on a Kendrick ship, made Logan queasy. The boy was the dearest thing in the world to him, and if anything had happened . . .

"It's a damn good thing I didn't know you were coming over," he growled at his grandfather. "I would have been a wreck."

Angus tapped the side of his nose. "Which is why I didna send word ahead. I knew ye would have worried like an old biddy."

"Marie agreed to this?"

Marie Pisnet, Joseph's grandmother, had raised the child from birth. Normally, she didn't let him out of her sight and had readily agreed it was best for Joseph to remain in Halifax, under her watchful and loving care whenever Logan was in Scotland.

Angus nodded. "It was her idea."

Joseph, who'd been hugging Logan around the neck, pulled back and wriggled a bit, as if wanting to get down. Logan eased his hold, propping the lad on his hip so they could look at each other.

"Aren't you happy to see me, Papa?" A troubling caution lurked in the boy's coffee-brown gaze.

Joseph had his mother's eyes. And like his mother, those eyes were open and honest, holding nothing back. Logan had always been able to read whatever Marguerite was thinking from her gaze, and he could do the same with his son.

And it made him feel like a worm.

"I'm *always* happy to see you, my dearest boy. I was just a little surprised, that's all."

Joseph's mouth tilted up at the corners. "But it's a good surprise. Grandda said it would be good."

"The best surprise," Angus said. "Yer da is just a wee bit upset because I didna write to him first."

Joseph grabbed Logan's collar. "Don't be mad at Grandda. He didn't want to tell you because you would worry too much."

He smiled at his son. "He was right. I would have been a gibbering idiot if I'd known you were at sea."

"But it was lots of fun. Grandda let me spend time with the sailors, and they taught me things, like tying knots. And they use *lots* of funny words."

"Oh, dear," Victoria said.

Logan scowled. "Really, Angus?"

"No need to talk about that now," his grandfather hastily replied. "We're here, and Joseph is happy to be in Scotland with his da. Aren't ye, laddie?"

Joseph's tentative smile suggested the matter was yet to be decided.

"Well, I am very happy to see you," Logan said, hugging him close again. "I missed you more than anything in the world."

Instead of returning his embrace, Joseph wriggled. "Thank you, Papa. Can I get down now?"

Logan's heart sank. "Of course, my boy." Emotion made his voice gruff, so he tried to lighten the moment by flashing a broad smile as he set his son down.

The boy straightened his little wool vest and gave Logan an apologetic grimace. "It's just that you smell, Papa."

Logan had to laugh. "I just spent three days on the road, and not in the best of conditions."

"Why don't you go have a wash and a change?" Victoria suggested. "We'll have tea while we're waiting for you. Nicholas had an appointment with his banker, but he should be home within the hour."

Logan gave her a quick, meaningful glance. "So, he doesn't know Angus and Joseph are here?"

Her smile was reassuring. "No, but he'll be delighted to see his grandfather and to finally meet his nephew."

His sister-in-law knew exactly why he was concerned. Nick had been a widower when he met Victoria, one still mourning the death of his four-year-old son, Cameron. Nick had blamed Logan for little Cam's death, and not without reason. While it had been a terrible accident, Logan should have foreseen it. He would carry the blame with him always, and it had been the reason he'd exiled himself to Canada.

Over there, Logan had felt too guilt-ridden to tell his family in Scotland that he'd married and had a son. Only when he'd returned home had he finally revealed that he was a widower with a boy of his own. Nick had been stunned that Logan had withheld such important news, but he'd grieved to hear of Marguerite's death and had offered Logan his deep sympathy. And he'd seemed pleased to know he had a nephew.

Still, Logan couldn't help being fashed. He had a son, when Nick had lost the child he'd loved more than anything. It wouldn't be easy for Nick to meet Joseph, when his own boy had been taken from him because of Logan's horrible mistake.

A gentle hand on his arm pulled him out of the grim reverie.

"Everything will be fine, dearest," Victoria said. "I promise."

He mustered a smile. "Yes, of course you're right."

"Are you sure Lord Arnprior won't be unhappy to see us?" Joseph asked Logan in a worried voice. "Uncle Royal told Grandda that Uncle Nick doesn't really like surprises."

"Only bad surprises, and we're definitely good ones," Angus said, ruffling the boy's hair. "The laird will be delirious to see me, ye ken. I canna imagine how the poor lad has been managin' without me."

"I can," Logan said tartly.

Before Angus could bristle up, Logan crouched down to eye level with his son. "Lord Arnprior will be delighted to see you. Aunt Victoria already said so, and one thing you'll soon learn is that she's never wrong."

"I always knew you were the smartest Kendrick," Victoria said with a twinkle. "Joseph, darling, believe me when I say we are all very happy you've come to live with us."

Logan smoothed a tender hand over his boy's head. Joseph had his mother's hair—sleek and black as a raven's wing. In so many ways he was a miniature of Marguerite, especially in his sweet, gentle nature. In this case, however, that nature was worrisome. Joseph was a sensitive boy, and now he'd been transported into a new and confusing world, unmoored from everything he'd ever known. Logan would do everything he could to protect his son from the negative consequences.

Starting now, by showing how happy he was to see him.

"Aye, it's officially the best day ever, now that you and

Grandda are here." He dropped a kiss on his son's button nose and stood. "I'm going to wash and change now, so I don't smell like a polecat anymore. Is that all right?"

Joseph giggled and nodded.

Victoria held out a hand to the lad. "Shall we go in and have some of those lovely tea biscuits, Joseph? I'm quite sure I saw a plum cake on the tea tray, as well."

"Can we give some cake to the dogs?"

Angus chuckled. "Aye, we can. The laddies love plum cake."

As Victoria led Joseph off to the drawing room, Logan snagged Angus by the sleeve.

His grandfather raised a hoary eyebrow. "What's amiss, lad? Ye are happy to see yer son, aren't ye?"

"Of course I am, you old goat, but why the hell did Marie agree to this? We agreed—we *all* agreed—that Joseph should remain with his grandparents, especially since you, Royal, and Ainsley were there in Halifax to help, too."

Angus pulled a letter from the inside pocket of his coat and handed it to Logan. "Times change, lad. Times always change."

Chapter Thirteen

Logan slowly descended the staircase, the letter from his mother-in-law in his hand. The news had rocked him so profoundly that he'd sat on his bed for fifteen minutes, choking back emotion.

Joseph Pisnet was dead.

It wasn't a complete surprise. His father-in-law's health had been fragile after he'd suffered a stroke some years ago. Still, he'd seemed quite hale when Logan was in Halifax last year. But the old man had been stricken with another stroke a few months ago, one that had killed him.

Joseph had been his first friend in Canada, a wise counselor and excellent business partner. Without his guidance, Logan probably would have died that first winter, a victim of his own arrogant stupidity. But the Acadian trapper had taken him under his wing and taught him how to survive in the wilderness, and how to navigate a cutthroat business.

More importantly, he had saved Logan from the worst of himself by believing in him and accepting him into his family. Because of Joseph, Logan had met Marguerite, the kindest lass God had put on this green earth. She'd been the saving of him, too.

And now they were both gone, taken from those who loved and needed them most, especially Logan's little boy.

No wonder his son had been so solemn. Little Joseph had adored the man who'd been more of a father to him than Logan ever had. Under the circumstances, he worried that separating the boy from the only life he'd ever known could be a disaster. But Marie had been adamant in her letter that it was time for Joseph to be with his father, and it was time for Logan to get off his backside and start acting like a proper parent. His mother-in-law had a knack for making a man feel guilty, and in this case she'd taken no pains to spare Logan's feelings.

Well, it was time to own up to his mistakes and redress the ones that he could.

He was halfway across the hall when Angus slipped out of the drawing room.

Logan frowned. "Is Joseph all right?"

"Aye. Kade and the dogs are playing with him. Graeme came home a few minutes ago. He was that surprised to see us, and I—" He had to stop and clear his throat.

Logan squeezed his grandfather's shoulder. "I know you missed the twins, and Kade especially. I'm glad you're home."

"I missed *all* of ye, ye ninny."

"Thank you for taking care of Joseph. I'm indebted to you."

"That lad is as quiet and good as ye can imagine, but too quiet now. He's missing his grandfather, ye ken."

Logan glanced at the letter in his hand. "They were very close."

"Pisnet was a fine man, and Marie is a fine woman. But she was feelin' the loss and wanted to return home to her people in Cape Breton."

"Still, I can hardly believe she would wish to be separated from her grandson. She all but raised him."

Angus poked him. "She *did* raise him, and now ye need to take over."

"Believe me, she made that clear, especially since Royal

and Ainsley have another baby on the way." He smiled. "Royal must be happy about that."

"Over the moon, the pair of them. But the Halifax house was feelin' a wee bit crowded already."

"Marie and Ainsley didn't always see eye-to-eye, I take it."

Angus snorted. "The house was barely big enough to hold the two of them, and that is a big house ye have there in Halifax. Ainsley truly loves Joseph, but she's better with little girls than boys. Joseph is six years old now, and he belongs with his da and the rest of his family. Marie knew that."

"Agreed, but I'm not sure he'll feel at home in Glasgow. Our good citizens are not a particularly tolerant lot. They barely put up with the Irish immigrants, much less . . ."

"A boy with Mi'kmaq blood?" Angus bluntly finished. "Ye'll need to throw it back in their faces and stop pussy-footing around it."

Logan scowled. "I'm not ashamed of my son's heritage, if that's what you're suggesting."

"Don't be daft, but the wee lad might get other ideas, if yer not careful. He already thinks ye don't want him here."

"That's ridiculous. Why would he think that?"

"Because yer livin' in Scotland and he was livin' in Canada?"

It was hard to ignore that logic. "I've made a mess of everything, haven't I?"

"Now ye have a chance to fix it, laddie."

Victoria popped her head out of the drawing room. "Are you two coming in? Graeme is eating all the plum cake, and Joseph is asking for his father."

As Logan followed Angus, Victoria stopped him with a touch. "I was sorry to hear about your father-in-law."

"Thank you. He was the best of men."

"Joseph is a terribly sweet boy. I'm so glad he's come home to us. To *you*."

Logan watched his son, sprawled on the rug with Kade and the terriers.

"As am I," he said in a voice tight with emotion.

Kade waved an arm. "Logan, come join us."

The youngest Kendrick brother was now seventeen, a tall beanpole of a lad. He'd grown strong these last few years, finally leaving years of sickness behind. It was because of Logan that Kade had taken ill as a boy—the consequence of that terrible day by the river. But Kade had never held it against him. The lad had a huge, loving heart, and it seemed he was well on his way to loving his new nephew, too.

Logan hunkered down on the plush Aubusson rug where the boys played with Toby and Daisy, the youngest of the terriers.

Joseph glanced up with a smile. "They're very nice dogs, Papa, don't you think?"

Nice was the last adjective anyone but Angus would likely use to describe the dogs. They were yappy, disobedient, and had a tendency to roll in whatever disgusting muck they could find.

"They are indeed," he said, returning the smile.

He had to repress the instinct to sweep the boy into his arms and hug him tight. Despite Angus's advice, Logan's instincts told him to go slow. Joseph was grieving the separation from his grandmother and now the loss of his grandfather. He needed patience, love, and the time to regain trust in the father he'd not seen in over a year.

Whatever his son needed, Logan was determined to give.

Angus settled into one of the needlepointed wing chairs beside the fireplace and pulled out his battered clay pipe. "Those two were just pups when I left, and now they're as fine as any terriers I've seen. Ye did a grand job with all the dogs, Kade. I thank ye for lookin' after them."

Angus had been heartbroken to leave his darlings when he fled Scotland. Only Kade's promise to care for them had prevented the old fellow from trying to smuggle the whole pack onto the boat.

Kade touched his grandfather's knee. "I'm sorry about Bruce and Bobby. I took very good care of them, but they were already old when you left."

"I know, but I still canna believe they're gone," Angus replied in a doleful voice.

"Tina has had another litter of puppies," Kade brightly added. "Six in all, and each in perfect health and scrappy as anything."

"As you can imagine, Taffy is simply thrilled," Victoria said wryly.

Taffy, the housekeeper at Castle Kinglas, had been managing the place with the precision of a drill sergeant for decades.

"Och, she'll get used to them," Angus said with a casual wave of his pipe. "She always does."

That was debatable, but the rest of them tactfully refrained from saying so.

"Can I have one of the puppies?" Joseph asked his great-grandfather in a hopeful voice.

"Ye'll have to ask yer da, but I ken he'll say yes."

When Joseph shot a wary glance his way, Logan swallowed a sigh. "Of course you can, son. You can pick out whichever one you want, and that pup will be yours from now on."

Joseph's shyly grateful smile twisted his heart with guilt.

"You look like you could use this," Graeme said, handing Logan a generous tot of whisky.

His half brother had been sitting quietly on the settee next to Victoria, before rising to pour out the drinks.

Graeme, once the biggest hellion in the family, was finally settling into a semblance of maturity now that he was well into his twenties. Unlike Grant, his twin, Graeme was still a restless soul, unsure what he wanted to do with his life.

He returned Logan's smile then carried a glass to his grandfather.

Angus took a sip. "Not bad, but nothin' as good as we used to brew—"

"Ahem," Victoria loudly interrupted.

Angus and the twins had once run an illegal still on Kendrick lands. It had been a sore spot for Nick, who'd been forced to pay a large fine when excise officers stumbled across the operation.

"We don't do that sort of thing nowadays, Grandda," Graeme said.

Angus heaved a sigh. "It was grand while it lasted. Our brew was miles better than this Glasgow stuff."

"It made a great deal of trouble for Nick," Graeme replied. "We try to avoid that now."

"It's true," Victoria said. "I can't remember the last time you and Grant engaged in a brawl or had an unfortunate encounter with the local constables. You haven't even broken any furniture."

Angus thoughtfully eyed his grandson. "Ye've changed, lad. I hardly recognize ye."

Graeme shrugged his broad shoulders, looking uncomfortable with the attention. "Everyone's got to grow up eventually, Grandda, even me."

Joseph stared up at his uncle, wide-eyed. "You look very grown up to me. You're almost as big as Papa, and he's a giant."

Graeme squatted down and ruffled his nephew's hair. "No one's as big as your da, Joseph. But I'm thinking you'll grow up to be as big as he is one day."

"Do you work with my papa too, like Uncle Royal and Uncle Grant?"

Graeme straightened up. "No. I . . . I'm still thinking about what I want to do."

"Trade isn't for everyone, Graeme. There's no shame in that," Logan said.

"You never worked for Papa, did you?" Joseph asked, looking up at Angus.

The old man snorted. "Ye wouldna catch me dead working in some dusty old office in the city, lad."

Logan had to swallow a tart reply.

"Grant and Royal enjoy working with your papa," Victoria said to Joseph. "They're both very good with numbers and organizing things."

"I'm not exactly a booby with such matters," Angus indignantly exclaimed. "Dinna forget I managed Kinglas when Nick and Royal were away fightin' the war."

"And splendidly, too," Victoria said without batting an eyelash. "Nicholas would have been lost without you."

The family maintained the fiction that the old fellow had done a bang-up job.

"Graeme has other talents," Victoria said to Angus. "His work was invaluable in helping to clear your name after, er, after that regrettable incident with the Marquess of Cringlewood."

"Do you mean the scaly *Sassenach* that Aunt Ainsley almost killed?" Joseph asked.

Logan almost spit out his mouthful of whisky. It took him a moment to wrestle it down his gullet. "Joseph, who told you about Cringlewood?"

"Grandda. He said the scaly *Sassenach* tried to kidnap Auntie Ainsley and Tira. And he almost killed Uncle Royal, except Auntie Ainsley shot him."

"And what else did Grandda tell you?" Victoria asked in a deceptively mild voice.

"Oh, nothin' worth mentionin'," Angus hastily butted in.

Joseph frowned at his great-grandfather. "But you told me you killed the other bad *Sassenach* with your dirk. That's why you had to leave Scotland so fast." He glanced at Logan. "You were there too, Papa. Grandda said you threw a man out a window."

Trust Angus to embellish any story.

"I just pushed him against a wall." Logan had used quite a bit of force, but Joseph didn't need to know that. "And your grandfather did not kill anyone with a dirk."

Angus pointed his pipe at him. "But I *did* kill him, ye ken."

Joseph beamed up at his grandfather.

Logan pressed a hand to his eyes. "I cannot believe you told him all that."

"I dinna like to lie," Angus said in a pious tone, "especially not to bairns. Sets a bad example."

With the exception of Kade, who was trying not to laugh, everyone stared at the old man with disbelief. Angus was the most accomplished liar in the family—probably in all of Scotland.

"Thankfully, those sad events are now behind us," Victoria said, clearly anxious to redirect the conversation. "Graeme was tireless in helping to track down the rest of Cringlewood's men and gather evidence for the magistrate. In fact, my brother thinks he would make a splendid investigator."

That was high praise indeed. Victoria's half brother, Aden St. George, held a rather mysterious senior position at the Home Office and wielded a great deal of influence at the highest levels of government.

Graeme actually blushed. "I just wanted to help."

"And I'm that grateful to ye, lad," Angus said. "It's no fun havin' a murder charge hangin' over yer head."

"Perhaps we can talk about something else, Grandda," Logan said, aware that his son was hanging on every word of the wildly inappropriate conversation.

The old man rolled his eyes.

"How is little Tira?" Victoria asked Joseph.

"She's all right for a baby, but she's noisy and still spits up sometimes."

"Not such a baby now," Angus said. "She's almost three and poppin' up like a weed."

For a moment, the old fellow looked stricken. He'd helped

raise Ainsley and Royal's daughter from birth and was devoted to the little lass.

Joseph wriggled closer and took his great-grandfather's hand, squeezing it in silent comfort. The boy had a grand, kind heart, just like his mother, and Logan felt his throat grow tight.

"Auntie Ainsley said I had to take care of Grandda, because he would miss Tira something fierce," Joseph said in a serious tone to Victoria.

Angus smiled. "I do miss her, but I'm glad to be with ye, laddie. And glad to be home with my family."

"And what about Aunt Ainsley?" Logan asked Joseph. "Do you like her?"

His son's gaze lit up with the expression of a devoted acolyte. "Oh, yes. She's so pretty and always smells so good. Uncle Royal thought so, too. He would make sheep's eyes at her. Grandda and I used to laugh when he did that."

Logan smothered a chuckle. Ainsley was quite the loveliest woman he'd ever met—until Donella Haddon. Even dressed like a disheveled urchin, Donella's beauty had shown through like a rising sun breaking through the mist.

And why the hell are you thinking about Donella? God knew he would likely never see her again.

"Papa, are you all right?" Joseph asked.

Logan blinked. "Yes, I'm fine."

The dogs suddenly dashed for the drawing room door, yipping with excitement.

Victoria shot Logan a glance. "That will be Nicholas."

"Oh, good." Kade scrambled up. "He'll be so surprised and excited to see Grandda and Joseph."

Logan, Graeme, and Angus exchanged swift looks. Clearly, they were all thinking that same thing—that this meeting might very well be difficult for Nick.

Joseph tucked his legs under him and slowly stood, staying close to Angus. He'd once more adopted a tight, wary expression, as if expecting the worst from whatever was about to happen.

A solemn, too-mature child had stolen in and taken the place of Logan's happy little boy. The change was mostly to be laid on his doorstep, and he had no bloody idea how to make it better, at least not right now.

"Nicholas will be thrilled to see Angus again," Victoria said cheerfully. "And he'll be so eager to meet his nephew."

"Really?" asked Joseph.

Angus scoffed. "Och, he'll be delirious to see us both. He's been missin' my help at Kinglas. Poor lad's been in a lather without me, not knowin' one end of a ledger from another."

Joseph's pursed lips started to ease into a smile until the door opened and Nick strode in.

The Laird of Arnprior paused, his steely blue eyes sweeping the room and its anxious occupants.

Every muscle in Logan's body urged him to sweep his son into his arms, holding him protectively close. Nick was the kindest of men, but he was laird and chief of his clan. His word was law, and that word would set the tone for Joseph's life in Scotland.

"No wonder Henderson was in a flap," Nick said. "This is quite the surprise."

Chapter Fourteen

Angus hauled himself up. "Aye, it's yer grandda, come home to help ye out of yer troubles. I knew ye'd be lost without me."

Nick snorted but opened his arms wide for a hug when Angus stomped over to him. Joseph hung back, clearly more than a little anxious about meeting his uncle.

Logan moved to stand beside his son. When Joseph's hand reached up and clutched his, Logan's heart throbbed with love and concern for the wee lad.

"Yer lookin' grand," Angus said, clapping Nick on the shoulder. "Except for some gray hairs, I see. Yer workin' too hard, so it's a good thing I'm back to help."

"Kinglas will muddle on a bit longer without you, Grandda," Nick said with a wry smile. "You can take all the time you need to recover from what I'm sure was a taxing sea voyage."

"Och, we were bored out of our skulls, ye ken." Angus rubbed his hands. "I'm ready to get back to work."

It was a running joke that Nick's worst nightmare was Angus getting back into estate business. To say their grandfather was old-fashioned and disorganized in his management techniques was an epic understatement.

"Nick's right, Grandda," Graeme said. "I've been helping

around the estate, and Victoria works on the books. You can relax as much as you want."

"Uh-oh," Kade muttered, when the old man started to bristle.

"Well, that'll be enough of that nonsense," barked Angus. "Estate steward is *my* job, and ye'll nae be takin' it away from me, ye cheeky lad."

Graeme winced. "I can hear you, Grandda. You're only three feet away from me."

Joseph tugged on Logan's hand. "Auntie Ainsley never let Grandda yell in the house. It was a rule."

"We tend to have a bit more yelling in Scotland, Joseph, but it's harmless."

"There's plenty of work to go around," Victoria said. "Between giving Kade lessons and taking care of my daughter, I am quite busy." She flashed Angus a smile. "I'll be happy to have your help, Grandda. You're so good with babies."

Angus was instantly diverted. He adored babies and was as good with them as he was with boisterous little boys.

"Whatever I can do, lass." He winked at Nick. "We were all that thrilled when ye wrote us with the news."

"Thank you, Grandda. Rowena's birth was a truly splendid day." Nick's voice was gruff with emotion.

The arrival of Rowena Caroline Kendrick five months ago had brought immense joy to the household, especially to her father. For Nick, many old wounds had been healed that day. He would never truly get over the loss of Cam, but now he had another child to love with a free and open heart.

"Rowena's a pip," Kade said.

"What are we waitin' for?" Angus enthused. "Let's go have a look at the bairn."

"In a bit," Nick said. "Besides, you've all been quite remiss when it comes to introductions."

Joseph glanced up at Logan. "What does that mean?" he whispered.

"It means your uncle Nick is anxious to meet you, son."

"I am at that," Nick said with a smile.

While the others silently watched, Nick approached Logan and Joseph. He cast Logan a sharp, assessing glance, then hunkered down so that he and the little boy were on eye level. Joseph regarded his brawny uncle with the sweet gravity that was so much a part of his character, and so much like his mother that Logan could barely breathe.

"Hello, lad. I'm your uncle Nick."

"Hello, sir. I'm Joseph Kendrick."

Nick pressed a finger to his mouth for a second, as if holding back a chuckle, then he extended a hand. "It's a pleasure to meet you, Joseph. Welcome to Kendrick House."

The boy glanced up at Logan.

"Go ahead, son. Shake his hand."

Still holding on to Logan, Joseph tentatively reached out. His small hand disappeared into Nick's.

"Thank you, sir," the boy said. "Grandda told me all about you on the trip."

"Did he now? And what did he say?"

"That you're the laird." He said *laird* carefully, as if trying it on for size. "And you're the clan chief, too."

Nick stood, still holding on to the boy's hand. "That I am."

"Grandda says it's a great honor, and that I must treat you a . . . accordingly."

Nick threw Angus an amused glance. "I'm honored to hold the title, Joseph. I try to do the best I can, but I don't always get it right."

Angus scoffed. "Och, yer the best laird the title's ever had."

"Since you're the head of Clan Kendrick, that means you're my chief, too," Joseph said.

"That's very true. You're definitely a member of the clan."

Logan could see the tension dissipate from his son's little body. Joseph smiled at his uncle, looking genuinely happy.

"I told ye not to worry, lad," Angus said. "The laird will take care of ye, just like he takes care of the rest of us."

"From the day you were born, Joseph, you were a member of this family and clan." Nick raised his eyebrows at Logan. "There was never any need to worry."

Logan was embarrassed to have ever thought his brother would have a whit of trouble welcoming the lad into the family fold. For one incredible moment, with Joseph standing between them and holding their hands, Logan experienced a sense of peace he'd not felt in a long time.

The boy tugged on his uncle's hand to reclaim his attention. "Grandda says you'll teach me everything I have to know to be a good member of the clan."

Nick appeared much struck by the notion. "I do believe that's true."

"You wouldn't mind?" Joseph asked, suddenly shy.

"It would be my great honor, laddie."

"Drat," Victoria muttered. "I never have a hanky when I need one."

"Take mine," said Graeme, extracting one from his inside pocket.

Victoria narrowed her gaze. "Is it clean?"

"Er, mostly."

"I'll make do without one," she dryly replied.

Logan suppressed a laugh.

"I have a chief back in Canada," Joseph said. "He's Mi'kmaq, like my mother was."

"Is he now?" Nick said. "I hope you'll tell me all about him while we have tea."

Joseph let go of Logan's hand. "Really?"

"Indeed," Nick said, ushering the boy to the chaise. "We clan folk have to stick together."

Joseph plunked down on the chaise, beaming up at his uncle, who beamed right back at him.

For a moment, Logan didn't know what to feel. His son seemed more comfortable with Nick than he did with him.

Then he mentally kicked himself. For so long, he'd been worried if Nick would truly accept his son. Now it was clear that the powerful shield of Lord Arnprior's protection would surround the most vulnerable member of the family. It was all Logan could wish for and more.

Angus returned to his chair by the fire. "Aye, we Highlanders have to stick together, especially against the *Sassenachs*. Those bloody bas—"

"A-*hem*," Victoria loudly interrupted.

"Give it up, lass," Logan said. "I suspect Joseph has heard worse from Angus."

"Auntie Ainsley told Grandda not to swear, but sometimes he forgets," Joseph piped up with fatal candor. "On the ship, he and the sailors swore a *lot*."

Logan snorted. "I can see you've been a splendid influence on my son, Grandda."

"At least I was there, ye ken. Unlike some people," Angus pointedly replied.

Logan had to struggle to keep his voice even. "Not because I didn't want to be."

"It's all right, Papa," Joseph said with an odd grimace. "I know you wanted me to stay with Meme Marie. You thought I would be happier with her."

God, the boy was killing him. "I *always* wanted you with me, Joseph. I missed you every single day."

"I know, Papa."

Nick shot Logan a glance before ruffling Joseph's hair. "Your papa missed you very much, just like we all miss Royal and Ainsley and little Tira. Family always misses family when they can't be together. But this is your home now, Joseph. We want you to be very happy here."

Joseph studied his uncle with a seriousness that prickled the back of Logan's neck.

"What is it, son?" Nick gently asked.

"Papa told me you had a little boy too, but he died. He said you were very sad."

Logan suddenly felt paralyzed. He desperately tried to remember exactly what he'd told Joseph about Cam.

Nick regarded the boy with equal gravity. "Yes. I was very sad when Cameron died."

"So was Papa for a long time. He tried not to show it, but everyone could tell."

"I know," Nick said gently, avoiding Logan's eye.

And thank God, because Logan was all but choking on his emotions.

"Goodness," Victoria said, making a show of peering at the clock on the mantelpiece. "It's late. I'm sure Rowena must be finished with her nap by now."

Nick flashed her a grateful smile before again ruffling Joseph's hair. "Would you like to meet your cousin now? She's very sweet, if a bit noisy at times."

The lad scrunched up his face. "Will she spit up on me? Tira used to spit up a lot, sometimes on Auntie Ainsley's best dresses."

The adults chuckled with relief that the fraught moment had passed.

"Rowena is quite good at *not* spitting up." Nick stood and held out a hand. "Let's go meet her, shall we?"

Joseph smiled and stood to take his uncle's hand. Clearly, Logan's big brother was better at dealing with little boys than he was.

"I'll just go warn Nurse that she's about to have visitors," Victoria said. She winked at Logan before hurrying out of the room.

Following her with Joseph, Nick paused at the door and

turned, lifting an imperious eyebrow. "Are you coming, Logan?"

"Do you want me to come?"

"Pinhead," was his brother's only reply.

"You'd better come, Papa," Joseph said earnestly. "Uncle Nick wants you to."

"Of course, son. I'll be right up."

"Get to it, lad," Angus said with a smirk. "Don't want to get left behind."

Logan shot him a dirty look and stalked out after his brother.

Families. They were a royal pain in the arse.

Chapter Fifteen

Families could certainly be a pain in one's backside.

"Uncle," Donella said, trying to be patient, "I'll simply remain quietly at Blairgal until any gossip dies down. Then I can decide what I want to do next."

Join another religious order, if she got her way.

Her great-uncle, ensconced in the old baronial chair by the fireplace, scowled. "We'll discuss it as a family, Donella. It's the way we've always made our decisions."

While the family's traditional methods of decision-making hadn't exactly worked in the past when it came to her, her uncle would thunder if she objected. If there was anything Donella couldn't abide, it was a thundering male.

Uncle Riddick, truly a good man, was both stubborn and her laird, which made for a tricky combination. She was used to obeying him and had done so for most of her life. But she was determined to hold fast on this one, no matter what he thought.

Besides, what else could she do with her life but become a nun? She obviously wasn't cut out to be a wife, and the idea of dwindling into spinsterhood, dependent on her family, was a humiliating prospect. By joining another religious order she could still be of use to the world, either through a life of contemplation and prayer, or by good works. She would have a purpose, not just rattle around Blairgal Castle like a boring old ghost, useless to everyone.

Her anxiety spiked at the vision of such a future, and her mind involuntarily searched for a reassuring image.

Somehow, Logan Kendrick's face popped into her brain. He was the most irritating man she'd ever met, and yet she'd felt safe with him. When they'd finally reached the security of her great-uncle's lands, Donella had been reluctant to say good-bye, as if in doing so, she was losing something important.

Something that could have been *something,* if given a chance.

Heat rushed into her cheeks at the memory of their leave-taking. She was not the demonstrative type, and yet she'd kissed him, clearly catching both Logan and herself off guard.

"You're looking a bit red in the face, lass." Her great-uncle peered at her with concern. "You've just suffered a great shock to the system, you know. Mayhap we should send for the physician again."

Donella had the constitution of a draft horse. Uncle Riddick, however, was hypochondriacally inclined and fretted about everyone's health, especially his own.

The real reason she'd gone red had nothing to do with illness and everything to do with the inappropriate thoughts she'd been having about Logan Kendrick these last three days.

She stood to replenish his cup from the tea service. "I'm very well, sir. I'm just sitting too close to the fire."

It was a convenient excuse, since there was a roaring blaze built up in the gigantic stone hearth. Family meetings were always held in the great hall. With its medieval suits of armor, heraldic banners, and ancient weaponry, it was an impressive if rather overdone testament to the Haddon family's history and traditions.

Uncle Riddick was very big on tradition. He was also a master manipulator and was doing everything he could to remind Donella of who she was and what she owed to her family.

As if I could ever forget.

She glanced at the longcase clock. "I suppose the others will be arriving shortly."

"Alasdair and Eden should be down soon. But I told them I wanted to speak with you first."

Donella froze. "You didn't tell them why, did you?"

He impatiently waved her back to her chair. "Of course not."

"Alasdair wouldn't stop pestering me about the Murrays. I had to pretend to fall asleep in the carriage."

Her great-uncle's rheumy gaze grew sharp. "You leave Alasdair to me. Your secret has been safe for ten years, and I intend to keep it that way."

Uncle Riddick remained a powerful laird who commanded respect, but he was old and in failing health. In fact, she'd been shocked by the physical changes wrought on his body during her years away. While he still had a sharp mind and an iron will, he'd grown wizened and frail. He'd turned most estate and business dealings over to Alasdair, who was assisted by Donella's brother, Fergus.

She had serious doubts now that he could manage the situation with Mungo Murray after all.

"Obviously Alasdair was away at the time of the incident," she said with some hesitancy. "But Fergus was here, as was Uncle Walter. Perhaps it might be best to enlist their help."

"And what do you think Fergus would do if he found out what *really* happened between you and Roddy Murray? Mungo would be the least of our worries if it came to light."

She winced. "Fergus would challenge poor Roddy to a duel."

The oldest son of Mungo Murray, Roddy had been smitten with Donella and had wanted to marry her. Uncle Riddick's terse refusal had resulted in thinly veiled accusations regarding Donella's character.

A feud had only narrowly been avoided due to the intervention of several chiefs from branches of both clans. Uncle had also made some thinly veiled accusations of his own that seemed to shut the matter down.

That Mungo Murray had never forgotten the insult to his family's honor was now abundantly clear.

"Only a few people know the truth of that situation, Donella, and it has to stay that way. Alasdair and Fergus would kick up a fuss, and your reputation would end up in tatters. Not that it's in the best of shape at the moment, ye ken," her uncle tartly added.

She couldn't blame him for being annoyed. "I'm so sorry, Uncle. You must want to throw me off the highest turret of Blairgal."

His expression softened into a wry smile. "You think you did us all a favor by hiding away in that convent, but you were sorely missed. We're that glad to have you home where you belong."

"I missed all of you too, Uncle. And I have to admit it's lovely to be home. Everyone's been pampering me to a disgraceful degree. If I'm not careful, I'll grow very spoiled and never want to leave."

"You'll not be leaving anytime soon, young miss, and that's an end to it."

"But—"

"And you'll not be saying anything about the Murrays beyond what I've told you to say. Are we clear on that?"

There was no point arguing with him. "Yes, sir."

"I've already written to Mungo and instructed my lawyers

to pay him a little visit. We'll not be having any more troubles on that score."

Instinct told her such would not be the case. In any event, she intended to be gone from Blairgal Castle sooner rather than later. Once she reentered the convent—any convent—Mungo and Roddy would cease to be a problem.

He extracted his watch and scowled at it. "Where is everyone? We have a great deal to talk about, and I have no intention of holding up dinner."

Donella rose. "Do you want me to ring for a footman to fetch them?"

"No need," said Uncle Walter as he stepped down from the spiral staircase at the end of the hall. "I'm here, and Edie and Alec are right behind."

With his spectacles and slightly stoop-shouldered physique, Walter looked exactly what he was—a scholar. He was also the kindest man Donella had ever met. He was Alasdair's father—stepfather, in truth, although that was another of the family's deep secrets. When she was young, Alasdair's mother had engaged in a brief, adulterous affair with the Duke of Kent, one of the king's sons, and Alasdair had been the unexpected result of that liaison. Walter had selflessly accepted the blame for not protecting his young wife from the rakish prince. And he'd accepted the babe as his own son, raising him with love and devotion after the death of his wife.

Alasdair, in turn, had always insisted that Walter was his true father and was equally devoted to him.

Her family was really quite wonderful. They stuck together through thick and thin, even when Donella's deranged mother had tried to murder Alasdair—certainly a low point in the Haddon family history.

Uncle Walter bent down to kiss Donella's cheek. "How

are you, my dear? Are you feeling quite up to this? You look rather flushed to me."

She had to resist the urge to roll her eyes. "I'm fine. It's just blazing hot in here."

"It seems quite chilly to me," Walter said. "I wonder if we should move to the library. It's much cozier in there."

"Give it up, Father," Alasdair said in a humorous tone. "It's a family meeting, so it's the great hall. And that means we have to huddle around the fire and roast ourselves like capons or sit a few feet away and freeze to death."

"We're Scots, lad," barked Uncle Riddick. "Not a bunch of namby-pamby *Sassenachs* who can't take a bit of the cold."

"This particular *Sassenach* never gets cold," Eden said in a cheerful tone as she joined them. "I love winter in the Highlands. It's invigorating."

"Well, *this* particular Englishwoman finds nothing invigorating about Scottish winters," said Lady Reese, who'd followed her daughter into the room. "How anyone can prefer a dreary winter in the Trossachs to the healthy English climate is beyond me."

"Aye, and after one season in London, a body will cough up its lungs onto the floor," Uncle Riddick dourly replied.

"What an unpleasant image," Walter commented. "Alec, why don't you fetch your mother-in-law a chair so she can sit near the fire, too."

Lady Reese gave Walter a gracious smile. "You are always so kind, dear sir, worrying about everyone else's welfare. Unlike some other people I could mention."

Uncle Riddick let out a derisive snort.

Lord Riddick and Lady Reese, once mortal enemies, had actually grown quite fond of each other once Alasdair and Eden were married and various members of the family stopped trying to murder each other. They were often found in Lord Riddick's library, drinking whisky while arguing the merits of English versus Scottish culture. Poor Walter was often forced to play referee.

Donella rose. "Sit here, my lady. It's a bit warm for me."

"You are looking flushed," Lady Reese said with a frown. "I do hope you're not falling sick again. Perhaps we should call for the doctor."

Donella briefly contemplated screaming and running from the room.

"I agree," Walter said. "One cannot be too careful."

Her ladyship shook her head. "How the poor girl survived that godforsaken convent is beyond me. It's a miracle she didn't expire from some sort of dreadful contagion."

"Mamma, by definition, a convent cannot be 'godforsaken,'" Eden said.

Her mother bristled. "Why not?"

"Because it's a *convent*."

"And if a miracle's going to occur, that's as good a place as any," Alasdair said, amused.

Uncle Riddick scowled at Lady Reese. "This conversation is entirely daft. And why the devil are you here? This is family business."

"I'm Eden's mother, which means I am a de facto member of your family. And may I remind that I was the one who not only cured Fergus of his melancholy but found him a wealthy wife."

That was all true, although Fergus hadn't really been melancholy. He'd been guilt-ridden about their mother's criminal behavior. Donella and Fergus had dealt with that guilt in different ways—she by entering the convent, and he by practically working himself to death to make up for their mother's misdeeds.

"She's got you there, Grandfather." Alasdair settled next to Eden onto the red velvet settee. "Lady Reese is a capital matchmaker."

"Excuse me, but I don't wish to get married," Donella said.

Lady Reese looked offended by the very notion. "All sensible women wish to get married."

"That's not true, Mamma," Eden said. "Many girls prefer the single state."

"For example, Donella," Alasdair said. "She had the good sense not to marry me, and bully for her."

"Only because you two were so poorly matched," Lady Reese retorted. "That entire debacle could have been avoided if the rest of you had only listened to the poor girl in the first place."

Donella jumped in. "Very true. I didn't want to get married then, and I don't want to get married now."

"Nonsense, child. You just haven't found the right man yet."

"There is no right man."

Possibly there might have been, and his name was Logan Kendrick. Now that chance was gone—thankfully, she told herself, since he'd likely not given her a thought since the day they parted. She'd discovered from Eden that Logan had a son—really, the dratted man had been ridiculously close-mouthed—and a rapidly expanding business that consumed all his attention. A man like him wouldn't waste a moment of time on a woman like her.

"Ah, here's Fergus," Walter said, sounding relieved.

Donella's brother hurried in from the anteroom. "Sorry I'm late. Did I miss anything?"

"Just reliving a bit of family history," Donella said, going to greet him.

He shot a quick glance around the room. "That bad, eh?"

"You have no idea."

Fergus enfolded her in a hug. "I'm here now, Sis. I won't let anyone badger you."

Donella hid a smile against his shoulder. With the exception of her uncle, Fergus badgered her more than anyone. All in the name of brotherly love, of course.

She pulled back and fondly patted his cheek. Like her,

Fergus had dark red hair, green eyes, and a dusting of freckles across his nose. When she left for the convent three years ago, he'd seemed hollowed out by the events that had almost torn their family apart. Now he was the picture of health, at peace with himself and devoted to his pretty English bride.

"Have I told you yet how happy I am for you?" she asked.

"Not as happy as I am to have you home—although you should be staying at Haddon House with Georgie and me. It's where you belong, Donella. Not up at the castle."

"It's Georgie's house now. She doesn't need me looking over her shoulder, telling her what to do."

Haddon House, Donella's family home, was a small but lovely estate a short ride from Blairgal. Before entering the convent, she'd all but run the place, since their mother had never been comfortable with the responsibility.

"Now, Sis—"

"Stop your palavering and come join the rest of us," their uncle interrupted.

"Why didn't Georgie come with you?" Donella asked as she drew him to an empty chaise.

"She thought you would have enough family telling you what to do without in-laws chiming in." Fergus pointedly looked at Lady Reese.

Her ladyship sniffed with disdain. "I, for one, would welcome Georgette's input. She's a very sensible girl."

"You like her because she never contradicts you," Fergus said.

"As I mentioned, she's very sensible."

"Perhaps we might get started?" Walter tactfully said.

"I'd like to start with a discussion about those bloody Murrays," Alasdair said. "I'm tired of waiting for answers."

"You'll mind your business, if you please," Uncle Riddick sternly replied. "I have the matter well in hand."

"I don't mean to start an argument, Grandfather, but—"

"Then don't."

"But I doubt a stern letter will solve the problem," Alasdair firmly went on. "If not for Logan Kendrick, Donella would have been kidnapped."

Eden shook her head. "I don't understand why they'd do something so deranged."

"I believe the answer is simple," Walter said. "When Donella was seventeen, Mungo Murray wished her to marry his son, Roderick. Since Donella was betrothed to Alec at the time, the offer was refused. Mungo saw that as an insult to his family's honor."

"We would have refused it regardless of Alasdair," Uncle Riddick snapped. "Roddy Murray is as thick as a plank, and his father is no better. Dolts, the lot of them."

"Roddy was quite sweet, though. Not at all like his father," Donella said, compelled to defend her long-ago suitor.

"And very handsome, as I recall," Walter thoughtfully added.

It was Roddy's handsome looks that had run Donella into trouble in the first place—not that she could admit it.

"That certainly didn't excuse the lies he told about my sister," Fergus said. "I should have shot him back then, like I wanted to."

Alasdair frowned. "What sort of lies were they?"

Oh, Lord.

"It doesn't matter," Donella said.

"The kind no gentleman should make about a lady," Fergus darkly responded.

Alasdair looked blank for a moment, then guffawed. "That's totally ridiculous. Donella cutting up larks with—" His wife elbowed him. "Um, Donella would never do anything inappropriate. She wanted to become a nun, for God's sake."

"It's immaterial," Uncle Riddick said. "The Murrays need

to realize once and for all that Donella will never marry Roddy."

Eden pressed a hand to her chest. "Do you mean to say that Mungo Murray tried to kidnap Donella to force her to marry his son? That's positively medieval."

"It's an old tradition in some Highland clans," Walter explained. "Although I've not heard of such a case in many years." He shot Donella a troubled glance. "They obviously heard you were leaving the convent. Just as obviously, Mungo Murray now feels that his son has a claim on you."

"As if the poor woman doesn't have a say in her own life," Eden huffed.

"Right. I've had enough of this," Alasdair said. "Fergus and I are riding north to pay Mungo Murray a visit."

Donella almost fell off the chaise. "No. I absolutely forbid it."

"We have to do something, Sis," Fergus said. "This cannot go unanswered."

"I don't want the past dredged up again. It was humiliating enough the first time."

"Donella is right. You'll only cause more trouble," Uncle Riddick said.

Alasdair made an exasperated sound. "But, Grandfather—"

Lady Reese leaned over and whacked him with her fan. "That's enough, Alasdair. Lord Riddick has made his decision, and the rest of you will abide by it."

"Who died and left you in charge?" Fergus muttered under his breath.

Her ladyship narrowed her gaze, as if deciding whether to whack him, too.

Donella mentally steeled herself. "The point is moot. I intend to write to the Mother Superior of an order of Franciscan nuns in Galway. Whatever problem there is with the Murrays will go away after I enter that convent."

That pronouncement resulted in a stunned silence. Not for very long, however.

"No niece of mine is going off to Ireland," thundered her uncle. "Much less to Galway."

"I should say not," Fergus chimed in. "You're staying right here with us, Donella. In fact, you're moving back to Haddon House today."

Donella repressed a wince. "No."

He paused. "No . . . to what?"

"All of it."

Her brother rubbed his forehead, looking frustrated and hurt. "Donella, don't you want to stay with us? Georgie would be thrilled, you know."

How could her brother understand what it felt like to be a hanger-on in one's own house? "That's terribly sweet, Fergus. It's just that . . ."

"It's just that Blairgal is a big, beautiful castle," Eden cheerfully finished for her. "Who wouldn't want to live in a castle?"

"And you and Georgie are still newlyweds, Fergus," Donella said. "You deserve time alone together."

"Oh, very well," he grumbled. "But that doesn't mean you have to run off again. Besides, you just got kicked out of the convent."

"I did *not* get kicked out."

"You rather did, dearest," Eden said apologetically.

"That doesn't mean *some* order wouldn't want me," Donella insisted.

"I think you should stay with us for a spell before making any final decisions," Walter said. He smiled at her. "After all, we missed you very much, and it's splendid to have you back."

"I missed you too, Uncle Walter."

Donella had always been surprised by how homesick

she'd been at the convent, and how much she'd missed her old life.

Perhaps Reverend Mother had been right about me all along.

Her mind immediately rejected that notion. She'd fought too hard to chart her own path only to give up now. And then the Murray problem was bound to blow up in her face, sooner or later.

Uncle Riddick, who'd been carefully watching her, finally spoke up. "If you agree to wait six months before making a final decision, I will support you." He leaned forward, lifting a hand. "But you will *not* go to Galway. We'll find you a respectable convent in England, if need be."

She sagged with relief. It was a partial victory and didn't seem . . . awful. After all, she'd made a thorough hash of things with the Carmelites. Taking time to make a careful decision about where she would go next made sense.

Of course, that still left the Murrays.

"And I'll take care of Mungo Murray," her uncle said, reading her mind.

She gave him a grateful smile. "Thank you, sir."

He pointed a gnarled finger at her. "Now, you cannot be hiding here at Blairgal, like a hermit. Go down to Glasgow with Eden and Alasdair for the holidays. Get out and do some socializing. Play cards, go to dances, and talk to nice fellows."

She gaped at him, appalled. "But—"

"Donella, you will not lurk about here for six months and then scamper off to a convent to escape us. You're going to do what all young ladies should do—have fun."

"But I don't know how," she blurted out.

Donella *hated* socializing and was an absolute failure when it came to flirting and other normal female activities. Aside from her relatives, she hadn't a clue how to talk to men.

You could talk to Logan Kendrick.

"Capital idea, Grandfather," Eden enthused. "I could truly use Donella's help planning the Christmas and Hogmanay parties. I love doing it, but it's always quite the undertaking, especially now that we have fewer staff at the manor."

Breadie Manor, a tidy estate just outside Glasgow, was the family's base when they visited the city. There, Eden and Alasdair hosted annual parties that were always tremendously successful. Donella had never been to one of those celebrations and had no desire to start.

"I haven't the foggiest clue how to plan holiday parties," she said. "We never did anything like that at Haddon House."

Socializing had always happened at Blairgal, overseen by her uncle and the castle's competent staff.

"Our housekeeper can get you started," Eden said. "In fact, I think you should go down early. Alec and I can join you in a week or so."

Alasdair frowned at his wife. "Why don't we all just go down at the same time?"

"Because Elizabeth has developed the sniffles, and Callum is teething. They're in no condition to travel."

Alasdair jerked up straight with alarm. "Lizzie has the sniffles?"

Lizzie was Eden and Alasdair's adopted daughter, an adorable and rambunctious three-year-old. Callum was their son, a robust baby who would no doubt weather the half-day journey to Breadie in good order.

"Nurse told me just a short time ago," Eden said with a vague wave.

Donella was hard-pressed not to roll her eyes. When she saw Lizzie a few hours ago, her little niece had seemed in perfect health.

"Then she cannot step foot outdoors until she's better," Alasdair exclaimed.

Alasdair Gilbride, once a fearless spy for the Crown, turned into a wreck when anything was even slightly wrong with his children.

"Sorry, old girl," he said to Donella. "You'll have to start the holiday folderol without us for a bit."

"But we don't even celebrate Christmas," she protested. "And we can certainly wait a few weeks before planning the Hogmanay celebrations."

Scots generally didn't fuss about Christmas, saving most of their holiday spirit for Hogmanay, when they rang in the New Year.

"We celebrate Christmas now," Alasdair said, winking at his wife.

"Aye," said Uncle Riddick, sounding slightly disgruntled. "With Eden and Georgie in the family, we don't have much choice."

"Which is exactly why we hold the parties in Glasgow," Eden said. "So you don't have to put up with our *Sassenach* fuss and nonsense." She smiled at Donella. "You'll see. It's great fun."

"And you're a Catholic now, old girl," Alasdair said. "Celebrating Christmas is obligatory."

"I suppose, although it's beastly that you're using my conversion against me," she grumbled, annoyed by their ruthless manipulation.

"But you love Christmas, Sis," Fergus said. "You told me that in one of your letters."

Christmas *had* been her favorite time of year in the convent. Festivities there had been simple, lovely, and heartfelt. The sisters had taken great joy in decorating the church and dining hall, and had even held a special dinner on Christmas night to celebrate the Savior's birth.

Alasdair beamed at her. "There you go. All settled."

Well, she couldn't stand up to the entire family. And

perhaps leaving Blairgal wasn't such a bad idea. She'd have the manor house to herself and could spend time planning her next steps without everyone trying to coax her out of them.

"Very well. I can leave in a few days. The rest of you can come down when you're ready."

"There is the issue of a chaperone, however," Walter said, frowning. "You won't have one at Breadie Manor until Eden arrives."

Ah, the perfect excuse to avoid socializing.

"The housekeeper will be there, and I promise I won't leave the estate. Besides, I'll be too busy planning the parties to do anything."

"Goodness, pet," said Eden, "you're not a servant. We want you to have fun, not just work."

Alasdair suddenly looked crafty. "Maybe dear Mamma-in-law could go with her. No one could possibly object if Donella was chaperoned by Lady Reese."

Donella was too horrified by that idea to even respond.

"Certainly not," Eden firmly replied. "I need Mamma's help with the children."

Most of them blinked at that remark. Lady Reese, while fiercely loyal to her family, was the least maternal woman one could imagine.

Her ladyship pressed a soulful hand to her bodice. "I couldn't *think* of abandoning Eden in her time of need."

"Good God," Fergus muttered.

"Then I suppose I will just have to stay here," Donella said, trying to sound regretful.

Eden beamed at her. "Not to worry, dearest. You can stay with the Kendricks. I wrote to Cousin Victoria just this morning, and she's expecting you in Glasgow by the end of the week."

Donella stared at her, once more too aghast to utter a sound.

And when Eden and Uncle Riddick exchanged a quick glance, she finally realized that the pair of them—assisted by Lady Reese—had been ten steps ahead of her, all along.

She was going to Glasgow, whether she wanted to or not.

Chapter Sixteen

Donella snuck down the stairs of Kendrick House to find the hall empty. She'd arrived at lunchtime to encounter an entire household determined to pamper her into submission. It had been much the same at Blairgal, to the point where she'd been happy to escape the parade of servants and family ready to leap to her assistance at a moment's notice, whether she wanted it or not.

She'd grown used to self-sufficiency. In the convent, Donella had performed every chore, from the endless washing of floors to long hours tending the kitchen garden under a hot sun. So as lovely as it was to be spoiled, she'd had enough, since it was beginning to make her feel useless and guilty.

The sooner she could begin her work at Breadie Manor, the better.

Escaping there for most of every day would also minimize her contact with Logan. The idea of seeing him again, especially after that ridiculous good-bye on her part, made her cheeks flame with heat and her stomach go topsy-turvy. God only knew what he thought of her, especially after that embarrassing scene with Alasdair at the crofter's cottage.

And yet here she was, living under the same roof with the man. It was the perfect illustration of just how much control she'd lost over her life.

Six months. You only have to stick it out for six months.

Then she'd be free to do what she wanted.

She made her way to Lord Arnprior's library, hoping to avoid the notice of the butler or a footman. Clearly a conspiracy was in the works between Kendrick House and Blairgal Castle, one that involved a great deal of well-intentioned meddling that was sure to drive her insane before the holidays even arrived.

What she needed more than anything else was peace and privacy, and she hoped to find that in the study. The only other alternative was her bedroom, where her assigned maid was fussing over her clothes. Donella didn't need a lady's maid, especially since she had so few gowns, but Victoria had insisted—just like she'd insisted on a shopping expedition tomorrow.

"You'll need a new pelisse, some day gowns, at least three dinner dresses, and a ball gown," her hostess had said after examining the meager contents of Donella's trunk. "Lord Riddick was quite clear. He's opened accounts for you at several stores and expects me to properly kit you out."

"It's entirely unnecessary," Donella had said, trying to sound firm. "I'll be too busy planning Eden's parties to socialize."

"Oh, I promised Edie I'd help you with that, too. So you'll still have plenty of time for socializing."

"But—"

"I have my orders, Donella. You are to buy some pretty dresses and enjoy your time here in Glasgow. His lordship was perfectly clear on that point."

And that, apparently, was that. She was to have fun, even if it killed her.

If she didn't first die of embarrassment when she saw Logan Kendrick.

Victoria had assured her that the study was empty, so she didn't bother knocking before slipping into the room.

Breathing a sigh of relief, she was about to head for the bookshelves that rose to the ceiling behind Lord Arnprior's desk when she caught sight of a small boy curled up in front of the fireplace, reading a book. He suddenly jerked into a sitting position, dropping the leather-bound volume to the floor.

Donella halted in the middle of the carpet as the boy scrambled to his feet.

"I'm sorry I startled you," she said. "I didn't mean to barge in like that."

The little boy tucked his hands behind his back, looking a bit wary. "That's all right. And you didn't really barge in."

She waggled a hand. "Perhaps just a bit?"

That won her a hint of a smile. "Maybe a little."

For a few moments, they eyed each other. The study was quiet but for the hissing of coals in the grate and the tick of the gilt and porcelain bracket clock on the mantel.

He was a handsome child, with jet-black hair and skin the color of bronze. His dark eyes were big and thickly lashed. He regarded her with a solemnity that seemed beyond his age, which she guessed to be about six. He was at that endearing, awkward stage when a boy was a few years out of the toddler stage but not yet old enough to enter the schoolroom.

When it became obvious that her little companion was content to stand and stare, studying her with open curiosity, Donella bit back a smile.

"I'm Donella Haddon. I've just arrived for a visit."

His eyes lit up. "Oh, you're the almost-nun Papa told me about. You had to leave the convent. Aunt Vicky said you might be coming for Christmas."

She mentally winced to learn he was Logan's son. The resemblance was quite strong, including the stubborn line to the jaw and the high forehead ending in a slight widow's peak. Then there were the gangly arms and legs that hinted he would grow up to be a tall man, just like his father.

Still, it was hard to believe that such a solemn child could be the offspring of the bold Highland warrior who tossed would-be kidnappers off bridges.

"Then you must be Joseph Kendrick."

He came forward and bowed over her hand forcefully. Unlike his father, he showed excellent manners.

"It's a pleasure to meet you, Miss Haddon."

She dipped into a curtsy. "And it's a pleasure to meet you, Mr. Kendrick."

"You'd better call me Joseph," he said with a shy smile. "There are an awful lot of Mr. Kendricks in the house."

"I'll be happy to call you Joseph, if you promise to call me Donella."

He crinkled his forehead. "Shouldn't I call you Miss Haddon?"

"Only if you want to. But I'm not really used to that name anymore."

"Because you were in the convent. You don't keep your regular names in a convent."

"Correct," she said, surprised he knew such a detail.

"What was your name before they kicked you out?"

Donella sincerely hoped she wouldn't spend the rest of her life known as the girl who got kicked out of the convent.

She gestured toward the velvet settee, inviting him to sit with her.

"My religious name was Sister Dominic."

Joseph perched next to her, tucking his feet close together and folding his hands in his lap. "That's a funny name for a girl."

She almost grinned. Perhaps he had a bit of his father in him, after all.

"True, but Saint Dominic was a great man who accomplished much in his life." She wrinkled her nose. "While I picked him as a good example for me to follow, it unfortunately didn't stick. I suppose that's why they kicked me out."

She mentally froze, surprised both by the words and the

effect of them. It was actually a relief, because it was the truth. How strange was it that it had taken a child to finally get her to admit it to herself.

His mouth twisted with sympathy. "They don't sound very nice, if you ask me."

"No, they were nice. I just wasn't a very good nun."

His eyes went wide. "Did you do anything naughty, like put frogs in the other nuns' beds or refuse to eat your turnips?"

This time, she did grin. "Sadly, no. Although now that you mention it, I can think of one nun who quite deserved a frog in her bed. And I like turnips," she added.

"Papa says I have to eat them so I grow up to be as big as he is," he said morosely.

"You can give your turnips to me. I'll eat them for you."

He brightened for a moment before that oddly wary expression shuttered his gaze. "You won't tell Papa, will you? I don't think he'll like it."

Surely the boy wasn't afraid of his father? Logan was a big, brusque man, but from what little he'd said to her, he clearly loved his son.

"Does your father know you don't like turnips?"

He shook his head.

"Then I would advise you to tell him as soon as possible, and also that I'll eat your turnips from now on."

She was again rewarded with that lovely, shy smile.

"I will." He cocked his head and pointed to her throat. "I like your necklace."

She touched the Celtic cross on its silver chain. Donella had given away most of her jewelry when she joined the Carmelites. Her brother had saved a few of the more important pieces, though, like this cross. She was slightly ashamed that she'd shed a few tears when Fergus had pulled it from his waistcoat pocket and given it back to her.

"It's a very old family heirloom, Joseph. It was a gift to my great-grandmother from her grandmother."

He apparently tried to work out the convoluted ancestral connection before giving up with a shrug. "I have a cross, too." He fished a chain out from under his shirt.

Donella rested the expensive gold cross in her palm. There was a delicacy to it, as if it had been made for a woman. "It's beautiful."

"It was my mama's. She died a few months after I was born."

"I'm so sorry. That's terribly sad."

"I don't remember her." He tucked the cross back under his collar. "But Papa saved this special for me. He gave it to her when they got married."

Donella had to struggle against a constriction in her throat. "I think it's a splendid gift. I'm sure your mama would be very proud to see you wear it."

"Mama was a Catholic, like me." His smile suddenly flashed bright. "And like you."

"I see."

"Mama's entire family was Catholic. I used to live with them in Canada." He looked at her with expectation, as if his words conveyed special meaning.

"That's nice," she said cautiously.

"Catholics have Christmas, even in Scotland, don't they?"

"Yes, although the festivities aren't as big as they are in England and France."

He blew out an unhappy breath. "But they still give presents and toys, don't they? And have treats and special cakes and things?"

Now she understood. He was afraid his Scottish relatives wouldn't properly celebrate Christmas. Not like he was used to, anyway.

She leaned in closer, as if imparting a great secret. "Well, I'm going to celebrate Christmas, no matter what. And there *will* be presents. In fact, I'm planning a big Christmas party for my cousin. She's English and loves Christmas. Would you like to come to our party?"

He wriggled with excitement, almost toppling off the settee. Donella righted him with a swift hand, returning his big smile.

"Really?" he squeaked. "I can come to your party?"

"Miss Haddon is having a party, is she?" came a deep, brogue-laced voice from the door. "I wonder if she'll give me an invitation."

Donella jerked around to stare at him, her cheeks flushing pink. Logan was stunned to find her sitting in his brother's study, comfortably chatting with Joseph.

His son sighed and rolled his eyes, as if annoyed by the interruption. The lad found his papa something of a pest these days, and he got along better with everyone else in the household, including, it would appear, Donella Haddon.

Logan had poked his head into the study, hoping to play a game of Fox and Geese with his son before dinner. Finding Donella, a woman he'd thought never to see again, was yet another in the string of surprising events of the last few weeks.

And why the *hell* hadn't anyone told him she would be here?

"Oh, ah, Mr. Kendrick," Donella stammered, rising quickly to her feet. "I didn't hear you come in."

Her cheeks were now glowing, and she looked more flustered than he'd ever seen her.

Perhaps she's thinking of the kiss she gave you when she said good-bye.

He'd thought quite a lot about that sweet kiss.

Joseph also came to his feet. "Papa *is* very quiet for a big man. Grandda said it's because he was . . ." He frowned, searching for a word, then nodded with satisfaction. "A hellion. Papa had to learn how to be quiet so he didn't get caught when he was being bad."

"Papa had to learn to be quiet when hunting in Canada," Logan said dryly, "so as to avoid being eaten by a bear."

Joseph wrinkled his brow. "That's not what Grandda said."

By now, Donella was pressing a finger to her lips, obviously holding in laughter.

"And I'll be having a little chat with Grandda about that."

In a blink, his son adopted the anxious look that never failed to send Logan's heart plummeting to the soles of his boots.

"Papa, please don't get mad at Grandda. He just likes to tell stories about when you and my uncles were little."

Logan hated that his son no longer trusted him to do the right thing.

"Och, laddie," he said, mustering a smile. "Your grandda is more likely to get mad at *me* for scolding him. He'll no doubt threaten me with a good paddling."

Joseph snickered. "You're much too big for a paddling."

"That would not stop Angus from trying." Logan moved to greet Donella. "Now, I see we have a visitor."

The lass gave him a graceful curtsy and a polite smile. After her initial flustered response, she'd adopted the self-contained persona she often wore when she was feeling most unsure of herself.

"Yes," Joseph said. "Aunt Vicky said Donella might come for a visit, and here she is. She's come for Christmas."

Logan raised a brow. "Has she now? That's a grand surprise."

"I take it you were not aware I'd be coming to stay," she said with a slight wince.

"No, but I rarely know what's going on around here. Just ask my son."

Joseph rolled his eyes again. "That's because you're always at work, Papa."

Logan rubbed his chin. "Hmm. I'll have to remedy that, but I'm certain that your aunt Vicky did not tell me about Miss Haddon's impending visit."

"I'd planned on staying at Breadie Manor, but Alasdair and Eden aren't yet ready to come to town. Eden wrote to Victoria and asked if I might stay here until they do." Her smile was apologetic. "I do hope I'm not putting anyone out."

"Lass, of course not. You're most welcome, and I'm sure Victoria is happy to have another woman in the house."

Her smile became more genuine. "I did get that impression."

"The Kendrick men can be a wee bit overwhelming. It's a wonder we don't burn the house down on a regular basis."

Joseph shook his head. "Not me. Aunt Vicky said I'm the good Kendrick."

Logan ruffled his son's hair. "That you are."

When Joseph carefully smoothed his hair back into place, Logan had to repress a sigh. Where was the fun-loving tyke who would throw himself into his father's arms, shrieking with laughter whenever Logan hung him upside down or tossed him into the air? He didn't know how to reach that boy anymore and feared he was gone forever.

He caught Donella studying them, as if she'd glimpsed the tension.

"So, Miss Haddon," he said, gesturing her to resume her seat, "what brings you to Glasgow?"

She settled gracefully onto the settee. Joseph plopped down next to her, appearing comfortable in her presence. Logan couldn't blame him. Some might think Donella haughty, but during their time together, he'd seen through to the heart of her. She was truly a bonny lass, both brave and kind.

"Donella's come to Glasgow to have a Christmas party," Joseph said with excitement. "One with presents, and treats, and *everything*."

"Well, that's splendid," replied Logan as he propped a

shoulder against the mantelpiece. "But don't you think you'd best call her Miss Haddon? You just met her, son."

When Joseph ducked his head, Logan wanted to kick himself. He should have waited until they were alone to correct the boy's manners. As usual, he'd made a cock-up of the simplest parental task.

"It's my fault," Donella quickly said. "I asked him to call me that."

"I'm sorry, Papa," Joseph said in a small voice.

"No, *I'm* sorry, lad," Logan replied. "If Miss Haddon gave you permission to use her given name, you can certainly do so."

His son frowned. "But you call her Miss Haddon, and you met her way before I did."

Logan fumbled for a sensible answer. "Well, you see—"

"Your papa must certainly call me Donella from now on," she interrupted, patting Joseph's hand. "After all, your aunt Vicky and my cousin, Alasdair, are close relations. So, it's like we're all family."

"Then *you* must call me Logan, of course," Logan firmly said.

Her eyelid twitched at his little push for intimacy. She'd been caught in her own trap, but he wouldn't tease her. After all, she'd done it to make his son feel better.

"Papa, Donella said I could come to her Christmas party," Joseph said, returning to the obviously most important subject.

"And as I mentioned, I hope I get an invitation, too."

One corner of her lush mouth tilted up. "I'm sure we can arrange that."

"There are going to be presents, Papa." Joseph gave him an intent look. "*Proper* presents, the kind you're supposed to have at Christmas."

Ah. So that's what the wee lad had been fashed about. "There will be proper presents here too, Joseph. Your aunt Vicky will see to that."

His son pulled a face. "Grandda said that proper Scots only celebrate Hogmanay."

Logan flexed his shoulders against the mantel, getting more comfortable. "We'll celebrate Hogmanay, but Aunt Vicky is English, so she's rather big on Christmas. They'll be plenty of parties, especially if Donella is planning one, too."

When he smiled at her, he was surprised to see her cheeks turn pink again. Then he realized her gaze had been stuck on his chest and shoulders, as if she were inspecting them.

Interesting.

Apparently, there just might have been something to that good-bye kiss she'd given him. He'd suspected as much.

"With proper presents," Joseph said with the dogged emphasis of a child.

Logan reached down to tap his son's nose. "With proper presents, I promise."

The grin that split Joseph's face triggered a corresponding burst of happiness in Logan's heart. He'd have to find time to Christmas shop for his son. Better yet, he'd take Joseph and let the lad pick out his own gifts. If bribery helped to smooth over the awkwardness between them, Logan was more than ready to empty his pockets.

"Whew, that's good." Then the lad's smile faded. "Meme was always very good at Christmas, especially since Grandpapa loved it so much. He . . ." Joseph lost his voice, swallowing hard.

"I know how much you miss him," Logan said quietly. "I do, too."

The boy gave an awkward shrug, his gaze dropping to his lap.

Donella threw Logan a sympathetic glance before tapping Joseph's knee. "Since Christmas will be here soon, we'd best get to planning our party, don't you think?"

He looked up. "Our party? Does that mean you want me to help?"

"Yes, if your father will allow it. You'll have to come to Breadie Manor, though."

Joseph turned a pleading gaze on Logan.

"Of course, son. Donella will be glad for your help, I'm thinking."

The study door banged open, and Angus charged in with his usual lack of grace. "I've come to meet the Flower of Clan Graham. I just found out she's stayin' for a spell."

At least there was one other person who hadn't known about Donella's visit. Why it was all such a mystery had yet to be clarified.

Looking pained because she really hated that name, Donella rose to her feet.

"Miss Donella Haddon, allow me to present my grandfather, Mr. Angus MacDonald," Logan said.

Angus gave her a flourishing bow, his grizzled hair practically dusting the table in front of the settee. "It's an honor to meet ye, Miss Donella."

She bobbed him a curtsy. "Thank you, sir."

Joseph tugged on his great-grandfather's sleeve. "Why did you call her that, Grandda?"

"Because she's the prettiest and kindest of lasses and the pride of her branch of the clan, her chief dubbed her the Flower of Clan Graham."

Joseph seemed awestruck. "Is that true?" he asked her.

"It's true that the chief gave me that nickname. But the rest is not," she said with an embarrassed smile.

"Aye, ye were all that, until ye ran off to that convent." Angus let out a gusty sigh. "And a very bad business that was."

Logan jabbed his grandfather in the shoulder. "It's time for Joseph to change for dinner, isn't it?"

"Oh, aye, I'll attend to that," Angus said. "Come along, laddie."

"You'll be here for dinner?" Joseph asked Donella as he took his grandfather's hand.

She smiled at the boy. "Indeed I will."

"The Flower of Clan Graham restored to her rightful place and come to stay with the Kendricks," Angus said, giving Logan a broad wink. "I hope ye realize how lucky ye are, lad. How lucky we *all* are to have such a lady with us."

Logan didn't know whether to laugh or scowl at his grandfather's lack of subtlety.

Donella looked appalled.

"Ye have a nice chat, now," said Angus as he backed out the door with Joseph in tow. "I'll make sure no one disturbs ye."

"Good God," Logan muttered.

Donella switched her ire to him. "Is your grandfather suggesting what I think he's suggesting?"

He held up his hands. "Don't look at me. I didn't even know you were coming."

"Because I won't have it. We all went through a great deal of trouble to squash any rumors, as you will recall."

"My grandfather is always stirring up mischief. Just ignore him."

"He's not the only one I'll have to ignore." She sat down on the settee, her back as straight as a poker.

"What does that mean?"

She grimaced, as if she'd revealed something inappropriate. "Nothing, and would you please sit down? I'd rather not stare up at you. I'll get a crick in my neck."

Logan bit back a smile. He'd missed her little scolds.

He took the wing chair across from her, stretching out his legs so his boots were mere inches from her daintily shod feet. She'd abandoned her gruesomely unflattering garb in favor of a moss green, kerseymere gown that skimmed her elegant figure and flattered her vibrant coloring. Her auburn curls, shiny and sleek, were restrained by a gold bandeau. Donella would always be considered a lovely young woman, but now, so stylishly dressed, she was a stunner.

"From your cryptic comments, I take it your family wasn't keen on your plan to hike off to Galway."

"You'd have thought I'd suggested an expedition to the Amazonian wilderness," she said, disgusted.

"Well, Galway's not exactly the most thrilling spot on earth."

"But it's where I might be able to join a convent again."

"So, Lord Riddick thinks a bit of holiday merrymaking in jolly old Glasgow will change your mind? Seems a bit far-fetched."

She let out a reluctant laugh. "Not as far-fetched as me planning all the holiday parties for Eden. I haven't a clue how to go about it."

"Yes, party planning doesn't seem quite in your line."

"That's what I've been trying to tell everyone, but they won't listen."

"Families generally don't. But is that it? You help Edie and Alec throw their insanely extravagant holiday parties and then hang about Glasgow for a spell? You'll be bored out of your skull in no time."

"My uncle insisted I give it six months before I make any permanent decisions about my life. Oh, I forgot. I'm supposed to have fun, too," she finished.

Logan could think of several ways to show her how to have fun—none of them appropriate.

"I take it you're not thrilled with that plan. You'd rather bury yourself away in Galway forthwith."

For a moment, she looked ready to take offense. Then she wrinkled her nose. "To be honest, I'm not sure what I want to do. I did rather muck things up last time, didn't I?"

Logan was relieved to hear that admission—a revelation he would keep to himself. "At least you don't have Sister Bernard breathing down your neck anymore. She sounded worse than Medusa."

"And not as cheerful."

When Logan started to laugh, she reluctantly smiled. "I told you I wasn't a very good nun."

"You'll find something else to be good at."

"I hope so. For now, I will do my best to plan parties and have fun."

"You deserve a little fun, lass, after everything you've been through."

She shot him a sweet, almost shy glance through her long lashes, and he felt it go straight through to his groin. He had to resist the urge to shift in his chair.

"I haven't yet thanked you for taking Joseph under your wing," he gruffly said. "He's a grand boy."

"He's a darling, and children really are the best part of Christmas, you know. They make it so lively."

"I'd forgotten how much he loved Christmas," he said ruefully. "I'm an idiot."

Donella held her thumb and forefinger an inch or so apart. "Maybe just a wee bit."

"Don't hesitate to be brutal, lass."

She grinned. "Sorry. You're a very busy man, so it's understandable it might slip your mind. Women usually manage that sort of thing, anyway."

"Like his grandmother did. But I do need to spend more time with him."

"I'm sure he'd like that."

He waggled a hand. "Maybe. The poor lad's had a hard time since coming here. Glasgow might not be the best place for him."

"Because he's a Catholic?"

"Told you that, did he?"

"He did."

"It's also because he's of . . . mixed heritage."

Her brow knit in confusion. "Because his grandparents are French speakers?"

He hesitated. "Partly. His grandfather was mostly Acadian,

and his grandmother is primarily Mi'kmaq, one of the native tribes of that part of Canada. People are not always accepting, shall we say."

"People can be stupidly intolerant, and the Scots are no saintlier than anyone else. Except maybe the *Sassenachs,*" she added with a glimmer of a smile.

He let his smile cover a rather staggering sense of relief that she so easily understood his worries. "Angus would certainly agree with you. But Joseph is a sensitive boy, and he's already suffered a few snubs."

She grimaced. "That's dreadful. I'm guessing, however, that you don't exactly turn the other cheek."

"I do try to refrain from tossing people off bridges, if that's what you're asking. But turning the other cheek generally doesn't work in the real world."

"It does if you tell your son that those who snub him are small-minded and best ignored. Better yet, pitied for the fools that they are."

"I'll be sure to try that the next time it happens."

She rolled her eyes, the cheeky lass. "Then I suppose the next best thing is to offer Joseph a distraction, like helping me at Breadie Manor."

"He'd obviously be thrilled. But you're supposed to be having fun, not taking care of lonely little boys."

"You do realize I'm not very good at fun. I just got out of a convent."

"Then all the more reason to kick up your heels. Wouldn't you like to go to a few balls, for instance? Dance a bit, flirt a bit, drink a little champagne?"

"I haven't danced in years, I don't like champagne, and I'm positively dreadful at flirting."

For the life of him, Logan simply couldn't resist. He leaned forward, bracing his forearms on his thighs as he fastened his gaze on her pretty mouth. "Then perhaps I'll have a go at teaching you," he said, dropping his voice to a rumbling purr.

Her emerald eyes went wide. "Ah, teach me what?"

"To flirt."

Donella starched up. "*Mr.* Kendrick—"

"Logan."

"Mr. Kendrick," she said more firmly, "I do not—"

The door to the study opened, cutting her off. Logan sighed and came to his feet. He'd been looking forward to another of her entertaining scolds.

"Forgive me for missing your arrival, Miss Haddon," Nick said as he joined them. "I was called away on business."

"So you knew she was coming, did you?" Logan sardonically asked.

Nick ignored him to bow over Donella's hand.

She dipped into a curtsy. "Thank you, my lord. It's a great honor to be staying with your family."

"The honor is ours," Nick replied. "And Logan is, no doubt, especially thrilled to have you visit. He's extolled your virtues at some length since your little adventure together."

That ridiculous comment brought the color flying back to Donella's cheeks and made Logan want to throttle his brother. It would indeed appear that there was a conspiracy afoot.

While Donella's suspicious gaze flickered between the two of them, thankfully she refrained from replying.

"How long will you be staying?" Nick prompted. "I hope through the holidays, at the very least."

"I . . . I don't know." She was looking more alarmed by the second.

Nick gave Logan a gentle smile. "We'll have to insist on it, won't we, Logan? You will no doubt wish to further your acquaintance with Miss Haddon."

"I think I'd better get ready for dinner," Donella said.

After another curtsy, she fled the room with impressive haste, all but leaving a dust trail in her wake.

"You're an idiot," Logan said. "And you embarrassed the poor girl. You're worse than Angus."

Nick grinned. "Nobody's worse than Angus."

"It won't work, you know. I have no intention of getting married again." As much as Logan was attracted to Donella, he'd made that decision long ago.

His brother strolled over to his desk. "She's a perfectly lovely girl from a splendid family. And from what I've heard, you get along exceedingly well."

"Who the hell told you that?"

Nick sat down and started sorting through his mail. "You need a wife, Logan, and Joseph needs a mother."

"Joseph has all the family he needs. And if you start playing matchmaker, I'll toss you out the bloody window."

"Victoria likes her, too," Nick said as he slit open a letter and began to read.

Logan waved an arm. "Donella wants to become a nun, for God's sake."

"Perhaps you could change her mind," Nick absently replied.

Logan stared at him with disbelief before turning on his heel and stalking from the room.

Chapter Seventeen

Logan listened to Donella and Joseph chat like old friends. His son was wedged between them in Logan's curricle, and the lad's attention was all for his new favorite as Logan drove them back from their outing at Mugdock Castle.

He'd arranged the visit as a special treat, hoping to spend time with both his son and Donella. But Joseph had largely ignored his father, holding Donella's hand as she'd shown him about the ancestral home of Clan Graham. The two had had a splendid time, while Logan had served as the mostly silent coachman and escort.

True to her word, Donella had involved Joseph in planning the Gilbride holiday parties. Logan had only discovered today that his son lurked outside Donella's door every morning, waiting for her to appear. She didn't seem to mind, clearly returning Joseph's affection.

Idiot that he was, Logan was jealous, and not simply because Joseph preferred Donella's company. As much as he wanted to be with his son, he also wanted to spend time with Donella—a lot of time.

It was Nick's fault, damn him. Ever since his brother suggested that Logan should marry the lass, he couldn't get the notion out of his head. When he wasn't worrying about Joseph, he was thinking about Donella.

The same could not be said about her. Donella had no problem keeping her attention firmly away from him, avoiding his presence whenever possible.

A small elbow dug into his side. "Papa, are you listening to me?"

Logan transferred the reins to one hand and patted his son on the knee. "Laddie boy, I always listen to you."

The boy raised a skeptical eyebrow in a dead accurate imitation of the look Donella often leveled at Logan.

"Then what did I just say?"

"You were speculating on the likelihood of stopping at the sweet shop for some cake."

"Well done, sir," Donella said, amused.

"I am capable of doing more than two things at once. On rare occasions, even three."

"I will file that for future reference," she dryly replied.

"So, we can stop for a treat?" As always, his son remained focused on his priorities.

"If Donella doesn't object."

"I'd love a treat," she said.

Logan's kind of treat would involve smooth, pale skin, shiny auburn curls, and lacy underthings.

Get your mind out of the gutter, man.

He refocused on his son. "Then the pastry shop it is."

Joseph wriggled with delight, sending his lap blanket sliding off. "Aunt Vicky says Monroe's has the best French pastries."

Donella retrieved the blanket and tucked it securely around Joseph's waist. Given the unusually mild weather for December, the wool plaid was barely necessary. Up at Castle Kinglas, snow would already be dusting the peaks around Loch Long. Glasgow, however, was enjoying a bout of temperate weather that boded ill for little boys longing for sledding and skating. Joseph had become so worried about the lack of snow that Logan had been forced to reassure him that they would travel to Kinglas immediately after the holidays.

"Since your aunt Vicky is invariably correct about everything," Logan said, "we will repair to Monroe's."

Joseph tilted his head to study him. "Papa, sometimes you talk funny."

"Funnier than Grandda?" Logan teased.

Joseph looked straight ahead. "I like the way Grandda talks. And *he* always tells me the truth."

Logan looked at his son, startled by the lad's solemn tone. "Joseph, I always tell you the truth, too."

"Whatever you say, Papa."

The response was so quiet Logan could barely hear it, and it made his heart sink. He'd never lied to his son, at least not deliberately. Had someone suggested he had?

Frustrated, he repressed the urge to question the boy. This wasn't the time or place, and he didn't want to ruin the day. But when he glanced at Joseph again, and saw his lower lip quivering, his gut turned inside out. It seemed he'd lost the knack of being a parent—if he'd ever had it.

After throwing Logan a troubled glance, Donella put her arm around Joseph's shoulders.

"Have you thought about what you'd like to order at Monroe's?" she brightly asked. "I'm going to have trouble choosing, because everything there is so good."

Joseph gave her a cautious smile. "What sort of treats do they have?"

"Let me think," Donella said in a pondering tone. "There are the éclairs, which are splendid. And the macaroons are also delicious. I don't know that I've ever had better."

Joseph perked up. "I've never had an éclair. What's it like?"

Donella rattled off descriptions of éclairs and other pastries, explaining each one in delectable detail. By the time they reached Glasgow, Joseph's good humor was restored.

The woman was a miracle worker, and as sweet as one of the pastries she described.

They pulled up on a busy street lined with shops. The groom jumped down to help Donella and Joseph to the pavement, and then climbed into the driver's seat after Logan gave him instructions to take the carriage back to Kendrick House.

"I hope you don't mind walking," Logan said to Donella. "But I'd rather the horses not stand about, waiting for us."

She winked at Joseph. "The walk will do us good after we've stuffed ourselves, don't you think?"

The boy nodded enthusiastically before taking Donella's hand and pulling her into Monroe's without a backward glance at his father. Logan shook his head and followed them into the sweet shop.

Monroe's bustling front room was filled with elegantly dressed ladies and mostly elderly gentlemen. An aisle ran between the tables and the glass display cases loaded with elaborate pastries and cakes. Waiters rushed back and forth, bearing silver trays with tea services and tiered cake plates.

Logan followed Donella and Joseph to the back room, which was more spacious than expected and filled with parquet tables and delicate, shield-backed chairs. The walls were painted in pale shades of pink and green and hung with framed prints of Parisian scenes. The establishment obviously catered to the Glasgow elite, unlike the coffee shops he tended to frequent. Those mostly served businessmen and merchants.

A harassed-looking waiter in a starched apron edged in front of him.

"Can I help you?" he haughtily asked, flicking a glance over Logan's driving outfit. "Sir?"

Logan swallowed a snort. Clearly, the staff at Monroe's took themselves a little too seriously.

"I see my party is already seated in the back. Your help is not required."

The waiter barely nodded before rushing off.

Joseph waved to him. "Hurry up, Papa."

Logan gingerly settled into one of the absurdly delicate chairs, praying it didn't collapse under his weight. "Hungry, are we?"

"Famished," said Joseph with all the drama of a six-year-old. "And Donella is, too."

"I could eat half the contents of the display case," she said, smiling at the boy.

"I could eat the other half," Joseph replied.

"No doubt, but we'd best leave room for dinner, or your aunt Vicky will make us eat gruel for a week."

Joseph giggled and reached across the table to take her hand. "Now you're just being silly."

She closed both her hands over his little fingers. "I do tend to be silly when I'm hungry."

Joseph's boyish adoration for Donella was both heart-warming and unnerving. Logan's son had attached himself to the lass, just as he had to his uncle Nick. The difference was that Nick would always be there for Joseph, whereas Donella's future was still uncertain.

Her impending departure, whether to a convent or even back to Blairgal, would hold negative consequences for the lad. She could be yet another terrible loss for him, because Donella had somehow reached the lonely place inside Joseph that no one else had been able to touch.

He needs her, which means you need her, too.

Donella gave Logan a quizzical smile. "Is something wrong, sir?"

"Just wondering where the bloody waiter is."

She raised a hand to catch a waiter's attention. "Language, Mr. Kendrick."

When Logan blew out an exaggerated sigh at the mild reprimand, Joseph giggled again.

God, it was *so* good to hear his son laugh and once more be the little boy who needn't worry about anything but whether there would be snow for Christmas.

Logan watched the wee tyke who meant everything to him and the almost-nun who'd turned his life upside down, and finally admitted the stark truth. He would do whatever it took to keep Joseph happy. If that meant keeping the bonny lass in their lives, by hook or by crook he would do it.

"I cannot say I am much impressed with the service," Donella said when the waiter ignored her. "I do hope the pastries make up for it."

Logan twisted in his chair, glaring toward the front room. Fortunately, another waiter came through the doorway and hurried toward them, apologizing for the delay. After taking their order, he returned shortly with the tea things, then hurried off to fetch their sweets.

Logan and Donella chatted amiably about her progress on the holiday parties. He was so busy thinking about how pretty she was—and planning his campaign to persuade her to marry him—that it took some time to notice that Joseph had fallen silent.

"What's the matter, lad?" he asked when he caught the boy peering uncertainly at one of the other tables.

"Papa, why is that woman scowling at us?" Joseph whispered.

Logan resisted the temptation to turn around and look.

"I'm guessing it's because I'm such a big lummox, and she's wondering if I'm going to break my chair. We Kendricks are rather famous for destroying the furniture, you know."

It was a standard joke around town that hostesses quaked in fear whenever the twins arrived at a party.

"I don't think that's why," Joseph said.

Donella leaned sideways so she could see around Logan.

"Oh, I see who it is. Just ignore her, Joseph. That particular woman is always glaring at someone."

Even though her tone was mild, Logan couldn't miss Donella's suddenly stiff posture. Nor could he miss the way his son was shrinking back in his chair, as if trying to disappear.

Slowly, he turned to meet the malevolent gaze of one of the biggest gossips in Glasgow. Seated with two other ladies, Mrs. Ferguson was the wife of a wealthy landowner from Dumfries. She'd tried to cause trouble for the Kendricks a few years ago by spreading ugly rumors about Royal and his adopted daughter, Tira. Nick had delivered a stern message to Mr. Ferguson, putting an immediate end to the worst of it, and the remaining gossip had eventually died down.

From her expression, it was obvious the woman loathed the Kendricks as much as ever.

"Good afternoon, Mrs. Ferguson," he drawled. "You appear to be suffering a touch of dyspepsia. Maybe you'd best go home and lie down."

Her eyes narrowed to outraged slits, and her complexion turned blotchy.

"Well, I never," huffed one of her companions, a middle-aged woman wearing an overtrimmed bonnet. "Such deplorable manners. So typical."

Logan casually braced an arm on the back of his chair. "Forgive me, ma'am. Do we know each other?"

"We do not, sir," she replied stiffly.

Logan flashed her a toothy smile. "How fortunate for both of us."

"Mr. Kendrick, your tea," Donella said in a firm voice.

Logan narrowed his gaze on the women, letting it linger for a few seconds before turning back to the table. Donella held out his teacup with a long-suffering expression. Joseph looked like he wanted to crawl under the table and hide.

"Thank you." He took the cup. "And Donella has the right of it, lad. Just ignore them and enjoy your tea."

Joseph stared down at his cup. "Those ladies don't seem to like us very much."

"Och, just a pair of old biddies. Best not look at them or you'll turn into stone."

Joseph blinked, obviously confused by Logan's observation.

Donella patted his hand. "Your father is just being silly, dearest. It's probably best that you ignore him, too."

"Excellent advice, because you never know what shocking things I'm going to say next," Logan said, winking at his son.

"Or do." A subtle warning laced her tone.

Don't make a scene.

Making a scene happened to be a Kendrick specialty.

Fortunately, their waiter arrived with a tray laden with pastries and cakes. They'd gone rather overboard on the ordering, but Logan was determined to spoil his son.

Donella smiled at Joseph. "My goodness. You'll have to roll me out of here if I eat more than my share of these."

Logan had a sudden vision of Donella rolling around in his bed. Naked, of course, because that's the way his brain worked.

He closed his eyes, trying to control his idiotic imaginings. He was on a public outing, with his son, no less, and yet he was visualizing how he would bed the primmest woman he'd ever met. There was only one explanation—he was losing his mind.

"Papa, is something wrong?"

Logan opened his eyes. "I'm trying to decide where to start. What do you think? The éclairs?"

When Joseph enthusiastically nodded, Logan transferred an éclair, two macaroons, and a piece of plum cake onto the boy's plate. Joseph picked up the gooey éclair and crammed half of it into his mouth.

"Careful, laddie," Logan said, trying not to laugh. "You'll choke yourself."

Blissfully unaware of the chocolate smeared on his lips, the boy nodded, his mouth too full to speak.

Donella dabbed at his face with a serviette. Joseph suffered it before taking another huge bite.

For a minute or so, Logan was too busy enjoying his son's pleasure to notice the buzz of rising voices in the room. But then he mentally slammed into a wall when one particular word seared his brain. Donella's gasp told him that she'd heard it, too.

As had Joseph, since the boy's fork clattered to the plate. He wiped a hand over his mouth, then stared fiercely down at the table, trying not to cry.

Fury rose inside Logan like a raging summer storm. He came to his feet and turned to face what he hated most in the world—someone who robbed his sweet boy of innocence.

"What did you call my son?" he asked Mrs. Ferguson.

He didn't raise his voice. He didn't need to, as her frightened expression revealed. But quickly self-righteous hatred replaced her fear, contorting her features into an ugly mask.

"You heard me, sir," she said. "No decent person would bring such a child into a civilized establishment."

Every other patron in the room froze. Their waiter rushed in from the other room, but one glance from Logan stopped him dead in his tracks.

"Mrs. Ferguson, I asked you a question," Logan said. "I insist on an answer."

The woman's companion laid a warning hand on her arm. "Dorothea, perhaps you shouldn't. He seems like a thoroughly rude and unpleasant man."

The old harpy shook off the restraining hand and glared at Logan. "I will not be driven off by you and your . . ."

"My?" he prompted.

"Heathen child," she spat out.

Logan took a step forward, but a sharp tug on his sleeve brought him up short. Joseph had slipped from his chair and now clutched his arm.

"Papa, please don't," he whispered.

Truthfully, Logan hadn't been sure what he was going to do, consumed by the anger roaring through him and the pain of seeing his son's pale, anguished face. He wanted to make the world safe for Joseph, to shield the lad from those who hated him simply for who he was.

And he hadn't a damn clue how to do that.

"Joseph, please come sit by me," Donella said, reaching over to take the boy's hand. She glanced up at Logan. "Mr. Kendrick, your tea is getting cold."

Her challenging gaze silently urged him to step back from the brink—to think of Joseph before his guilt-fueled anger.

He mustered a smile as brittle as thinning ice and patted his son on the head. "Aye, go sit with Donella, lad."

Logan resumed his seat and forced himself to take a gulp of his tepid tea. Donella laid Joseph's serviette across his lap, all the while talking soothing, cheerful nonsense. He barely heard the words, too busy watching his son.

When Joseph refused to meet his gaze, Logan's heart plummeted right through his heels and drilled into the floor. What a cock-up he'd made of things—again. Only Donella's quick action had saved him from doing something monumentally stupid.

The waiter approached their table, nervously smoothing his hands over his starched apron. "Is there anything else I can get you, sir?"

"Just the bill, thank you."

With alacrity, the man returned with the receipt. Logan paid, then rose to usher Donella and Joseph out.

"Joseph, go with your father," Donella said. "I'll follow you in a moment."

When Logan frowned, she simply gave him a bland

smile. He took Joseph's hand, taking care to keep him well to the other side as they passed near Mrs. Ferguson's table. When the old shrew cast Logan a triumphant smile, he had to throttle back on the overwhelming desire to dump the contents of the teapot over her head, especially after he heard Joseph quietly sniff.

While he'd had worse moments in his life, ones of tragedy and despair, this incident brought out a deep, quiet sorrow. It was as if something small but precious had been snuffed out before it truly got a chance to grow.

A tremendous crash sounded behind them, followed by outraged shrieks.

Holding fast to Joseph, Logan turned to find Mrs. Ferguson and her companions wearing the contents of their tea service. Mrs. Ferguson's bodice was particularly drenched, but all three women sported bits of cakes, tarts, and creams down the fronts of their gowns. Broken plates and teacups were strewn about the floor in a thorough mess.

Donella looked only mildly regretful as she surveyed the wreckage.

She righted the small table, which had apparently toppled dead-on into Mrs. Ferguson's lap. "Dear me, what a dreadful mess. However did that happen?"

Mrs. Ferguson, dripping both outrage and clotted cream, heaved to her feet. "You deliberately tipped the table onto my lap. I saw you do it."

Donella pressed a neatly gloved hand to her chest. "Surely not. That would be a *terribly* rude thing to do to someone. Rather like calling them horrible names."

Mrs. Ferguson swelled up like a turkey as she glared at Donella. Logan expected her to begin gobbling like a turkey, too. At the moment, however, she seemed too furious to get another word out.

Their waiter bolted back into the room, gaping in dismay at the level of damage.

Logan snagged him by the elbow. "I'll pay for the damage," he quietly said. "And a little extra, if you can minimize the fuss."

The waiter shot him a sharp glance, then winced when one of Mrs. Ferguson's companions let out another shriek.

"Raspberry jam stains on my best pelisse," she wailed. "And I just bought it the other day. It was *frightfully* expensive."

Logan and the waiter exchanged another glance.

"Send *all* the bills straight to me at Kendrick House," Logan said.

"Understood, sir," the man dryly replied before hurrying off to deal with the mess.

Donella handed him the remnants of a broken teacup she'd retrieved from the floor.

"Thank you, miss. I'll take care of all this."

She gave him a sweet smile before again addressing Mrs. Ferguson and her friends. "Ladies, my sincere apologies. I do hope I didn't ruin your afternoon. Why, I would never forgive myself in such a case."

Mrs. Ferguson let out an angry snort. "It's no wonder Lord Riddick packed you off in disgrace. Why he allowed you to come home now is beyond me. You should have remained in that stupid convent, out of sight. Just like your mother, you are. Not fit for decent company."

Donella flinched and took a step back.

"You'd best think carefully about what you're going to say next, madam," Logan growled, preparing to intervene.

Donella quickly recovered. "What an ugly comment to make, Mrs. Ferguson, especially when the season of charity and mercy is upon us."

"How dare you lecture me, you unrepentant hussy," Mrs. Ferguson retorted.

Hussy? What the bloody hell was the woman talking about? The lass had almost become a nun, for God's sake.

Donella sighed. "The quality of mercy is *generally* not strained, ma'am. In your case, however, it seems to be broken.

How unfortunate for your husband. I absolutely pity the poor man."

Logan had to swallow a laugh, because the lass had hit the nail on the head. Everyone knew old Ferguson lived in mortal terror of his harridan wife.

Donella turned to Logan and Joseph. Her expression was placid, but he saw turbulence roiling in her emerald gaze. "Are we ready to go, gentlemen?"

"After you, Miss Haddon," Logan said.

She took Joseph's hand and led him from the shop. Logan followed, smiling blandly at the avidly curious patrons. The scene was sure to generate astounding levels of gossip.

In other words, it was another typical day for the Kendrick family.

Chapter Eighteen

Joseph tugged on Logan's hand. "Slow down, Papa. I can't keep up."

"Sorry, laddie. I keep forgetting you're not as tall as I am yet."

"No one's as tall as you," Donella said with a wry smile as Logan slowed his pace.

"Grandda says you're like one of those giants from the stories about the ancient"—Joseph frowned, searching for the word—"Picts."

Thank God the lad was talking again. After leaving Monroe's, Joseph had withdrawn into himself, head down and gaze fastened on his feet. Donella, bless the lass, had kept up a cheerful stream of comments on harmless subjects, as if she'd not just upended a table on a bunch of old biddies.

Logan had also fallen quiet, thinking through how to manage the gossip sure to arise from today's ugly episode. He also couldn't help pondering Mrs. Ferguson's cryptic remark about Donella's mother. That veiled dig had obviously hit Donella full on. He had no idea why, since he didn't know much about the girl's history.

No one in Riddick's family had ever mentioned Mrs. Haddon. There was obviously a reason for that, and he guessed it wasn't a happy one.

"A Pict, am I? Let's be grateful I don't run around the house with blue paint on my face."

"Maybe we should all wear blue paint on our faces," Joseph said, perking up. "That might be fun."

"I bet you the twins would agree," Logan said.

"Not the ladies, though," Donella said. "I don't think your aunt Vicky and I would look very nice in blue paint."

Joseph shot her a worried glance. "We don't have to do it if you won't like it."

Donella smiled. "I'm teasing. You can wear as much blue paint as you like."

"I want you to have fun, too," Joseph earnestly said. "So you'll keep staying with us."

She took the boy's free hand as they crossed the street into a quiet square. "Of course I'll keep staying with you. And you and I always have fun, don't we?"

Joseph gave her a tentative smile.

Time to start putting it out there, old boy.

"We both hope Donella will stay with us for a very long time, son." Logan glanced over to meet her gaze. "And I'd also like to note that I can be fun as well."

She frowned at him, clearly a bit fussed by his remark. He simply gave her a bland smile in return.

For a few minutes, they walked in silence, and Logan found an odd sort of peace settling over him. To be strolling down a quiet, tree-lined street, his son safely tucked between them, felt . . . right. It seemed like something almost forgotten had slipped into place, like a missing puzzle piece found between the cushions of an old sofa and put back where it belonged.

"Papa."

"Yes, son?"

"Why did that lady have to be so mean? She doesn't even know me."

Donella's quiet sigh echoed his own. Joseph was too

smart and too sensitive to let the matter go, especially now that he was getting older.

"I expect it's because Mrs. Ferguson is an unhappy person," Logan said, trying to feel his way through the morass. "Unhappy people try to make other people unhappy. For some reason, they think it will make them feel better."

"She called me a heathen, but I'm not." Joseph blew out an exasperated breath. "I'm just me."

"There is *nothing* wrong with you, son," Logan said. "And there was nothing wrong with your mother, or your grandparents, or the Mi'kmaq, or the Acadians, or the Scots, or anyone else. Sadly, people like Mrs. Ferguson find all sorts of reasons to hate other people. For the longest time, the English hated the Scots, especially Highlanders. Some *Sassenachs* still do."

"Which is probably why we shouldn't call them *Sassenachs,*" Donella pointed out.

"Tell that to Angus."

She ignored his feeble joke. "Joseph, sometimes people are afraid of what they don't know. It's a great shame, because often when we talk to people we're a little afraid of, we discover they're actually quite nice."

"I don't think Mrs. Ferguson would want to talk to me even if I tried to be nice to her," the lad quietly replied.

"Well, as Grandda always says, 'Ye canna argue with stupid'," Logan said. "There's no point in wasting your breath on the Mrs. Fergusons of the world, son. Best ignore them."

"And try to forgive them for their ignorance," Donella added.

Logan snorted. "I noticed how forgiving you were when you dumped that table on her."

"An unfortunate accident," she said, shooting him a look.

"But I saw you hook your fingers under the table and tip it," Joseph said.

Donella's cheeks flamed pink. "Oh, dear. I didn't want you to notice that."

Logan smothered a laugh. "Fair warning, lass. Joseph has eyes in the back of his head."

"Joseph, it was very wrong of me to lose my temper," she ruefully admitted, "and just as wrong to pretend that I didn't."

The boy glanced up at Logan. "Do you think she was wrong to do that, Papa?"

He hesitated. "It's tricky, son. Sometimes you have to stand up for yourself. To fight back against something you know is unfair or wrong."

"By hitting people?" Joseph asked in an uncertain tone.

"It's usually best to avoid that sort of thing, if you can. Donella's method was much more effective."

"But *you* looked like you were going to hit the mean lady."

"Your father would never hit a woman," Donella said firmly. "No matter how nasty she might be."

Joseph rolled his eyes. "I know that. I just said it looked like he wanted to."

Logan felt like an utter worm. "Mrs. Ferguson doesn't like the Kendricks, and she makes a point of showing it. But I shouldn't have lost my temper, either."

"Why doesn't she like us?"

"It has to do with Uncle Royal and Auntie Ainsley," he said vaguely. "Mrs. Ferguson kicked up some mean talk when they got married."

"Oh," Joseph said. "You mean because Uncle Royal pretended to be Tira's real father, even though he isn't."

"What?" Donella blurted out.

Too late, Logan remembered that she'd been sequestered in her convent during that particular family debacle.

He shook his head at Donella, trying to warn her away from impending danger.

Joseph, however, had no compunctions about sharing.

"Auntie Ainsley's fiancé put a baby in her tummy when he wasn't supposed to. But he wasn't a nice man, so Auntie Ainsley gave Tira to Uncle Royal, who pretended to be her father. But then they got married, so Uncle Royal now really is Tira's father. So it's all fine."

Logan winced at the stunned expression on Donella's face. "Ah, I don't think this is an appropriate topic of conversation, son."

Joseph glanced up at him. "Which part?"

"All of it."

The boy looked perplexed for a moment before rolling his eyes. "Papa, *everyone* knows how babies are made, probably even Donella."

The woman in question pressed a hand to her lips, trying to stifle a laugh.

"You know, for an almost-nun, you're not very well behaved," said Logan.

"I suppose that's why they kicked me out of the convent."

Joseph let out a dramatic sigh. "I wish I knew why they did that. I bet it was for something jolly, like putting salt in the sugar bowls."

"Or something truly naughty," Logan said, getting his revenge. "After all, this *is* a woman who goes around tipping over tables in sweet shops."

Donella shot him an evil glare but refrained from rising to the bait.

As they crossed the square that fronted Kendrick House, the wind swirled around their feet and sent dried leaves scudding in front of them. The chill in the air hinted at an end to the mild weather. Joseph might get some snow in time for Christmas, after all.

Donella ushered the boy up the marble steps and reached for the door knocker.

"No need," Logan said, fishing in his pocket. "I've got a key."

He stood a step below her, breathing in the faint, lemony scent of her hair. The russet curls were only partly confined by her small hat. Pale skin, dusted with freckles, peeked above the collar of her pelisse. Logan had to fight the urge to lean in and kiss her there, convinced she would taste delicious, like a creamy lemon tart.

"Papa, are you going to kiss Donella?" Joseph was peering up at him, wide-eyed.

Good God.

Before he could issue a denial, Donella jumped as if he'd just goosed her arse. She turned around and gave him a stare cold enough to freeze his bollocks.

"Certainly not," she said tersely. "The key, Mr. Kendrick."

Logan meekly handed it over. She unlocked the door and propelled Joseph inside.

Clearly, his courtship skills needed more than a bit of work.

He stepped inside to see his brother standing in the center hall, accepting a stack of mail from Henderson. The butler then came over to help them with their coats.

"There you are," Nick said with a smile. "I hope you had an enjoyable outing. The weather was quite fine for a trip up to—"

He broke off when Joseph dashed over and threw his arms around his waist. The lad burrowed his face into his uncle's waistcoat. Nick lifted an inquiring eyebrow at Logan, who just sighed and shook his head.

"Now, what's all this?" Nick asked, bending down over his nephew.

"Nothing," came the muffled reply. "I just missed you."

Donella cast Logan a sympathetic glance. He mustered a smile, trying to pretend it didn't shred his heart that Joseph had run to his uncle for support. Sometimes, the irony of it just about killed him.

"I missed you too, laddie." Nick eased Joseph back so he could study his face. "Did you enjoy your visit to Mugdock?"

"It was nice."

That careful reply drew another inquiring look from his brother.

"It's been a bit of a long day," Logan said. He glanced at Donella. "Tiring for all of us, I imagine."

She readily took the hint. "I don't know about Joseph, but I'm exhausted from climbing up and down those stairs at Mugdock. Rest and a cup of tea would be just the thing."

"Your aunt Victoria is in the nursery with Rowena and Angus," Nick said to Joseph. "Why don't you go up and have tea with them?"

"Rowena's too young to drink tea. And she drools." Joseph's tone suggested drooling was an act of high treason.

"That's because she's teething," Nick said. "Drooling is a requirement at that stage."

"Grandda will be happy to see you," Logan said. "And he doesn't drool. Most of the time, anyway."

"That's not very nice, Papa."

He tried again. "Grandda will want to hear all about Mugdock, though. It's one of his favorite places."

Joseph rolled his eyes but took Donella's hand and headed up the stairs.

"Having a little trouble, are we?" asked Nick.

"You have no bloody idea."

"Then come to my study and tell me about it. You look like you could use something a little more fortifying than tea."

"Just give me the whole damn bottle." Logan followed his brother down the hall.

Nick tossed the bundle of mail onto his desk and went to the drinks trolley. Logan settled into one of the needlepoint wing chairs in front of the fireplace. When Nick handed him a glass of whisky, he downed a generous gulp. Sighing, he leaned back in the chair, letting the warmth of the whisky seep through his body.

Nick settled into the matching chair, stretching his booted legs to rest against the firedogs in front of the hearth. "Trouble at Mugdock?"

"Mugdock was fine. In fact, Joseph loved it. The house-keeper made a grand fuss over him, and I took the lad and Donella to the top of the old tower so we could see the view."

"I loved that place as a boy. It's like going back in time, when the old clans still held sway over Scotland."

Logan scoffed. "You mean when we were all trying to kill each other. But it was grand to see Joseph having so much fun, for once."

"And what about Donella? Did she have a good time as well?" his brother casually asked.

"Don't pretend you're simply making a polite inquiry. I know exactly what you're up to."

Nick gave him a lopsided smile. "I'm only looking out for your interests, old man. It's my job, as both your older brother and your laird."

"And you've decided that Miss Donella Haddon is in my best interests, Lord Arnprior?"

"Victoria certainly thinks she is."

"Well, if Lady Arnprior has decided, then I suppose everything is settled," Logan sarcastically replied. "In that case, I hope she'll make the lady in question privy to her decision, since she won't take it well from me."

Nick laughed. "All right. Tell me what happened."

Logan stacked his boots heel to toe. "It was a good day. Joseph and Donella enjoyed the outing." He flashed his brother a rueful smile. "The two of them get along famously."

"She's very good with him."

"Almost as good as you are." Logan regretted the words as soon as they were out of his mouth. "Sorry, I didn't mean—"

Nick leaned over and gave him a light punch in the shoulder. "Of course you did, idiot. And it's fine. Joseph is simply looking for some guidance. I'm the laird and the head of the clan. Something in that obviously appeals to him."

"He's supposed to be looking to me for guidance," Logan said tersely.

"He will, once you remember how to be a parent again. Ainsley had the same problem when she was separated from Tira for all those months. Sometimes it takes a while to regain one's bearings."

Logan stared gloomily into the fire. "Or sometimes one is just bad at the whole thing."

Nick let out an exasperated sigh. "Are you going to wallow in self-pity, or tell me what happened?"

"Who died and left you in charge of everything?"

"I believe our father did. And may I remind you, it's not exactly a picnic looking after the lot of you."

"Poor you. Very well, if you must know, I made a complete hash of things again. Donella, fortunately, came to the rescue."

"How so?"

Briefly, Logan recapped the scene at Monroe's. As soon as Nick heard about Mrs. Ferguson, he growled out all sorts of social retribution. But when Logan explained how Donella handled it, his brother practically choked on his drink.

"She did what?" he spluttered.

"She tipped the contents of the entire bloody table onto their laps."

"Well, that is splendid. Kudos to the lass for her quick thinking."

"For a girl who spent three years in a convent, I must say she's full of surprises. Her actions certainly took the focus off poor Joseph and placed them squarely on her." He frowned.

"Actually, I'm a bit worried about that. Ferguson and her pack of hens are bound to spread tales about the lass."

"She certainly gave them ample material. How many witnesses?"

"The shop was full."

His brother shook his head. "We'll do what we can to contain the gossip. And you can be sure I'll be having a chat with Mr. Ferguson about his wife's behavior. I will not allow her or anyone else to badger Joseph or subject him to bigotry."

Logan grimaced. "I'm grateful for your help, but I feel like hell that I can't seem to protect my own son."

"You do protect your son, but this is different, Logan. Victoria and I have greater social influence than you do. We'll come up with the best way to indicate to the Fergusons and all of Glasgow that Joseph must be treated with the degree of courtesy I expect for all of my family."

"Even the twins?"

His brother flashed a smile. "Even the twins. You're not to worry, laddie. I'll take care of it."

"Thank you, old man." Emotion had made his voice gruff, but his brother would understand his true feelings.

"You're welcome." Nick cocked his head. "Now tell me what else is bothering you."

He hesitated a moment. "I'm worried how this will affect Donella."

"Tempest in a teapot, I think. After all, she's Riddick's niece, and she's under my protection, as well. Mrs. Ferguson is not a popular woman, so I'm sure any fuss will die down soon enough."

"I'm not so sure. She made a comment about Donella's mother that seemed to upset the lass."

"What sort of comment?"

"Something about how Donella was just like her mother and should be sent away."

"Ah." Nick rubbed his chin. "That's unfortunate."

"Is her mother still alive? I got the impression she'd died a few years back."

"She's alive, but not well. Mrs. Haddon currently resides very quietly in the outskirts of Edinburgh, under the care of a private physician."

Logan frowned. "What the hell does that mean?"

Nick tapped his skull.

"Damn, you mean she's dicked in the nob?"

"Unfortunately. Mrs. Haddon's condition was such that the family believed it best to put her in the care of a well-respected and suitable physician."

"That's a bloody awful thing to have to deal with." No wonder poor Donella had been so rattled by the biddy's mean-spirited comments. "Must have been a dire situation to take that sort of action instead of keeping the poor lady at home."

"I'm not privy to the details, so you'll have to ask Miss Haddon for more."

"Right," Logan scoffed. "By the way, lass, I heard your mamma is queer in the attic. Anything you want to tell me?"

Nick grimaced. "If today's incident blows up to the level of a scandal, you might have to talk to the poor girl about it. You're the one who got her into this mess, after all."

"I bloody well did not. I was just trying to take care of my boy."

"Not very effectively, if Miss Haddon was forced to intervene."

Logan gave his brother the look that usually caused grown men to flee. Nick, as usual, was unimpressed.

"Oh, very well," Logan finally admitted. "You're right, of course."

"I usually am."

"That doesn't make it any less annoying." He sighed.

"Nick, what the hell am I going to do with Joseph? He's my life, but I can't seem to get it right."

"You're trying too hard. Just relax and be his father."

"I'm not sure I know what that means anymore."

"For one thing, you should stop being so cautious with him. He's a little boy, not a piece of china. He won't break."

The room seemed to shift sideways, and suddenly all Logan could see was the lifeless body of his nephew as he carried him from the raging, unforgiving river. He *had* broken a child that day. He'd stolen Cam's life from the entire family, because he'd been too stupid to pay attention to what really mattered.

His brother's hand landed on his forearm, jerking him out of the soul-destroying memory. "Stop that right now, Logan."

"I'm sorry, Nick," he whispered. "So sorry for everything."

"Look at me, lad."

Logan forced himself to meet his brother's gaze. Nick's eyes, a mirror of his own, were filled with a father's deep sorrow, tempered by wisdom and love.

"You were young and foolish. It was an accident—a terrible one, but an accident nonetheless. I forgave you, Logan. Now it's time you forgave yourself."

"But I break things, Nick," he said hoarsely. "And I'm so bloody afraid of breaking Joseph, too."

Now his brother began to look stern, like the laird he was. "Joseph is a strong boy. You won't break him, I promise. For one thing, I won't let you. To quote Angus, 'Yer not too big for me to paddle yer bum if ye make a mess of things.'"

Logan let out a strangled laugh. "I don't know what I did to deserve a brother like you."

"Och, don't be a silly bugger, man."

Nick's gaze was warm with a deep and abiding affection. While tragedy had all but smothered that affection, it had never died. It had only been waiting for light to seep back into their lives, opening their hearts and healing them all.

"My little Cam loved you, laddie," Nick gently said. "He loved all of us. That's what you should remember. That's what we all owe my son and ourselves."

It took Logan several moments to choke down his emotions. God, he was a lucky bastard to have the family he did.

"When did you get so damn smart?" he managed.

Nick reached for his glass. "I've always been smart. You were just too thick-headed to notice."

"All right, wise one, what do I do about my son? And about Donella?"

"I've already told you how to deal with your son. As for Donella . . ."

"Yes?"

"Marry the girl, of course. You'll get a fine wife *and* a splendid mother for Joseph. They clearly have a great deal of affection for each other."

"He certainly prefers her company to mine."

"Think how pleased Lord Riddick and his family would be, too," Nick added. "It could only help your business dealings with the old fellow."

Logan raised his eyebrows. "Are you suggesting I marry the girl to nail down a business deal with Riddick?"

"Of course not. It's simply an added incentive."

"Oh, she'd be thrilled to hear that."

"Logan, it's clear that you're quite taken with the girl. It is also clear—despite her continued insistence on becoming a nun—that she is quite taken with you, as well."

"I don't think so."

"Then you haven't been paying attention. And Victoria would tell you the same."

"Huh."

"You can be quite charming, when you're not being an idiot."

Donella did seem quite aware of him as a man, which could be viewed in a positive light. And he was more than aware of her as a woman.

"I'll think about it."

"Don't think too long, because you're not *that* charming," Nick said. "She just might choose a nunnery, after all."

Chapter Nineteen

Donella stole a glance at Logan as he expertly steered her through another turn of the waltz. The other dancers swept by them in a swirling array of silks and satins, the sparkle of jewels glittering like tiny stars under blazing crystal chandeliers.

For a few moments, she felt light-headed. It was like tumbling through a rainbow, and had less to do with the dance than with the man holding her close.

"Are you all right?" Logan murmured.

She managed a smile. "I'm just a bit out of practice."

"Och, you're the most graceful lass on the floor." He leaned closer, whispering in her ear, "And the prettiest, ye ken."

She barely managed to avoid tripping over her feet.

Waltzing with Logan Kendrick was like nothing she'd ever experienced. *Stimulating* probably described it best, especially earlier when he wheeled her through a turn and she made a startling contact with his lower body. Everything about him felt big and hard, including what was hidden beneath the drape of his kilt.

The entire evening was turning out to be rather mind-boggling, because she was beginning to think Logan was courting her. Even more mind-boggling, she was beginning to *like* the notion, though she hadn't a clue why he'd wish to do so, much less publicly.

After the gruesome episode last week at the sweet shop and the resulting nasty gossip, Donella had expected the entire Kendrick household to lay low for a while. Yet according to Victoria, an opposite strategy had been formulated. The Kendricks would brazen it out, making it clear that little Joseph had their full protection and Donella their full support.

That strategy seemed to include a great deal of attention on her from Joseph's father, if the last week was any indication. Whenever she left the house, Logan almost invariably accompanied her. If his intention was to show the denizens of Glasgow that she enjoyed his protection, he was making a splendid job of it.

Still, the ugly glare she'd just gotten from a familiar-looking couple on the side of the dance floor suggested the plan hadn't been entirely successful. She stumbled a bit, and it took a moment to regain her rhythm.

Logan glanced at her face, then eased her to the side of the floor and behind a massive column as the strains of the waltz faded away. "You're not all right, are you?"

Truthfully, she was getting quite tired of strangers giving her the evil eye, even if she had dumped a table onto three unsuspecting women. It hadn't been the proudest moment of her life, but she found it hard to regret. Even so, she thought it would be best to stay out of the public eye for the time being. Logan and the rest of the Kendricks, however, clearly did not agree.

"I'm fine," she tersely replied.

Logan crossed his arms and propped his brawny shoulders against the column. Really, there should be a law against a man looking so splendid in clan dress, especially in evening kit. It was exactly the sort of distraction she didn't need.

"That's a load of old cobblers, Donella. You're fashed

about something, and I refuse to believe it's because some old tabbies and muckrakers can't keep their silly mouths shut."

The gossip did bother her, but she'd rather die than admit to something so shallow. "Mr. Kendrick, I have asked you repeatedly not to employ such vulgar language."

"And I call bollocks to that bit of prevarication, too."

She scowled. "You really are the most irritating man."

"Aye, it's a rare talent." He tipped up her chin with a gentle forefinger and held it there. "Out with it, Donella. What are you upset about?"

When two ladies strolling by arm in arm looked scandalized, she tried to push his hand away.

"Are you *trying* to destroy what little reputation I have left?"

Logan wrapped his fingers around hers, refusing to let go.

"If you keep this up, I won't have any choice left but to enter a convent," she groused. "I'll be a complete social leper."

His mouth—which she spent too much time looking at—curved up in a seductive smile. "Something tells me that's not your only choice."

When she realized what he was suggesting, she yanked her hand away. "You shouldn't tease like that. It's not nice."

Now it was his turn to scowl. "I'm not teasing you. You're not the sort of girl for that."

"That is something I am well aware of."

"I think you've got the wrong end of the stick, lass."

"Then perhaps you can give me the right end, because I don't know what to think about any of . . . of this." She felt like her face was on fire, and her skin was prickly under her stays. "If I didn't know any better, I'd think you were . . ."

She couldn't bring herself to say the words.

"Courting you?"

"It's a ridiculous notion, and you know it."

Amusement gleamed in those blasted blue eyes of his

before his gaze turned uncomfortably penetrating. Helpless, Donella stared back. The noise of the ballroom faded to a tuneless buzz, easily ignored. Only Logan was real. He was so full of energy and life, drawing her to him with an irresistible force. Her heart began to pound with an erratic beat, and the hot flush seeped into the very depths of her being.

This simply cannot be happening. Not to me.

No man had ever looked at her like he did, not even Roddy. But the expression in Logan's eyes practically devoured her. It made her feel almost . . . wild.

Then he blinked and straightened up, putting space between them. The din of the room came rushing back and, for a moment, Donella felt overwhelmed by the frantic gaiety of their surroundings.

"I need a drink. We *both* need a drink before finishing this conversation," Logan said in a husky voice.

She expelled a shaky breath. "I don't think we need to finish this conversation at all."

He waved to a nearby waiter carrying a tray of wine goblets.

"Here," Logan said, handing her a glass. "You look like you could use it."

She could, so she dutifully took a sip, hoping it would steady her jangling nerves.

Logan tipped the waiter and took a cautious sip from his goblet. "God, they do serve ghastly stuff at these affairs, don't they?"

"Any sort of alcohol makes me feel tipsy," she admitted. "We drank only cider and a bit of ale in the convent."

He grinned. "I'd quite like to see you get tipsy, Miss Haddon. Perhaps you'll finish my glass, as well?"

"One will be quite enough, thank you."

"Then let's get back to our very interesting conversation."

Donella didn't wish to continue, at least not in a public

venue. If he said he was courting her, she'd probably faint from shock. And if he said the opposite, she'd be humiliated for making such an outrageous assumption about him.

She peered around the column. "We should return to our party. Victoria and Lord Arnprior will be looking for us."

"No, they won't."

Donella was about to insist when she noticed someone staring intently at them from a few yards away. More correctly, she was staring at Logan. A lovely blond woman, dressed in the first style of elegance, was studying him with an avid expression. There was something about the woman's regard that was almost unnerving.

"Are you even listening to me?" asked Logan, sounding exasperated.

"Forgive me, but there's someone staring at us. At you, to be precise. She seems to know you."

"That dodge won't work, Donella. I know scads of women in Glasgow."

When she lifted an eyebrow, he grimaced.

"That didn't come out quite right," he said.

"Perhaps you should acknowledge her."

Muttering under his breath, Logan followed her indicating nod and promptly spilled half his drink. He stared at the young woman, his expression thunderstruck and oddly blank.

Donella plucked the glass from his hand. "Mr. Kendrick, is something wrong?"

He didn't seem to hear. When the lady smiled at him—a charming, winsome smile—Logan simply blinked, apparently held in place by invisible bonds.

Donella set both glasses on a side table and handed Logan a handkerchief from her reticule. He absently wiped the wine from his fingers and then handed it back to her.

"You're welcome," she said sarcastically.

That finally caught his attention. "Oh, sorry."

"You look like you've seen a ghost."

His laugh was rough and held a note of disbelief. "I think I have."

"I don't—"

Victoria suddenly emerged from the crowd, dodging around a portly gentleman to reach them. "There you are." Obviously sensing something amiss, she followed the direction of Logan's gaze. "Oh, blast."

"What is going on here?" Donella asked.

"Ladies, if you'll excuse me," Logan said.

He strode off, forging a path through the crowd to the young woman, who'd been clearly waiting for him to do just that. As he took her gloved hand and raised it to his lips, her expression seemed almost triumphant to Donella.

She, meanwhile, felt her insides curl up and began looking for a nice, dark corner to hide in.

"Who *is* that?" she asked Victoria.

"Mrs. Jeannie MacArthur, a widow from Edinburgh," Victoria grimly replied.

"She's . . . she's certainly very dashing."

The woman's guinea-gold hair shimmered under the lights. She had enchanting, lively features and a perfect rosebud mouth. Although some might uncharitably call her short, she carried herself with elegance and grace.

She also had, if one were inclined to comment on such a thing, an ample bosom, well displayed by the fashionable but daring cut of her bodice. That Logan was also noticing Mrs. MacArthur's bosom was quite evident.

"Apparently, she's just come out of mourning and is now visiting with family in Glasgow," Victoria said. "She's also trouble—which I hoped to avoid by reaching you before Logan noticed her."

"Too late," Donella dryly replied.

Victoria flashed a sympathetic grimace. "I'm sorry, dearest. This is an unwelcome complication."

Donella affected a casual shrug. "Mr. Kendrick is free to associate with whomever he likes."

"Not if he knows what's good for him." Victoria hooked a hand through Donella's arm. "Come on, we have to find Nicholas and the twins."

Donella cast a glance over her shoulder as her friend towed her away. Logan was now leading Mrs. MacArthur onto the floor for the next set of dances. And by the way he was gazing at her, it was clear he'd forgotten everyone but the woman on his arm.

So much for making a declaration of courtship.

As they wended their way through the crowd, Donella did her best to ignore the curious glances that followed them. One moment, Logan had been openly flirting with her in the middle of a ballroom and the next he'd abandoned her for another woman. It was humiliating, but at the moment she simply felt numb.

With her usual brisk competence, Victoria soon had them down the staircase and into the entrance hall. Lord Arnprior was waiting there, holding their wraps and looking even more grim-faced than his wife.

"Did you find the twins?" Victoria asked.

"I sent them to fetch the carriage."

Arnprior helped them on with their cloaks and then ushered them through the doors into the cold December night. The twins were standing beside the family's town coach, pulled first in line.

"Here, Miss Donella," Graeme said with a sympathetic grimace. "Let me help you."

Mentally sighing, she took his hand and climbed into the coach. It would appear the Kendricks had also been making assumptions about her and Logan—assumptions obviously far off the mark.

Victoria came in next, followed by her husband.

Arnprior leaned out the door to speak to his brothers. "One of you needs to find Logan and get him the hell out of there."

Donella had never heard his lordship utter so much as an oath.

"I'll do it," Graeme said.

"Tell him I need to see him *immediately*."

His brother nodded. "I'll see to it."

As Graeme disappeared, Grant climbed in and settled next to Donella.

"Nick, I don't think—" Grant clamped his lips shut when he encountered his brother's furious stare.

"Let's wait until we get home, dear," Victoria said gently to Grant.

Kendrick House was thankfully but a short ride away, because the atmosphere in the carriage was fraught. The earl was barely holding his temper in check, and Grant and Victoria were almost equally disturbed.

Whatever it was about Logan and that woman, it must be bad.

After they reached the house, Henderson hurried out from the back of the hall to assist the junior footman with their outerwear.

"I beg your pardon, my lord, my lady," said the butler. "I didn't expect you home so early. Would you like tea in the drawing room?"

"I'll be in my study," Arnprior said. "Send Logan in to me as soon as he gets home."

Then he stalked off down the hall.

"Oh, dear," said Victoria.

Grant shook his head. "This is bad."

"That, dear boy, is a capital understatement," replied his sister-in-law.

By now, Donella had recovered from her shock and was beginning to experience *quite* a bit of curiosity.

It's none of your business.

She moved toward the staircase. "I think I'll just go up to my room."

"I'm so sorry for ruining your evening," Victoria said.

Donella paused, one hand on the polished bannister. "Truly, you didn't."

"No, Logan did that," Grant said with fatal candor.

One could always rely on the twins for blurting out the unwelcome truth.

She managed a smile. "No harm done."

"I wish that were true," Victoria said. "And when the gossip was *finally* beginning to die down."

Angus clattered down the stairs to join them. "I just got Joseph off to bed. I didn't expect ye for hours. What's amiss?"

Victoria threw Grant a clear warning glance—without effect.

"Jeannie Campbell is what happened," Grant baldly stated. "At the ball, and she went smash up to Logan, brazen as anything."

"Rather the opposite, I'm afraid," Victoria said.

"Jeannie Campbell." Angus's eyes bugged out. "I thought that lass was married and safely stowed away in Edinburgh."

Victoria pressed two fingers between her eyebrows, as if trying to stave off a headache. "She's now a widow and not safely stowed, as tonight illustrated."

Angus let out a string of oaths both shocking and inventive. The fact that Victoria didn't bother to reprimand him told Donella how bad things were.

"How did Nick take it?" Angus said, finally winding down.

"About as well as you might expect," Grant dolefully replied.

"Where's Logan now?"

"Graeme went to fetch him," Victoria said. "He's to bring him straight home."

"Well, I'd best go see to Nick," Angus said. "The last thing we need is the lads tryin' to kill each other again."

Victoria scowled. "It will *not* come to that."

Angus snorted, then regarded Donella with an all-too-familiar sympathy. "Sorry ye had to see this, lass."

She spread her hands. "I'm truly not sure what I saw."

"I'll come up and explain everything later," Victoria said, "once I prevent the impending mayhem."

"I assure you, my lady, that an explanation is not necessary."

"You'll hear it all, anyway," Grant said in a gloomy tone. "There's bound to be a *lot* of yelling once Logan gets home."

Chapter Twenty

The yelling was muffled, since much of it occurred in Lord Arnprior's study, but Donella had heard it almost as soon as Logan walked through the front door. Angus was the first to raise his voice, then Lord Arnprior, then the guilty party himself, and finally the twins.

She had to give the countess a great deal of credit, because she could yell almost as forcefully as the Kendrick men. According to the talkative maid who'd helped Donella unlace her dress, her ladyship had threatened to bash a fireplace tool over the heads of various male relatives, including her husband.

It was a right, royal mess. Thankfully, Eden and Alasdair were now in Glasgow. Eden had sent round a note earlier this evening to announce their arrival, and that meant Donella could escape to Breadie Manor first thing in the morning.

The deep bong of the longcase clock sounded the late hour. Although exhaustion and a vague sort of sadness pulled at her bones, Donella knew she'd be unable to sleep. Better to spend time packing.

As she sank down onto the dressing table stool to organize her toiletries, she glanced at her reflection in the pier glass. She looked dreadful, with a pallid complexion, shadowed eyes, and hollowed-out cheeks. Her short curls added to the impression that she was a half-starved street urchin instead of a mature woman. It was no wonder Logan had taken one look at Jeannie MacArthur and promptly forgotten her existence. As far as womanly attributes were concerned, she'd lost the race before it started.

Stop feeling sorry for yourself.

It wasn't as if she'd ever expected to marry Logan Kendrick. She didn't intend to marry anyone. Her original plan—wait six months and enter a convent—still stood.

Ignoring the ache in her chest, she rummaged through the table.

She glanced up when a quiet knock sounded on the door. "Come in."

Still garbed in her evening gown, Victoria slipped inside. "I decided to take a chance that you were still awake."

"It was a wee bit difficult to sleep through the battle of the clans going on downstairs, ye ken."

"Ugh. Highlanders can be *so* annoying." Victoria flopped into an overstuffed, floral armchair in front of the fireplace. "Present company excepted, of course."

Donella swiveled to study the countess, who was staring gloomily into the crackling fire. "Rumor has it that Englishwomen are more than capable of handling boisterous Highlanders."

"Did one of the maids tell you that? No doubt the servants heard just about every word of that revolting discussion."

"I suspect they couldn't avoid it, even if they tried."

"And I suspect they didn't try very hard."

Donella smiled and went back to stacking her bandeaus and ribbons in a neat pile.

"So, you've decided to leave us," Victoria said after a short silence.

"Eden and Alasdair arrived in town this evening, and I

can work more efficiently if I'm staying at Breadie Manor. There's still a great deal of work for the Christmas party."

Victoria sighed. "I'll miss you, but it's no wonder you wish to leave. Logan has made a complete ass of himself. All I can say is that there *is* a reason for his ridiculous behavior tonight. One that makes quite a lot of sense."

"I'm not owed any explanations, Victoria."

"Of course you are, dear. We all know Logan was courting you. He'd been making quite a show of it. Trust me—everyone noticed."

Donella looked down to see she'd crumpled some of the ribbons she'd just folded. "It . . . it doesn't matter. He obviously doesn't wish to—"

Victoria stood. "Since you're still awake, I wish you'd come to the nursery with me."

"But—"

"Nurse says Rowena is fractious this evening, and I want to check on Joseph, too."

Donella's heart jammed in her throat. "Oh, dear. I hope Joseph didn't hear the argument. He's so sensitive about anything to do with his father."

Victoria headed for the door. "Let's go find out, shall we?"

When Donella hesitated, the countess tilted her head. "Joseph will surely wish to see you if he is upset. You have a splendid knack for making him feel better when he's out of sorts."

Donella smiled wryly. "You're quite good at that."

"What?"

"Making people feel guilty."

Victoria chuckled as she led Donella out of the room. The long corridor was hushed and dim, lit only by a few lamps on half-moon tables.

"I hope I don't run into anyone, dressed in my nightrail and wrapper," Donella said.

"I ordered all the men upstairs. Everyone's finally in bed, thank goodness."

They took the stairs to the nursery floor, where the schoolroom and music room were also located. Kendrick House was a lovely, spacious mansion, which amply served the comings and goings of a busy family. It was a home in the best sense of the word—warm, welcoming, and usually a great deal of fun.

For a moment, Donella couldn't help missing Blairgal Castle and her own family. Yet Blairgal no longer felt like home. While she'd been in the convent, her relatives had moved on with their lives, getting married and starting families. Oh, they'd welcomed her back with open arms, but she no longer really fit in.

Victoria opened the door to the nursery. "Good evening, Lucy. How is my daughter this evening?"

The head nursemaid was sitting in a rocker next to the rosewood cradle. She glanced up with a grimace. "I think the wee mite has a new tooth comin' in, my lady. She's still fussin'."

Victoria crossed the long room, cozily tucked up under the eaves of the big house. Bookcases and shelves lined the walls, each one stacked with toys, puzzles, dolls, and chalkboards. The floor was covered with a thick-piled carpet, perfect for a baby to crawl upon or for a little boy to play with a set of toy soldiers. Joseph's set took pride of place in front of the hearth. The little wooden soldiers were lined up in neat rows, ready to march off to whatever adventures awaited them.

The countess peeked into her daughter's cradle and chuckled. "Wide awake, I see."

Deftly wrapping the bairn in the light blanket, Victoria scooped her up.

Rowena Caroline Kendrick was five months old and an

absolute darling. A plump, happy baby, she had her father's black hair and her mother's sapphire eyes. She laughed a good deal more than she cried, and never protested when a boisterous Kendrick male hoisted her over his head or planted bristled kisses on her cheeks.

Her favorite, naturally, was her papa. Normally a serious, dignified man, Lord Arnprior's face lit up like a blazing comet whenever he saw his daughter. He spent a fair amount of time with her, more so than the average aristocratic male, in Donella's experience. The earl sometimes seemed a bit sheepish about his tendency to haunt the nursery. According to Victoria, it annoyed the nursemaids, but Donella found it to be an endearing quality in such a powerful, busy man.

"Lucy, why don't you get ready for bed?" the countess said. "I'll rock Rowena and see if I can get her to sleep."

"Very well, my lady." She bobbed a curtsy and disappeared through the door that led to the nursery staff's rooms.

Victoria glanced at Donella. "Would you mind checking on Joseph?"

Donella crossed to the door on the opposite side of the nursery. Carefully, she cracked it open, letting a sliver of light seep into the small room.

The bedroom's comfortable furniture was perfectly sized for a little boy. The bed, tucked near the fireplace, was normally piled high with thick wool blankets and several pillows. Tonight, Joseph had kicked off most of the blankets and scattered most of the pillows onto the floor.

Sprawled on his stomach with one leg half off the bed, he hugged the remaining pillow to his chest. He was sound asleep and didn't stir when Donella gently moved his leg back onto the bed and rearranged the blankets over his slight body.

Reaching down, she smoothed a hand over his thick hair. Her chest went tight with longing, and she had to resist the urge to lie down beside him and bring him into the shelter of her arms.

While she'd come to love this sweet child in such a short time, Donella now realized how foolhardy it was to grow so attached to him. Soon, she must say good-bye. She could only hope that Joseph would forget her a great deal more quickly than she would forget him.

Or forget his father.

"Everything all right?" Victoria asked softly from the door.

Donella tucked the blanket a little closer around Joseph's shoulders.

"He's sound asleep," she whispered as she returned to the nursery and closed the door. "I'm sure he slept right through the, er, episode."

"Epic disaster, you mean," Victoria said as she gently rocked her daughter in her arms.

Donella rested a hand on Rowena's head. The babe turned her cheek and gave her a sleepy grin, punctuated by a huge yawn. "She's so beautiful, Victoria."

"Why don't you hold her?"

"But—"

The countess plunked her daughter into Donella's arms. "Take the rocker while I tell you about the epic disaster."

"Don't you want to sit? You must be exhausted."

"I'm too annoyed to be tired."

"You seemed to calm everyone down, though."

"It's only an armed truce, one that's barely holding. I haven't seen Nick and Logan this angry with each other in a very long time." Victoria crossed her arms and lowered her gaze, lost in thought.

"You don't have to tell me if you don't want to," Donella said. "It's truly none of my business."

Victoria began pacing the long room. "I'm trying to decide where to start. It's a complicated story."

"I'd imagine it has something to do with the breach between Mr. Kendrick and Lord Arnprior, and his move to Canada?"

"You knew about that?"

Donella glanced at the baby in her arms. Rowena's eyelids were at half-mast. "I do recall my uncle talking about an unfortunate series of events that befell the family, and that Lord Arnprior had essentially sent his brother away. But it was years ago, and I'd never met any of the Kendricks, so it didn't mean much to me."

"Nicholas did more than send Logan away. He told him that if he ever set foot on Arnprior lands again, he would kill him."

Donella stared at her friend. "Did he actually mean it?"

Victoria looked grim. "At the time, he did."

"I . . . I don't know what to say." It seemed so out of character for such a kind and just man.

"You know I'm my husband's second wife."

"Yes, I understand that his first wife died quite young."

"She did." Victoria hesitated. "It was not a happy marriage, for many reasons, and the first Lady Arnprior suffered from . . . poor health."

"That must have been difficult for his lordship," Donella cautiously said.

"It was. The one good thing that came from the marriage was their child, a little boy named Cameron."

"I didn't know he had a son." Then Donella realized what that meant. "Oh, no. Please don't tell me . . ."

Victoria moved to sit in the padded twill armchair on the other side of the fireplace. "From the first, Cam was the light of my husband's life—even more so after his wife died. The entire family adored the child. According to Angus, he was what saw the family through some very difficult times. Logan, Royal, the twins . . . they all doted on the boy. But to Nicholas, Cam was everything."

Donella could feel the pain gathering in her heart. "What happened, Victoria?"

"Angus would say Jeannie MacArthur happened. Or, as she was known back then, Jeannie Campbell."

She remembered the look on Logan's face when he'd first spotted the woman. "I take that she and Logan were close?"

"Logan was mad for the girl. That wasn't particularly unusual for him. He was a terrible flirt when he was younger and fell in and out of love quite easily."

"Naturally, I'm shocked to hear that."

Victoria flashed her a brief smile. "I know. But he's nothing like he used to be, that I can tell you."

Until tonight, if his reaction at the ball was any indication. "But things were different with Jeannie Campbell, I take it?"

"Apparently he was going to propose to her."

Something nasty and mean-spirited twisted Donella's stomach into a knot. She forced herself to ignore it. "Obviously, he didn't."

"Nicholas and Angus didn't approve of her, which in itself is quite surprising. Angus rarely objected to anything Logan did and spoiled him terribly. But this time, he and Nicholas were in agreement that Jeannie was not a suitable candidate for a wife."

Donella tried to be fair about it. "I wonder why. She seems lovely and elegant, and very much a lady."

Victoria looked disapproving. "Elegant? More like flashy, if you ask me. In any case, Angus and Nicholas thought her flighty, spoiled, and very vain. But Logan wouldn't listen, and her family background was excellent. Her father is closely related to the Campbell clan chief. Since the Campbells were in favor of the match, that also made it tricky."

To Donella, nothing was more important than character.

Sadly, clan relations often trumped other considerations. "If there was no true impediment, what happened?"

"Tragedy," Victoria said with an unhappy sigh.

"Lord Arnprior's son?"

"It happened in late spring, up at Kinglas. Logan got Cam fishing gear for his fourth birthday—a miniature pole and tackle. As a special treat, he and his brothers wanted to take the boy fishing in the river that runs down to the loch." She paused for a moment, as if gathering herself. "Nicholas was busy that day and couldn't go with them. At first he wouldn't give his permission, since the river runs high at that time of year."

Because of the snowmelt, Highland streams that were slow and gentle in the fall ran fast and high—and often deadly—in springtime. Already she could guess the outlines of the tragedy, and it made her sick.

"Logan talked him into letting Cam go," Victoria continued. "In fact, he promised Nicholas that he would never let Cam out of his sight."

"Oh, no," Donella whispered.

"At first, everything was fine. Logan was very good with Cam, and the boy adored him. He looked up to Logan almost as much as he did to his father. So even though Cam was quite rambunctious that day, Logan had kept him under firm control. Until . . . he was distracted."

"By Miss Campbell?"

Victoria's mouth briefly thinned. "Yes. She happened to come riding by on the trail that goes along the river. She stopped to speak to Logan. That led to his . . ."

"Distraction." Donella had to struggle with a flare of rage that made her want to strike something. Strike *Logan*. "But he gave Lord Arnprior his word. He should have *told* her that he had to keep a close watch on the child."

"According to Angus, he did try. But Miss Campbell

was not someone to take no for an answer. She was used to Logan's attention and wasn't best pleased when he put her off."

"Still—"

Victoria leaned forward in her chair, looking earnest. "You mustn't think that Logan neglected Cam. He didn't. And the others were all there too, and not far from the boy. But Logan did turn his back for a few moments, and that was enough. It all happened so fast."

Donella hated to even ask. "How did it happen?"

"Cam tried to stand on a wet rock and fell into the river. Kade, who was only nine at the time, was the closest and immediately jumped in. Unfortunately, he was swept away, too."

If Donella hadn't been holding the baby, she would have covered her mouth in horror. Victoria looked sick, too.

"Logan immediately went in after Cam, while Royal swam for Kade. Royal was a very strong swimmer, but he was barely able to keep himself and Kade from drowning. Cam was swept farther downstream toward the loch, and it took Logan quite some time to reach him, in the most punishing of conditions. Angus said he never gave up, even when they all knew it was too late to save the boy. But Logan was going to get his nephew or die in the attempt." She breathed out a wavering sigh. "Even now, I think the poor man sometimes wishes he'd died with Cam."

Carefully, Donella adjusted the now-sleeping baby before wiping away her tears. "What a horrific, senseless tragedy."

"Royal told me once that what Logan did was nothing less than heroic. But it was too late. All they had left to bring home was that sweet boy's lifeless body."

"I cannot imagine Lord Arnprior's pain."

"Nicholas blamed Logan, and . . . and they fought. Only Royal's intervention prevented them from killing each other." Victoria grimaced and shook her head. "Correction.

From Nicholas trying to kill Logan. Logan only defended himself. I'm sure he could have throttled Nicholas with his bare hands had he wanted to, even though my husband is a *very* strong man."

Logan topped his brother by a few inches, and out-weighed him, too. It must have been a nightmarish scene.

"Then we must all be grateful for Royal," Donella said stoutly. "From everything I've heard, he sounds like a perfectly splendid man and a blessing to his family."

Victoria managed a smile. "Royal is, well, *splendid* doesn't even begin to describe it. He has saved this family—and my husband—countless times."

"I take it he was able to convince your husband not to kill Logan?"

"Yes, and he also convinced Logan that he needed to leave Kinglas. It was the only way to keep Nicholas from falling completely apart. So, for the sake of the family, Logan sailed for Canada and didn't return for six years."

Donella grieved for Lord Arnprior's terrible loss, and for the sorrow and guilt that Logan must have suffered. Most men would have completely buckled under the strain.

She was discovering, however, that the Kendricks were not most men.

Logan's behavior now made more sense. Despite his brash, confident exterior, he was a guarded man who instinctively protected himself. So many grievous losses were bound to have an effect on one's heart. While she'd not suffered one particle of the grief Logan had, she understood how it had affected him. That kind of pain made it hard to trust—and without trust, there could never truly be love.

"But your husband obviously forgave him," she finally said.

"He rather had to after Logan rescued me from a murderer."

Donella gaped at her. "Someone tried to murder you?"

Victoria looked amused. "Yes, but that's a story for another time."

"And I thought my family was dramatic."

"Your family is quite lively, dear. Don't forget they're my family, too."

"I do tend to forget that. Which means you know where all the bodies are buried."

"And will remain safely buried," Victoria said firmly. "I am not one to tell tales. You deserve your privacy after everything you've gone through."

You don't know the half of it.

"Thank you. It's just that—"

The muffled chime of a clock in the hall interrupted her.

Victoria stood. "It's late. Let me put this wee one in her cradle, and then I'll finish the story. It won't take long to tell."

She obviously meant what had happened tonight. "It's fine. It's really none of my business, anyway."

"We consider you one of the family," Victoria said as she came over to retrieve her daughter. "Of course it's your business."

Donella didn't know how to respond to that. She simply handed Rowena over.

"Well done," Victoria murmured, as she smiled at her sleeping child. "Angus could come in and play his bagpipes, and she'd sleep through it."

As she watched the countess place the baby in her cradle, Donella was again filled with a sharp sense of longing. For years, she'd yearned for a life of quiet contemplation, sheltered from the world by high convent walls. After all, the world was so messy, and often more uncomfortable than not. But with a rapidity that stunned her, Donella now wanted more of the world, with all the messiness—and love—that entailed.

Victoria resumed her seat by the fire. "Where was I?"

"At Mr. Kendrick's exile from Kinglas."

"Ah, yes. Logan set sail for Canada almost immediately, and without ever seeing Miss Campbell."

Donella found that surprising. "That must have been difficult for both of them."

Victoria waggled a hand. "For Logan, yes. But from what I gather, he was half out of his mind with grief, and terribly guilt-stricken. He was in no condition to see the girl so soon after the accident."

"I can't help but feel sorry for her. To be so cruelly separated from the man she loved."

"I wouldn't feel too sorry," Victoria dryly added. "Logan wrote to her before he left Scotland and asked her to go with him—as his wife, of course."

Donella blinked. "She refused?"

"Quite readily. Oh, she blamed it on her family. The Campbells were no longer interested in the alliance, after Logan's estrangement from his brother."

Donella couldn't help starching up. "If she loved him, that shouldn't have mattered. She would certainly want to be with him in his time of trial."

"Then I suppose she didn't love him, did she?"

"She seemed quite taken with him tonight."

"And he seemed just as eager in return?" Victoria gently prodded.

Donella simply raised her eyebrows.

"I think he was more stunned than anything else," Victoria said.

"He looked like Odysseus encountering one of the sirens." She winced. "Sorry, that sounds awful. I don't even know the woman."

"That's exactly what Angus called her tonight. However, Logan claims he was simply being polite, paying his respects to an old friend who'd only recently put off her widow's weeds."

Donella couldn't hold back a snort. "Polite? That's one way to put it."

"I agree. I was tempted to box his ears for abandoning you so precipitously. It was exceedingly rude. Nicholas was also quite put out, and he made sure Logan knew it."

Donella winced. "How embarrassing."

"That was only one part of the argument, dearest. Mostly, we're worried that Logan will be susceptible to Jeannie's wiles again. Logan, of course, denies any such thing and grew quite heated at the suggestion."

"They seemed *quite* happy to encounter each other, if you ask me." Recalling the expression on Logan's face made Donella's heart hurt.

"I would wager that's true for Jeannie, because Logan is now a very rich man. He wasn't an eligible match six years ago, but he definitely is now. Half the mothers in Glasgow have been chasing him for their daughters ever since he stepped foot off the boat."

Donella had seen evidence of that at various social functions in the city. It had never bothered her before, likely because he'd always seemed immune to any attempts to engage his interest.

That, however, was no longer the case.

She stood. "It's certainly understandable that Miss Campbell—Mrs. MacArthur, I should say—would wish to renew her friendship. I'm sorry for Lord Arnprior's sake, however, and for the upset it caused the family."

"And for the upset it caused *you*," Victoria said with gentle emphasis as she rose.

Donella forced a smile. "Mr. Kendrick owes me nothing except a minor apology for his precipitous exit this evening."

"I'd say he owes you a great deal more."

"He doesn't," Donella said firmly. "I'm grateful for your candor, and I understand why you wished to tell me. But there is nothing to worry about, Victoria, I assure you."

"But—"

"If you'll excuse me, I'll bid you good night." She turned and fled the room, ashamed of the tears that lurked so close to the surface.

Chapter Twenty-One

He'd made a cock-up, all right. Even Angus was riding up Logan's backside, calling him everything from a jinglebrains to a turd-head. Grandda almost always defended him in any brangle he had with Nick, but not this time.

Not when it came to Jeannie Campbell.

Of course, she was now Mrs. MacArthur, a beautiful and experienced young widow.

If Logan didn't miss his guess, *very* experienced.

"The turn's comin' up, sir," his groom prompted from his perch behind.

"Oh, right. Thank you, Sam."

Distracted by his gloomy thoughts, Logan had almost missed the turn into Breadie Manor, Lord Riddick's small estate just outside the city. Although his lordship rarely visited, Alec and Edie were often in residence and had arrived yesterday for the holiday season. That unfortunate bit of timing had coincided with Logan's momentary but appalling lapse with Donella.

Nick had given him an earful about his behavior at the ball, and Logan couldn't blame him. He'd been a first-class idiot, all but abandoning poor Donella at the worst possible moment. The sweet, generous-hearted lass had been primed to tumble, and he'd have been more than happy to tumble with her.

But then he'd turned and seen Jeannie Campbell, the first girl he'd ever truly loved. Standing ten feet away, she glowed like a vision from a happier time, smiling that smile that had always and only been for him.

He'd promptly forgotten everything, including his own bloody name, and gone to her without hesitation.

It had taken only a few minutes for him to come out of his Jeannie-induced haze and realize what he'd done. Unfortunately, by then the family had decamped, and it had taken Logan some length of time to politely extract himself, even with an impatient Graeme hovering nearby.

That Jeannie was eager to resume their relationship was obvious from her flirtatious manner and semi-scandalous hints. At one point in his life, he would have responded like a slavering, idiotic lapdog. Not anymore. Not after the turmoil and grief of that fateful day by the river, and all the heartache that had followed.

For her part, Jeannie had made it immediately clear that she had no wish to rehash old tragedies. To her, apparently, they no longer mattered. Logan had been stunned by her terse dismissal of the past.

Still, he'd turned the girl's life upside down all those years ago, exposing her to gossip and humiliation. If nothing else, he owed her courtesy and respect, as well as an acknowledgment that they'd once meant a great deal to each other.

Trying to explain that to Nick and the rest of his family, however, had all but sent Kendrick House crashing down on their heads.

Things had gone from bad to worse at breakfast this morning, when Victoria informed him that Donella had already departed for Breadie Manor. At that point, Joseph had glared at him over a plate of ham, clearly blaming him for driving away his best friend. And that meant that Logan was now squarely in everyone's black book.

But worst of all was that he'd hurt and humiliated Donella. He could only hope the damage wasn't permanent.

When he pulled the curricle in front of the Palladian-style house, his groom jumped from his perch and came round to let down the step.

Logan had barely gotten his boots on the ground before the manor's front door flew open and Alec Gilbride stalked down the steps. Murder—or mayhem, at the very least— glinted in his steel-gray eyes.

Logan mentally sighed. "Take the horses around to the stables, Sam. I expect I'll be here for some time."

Or perhaps not if Alec just decided to shoot him and have done with it.

Sam flashed him a sympathetic grimace before climbing into the curricle.

He strolled up to the marble porch where Alec impatiently waited, arms crossed and a scowl blackening his normally genial features.

"You're looking a wee bilious this morning," Logan said. "Stomach troubles? Hope it's not catching."

"Sleeping troubles, as in, getting roused out of bed at the crack of dawn by Donella's arrival. What the hell did you do to the girl, you bastard?"

"I didn't do anything. I didn't even know she'd gone until Victoria told me at breakfast."

"That's not what I heard."

Logan dropped the casual pretense and scowled back at his friend. "What the hell did she tell you, anyway?"

Alec's gaze narrowed to stone-colored slits. "I'll thank you not to use such language when referring to my cousin."

"She's not even here. Now, tell me what she said so I can fix it."

"Donella didn't say a damn word about you. She just

stalked in and barked at me before disappearing into her room. Even Edie can barely get a word out of her."

"Then if she didn't say anything, why are you glaring at me like I'd just robbed the girl of her virtue?"

That brought Alec barreling forward into Logan's face. "Did you, in fact, rob her of her virtue?" he growled, jabbing a finger at his nose. "Because then I *will* kill you."

Logan gave him a shove. "Of course not, you moron. Is that really how you think I would treat her, or any woman for that matter?"

Alec retracted his horns a bit. "You did something to upset her at that blasted ball, and it apparently involved another woman. You'd better set it to right, because if I don't kill you, Edie surely will."

"How exactly do you know what happened? You weren't even at that stupid party, and Donella's not talking."

Alec flashed him a toothy grin that looked more like a snarl. "I used to be a spy. I do have my sources."

Logan shook his head in disgust. "Angus. He brought Joseph over this afternoon to visit. That old fool can never keep his bloody mouth shut."

"I never reveal a confidential source."

"Oh, bugger you."

When Alec smirked at him, Logan considered tossing his friend onto the drive. But that would hardly advance his cause with Donella. Not to mention that Alec would give as good as he got, and sporting a black eye or broken nose would hardly assist his wooing campaign.

"Are you two finished jumping about like bantam roosters?" came a sardonic voice from the top of the steps.

Logan swept off his hat and gave Edie an extravagant bow. "Mrs. Gilbride, you're looking as lovely as always this fine day."

"It's not fine. It's bloody freezing, so stop acting like nitwits and get in here."

"Edie, love," Alec replied, "I'm trying to determine if Logan's presence will disturb Donella even more. I won't have the blighter causing trouble."

Edie pulled her cashmere shawl closer around her shoulders. "That's for Donella to decide. Now, cease acting like Scottish oafs and get inside."

"Why your wife ever married you is beyond me," Logan said to Alec. "She's too smart and pretty for the likes of you."

"Oh, I can tell you *exactly* why she married me," Alec said, waggling his eyebrows.

"You're an idiot." Edie turned on her heel and disappeared inside the house.

"Yes, but I'm your idiot," Alec called after her.

Logan clamped a hand on his friend's shoulder and propelled him up the stairs. "She's right. It's bloody freezing out here, and I would like to see Donella at some point. My son, too."

"Fine, but you'd best fix this, Logan, or I swear I *will* murder you."

"That's why I'm here. Now if you would just get the hell out of my way."

"Now, gentlemen, no more fighting," Edie said as they joined her in the entrance hall. "You'll shock the servants."

Logan shot a glance at the liveried footman, who stood by the door with a hint of a long-suffering expression. "I suspect your staff is used to it by now."

"True enough," Alec said. "In fact, they'd probably faint dead away if we started acting like normal folk. Isn't that right, Robby?"

"If you say so, sir," the footman politely replied.

Alec cocked an eyebrow at Logan. "Care for a whisky in my study before you begin tempting fate?"

"Is that a euphemism?"

"For what?"

"Bashing my head in."

Alec snorted a laugh and shook his head. Clearly, Logan had passed muster, reassuring his friend he intended to do right by Donella.

"There will be no drinking," Edie said in a severe tone. "Not until you and Donella sort this out."

Logan couldn't resist. "Sort what out?"

"Do not tempt me, Logan Kendrick," she retorted. "I *will* bash your head in, if necessary."

"On second thought," Logan said to Alec, "she's the perfect wife for you."

Alec wrapped an arm around Edie's nicely curved waist, pulling her close. "I know that better than anyone. In fact, while Logan does his best to act like a normal human being, why don't we go upstairs and—"

His wife gave him a little shove and wriggled out of his arms. "You can be so annoying, Alasdair Gilbride."

Still, Logan didn't miss the blush on her round cheeks or the pleasure in her little smile. Quickly, though, she leveled another scowl in his direction.

"This situation is too serious to joke about," she said. "Donella is upset, as is Joseph. You need to fix things, and right now."

Logan sighed. "Obviously. Where are they?"

"Donella, Angus, and Joseph are in the drawing room, organizing the decorations for the Christmas party."

"Any chance you can get my grandfather out of the way, Edie? I can't do this properly if he's mucking everything up."

As if on cue, one of the doors off the wide hall flew open and Angus stalked out. He was looking especially deranged today, dressed in one of his oldest kilts and an ancient patched leather vest. Between the outfit and his white hair, frizzed out like a puffball, he looked like he'd just rolled out of an obscure Highland glen.

He stomped over to join them. "About time ye showed up. I was fair ready to come lookin' for ye."

"And good afternoon to you, Grandda. May I say you're looking particularly disreputable today? How in God's name did Victoria let you out of the house in that outfit?"

Angus whipped up a gnarly finger and wagged it at Logan's nose. "I'll have no sass from ye, laddie boy. Ye ken I'm here to help Joseph and the lass decorate the house. Ye canna expect me to be standing on ladders and hauling in greenery in my best finery."

"I'm sure the servants would be happy to stand on ladders. There's no need to go about dressed like a scrub." Logan frowned. "Besides, I don't want you climbing ladders. You're too old for that nonsense."

"I did try to make a similar point," Edie said. "Of course Mr. MacDonald did not agree with my assessment."

"Aye, because I'll nae be havin' ye put me out to pasture, like some broken-down old nag."

Knowing how chippy Angus was about his age, Logan tried a different tack. "Grandda, the servants are supposed to help with this sort of thing. You'll annoy them if you do their job."

"Fah. Lowlanders—what do they know about celebratin' Christmas?"

The Kendricks had never celebrated the holiday until Victoria joined the family. Logan refrained from pointing that out, however, since he was simply grateful that the old fellow was still talking to him after last night's donnybrook.

As if reading his thoughts, Angus narrowed his gaze. "But that's not what I wanted to talk to ye about. Ye have ground to make up, laddie. Miles of it."

Logan blew out an exasperated breath. "All right, but can we please not do this in front of an audience?"

"Don't mind us," Alec said. "We're happy to see you get your ar—"

Edie jabbed him in the side.

"Er, see your grandfather talk some sense into you," he finished.

"Well, not me," said Edie.

She nodded a dismissal to the footman, then took Alec's arm and started dragging him toward the stairs.

"Are we going up to the bedroom, after all?" Alec asked, ever hopeful.

"No," Edie tartly replied. "We're going to the nursery to spend time with your children. You've yet to see them today."

"Blast."

"Everyone knows how much you love your children, you big oaf," his wife pointed out. "Some days, I can't keep you out of the nursery. It drives poor Nurse demented."

"Which is why I'm suggesting we go to the bedroom first, so we can make some more children."

"I will box your ears, Alasdair Gilbride," Edie said. "What in God's name will our guests think of us?"

"That yer husband is a lucky man, lassie," Angus called after them.

"He'll be lucky if I don't shove him out a window," Edie called back.

She herded him up the stairs, scolding him as she followed. Alec being Alec, he teased her the whole way, their mock argument eventually fading.

"She's a grand lass, even though she's a *Sassenach*," Angus said.

"That she is."

"But she's nae too happy with ye," his grandfather said, going back to scowling. "We had quite the chat about it, first thing."

"Then she can join the club. Nick wouldn't even talk to me this morning, and Victoria acted like I'd killed her pet budgie."

Angus looked perplexed. "What? She doesna have a pet budgie."

Logan ground his teeth. "Can we please get this over with, so I can go in there and try to make amends to Donella and my son?"

Angus studied him for a few moments before nodding. "Ye ken ye made a right mess of things."

"I ken verra well," Logan said dryly.

"That Campbell girl, she's trouble. I told ye that from the first, but ye never wanted to listen to me—or to Nick."

"And as I told you both last night, I was simply trying to be nice to the woman. How did you expect me to behave? I all but demolished her life."

"Ye did no such thing. She went right on to marry that poncy, rich barrister in Edinburgh." Angus rubbed his fingers together. "Widower, ye ken, on the lookout for a young, pretty wife. Jeannie Campbell was more than happy to fit the bill."

His grandfather's trenchant assessment resonated more than he cared to admit. Still, he wanted to be fair.

"I expect she didn't have much choice after I ruined her reputation. Everyone knew I was going to ask her to marry me."

"As I recall, ye did ask her, and she refused."

"Then why are you looking so sour? You never wanted me to marry her."

"True, but I'll nae be havin' ye feel sorry for the girl. She didn't put up the least little fight for ye when it all went to hell. If the lass had loved ye, she would have."

Logan had once thought that too, but he was older now and wiser. "It would have meant leaving her family and leading a precarious existence. I can't blame her for refusing me."

"I can," Angus snapped.

"But it no longer matters, does it? And I hope her marriage was a happy one."

"Och, she's certainly a happy widow."

Logan reluctantly smiled. "And a rich one, I suppose."

"Ye'd be wrong about that. Why do ye think she's sniffin' aboot yer heels, ye booby?"

"What the hell are you talking about?"

"I've heard she's got only a small widow's portion. Her husband had a son and daughter from a previous marriage. They inherited, not yon widow."

"You gossip as much as any old biddy, Grandda. In fact, you *are* an old biddy."

Angus waved away the insult. "I'm right about this one, laddie boy. Trust me."

Logan couldn't help remembering that Jeannie *had* asked him a number of quite pointed questions about his business. He'd assumed it was simply her attempt to be polite.

"It doesn't matter," he replied. "I have no intention of getting involved with Jeannie MacArthur. You may rest assured."

"I'll nae rest on anything until ye get yerself into the drawin' room and make yer apologies to Donella."

"For God's sake, that is exactly what I've been trying to do ever since I got here."

"Then let's get to it," Angus said, bustling off ahead of him.

It was inevitable that he'd have a small but highly critical audience for his apology. Then again, the presence of his son and grandfather might cut down on the chances of Donella throwing a vase at his head.

But as soon as he could, he intended to get her alone. Then he would do whatever it took to convince her to forgive him.

"Dearest, why don't you let me do that?" Donella asked as she steadied Joseph on the ladder.

They were trying to drape swags of bay leaves around the portrait that hung over the fireplace, a splendid depiction of her great-uncle in full clan dress. The colors in his tartan would match perfectly with the greenery, especially once she finished it off with red velvet ribbon.

Unfortunately, Joseph wasn't tall enough to reach the top of the frame.

"If you'd let me climb to the top of the ladder, I could reach it," he said.

"I'm afraid it's too high. If you were to fall, your father might toss me off a cliff."

"I'd like to toss *Papa* off a cliff," the boy muttered.

She couldn't hold back a small chuckle, despite her dreadfully gloomy mood. Although she didn't regret her decision to leave Kendrick House, she hadn't anticipated how emotionally wrenching it would be. It was silly, since she was still close by, and it was lovely to be with Eden, Alasdair, and the children again. Breadie Manor was very familiar and should feel like home.

But it didn't. Kendrick House now felt like home.

Donella had always thought of herself as a rather dull person, and certainly not one given to emotional outbursts. But she'd actually started to sniffle before climbing into the carriage this morning. Only a promise from Angus to bring Joseph for a visit had staved off an embarrassing display of tears.

Blowing out an impatient breath, she silently ordered herself to stop acting like such a ninny.

"Your papa would be truly dismayed to know you thought that," she said. "He loves you very much and always does what's best for you."

The little boy scowled over his shoulder. "No, he doesn't."

His vehement reply startled her. "Why would you say that, darling? You know how much he loves you and worries about you."

"It's not that," he impatiently replied. "It's because he does stupid things."

Joseph turned back to the portrait, trying once more to hook the swag over the corner of the frame. Donella placed a hand flat on his back, keeping him from teetering.

"If that's so, I'm sure he doesn't mean to."

"Well, he did something stupid to upset you, and then you left Kendrick House." There was a suspiciously long pause. "I hate that you left."

Donella had to pause for a moment herself before she could reply. "Joseph, your papa did not wrong me in any way, I assure you."

"Grandda said Papa talked to the mean lady at the party, and it upset you."

Donella was going to have to have a little chat with Angus. As much as she liked the old fellow, he was too forthcoming with the little boy.

"Your father was simply chatting with an old friend. There's nothing wrong with that."

He threw her a skeptical glance. "But it's not just Grandda who doesn't like the lady. Uncle Nick doesn't, either. And I heard Aunt Vicky talking about it to Uncle Kade this morning, too."

Donella raised her eyebrows. "You shouldn't be eavesdropping on adult conversations, Joseph. It's not polite."

He shrugged. "Grandda will tell me, anyway."

"I'm beginning to think your grandfather is a *very* bad influence on you, young man."

That earned her a cheeky grin, which made her laugh again. But her laughter quickly faded when she thought of the good-bye soon to come when she returned to her former life.

It must have shown in her face, because his smile dimmed. "If it wasn't because of Papa, why did you leave, Donella? Don't you like us?"

She briefly rested her cheek on his back. "I like you all *very* much, and especially you. But it was time to come home to my family. I hadn't seen them for a very long time, not since I entered the convent. And Eden needed my help getting ready for the party."

He scrunched up his face. "Well . . . I suppose that's all right. But I hope you let me and Grandda come visit again."

"As often as you want, dearest. In fact, I'll need your help decorating for all the parties."

He turned back to his work, making yet another attempt at pitching the swag over the frame. "But what happens when all the parties are over? Will I get to see you as much?"

She didn't want to lie but wasn't yet ready to tell the truth. Just thinking about never seeing Joseph again, or Logan . . .

"Don't you worry about that," she briskly replied. "Now, I do think we're going to need help, so please come down."

"Let me try again. I can get it."

Stubborn, like his father. "Joseph, I don't think—"

When he stretched up on his toes and forcefully threw the swag over his head, it sent the ladder teetering. With a yelp, Donella grabbed him around the waist and thrust a leg out to keep the ladder from going over.

She was about to call for help when she heard the sound of a quick, firm boot tread. A pair of brawny arms reached around her and grabbed the wooden frame to hold it steady.

"I've got you, lass," murmured a low brogue.

She knew that voice, and she knew that body. She felt the heat of Logan everywhere, from the backs of her legs all the way to the top of her head. And, oh, how she longed to lean back into his strong embrace.

Joseph heaved a dramatic sigh. "I was fine, Papa. I wasn't going to tip the silly ladder."

"Of course not, my boy. But I think one of the legs is off balance. The entire contraption looks rather wobbly to me."

She and Joseph both craned sideways to look. If Logan hadn't been holding on to it—and her—the ladder would have crashed to the floor. Still, she didn't think it necessary for him to stand *quite* so close.

Sadly, her body didn't seem to agree with her brain.

"Angus, surely you see it," Logan said. "I shall certainly

have to speak to Alec about that. I might even have to give him a thrashing."

"Now you're being silly, Papa," Joseph said.

"Me, silly? Never."

"Now that ye mention it," Angus said, "that ladder does look a bit tippy. Ye best keep holdin' on to Miss Donella while she helps the wee lad down to the floor."

"I'll be happy to do just that," Logan murmured in her ear.

Since Donella's instinctive response was to wriggle closer to him, she compensated by giving him an elbow to the gut, which felt as hard as a washboard.

He chuckled. "You'll have to do better than that, lass."

Still, he took the hint and stepped back.

"I don't think it's the ladder," Joseph said as Donella guided him down. "It's just that my arms aren't long enough." He let out another dramatic sigh.

Logan ruffled his son's hair. "Och, you're sprouting like a weed. Soon enough you'll be taller than I am."

"Meme always said I take after my mother, and she wasn't very tall, was she?" Joseph asked as he handed the length of swag to his father.

"She wasn't tall, but she was very sweet and pretty."

His quiet, somber tone had Donella wishing she could somehow comfort him. Instead, she could only give him a sympathetic grimace.

"Ugh," Joseph said. "I don't want to be pretty. Only girls are supposed to be pretty and sweet."

The lad's comment, and his father's answering smile, chased away her melancholy moment.

"You'll be a braw lad, I promise," Logan said. "And thank God you take after your mother. We Kendricks are a sorry lot, always tumbling into trouble."

"That's certainly true," said Donella. "The stories about Clan Kendrick are legendary in this part of Scotland." She winked at Joseph. "And not for the right reasons, if you take my meaning."

He perked up. "What sort of stories?"

"You're too young to hear most of them, laddie boy," his father replied.

"It's all right, Papa," Joseph said. "Grandda has already told me some."

Logan narrowed his gaze on the old man. "I'll have to be talking to Grandda about that."

"I'm just tellin' the lad a wee bit of his family's history, is all," the old man protested.

"That's what I'm afraid of."

"I like Grandda's stories," Joseph said. "They're fun. *He's* fun."

Logan winced at the clear implication that he was not, in fact, fun.

Even though Donella was still annoyed with the blasted man, she couldn't help but feel sorry for him. For all his faults, he tried mightily to be an excellent father. Joseph certainly didn't make it easy for him.

"Why don't we get finished with this swag?" Donella said. "Then we can have some tea and cakes. I think we're done with this room, anyway."

"And ye've done a grand job, lassie." Angus cast an approving eye around the room. "Edie will be right pleased to see how festive ye've got it."

Donella took a moment to inspect the result of her labors. "They were mostly Eden's ideas. After all, she's the one who knows how to celebrate Christmas in grand style."

Still, she felt pleased with her work. The formal drawing room was spacious and elegant, with beautiful plasterwork in shades of cream and pale green offset by panels of red wallpaper. With its mahogany furniture, upholstered in matching shades of red, it made a perfect backdrop for the swags of laurels and bay leaves on the mantelpiece and picture frames, and the arrangements of holly wreaths and candles that dotted the tabletops. Eden had also suggested tying red velvet bows to the backs of the chairs and draping gold cloths over some of the smaller tables. When the lamps and candles were lit, the room would shimmer with a festive glow.

"Yes, but we've got a lot more to do," Joseph reminded her. "We still have to decorate the entrance hall, the staircase, and the dining room. The servants have to put up all the kissing boughs in the ballroom, too."

"Kissing boughs. My favorite," Logan said, waggling his eyebrows at Donella.

She scowled at him, trying to ignore the heat rising to her cheeks. Really, the man had quite the nerve flirting with her after last night's debacle.

"Yer losing yer touch, lad," Angus said to Logan.

Joseph looked suspicious. "What are you talking about?" Then his expression brightened. "Oh, are you going to kiss Donella under the mistletoe?"

Logan smiled. "Well, now that you mention it—"

"No," Donella blurted out. "You and your father are going to finish draping that swag, and then we're going to have tea."

"Spoilsport," Logan murmured.

He took the swag and climbed the ladder, his height and long arms making easy work of draping the frame. Joseph handed him the red bow for the middle of the swag, and the job was done.

"Now can we have tea and cakes?" Joseph hopefully asked.

"I have another suggestion," Logan said. "I'd like to take you Christmas shopping—to pick up some gifts for your uncles and Aunt Victoria. There's a jolly candy shop we might nip into, as well."

Donella's heart sank. She'd wanted to spend more time with Joseph—and with Logan, truth be told, now that he was here.

Still, she forced a smile, since it was important for Joseph to spend time with his father. "What an excellent idea."

"Can Donella come, too?" Joseph asked.

"I'm counting on it," Logan said. "She can help *me* do a little shopping."

She blinked at him. "Um, really?"

"Yes, really." His warm gaze slowly tracked over her.

"But—"

"And Grandda is coming, too," Logan added, smiling at his son. "He can help you pick out presents for Uncle Nick and Aunt Victoria, while Donella helps me find presents for you."

"That's a grand plan," Angus said with an approving nod. "Well done, lad."

It was a *terrible* plan. She might wish to spend time with Logan, but certainly not alone. "But how will we all fit in your curricle?"

"My groom can stay here. I can pick him up when I return you home."

"But—"

Angus took Joseph's hand. "Let's go fetch our coats."

"Huzzah," Joseph said, scampering out with his grand-father.

Donella stared at Logan and tried to marshal her scattered thoughts. "Sir, I don't need to do any Christmas shopping."

He calmly met her gaze. "I do."

"And you need *my* help?"

A roguish smile teased the corners of his enticing mouth. "Obviously, or I wouldn't ask."

Irritation finally got the better of her. "Perhaps you should ask Mrs. MacArthur. I'm sure she'd be happy to accommo-date you."

Almost immediately, her tangled emotions were over-ridden by the horror of her own stupidity. "I, uh . . ."

"Yes, about that," he gently interrupted. "That's why we need to talk."

Tendrils of panic swirled through her stomach. "It's none of my business, really."

His jaw took on a stubborn—well, more stubborn than usual—tilt. "I disagree. I need to explain some things."

When he took a step closer, she held up her hands. "Mr. Kendrick—"

"Are you coming, Donella?" Joseph asked, sticking his head back into the room. "Grandda said we might have time to go to the toy store and get a doll for Rowena. And look at the puzzles, too. But we have to go right now."

Logan simply lifted an eyebrow in gentle challenge.

Hell and damnation.

"Coming, Joseph," she said.

As she stalked past Logan, she threw him a seething glance. His only reply as he followed was a low, self-satisfied chuckle.

Chapter Twenty-Two

"Now that we're finally alone . . ."

Donella cut Logan off. "Sir, we are in the middle of a busy street."

When he unleashed his slow, seductive smile, their surroundings faded away. She gazed up into his eyes, caught as always by their extraordinary color. They reminded her of northern seas under a bright summer sky—hidden depths of blue that stretched to the horizon. Part of her longed to plumb those depths, while the other part wanted to hoist sails and head in the opposite direction.

Because she had secrets of her own, ones she needed to keep hidden safely away.

Logan dipped his head closer. "There's a park down that side street. We could take a quiet stroll, if you wish."

Donella resisted the competing urges to plant a hand on his chest and shove him away or grab his cravat and yank him down for a kiss. Instead, she tucked her hands inside her muff, wondering if she was losing her wits. It was an unfortunate prospect, since one insane woman in the family was already one too many.

When she caught a disapproving glance from a pair of elderly ladies, she stepped back. It was perfectly respectable for Logan to escort her, but Glasgow wasn't London. He'd been standing much too close, and he knew it.

"I have no intention of slinking off to a park with you," she replied. "So you can put that notion right out of your head."

"I didn't ask you to slink. I asked you to go for a walk, so we could talk more privately."

She took his arm and began steering him along the sidewalk. "That, of course, is why you sent Angus and Joseph haring off. But as I already said, there is no need for a private discussion."

He extracted his elbow from her grip. "I'm the gentleman, lass. I'm supposed to be escorting you, remember? Unless you wish to generate more gossip with your masterful ways."

He jerked his head to indicate a couple in front of a milliner's shop. They were eyeing her and Logan with disapproval. Since the pair looked vaguely familiar, Donella dredged up a smile. In response, the woman let out a censorious huff and disappeared with her companion into the shop.

"They never should have let me out of the convent," Donella said with a sigh. "I have absolutely no manners."

Logan chuckled. "Neither do I, but I suppose we should at least pretend we do while in public."

"This entire expedition is ridiculous," she groused. "You quite obviously do not want to go shopping with me. You simply wish to badger me, so you might as well get it over with."

He adopted a long-suffering expression. "That is exactly what I've been trying to do."

"Well, you don't need to drag me off to a secluded park to do so. That, I might add, would not help my reputation."

"Because it's a rather delicate subject, I was hoping for

some degree of privacy. But if you want to discuss it here in the middle of the bloody street, we certainly can."

"Since I'm not sneaking off for a clandestine conversation, that *is* your only choice."

His sideways glance held considerable frustration. "You can be an incredibly stubborn woman. Not to mention irritating."

She barely refrained from sticking her tongue out at him. *And what would Sister Bernard have said about that?*

The image of Sister's horrified reaction had her choking down a laugh and made her wish even more she could give in to her silly impulse. She'd certainly come a long way from her convent days.

They walked in silence down the street.

"Why don't we walk up to the church at the end of the street?" she asked, looking for a compromise. "It's not busy up there, so we should be able to talk without half of Glasgow giving us the evil eye."

He let out a sardonic snort. "I'd forgotten how small this town could feel. And how judgmental."

"I'd forgotten that, too. The Kendricks do have a special knack for generating tittle-tattle. It seems to be a particular family talent."

"Years of practice." He steered her across the street to a quieter stretch of pavement. "That brings me to the point of this discussion. I owe you an apology, Donella. I was a complete buffoon last night, and I cannot tell you how much I regret it."

Her heart slammed against her ribs. Whether it was from hope or dread, she couldn't yet tell.

Don't make a fool of yourself.

"Thank you," she calmly replied. "You were simply greeting an old friend you hadn't seen in a long time. Your surprise was understandable."

"That doesn't excuse my behavior. I all but abandoned you on the dance floor."

"We weren't dancing."

"Donella—"

She flapped her muff at him to interrupt. "Very well, sir. You made your apology and I accepted it. There's no need to discuss that business any further."

He shot her that narrow-eyed glare again, one that always indicated immense irritation. "There is every need to mention *that business,* because there has been some sort of misunderstanding about Jeannie and . . . I mean about Mrs. MacArthur and me."

Donella fixed her gaze on the tall steeple atop the church at the end of the street. "It's truly none of my business."

He gently pulled her to a halt and turned her to face him.

"It is your business," he said in a terse voice.

She avoided meeting his eyes. "I don't see why."

"If you don't see why, then you haven't been paying attention. Mrs. MacArthur is an old friend. Nothing more."

"But Victoria said—"

"I don't care what Victoria said. What happened with Mrs. MacArthur is long in the past and will remain there. I give you my word."

Rattled, she met his gaze. His irritation gave way to something much warmer, and that rattled her even more.

A smile twitched at his lips. "You really haven't been paying attention, have you?" He shook his head. "Or else I *have* made a complete hash of this. What a pair we are, my sweet lass."

Donella felt her mouth sag open. That turned his slight smile into a full-out grin as he tipped her chin back up with a gentle finger.

Annoyed that she'd been gaping at him like a half-wit, she scowled. "Are you saying that you're actually courting me?"

"I tried to make that rather obvious, but apparently not obvious enough."

"Good Lord," she whispered.

When he continued to regard her with amusement, she made an effort to say something coherent. "But *why*? It makes no sense."

"Doesn't it?"

"I'm so happy you find this amusing," she stiffly replied. "If I find out that Alasdair is bothering you about that stupid abduction attempt, I will murder you both. You need to stop acting like bacon-brained idiots. Absolutely nothing happened in that cabin, and you know it."

Liar.

"One of the things I most like about you is your brutally refreshing honesty," he said. "You think nothing of insulting a man to his face, even if he's courting you. *Especially* if he's courting you. It's a bold tactic."

Donella couldn't decide whether she wanted to slap him or herself for engaging in such a ridiculous conversation. How it had gotten so ridiculous, and so quickly, was a bit of a mystery. But now all she wanted was for it to end.

"When a man acts with such a complete lack of decorum, I don't know what else one should do. Now, if you're quite finished insulting me—"

He gently reeled her back when she tried to stalk past him. "Come back here, daft girl. By the way, I believe you're the one who's insulting me, not the other way around."

Even though his eyes still glittered with amusement, there was heat there, too—a seductive heat that fluttered her insides like a flock of sparrows.

Donella gazed up at him, feeling wooly-headed. "I . . . I don't know what you want from me."

"First, I want you to accept my apology for last night's stupidity."

"But I already did that."

"I mean *truly* accept it."

When she gnawed her lower lip, Logan's gaze flickered down to her mouth and caught there.

"I do," she hastily said. "Are we finished?"

"Not quite. I also need you to understand that I meant what I said about Mrs. MacArthur."

She resisted the temptation to chew on her lip again. Anxiety and a burgeoning hope were destroying her nerves. "It didn't seem so last night."

"I truly was surprised to see her," he admitted. "Mrs. MacArthur and I were once quite close."

"From what I heard, you proposed marriage."

His smile was wry. "Blunt, as always. I do like that quality."

She refused to be distracted. "You *were* going to marry her."

Now it was Logan's turn to stare up at the church spire. "Yes, but whatever we had back then, well, let's just say it's best left in the past."

Donella knew he was thinking about little Cam, and how he'd been unable to save him.

She fleetingly touched his chest. "I'm so sorry, Logan."

He turned to look at her. For a moment, his eyes seemed as cold and stark as winter. But as their gazes held, the cold faded away.

"Victoria told you," he said gruffly.

She simply nodded. For him, old wounds had been ripped open again, and she suspected he wouldn't wish to discuss it.

After a pause, he cleared his throat.

"Then you must see I have no wish to renew a relationship with Mrs. MacArthur." He rolled his eyes. "For a thousand reasons."

Donella's heart sank. "I understand. Your family wouldn't approve."

He frowned. "They wouldn't, but that's not what I meant."

"Of course, sir. I understand completely, truly I do." And now she was babbling. "We are finished this discussion, are we not?"

His gaze was so riveting she had to fight the impulse to look away.

"Oh, lass, we're not close to being finished," he murmured, his brogue going deep and rough.

Donella's stays suddenly felt tight, and she had trouble catching her breath. "We'd best get back. Angus and Joseph will be wondering where we are."

Mischief gleamed in his eyes. "Coward."

"And we *are* supposed to be Christmas shopping."

When she gave him a little shove to get moving, he huffed under his breath.

Taking her hand, he tucked it back inside her velvet muff. "Don't want your hands to get cold, love," he murmured.

She dropped her gaze, annoyed that she was no doubt blushing like a schoolgirl.

"And, yes," he added, "we're going shopping. I think I'll look about for a present for you."

"You'll do no such thing, Mr. Kendrick."

"Logan."

"*Mr.* Kendrick."

When he laughed, she couldn't hold back a reluctant smile. She was grateful when he asked her which shops she needed to visit, giving her a moment to recover her mental balance. To say her emotions were tumultuous would be to massively understate the case.

Was he truly courting her? And were his feelings for Jeannie MacArthur truly relegated to the past?

Donella's instincts about men—about life—had been wrong more than once. And since those instincts were now urging her to allow Logan to woo her—and possibly wed her—she truly didn't know how to respond.

The safest course would be the cautious one.

But I'm sick of being cautious.

"You mentioned that you wished to pick up snuff for Lord Riddick," he said as they strolled past the fashionable storefronts. "There's a good tobacconist just up ahead. Would you like to pop in?"

"Yes, please, something plain for my uncle. Spanish Bran, perhaps?"

"Excellent choice. No nonsense like Attar of Roses for a sensible Scotsman."

"I'm not familiar with that one. Then again, I'm not exactly fashionable, so I wouldn't be."

He paused before the door of a shop, smiling down at her. "You're as fashionable as you need to be, lass."

The man had a *lethal* smile. She could almost wish to unbutton her pelisse and fan away the flush of heat.

"Which is to say, not fashionable at all," she joked, trying to cover.

His reply was cut off when the door opened and a brawny young man hurried out, barely avoiding them. His thick shock of blazing red hair was instantly and *fatally* recognizable to Donella.

She could only pray he wouldn't recognize her.

"Och, excuse me," he said. "I didn't see ye—"

When he stuttered to a halt, his eyes going wide, Donella knew her prayers had gone unanswered. The young man gaped at her with utter astonishment.

All she could do was stare back in horror at the face she'd not seen in years. She would never forget it, nor would she forget the shameful secret his presence conjured up like a howling ghost.

"Is there a problem, sir?" Logan asked.

The sarcasm in his tone apparently did the trick. Roddy Murray awoke from his stupor and flashed Donella a wide smile that only served to increase the panic crackling through her brain.

"Miss Donella," Roddy said in his deep brogue. "I heard ye were out of the convent, but I had no idea ye were in Glasgow. We just got to town a few days ago, so I reckon it's no wonder I hadna heard about ye bein' here."

Her wits finally started to thaw. His comment surprised her, since the Murrays hated anything to do with the city. Generally, they tucked themselves away on their estate in one of the more remote corners of the Trossachs. And yet here they were, only a few weeks after her attempted abduction. That seemed entirely too coincidental, especially since Uncle Riddick had sternly warned the Murrays to stay away from the Haddons in general and Donella in particular.

Still, Roddy did seem genuinely surprised—and pleased—to see her. Had he not even been aware of that insane episode or known about her uncle's warning?

"Is your entire family here in Glasgow?" she managed.

"Aye. We've all come down for a spell, visiting with my mother's sister, ye ken."

"Your father, too?" she prodded.

Mungo Murray was the most likely suspect behind the abduction. Good-natured Roddy was incapable of designing any sort of complicated plan.

He looked confused, which wasn't unusual. Confusion was Roddy's natural state. In Donella's experience, most girls had been willing to overlook that unfortunate fact because he was both handsome, good-natured, and his father's heir.

"Where else would he be?" Roddy answered.

An upsweep of nausea forced her to close her eyes and suck in a breath. All her old sins had finally caught up with her.

"Are you all right, lass?" Logan asked.

She opened her eyes to meet his concerned gaze. "Yes, I'm perfectly fine."

He switched his attention to Roddy. "And who are you?"

Roddy blinked, obviously perplexed by Logan's rude behavior.

"Just a family friend from the old days," Donella blurted out. "It's getting late. Don't you think we should look for Joseph?"

Roddy looked like a kicked puppy. She couldn't help feeling a twinge of guilt.

Somehow, he mustered a smile and held out a hand to Logan. "I'm Roderick Murray, sir, of the Murray Clan. As Miss Donella says, an old friend."

Logan's hand froze in midair. "Murray?"

"Aye, sir. Roddy, to my friends." He grinned at Donella. "Ye always called me that, ye ken."

Donella had once read a book in which several characters were swept away by a monstrous tornado. When Logan's outstretched hand curled into a fist, she found herself wishing to see one whirling down the street.

Logan began to crowd Roddy in the doorway. Horrified, Donella wedged herself between them.

"Yes, I do remember," she said in a dementedly bright voice. "But we were very young, you know."

"Och, but ye *must* ken how glad I am to see ye now." He smiled at her with genuine pleasure. "Despite what happened with . . ." He twirled a hand.

Oh, God, please get me out of this.

"Roderick, it's lovely to see you, but we really must—"

"Who's yer friend, Miss Donella?" Roddy interrupted, frowning, apparently remembering that Logan had snubbed him. "He seems a mite fashed."

"As I mentioned, we need—"

Logan wrapped his hands around her shoulders and moved her out of the way.

She yanked her hands out of her muff and grabbed his arm. "Mr. Kendrick, your son is no doubt waiting for us."

He ignored her. "I'm Logan Kendrick, Murray. I'm the man who prevented Miss Haddon's kidnapping a few weeks ago. An attempt by your clansmen."

Roddy's stunned expression would have been comical if the situation wasn't so dire. "Murrays tried to abduct Miss Donella? Go on, man. That's daft."

Logan took a step closer, forcing Roddy to back into the glass of the shop door. The sound drew the attention of the shopkeeper and several customers.

"You'd best tell me what you know about it, or else," Logan said in a low, terrifying voice.

Roddy went from confused to indignant in an instant. "Are ye saying *I* had something to do with it? Why the bloody hell would I want to kidnap Donella?"

He was loud enough to capture the interest of an elderly couple strolling by. Donella's heart sank when she realized it was Lord and Lady MacTavish, high sticklers of the first order.

Donella again tried to wedge herself between the men, but Logan held her back.

"People are beginning to notice," she hissed.

"I don't give a damn," he said. "I don't want you anywhere near a Murray. Go down to the toy shop and find Angus and Joseph. Stay with them until I come to get you."

"Do you think Roderick is going to kidnap me right off the street, in broad daylight? Don't be ridiculous."

"I've never kidnapped anyone in my life," Roddy huffed. "And I'm verra fond of Donella, ye ken."

Logan's gaze narrowed to icy blue slits. "No, I dinna ken. Perhaps ye would like to explain it to me."

His lethal tone would have sent most men scrambling backward, right through the plate glass, if necessary. Sadly, Roddy was too dense to take the warning.

She once more tried to wedge herself between them, this time facing Logan. "He means nothing except the fact that the Murray and the Haddon families were once quite close."

Logan scoffed. "That's a bit rich, lass. Friends, generally speaking, don't abduct friends."

Roddy, being an idiot, agreed with him. "That's true. My da always hated Lord Riddick. Called him a churly grumbleguts, he did."

Beginning to feel like a piece of cheese smashed inside a scone, Donella wriggled around to glare at Roddy.

"Roderick, please be quiet."

"But—"

"Shut. Up."

He subsided with a grumble, looking wounded again.

She turned back to Logan. "You're causing a scene, sir. We need to go."

He tossed a glance over his shoulder at the small audience that had joined Lord and Lady MacTavish. "Having fun, are we? I suggest you bugger off before I really lose my temper."

That *bon mot* generated a round of outraged gasps. But since he *was* Logan Kendrick, his warning had the desired effect.

"You are a complete idiot," she said when he turned back to her.

"Got rid of them, didn't I?"

She jabbed a finger into his chest. "You are going to ruin what little bit of reputation I have left."

"You needn't worry about your reputation. I'll take care of that."

"You just did. Now, can we please put an end to this utterly humiliating scene?"

"Not before I'm convinced that this nincompoop didn't try to abduct you," Logan shot back.

"I keep tellin' ye I didn't," Roddy indignantly exclaimed. "And I'll darken yer daylights if ye say it again."

Donella twisted around. "Roddy, for your own sake, please *shut up*."

He grimaced. "But I canna have ye thinkin' such a thing. Ye must know that I would never hurt ye. Never."

Whatever his faults, Roddy didn't have a devious bone in his body. "I know. I believe you."

"Then what about your father?" Logan asked him. "Or others in the Murray Clan? Is there some reason *they* would want to hurt Donella or Lord Riddick?"

When the shopkeeper banged on the door behind them, poor Roddy almost jumped out of his boots.

"Would ye please stop blocking the door?" the man yelled through the glass. "My customers wish to leave."

"I'm sorry," Donella called back. Then she fixed Roddy with a stern look. "Roderick, go home. And do not mention this unfortunate encounter to your father. Understand?"

"But—"

"I mean it." She turned and planted a hand on Logan's chest and gave him a shove. "If you do not move, I will be forced to kick you in the shins. Which will definitely hurt me more than it hurts you."

Logan scrubbed a frustrated hand over his face. "Donella, I need to—"

"What you need to do is *stop*."

She took his arm and began dragging him away. Thankfully, this time he let her—but not without directing a scowl over his shoulder at Roddy.

"This isn't finished, Murray," Logan barked.

"Stop making a scene or I'll murder you," Donella hissed.

Perversely, that made him snort with amusement. "You know, for an almost-nun, you frequently sound quite blood-thirsty."

Now that she'd finally escaped the scene, the sheer horror hit her full force. Roddy had been only seconds away from blurting out enough of the truth for Logan to guess the rest. And that likely would have resulted in *real* murder, or at least enough bloodshed to cause a dreadful mess.

"No need to fall into a snit, lass," Logan said. "And you can hardly blame me, since we just ran into a man whose family tried to kidnap you. A man you were apparently *verra* close to, whatever that means."

She refused to look at him. "It doesn't mean anything. He's not terribly bright, as I'm sure you noticed."

"Donella, what aren't you telling me?"

She glanced up at him, exasperated. "Do you never give up?"

His answering smile managed to look both charming and feral. "Not when it comes to you."

Panic once more began to thread icy tendrils through her brain. "It's not your business."

"I think it's entirely my business, lass. After all, you're going to be my—"

"Donella, here we are!"

She felt weak with relief when Joseph pelted toward them, with Angus following at a more leisurely pace.

The boy skidded to a halt in front of her. "Grandda and I were looking everywhere. You've been gone ever so long."

She patted his shoulder, annoyed to see a slight tremor in her hand. "We decided to stroll up to the church at the top of the street."

Joseph frowned. "You didn't go Christmas shopping?"

"We . . . we ran out of time," she said lamely.

"Ran out of time, did ye?" Angus's gaze flickered between them. "Ye both look as queer as Dick's hatband. What's amiss?"

"Just an interesting encounter with an old friend of Miss Donella's," Logan said.

Joseph heaved a sigh. "Papa, are you being mean to Donella again?"

"Of course not. I'm never mean to anyone."

"Ha," Donella said.

"Ha," Joseph echoed.

Logan pointed a finger at Angus. "Don't even think about it."

The old man snorted. "Doesna seem like the lassie agrees with ye."

"The lassie would be wrong."

Donella decided it was time to marshal her loyal troops. "The lassie is not wrong." She looped her muff around one wrist and offered a hand to Joseph. "Would you and your grandfather like to walk me to Kendrick House?"

"Yes, please." Joseph looked at his father. "Papa, we left the packages at the toy shop. Grandda said you could fetch them and take them home in your carriage."

"Papa is supposed to be driving Miss Donella back to Breadie Manor, remember?" Logan scowled at her. "Where she now lives."

She waved her muff. "I'm sure Lord Arnprior's coachman can drive me home. Then he can pick up your groom on the way back."

"But that's ridiculous," Logan objected. "I'm right here, and my curricle is right down the bloody street."

Angus snickered. "Ye'd best pick up the packages while I walk the two of them back to Kendrick House. Oh, and stop at the sweet shop while yer at it. We had them set aside boxes of taffy for Kade, Braden, and the twins."

"So now I'm supposed to play footman to you lot?" Logan said, clearly exasperated.

"Seems so." Angus took Donella's arm. "Ready, lass?"

"I am indeed."

"I'm not done with our conversation, Donella," Logan said in a clear warning tone.

"I am." She turned and marched off with her faithful escorts.

Chapter Twenty-Three

Donella eyed her bosom in the pier glass over her dressing table and tried to tug up her bodice. It still seemed scandalously low, despite Eden's earlier assurances.

"You need to stop dressing like a prude or an antidote," her cousin-in-law had insisted. "You're much too young and pretty for that sort of nonsense, especially at a Christmas party."

While it was true that the gown was beautiful—plush green velvet lavishly trimmed with creamy lace and gold ribbons—Donella had almost fainted the first time she'd tried it on. It required her to wear a specially designed set of stays, because her regular ones would have stuck up over the top. Eden had taken care to order them in anticipation of her objections.

Dress troubles aside, she was feeling too rattled to celebrate anything with the Murrays in town and with Logan Kendrick now on the scent.

That Logan was deeply suspicious of Roddy Murray was undeniable. That Logan was deeply annoyed with her was also undeniable.

She'd spent much of the last week dodging him so as to avoid questions she couldn't answer. By sticking close to

Blairgal and throwing herself into final preparations for the party, she'd managed to minimize contact with her erstwhile suitor.

Joseph had been innocently helpful, coming to visit with Angus almost every day. Since Logan would never forbid his son to spend time with her, Donella had found herself protected by a very effective little chaperone.

It was sad, really, the methods she was forced to employ to protect her secrets.

"You'd have made a dreadful nun," she murmured as she again tugged at her bodice.

Eden's maid had been helping her mistress pick out fans, but now bustled over. "Miss Donella, if you don't stop yanking it, you'll rip that lovely dress."

"I'm not yanking, Cora. I'm just . . . fixing it."

Cora swatted her hands away. "Leave off and let *me* fix it."

Eden sank down onto a low, upholstered chair by the fireplace. "Best do what Cora says. She always wins."

"And don't you be flopping down like a nasty schoolboy," Cora said. "You'll wrinkle that gown something fierce, and then I'll have to listen to what-for from Lady Reese."

"Mamma stopped caring what I look like when I married the heir to a Scottish earldom."

"A rich heir," Donella added with a smile.

"And you gave him up for me, old girl. Have I thanked you lately for doing that?"

"You have, but I truly gave him up for myself. You were the nudge I needed."

"Well, it all worked out for the best. I got the man I love, and you're about to get the man you—"

Donella threw up a hand. "Don't say it. The very idea gives me hives."

Cora blew out a frustrated breath as she straightened

Donella's shoulders. "You girls wriggle about like worms on a hook. It's a wonder I can get you dressed at all."

"What a flattering description," Eden said in an amused voice. "But Donella looks absolutely smashing tonight, and you know it."

Cora finished retying the ribbons at Donella's back, then reached around to rearrange the gown's neckline. That put even more bosom on display.

"There," said the maid with satisfaction. "Now don't you be touching anything, Miss Donella, or you'll spoil it."

Eden rose and joined them at the vanity. "You do look lovely, pet. Logan will be thrilled."

"I cannot imagine why I'd even care."

Cora and Eden exchanged a furtive glance.

"I can see you in the mirror, you know," Donella dryly said.

"That will be all, Cora," Eden said.

"Yes, ma'am."

The maid couldn't resist fussing with Donella's hair one more time before gathering up some discarded shifts. She paused at the door to give her mistress a pointed look.

"You keep an eye on Miss Donella, now. She's not used to the ways of these townfolk."

"It's Glasgow, Cora," Eden said. "No one ever does anything shocking here. Besides, Mr. Kendrick will certainly look after her."

"That's exactly what I'm afraid of," Donella muttered.

After the door closed, Eden gave her a reassuring smile. "You look perfectly respectable and just as you should. And I love what Cora did with your hair. I have a feeling you're going to start a new style in boring old Glasgow."

Cora had pomaded and brushed Donella's short hair until it gleamed almost red in the candlelight. Then she'd wound a green velvet bandeau around her head, gathering most of the curls up in a fashionable tumble. The problem was it left her neck and shoulders completely exposed, like much of her chest.

"But I feel like there's really too much . . ."

"Bosom?" Eden finished.

Donella wasn't exactly well endowed, but the tops of her breasts were swelling above the green fabric. "There seems to be an awful lot on display, if you ask me."

"Fah. Just look at my gown. I'm all but falling out of it."

"You're nursing, so it's understandable that you'd still be rather . . ."

"*Buxom* is the term I think you're searching for," Eden said cheerfully. "I always was, though. Pregnancy and childbirth have simply made it ridiculous."

"Not that your husband seems to mind."

That comment was not at all the sort of thing a nun would ever say. But Eden was so easy to talk to, as was Victoria. Nothing ever seemed to shock them, nor did they judge or criticize her. It was refreshing and altogether wonderful.

"You might not be as amply supplied as I am in the bosom department," Eden said, "but I assure you that Logan is fully aware of your charms."

An unpleasant thought rose unbidden in Donella's head, one she couldn't seem to repress. "He seems quite aware of Mrs. MacArthur's charms, as well."

Eden batted that away with an impatient hand. "You shouldn't listen to gossip, Donella. It's almost always wrong."

"Is it?" She hoped so, but evidence might suggest otherwise.

"Yes, and it certainly is in this case. Logan doesn't give a hang about that dreadful woman. Please don't let such nonsense stand in your way." She paused. "You've grown quite fond of him, haven't you?"

Donella struggled not to fib. "You do remember I'm leaving for Galway at some point. To join another order of nuns?"

"Pet, you are no more joining a convent than I'm joining Astley's Circus."

Donella opened her mouth to issue a firm denial. Unfortunately, nothing came out.

Swallowing hard, she tried again. "I'm not?"

"You are definitely not," Eden said firmly.

She winced. "Well, I . . ."

Eden placed gentle hands on her shoulders. "Dear girl, I know something is troubling you. Something is holding you back from expressing your feelings. Feelings that are telling you that the convent is no longer your path."

Donella rubbed her forehead. "Drat. I was so hoping I was wrong about that."

"I'm not sure why. It's lovely to be in love, and Logan is a splendid fellow, you must admit."

"He is, but it's . . . complicated."

"Can't you talk to him about it?"

"God, no." He'd probably storm off and murder half the Murray clan—perhaps after murdering her first.

"Then what about Alec?" Eden asked. "Can you tell him?"

Uncle Riddick had suggested exactly that. After that awful run-in between Roddy and Logan, Donella had dashed off a panicked letter to him, asking for guidance. He'd replied that it was finally time to tell Alasdair about her history with Roddy Murray. Since the Murrays were now in Glasgow, it made sense for her cousin to deal with the situation.

Besides, it seemed clear that Mungo Murray had ignored her uncle's warning, and that meant drastic measures were necessary. While Mungo might feel confident enough to ignore an old man, facing down Captain Alasdair Gilbride was another matter entirely.

"I was planning on doing that," she confessed. "I'm just trying to work up my nerve."

"It's about something that happened when he was fighting in the war, isn't it? While you were still betrothed?"

She gave a miserable nod.

"Pet, Alec loves you. He would do anything for you, as would I."

Donella mustered a smile. "I know. Thank you."

"And if you think you can shock him, it's impossible. God knows I've tried over the years, too."

"He says you just drive him demented."

Eden laughed. "It's rather my mission in life, and I think you should make it your mission to drive Logan Kendrick demented, too. In fact, you're already doing a jolly good job of it, from what I can see."

"The opposite, I'm afraid. He's driving me insane."

"Then it sounds like you're perfect for each other."

"I . . . I don't know about that."

Eden took Donella's hands in a comforting grip. "All I can advise is to give yourself a chance and give Logan a chance. You might be surprised at what could happen."

Perhaps she was right. Perhaps it was time to stop being afraid.

"All right. I'll try."

Her cousin wagged a finger. "Obviously, that means you can't keep avoiding him."

"But it's so much easier that way," she said with a weak smile.

"Trust me. You can try, but the chickens *always* come home to roost."

Donella rose from the dressing table. "They already have, and I'm afraid they've made quite the mess."

Logan craned around, trying to spot Donella in the throng. Scots didn't make a fuss about Christmas, but that hadn't stopped what seemed like half the population of Glasgow from squeezing into Breadie Manor. The guests were quaffing enormous amounts of champagne, inhaling tables of food like locusts, and having a splendid time being shocked by Papist holiday extravagance. Between the crowd and the Christmas greenery that cluttered every available inch of space, it was a miracle anyone could see ten feet ahead.

The fact that Edie was also missing meant she'd probably gone upstairs to fetch her reluctant cousin. Logan had never had trouble courting a woman before, but Donella was making it a hell of a challenge.

The encounter with Roddy Murray had put the cat amongst the pigeons. Since then, Logan had been working to get to the bottom of the mystery between the Murray and Haddon families, although answers were elusive. He'd fully intended to call on Mungo bloody Murray and drag the truth out of him until Nick had forbidden it.

Not that Logan wouldn't disobey Nick, but his brother had pointed out that forcing a confrontation would embarrass Donella and would hardly help in the wooing department. Nick had then suggested writing to Lord Riddick, asking for guidance. When Logan did so, his lordship's reply had all but told him to sod off, stating it was Haddon family business and that Alec would deal with it.

Nevertheless, Logan intended to have a quiet little chat with Alec as soon as he could drag him away from his guests.

After another quick scan, he left the ballroom and headed down the crowded corridor to check the dining room for Donella. Even if he found her, however, there was no guarantee she would talk to him. It wasn't just the annoying Murray mystery that was holding her back. It was Jeannie MacArthur, too. Gossip had already spread through the city, not surprisingly, given they'd once been expected to marry.

And now that Jeannie was a widow and he was rich some people would naturally start making assumptions.

It hadn't helped that the one damn day Donella had stopped by Kendrick House to fetch Joseph was the very day Jeannie, along with her mother and aunt, had come calling. Victoria had not wished to appear rude, especially since Jeannie's aunt was married to a clan chieftain, so she received them.

Thank God Nick had been away. But Logan had been trapped with the ladies for a good half hour. It hadn't taken long to gain the distinct impression that Jeannie and her relatives were mentally riffling his pockets and calculating his financial worth. After making his escape as soon as he could, he had run smack-dab into Donella in the hall, preparing to leave with Joseph. When Logan suggested going with them, she'd all but given him the cut-direct, as had his son.

It was a damn mess, both with Joseph and the woman he intended to marry. He'd better get it sorted tonight or God only knew what would happen.

He reached the main drawing room, set up with a lavish buffet. Tables, covered in starched white linen and topped with silver candelabra circled by festive wreaths of holly and ivy, were grouped around the center of the room. All were occupied, as were the settees and upholstered benches— decorated with red and green velvet ribbons—tucked against the walls. Most of the younger ladies had taken to the settees, drinking champagne punch and fluttering their fans at the gentlemen who strolled by.

It was all so boring that he'd rather wrestle a bear in the middle of the Canadian wilderness.

He was about to retreat when he finally spotted Donella. She was standing quietly behind a large potted palm, doing her best to blend into the foliage. It was a hopeless attempt, because she was absolutely the prettiest girl at the party, though she generally downplayed her looks.

Not this night. Her plush velvet gown, which matched the color of her extraordinary eyes, hugged her gentle curves and displayed an enticing amount of bosom. Of course he'd known Donella had breasts; he'd just never seen much of them. Now that he had, his brain—and the rest of him—made the split-second decision it wanted to see more.

Much more.

Her slim neck and creamy shoulders were also on ample display, since her gleaming hair was swept off her neck and captured in a velvet bandeau. Logan's hands tingled with the need to explore that smooth, freckle-dusted skin and dip down below the gold trimmed edge of her bodice. She would have lovely soft nipples, rose colored, that would grow dusky and hard under his fingertips.

That wouldn't be the only thing growing hard if he persisted in this line of thought. If he didn't wish to erect a tentpole under his kilt, he'd best get his idiotic brain under control. Wooing Donella was the first order of business, and she would be decidedly unimpressed with rampant displays of masculine lust.

Seeing her as she was tonight, though, would certainly make it harder to keep his hands to himself.

Telling his blasted cock to stay down, he started to make his way over to her odd hiding place. As he got closer, however, it became clear why she was standing in the shadows, as still as a marble statue. She was as pale as one too, but for the angry flush coloring her cheekbones.

"Oh, my dear," said an attractive blond girl, seated on the bench in front of the large palm. "*Surely* you've heard about Donella Haddon and her mother. It's *outrageous*."

Her companion, a young woman with a large feathered

fan, leaned closer and flapped like a deranged parrot. "Not a word. Do tell."

"You mustn't say anything, because I promised Mrs. . . . er, the person who told me . . . that I wouldn't breathe a word."

"My lips are sealed," her friend solemnly affirmed.

Anger started a slow burn in Logan's gut. While Donella was obviously too embarrassed to do anything about the gossiping chits, he certainly wasn't.

But as he started forward, her glance darted over to meet his. She shook her head in clear warning. When he lifted an inquiring brow, she waved a hand, telling him to retreat.

No bloody way.

Since it was obvious she didn't want him interfering, he simply held his ground, biding his time.

"From what I heard," said the blond girl, "there was *quite* a horrendous scandal. And Lord Riddick was forced to cover it up with *quite* a bit of money."

The fan lady all but flapped up a gale. "You mean a scandal about Miss Haddon's mother? What happened?"

"It had to do with Miss Haddon's betrothal to Captain Gilbride. Which was *quite* another scandal, you know. Apparently, he didn't wish to marry her, so he ran away."

"I know that," Fan Lady said impatiently. "Then he came back ten years later with Eden Whitney. Imagine, bringing home the girl you intend to marry, right under your fiancée's nose."

"Yes, but that's not the truly shocking part."

"It seems *quite* shocking to me. I heard she became his lover, even before he broke if off with Miss Haddon."

Logan's anger flared hotter. They were gossiping about their host and hostess, whose hospitality they were happy to accept all while spreading ugly rumors about them.

As if sensing his fury, Donella again glanced over and gave a firm shake of her head. *Trust me,* she mouthed.

Logan answered with a terse nod, even though it went against every instinct.

"And Mrs. Gilbride is from London, you know," Fan Lady added. "She had quite the reputation before she arrived in Scotland."

"True, but that's not the really scandalous part," said the blonde. "It's the business after Miss Haddon broke off the engagement. Apparently, her brother challenged Captain Gilbride to a duel and almost killed him."

Donella rolled her eyes. Clearly, nothing of the sort had happened, or Logan would have heard about it, too.

"One can hardly blame her brother," said Fan Lady, looking dubious. "But I don't know about the almost-killing part. Gilbride and Miss Whitney were married only a few weeks after the betrothal was broken off."

Her friend waved an imperious hand. "Silly details. It's what happened next that's important."

"Well, what?"

The blonde leaned in close, although she didn't bother to lower her voice. "Miss Haddon's mother went insane. Apparently, the broken engagement and the subsequent duel were too much for her reason. She went *entirely* mad and had to be locked away."

Her friend slapped the oversized fan to her chest. "That's simply awful," she said in tones of delight. "Is she still locked away?"

"Yes, in one of those dreadful asylums where they stick mad people."

Now that was complete bollocks. Logan glanced at Donella again, but this time she refused to meet his eye.

Fan Lady looked dubious again. "That doesn't really

sound like something Lord Riddick would do. He's a very respectable man, and an earl, after all."

"I can assure you that I heard this from an unimpeachable source," the blonde insisted.

"If you say so. I feel a bit sorry for Miss Haddon. It can't be very nice to have your mamma locked away for being insane."

"Don't feel sorry for her, my dear. She's almost as unstable as her mother. Why else do you think Lord Riddick shipped her off to that convent in the middle of nowhere?"

"I assumed it was because Captain Gilbride broke her heart, so she took the veil."

This time, Donella looked at Logan and again rolled her eyes. His stomach unclenched a bit. She'd been looking devastated for a few moments, listening to that awful talk about her mother.

"Don't be silly," said the first girl. "The Haddons aren't even Catholic. Lord Riddick sent her off because Donella became hysterical. It would be rather too much to have both her *and* her mother in an asylum, so he consigned her to the convent instead. God knows why they let her out, since she's obviously a danger to herself and others."

Her friend flapped her fan with dizzying force. "I did hear something about an episode with Mrs. Ferguson, but I thought it was an accident."

"It was no accident. Miss Haddon deliberately attacked the poor woman." The blond girl shook her head. "It's entirely outrageous that they let her out, so she'd be free to roam about town attacking innocent ladies."

"Goodness," exclaimed Fan Lady. "Are you *truly* saying she's as demented as her mother?"

"My dear, I think it—"

"You think what?" Donella asked, stepping up behind them. "That I'm insane?"

Fan Lady let out a squawk, just like a parrot, and the pert

blonde almost tumbled off the bench. Donella sauntered around to stand before them, casually crossing her arms.

The blonde managed to pull herself together, although her friend looked ready to slide into a dead faint. Logan supposed he'd better make ready to catch the silly chit, although he didn't feel much inclined to do so.

"Miss Haddon, I didn't see you there," said the blonde, making a game attempt.

"Obviously. You did, however, seem to know quite a bit about me and my mother." Donella tilted her head, frowning thoughtfully. "Perhaps I am."

"Per . . . perhaps you're what?" stammered the blonde.

Donella leaned forward, pinning them with a bone-chilling stare. "Perhaps I *am* insane. I do have all sorts of disturbing thoughts, and I can't seem to control them."

The two gossips were now staring at her with undisguised horror. But as much as he appreciated Donella's tactics— God, he loved a ruthless lass—it was time to intervene before the nitwits began shrieking in terror.

Or before he burst into uncontrollable laughter, which would also cause a scene.

He strolled up to the bench. "Up to a little mischief, I see. Are you needing a hand, lass?"

Donella gave him an adorably haughty look. "I believe I have the situation under control, Mr. Kendrick."

The pert blonde jumped to her feet. "Oh, sir, thank God. Something must be done. Miss Haddon is . . . is . . ."

"Insane," Donella helpfully supplied.

Fan Lady staggered to her feet and clutched her friend's arm. "Perhaps you'd better take her away, Mr. Kendrick," she said in a quavering voice. "Before she does something . . ."

"Insane?" Donella again chimed in.

Logan choked back a laugh. "All right, Miss Haddon, I believe you've twitted these ladies enough for one night.

They're obviously a bit chicken-hearted. You'll send them off into a fit of hysterics if you're not careful."

"I do believe that was my intention," Donella replied.

The blonde, obviously the sharper of the two, finally twigged. "Do you mean you were making fun of us?" she angrily demanded.

Donella gave a slight shrug, as if barely caring enough to reply.

"I'd say you earned it too, from what I heard," Logan said. "You certainly didn't bother to lower your voices."

Fan Lady turned an unbecoming shade of puce. "You were eavesdropping on us?"

"I was standing several feet away and, yes, I could hear you." Logan narrowed his gaze on the blonde. "By the way, who was your supposedly reliable source? Because that was the most ridiculous palaver I've ever heard."

"It's none of your business," she snapped.

"It is, however, my business," Donella said. "So let me give you a word of advice—don't listen to gossip. You both sounded like silly dimwits, which is hardly an attractive quality in a respectable woman."

"You're one to talk, Miss Haddon," the blond girl indignantly replied. "I think you are quite awful."

"Awful," her friend echoed in a quavering voice.

"Naturally, I'm devastated to hear that," Donella said.

The blond girl took her friend's arm. "Come along, dear. I don't know why we came to this dreadful party in the first place."

"Don't forget to say good-bye to the Gilbrides on your way out," Logan said. "You know, your host and hostess? The ones you were gossiping about?"

The chits stormed past him, drawing a great deal of notice in their wake. In fact, even though they'd been relatively tucked away, he suspected their scene had drawn at least some attention.

Splendid. More gossip.

"Well, that was fun," he said, turning back to Donella.

She sank onto the deserted bench with a sigh. "No, it wasn't."

Chapter Twenty-Four

What in heaven's name is wrong with me?

Donella contemplated that question while staring at the tips of her dance slippers. If Logan hadn't appeared and forced her to pull in her claws, how far would she have carried her ghastly joke? Deserved or not, her behavior had been uncharitable and foolhardy.

"Mind if I join you?" Logan asked as he sat down beside her.

She cut him a sideways glance. "Do I have a choice?"

He flashed his devastating smile, not looking a bit concerned that she'd again caused a scene. Although it would not be as dramatic as the chatter about the sweet shop, gossip about this particular episode would surely circulate.

Of course, Logan also excelled at making scenes, so he was hardly in a position to criticize.

"I suppose you could flounce off and leave me here," he replied. "But that would probably draw even more notice, which I'm sure we're both eager to avoid."

The gleam of humor in his eyes sparked her temper.

"You certainly did your best to stoke the furnace, sir. Your comments were hardly helpful in defusing the situation."

His eyebrows went up in an incredulous tilt. "Lass, I pulled your pretty arse *out* of that furnace. Those two idiots were about to launch into a shrieking fit of hysterics. Well done, by the way. I was impressed by your tactics."

"Yes, I managed the situation quite skillfully. Every person in the room witnessed that ridiculous scene. One only has to look around to see the evidence."

So far, Donella had done her best to pretend she wasn't the target of avid interest. And no doubt more than a few of the guests had also heard the ugly remarks about her mother and what she'd said in return.

Logan made a point of scanning the room, letting his iron gaze linger on anyone who seemed a little too curious. Predictably, most of the guests hastily glanced away or struck up a loud conversation with their companions.

Enjoying the protection of an irate Kendrick male did occasionally have its advantages.

Logan returned his attention to her. "Dinna fash yerself, lass. No one will pay a mite of attention to those two twits."

It was her turn to be incredulous. "You did hear what they were saying, did you not?"

Now that he'd finished terrifying the room, Logan's gaze had once more turned warm and so kind that it brought a sudden sting of tears to her eyes. Because underneath her rage and contempt for those who would gossip with such callous disregard, lurked an endless pool of hurt and shame.

And when Logan finally found out the truth . . .

Donella pressed a hand to her lips to choke back a small sob.

"Och, lass," he murmured. "You'll not be having a bout of hysterics in the buffet room. Edie would kill me if I let that happen."

A flare of irritation snuffed out her incipient tears. "Since when did you ever see me fall into hysterics, Mr. Kendrick? When we were set upon by kidnappers, perchance?"

He rose from the bench and extended a hand. "That's my

girl. Now let's get a wee dram to settle you down. We definitely need to talk about this little episode."

"You said that on purpose," she grumbled.

"It worked, didn't it? Now don't make me stand here looking like a booby while you make up your mind."

"Very well, but only because we'd both look like boobies and generate even more gossip."

"Actually, I think we've cornered the market on gossip."

Given the rise in chatter as he led her from the room, there was little doubt of that.

"I don't suppose you could encourage the twins to do something outrageous?" she hopefully asked. "Something truly stupid that would draw attention away from us."

"Alec and Edie wouldn't be too happy if I did. The twins destroyed quite a bit of furniture at one of their Hogmanay parties a few years ago. Took Graeme and Grant months to pay off the damages."

"That's awful." She paused. "Do you think they would do it again if I asked them?"

He steered her toward a knot of soberly clad gentlemen. "You needn't worry about anything, Donella. I promise."

He was wrong about that. But since he was now exchanging greetings with the men who were obviously business acquaintances, she held her peace.

Besides, she wasn't exactly burning to reveal her gruesome family secrets, and especially not to him.

"If you'd like to speak with your friends, I won't mind," she said as he moved them along. "I can go find Eden."

He threw her an amused glance. "That is a pathetic attempt to avoid the matter at hand, sweetheart."

She scowled. "You really are immensely irritating."

"Years of practice."

Donella was so busy muttering under her breath, it took a

moment to realize he'd led her into the quiet cross-corridor along the back of Breadie Manor. "Where are you taking me?"

"To the library. Alec keeps his best whisky there, and it's quiet, so we can talk."

She skidded to a halt. "That is an exceedingly bad idea."

"Why?"

"Because we'll be alone."

Brawny, handsome, and temptation incarnate, he loomed over her. "We're just going to have a wee dram and a wee talk. Nothing scandalous about that."

"It's entirely scandalous, and you know it."

His eyes betrayed his exasperation. "Donella, we've been alone on any number of occasions, and our families have never objected."

"No? Alasdair all but threatened to murder you for maligning my virtue after that night in the crofter's cottage."

"I believe we agreed it was impugning, not maligning."

She looked around for a convenient vase to throw at his head.

"I'm very good at ducking, lass," he said, gently nudging her along. "And I promise to be on my best behavior. If I'm not, I further promise that you can bash me over the head with as many vases or candlesticks as you like."

"You're ridiculous."

"I know, but you like me anyway."

She refused to dignify that with an answer because, well, she did like him.

You more than like him.

Logan was right, and Eden had been right, too. She needed to give this a chance, and she needed to be as honest with him as she was able. Donella couldn't reveal everything about her past, but she could tell him about her mother. He certainly deserved that much.

The library was at the very end of the hall, far from the

service rooms and the more public parts of the house. It was blessedly silent, and Donella had to admit she was grateful to escape the heat and the press of so many people. After her years in seclusion, she still found crowds to be a formidable challenge.

She'd always preferred a quiet evening by the fire, spent with a book and a cup of tea, and sometimes a chat with family or close friends.

A sudden image of Joseph curled up by her side as she read him a story rose in her mind. Logan was close by, keeping watch over both of them. A sense of longing began to squeeze her heart so strongly that it was hard to breathe. God, she wanted that life. She wanted her own family, and a child to love.

And she wanted Logan. That was the most shocking revelation of all.

"All right, lass?" he murmured as he reached around her to close the door.

She forced out the breath that was stuck somewhere between her ribs. "Yes."

He tipped up her chin and studied her face for a moment. Then he dropped a quick kiss on her forehead. "We'll get it sorted, sweetheart."

"There's nothing to sort, I assure you."

He snorted by way of reply and led her to the apple-green velvet chaise tucked cozily into the alcove of the bow window. "I'll get us a drink."

She gratefully sat, given her wobbly knees.

He crossed the room that Eden had recently repapered in a crimson silk that handsomely set off the Grecian mahogany furniture. Splendid bookshelves flanked the large desk and the fireplace, rising floor to ceiling.

As far as Donella was concerned, the best feature of the room was this window alcove, which faced west toward the rising hills. The intimate little nook was her favorite place to read. Thanks to the fire burning brightly in the hearth, it was cozy now, too. For the first time all evening, her tense muscles began to relax.

But her heart started tripping over itself again when she heard Logan's quiet footfall returning to her.

"May I?" he asked, as he settled beside her.

She took the cut-crystal glass he offered. "I don't know why you bother asking, since you're going to do whatever you want."

His smile was crooked. "Probably, but Nick often tells me that I should be improving my manners."

"I'd say it's a lost cause." She sighed and set the glass on the low reading table before them. "Then again, so am I."

"That's why we're perfect for each other." He picked up the glass and handed it to her. "Drink, lass. Think of it as medicinal. It'll help warm you up."

She was already feeling *quite* warm, thanks to the giant sitting next to her. Nevertheless, she complied with his gentle command. The smoky beverage slid down her throat to ease her taut nerves.

"You were looking a little pale there for a while."

She managed a smile. "I'm sorry I'm being such a goose, and I really should thank you for rescuing me. Your intervention was most timely."

"I'm just sorry you had to hear their ugly nonsense."

"It's my own fault, eavesdropping as I was."

"I was rather surprised to see you lurking behind a potted plant in that nefarious manner. How did you end up there, anyway?"

She winced. It would be easier to dodge his question, but embarrassment was no excuse for cowardly behavior. "If you must know, I was looking for you."

His dark eyebrows shot up. "Hiding behind a potted plant? Not my usual habitat, love."

Donella plunked down her glass and crossed her arms under her breasts.

Predictably, his gaze snagged right on her bosom, which *was* rather popping up over the top of her bodice.

She hastily brought her hands down to her lap. "Don't be ridiculous. I was simply having second thoughts and needed time to compose myself. Things haven't exactly been easy between us this last little while."

Logan was obviously fighting a smile. "So you decided to duck behind the greenery for a bit of ruminating. Of course that makes perfect sense."

"It was a very nice plant, in case you failed to notice."

She sounded like a twit but she didn't care. Logan Kendrick had to be *the* most annoying man in the entire kingdom.

He reached for one of her hands, wrapping his long fingers around hers. "I did fail to notice, because I was busy looking at the extraordinarily pretty girl hiding behind the palm and I was wondering what she was doing."

His warm, gentle tone deflated her sails.

"I sound like a complete fool, don't I?" she said with a sigh. "And I did get my just deserts for eavesdropping. I didn't mean to, you know. I was simply going to sit in that window alcove when I heard those two, idio—er, girls talking."

"Idiots, I believe you were going to say."

"That would be very uncharitable of me."

He pressed a kiss to the back of her hand. The feel of his lips on her skin sent shock waves rippling through her body.

"It's just ugly nonsense," he said in a soothing tone. "You shouldn't listen to any of it."

Oh, dear. The last thing she wanted was his pity. She'd been an object of pity too many times, and she was heartily sick of it.

Better to make a joke of it. "They weren't entirely wrong. I've been causing one scene after the next about town—

rather like a circus act. No matter how hard I try to behave, I just can't make it stick."

That last bit ended on a quavering note that made her feel even more humiliated.

He scoffed. "Donella, there isn't a damned thing wrong with you, and don't let anyone tell you otherwise."

"You have to admit some of my behavior hasn't exactly been rational."

"Really? I hadn't noticed anything amiss."

It was her turn to scoff. "Logan . . ."

He took her other hand, holding both between his. "Donella Haddon, you are a brave and spirited lass with true Highland fire. If you'd been a man, you'd have been a warrior."

As she gazed up into sky-blue eyes that gleamed with humor, affection, and warmth that muddled her brain, Donella didn't feel brave at all. She felt terrified, because she was realizing she'd truly and finally fallen in love.

And that meant she had to own up to some very uncomfortable truths.

"I meant it when I said those girls weren't entirely wrong. When they were talking about my mother, and about me."

"Sweetheart, if you're trying to say you're queer in the attic, I'm not having it."

She glanced down at their joined hands. God, it was hard to tell him. Harder than she'd ever imagined.

"The truth can't be worse than the lies," he said.

She choked out a strangled laugh. "You'd be surprised about that."

"Donella, it's time I knew the truth about your poor mother's situation. I can help, if I know exactly what the problem is."

Her gaze darted upward to meet his. Instead of confusion or judgment, she saw only understanding. "You know, don't you?"

"That your mother is ill and under private care? Yes. Nick told me."

"Of course he would know. Victoria would have told him." And how embarrassing was it that his lordship had then gone on to tell Logan.

Logan shook his head. "He only told me because I was concerned by your reaction to the old Ferguson bat at the sweet shop. Nor has Victoria been telling tales. Nick has only the most basic details about your mother's condition, nothing else."

"Does anyone else in your family know?"

"Not to my knowledge. And it's no one's business but yours. I only wish to know because I want to protect you against the kind of ugly gossip we heard tonight."

He so obviously meant it that she found herself blinking back tears again.

"Och, lass," he said in a gruff voice. "None of that nonsense. Ye'll kill me if ye start up with that."

She pulled away one hand to briefly press her fingertips against her eyelids. "Sorry, I'm being silly. And I don't know if there's anything you can do, since the rumors are already circulating. We thought we'd scotched it after the original incident but apparently not." She sighed. "I suppose getting kicked out of the convent is what set it off again. My poor family. I give them nothing but trouble."

"If that was the case, they'd be shipping you off to another convent as quick as could be, and they are not."

She wrinkled her nose. "Maybe it would be better if they did."

Logan dipped his head and pressed an utterly possessive kiss to her lips. His mouth was warm and firm, lingering for a few delicious moments, long enough to set her heart hammering against her ribs. When he drew back, she found her hand resting on his chest, as if to find balance.

Because she'd never felt more off-kilter in her life.

"And we'll have no more nonsense about another convent," he said gruffly. "You're staying right here with the people who love you, understand?"

She blinked up at him, trying to gather her scattered wits. She wished she had the courage to ask if he was among those who loved her. Since that seemed presumptuous and entirely too risky, she simply nodded.

"Good girl. Now, do you think you could tell me about your mother?"

"Why not?" she said ruefully. "Everyone else in town seems to know."

"That's doubtful, and it wouldn't be accurate, anyway." He let go of one hand and reached for her glass.

"Are you trying to get me intoxicated, Mr. Kendrick?"

"Just trying to help you steady your nerves."

Donella took a healthy swallow, choking a bit as it went down. "At this rate, I'll be so relaxed I'll slide down to the floor."

"If you do, I promise to catch you."

And keep me, too. I hope.

"It's not a very nice story," she warned.

"I'm a Kendrick. We specialize in that sort."

"By Kendrick standards, I suppose it's probably not all that shocking."

He cupped her chin and gave her another brief kiss. "It's all right, Donella. Whatever you tell me, it'll be all right."

What she *should* tell him is to stop kissing her. Donella made herself promise that if he did it again, she would box his ears.

Or, at the very least, give him a severe scold.

"Very well." She took a deep breath. "My mother hired someone to kill Alasdair, and when that didn't work, she took it upon herself to try to kill Eden. And when *that* didn't work, she then attempted to shoot Alasdair herself."

Logan gazed blankly at her. "I hope you're joking."

"Believe me, I wish I was."

Obviously astounded, he stared at her for several long seconds before finally replying. "I must admit, even by Kendrick standards that's quite something."

Donella's heart shriveled a bit. "Yes, it's terribly off-putting. I do understand that."

Logan's eyes narrowed thoughtfully; then he tipped up her chin and kissed her again.

This time, he lingered over her mouth and gently explored the seam of her lips with his tongue before finishing up with a gentle nuzzle. The kiss sent a flush of heat prickling beneath her stays, and all she could do was clutch at him, trying not to shake.

"Sir, you really must stop doing that," she quavered after he drew back.

It was a pathetic scold. As for boxing his ears, she supposed it was no surprise that she'd lost any desire to do so.

Obviously, the sisters had been dead accurate in their assessment that Donella did not belong in a convent.

"Daft girl," he said gruffly. "As if anything your mother did would scare me away."

She swallowed. "This is a very improperly conducted conversation, in more ways than one."

"You can give me an excellent scold later on that point. But for now I would be grateful if you could explain why your mother would behave in so deranged a manner."

"Because she's deranged?"

He winced. "Sorry. That was a wee bit clumsy of me."

"It's not your fault. The whole thing is so far-fetched it's impossible to discuss in a rational manner. And to tell you the truth, I hate talking about it."

He reached out and grabbed her glass again, handing it over. "Just tell me what you feel able to."

Donella took another fortifying sip. "My mother was always high-strung and volatile. She grew worse after my father died, but we always made excuses for her." She tried for a smile. "It's rather difficult to imagine that one's nearest relation could become so dangerously unhinged. We should certainly have paid better attention. My brother, especially, still feels terrible guilt over the whole thing."

"Fergus does wear his heart on his sleeve. But thank God that your mother didn't hurt anyone."

Donella waggled a hand. "She did hurt someone."

Logan frowned. "Who?"

"Me."

"What?"

She winced. "You needn't yell, sir. I'm right here."

He plucked her glass away and put it on the table, again taking both her hands. "Please tell me yer all right, lass."

The brogue had come out again, indicating he was truly upset. He'd gone pale under his tan, which certainly suggested that he really did worry about her.

"I'm fine. Truly, it was just a minor wound."

"Tell me exactly what happened," he tersely said.

"It happened in a small, back garden of Blairgal Castle. There's an old wall that marks the edge of the garden, blocking a very steep drop into a ravine. Mamma had forced Eden up onto that wall, and was going to make her jump. Then she'd tell everyone she'd committed suicide."

"God, that's awful. I'm so sorry. It was about you and Alec breaking it off, I take it."

"For Mamma, that was the final straw. She'd always resented Alasdair and believed Fergus should be heir to the earldom, especially since he'd taken on the duties of estate steward after Alasdair ran away and joined the army."

"Fergus was next in the line of succession?"

Donella nodded.

"I suppose I can see a certain logic to that," Logan said, "but then why kill Edie?"

"Mamma was convinced that, in his grief, Alasdair would turn to me for comfort and eventually ask to marry me. I would then become Countess of Riddick after my uncle died."

"But what about Fergus and his claim to the earldom?"

"Mamma intended to do away with Alasdair at some point. That way I would be a wealthy dowager countess, and Fergus would still inherit."

She could see Logan trying to puzzle the mad scheme out. After a few moments, he shrugged. "Sorry, sweetheart, but it makes no bloody sense. It's the most convoluted plot I've ever heard."

"I told her that. I made it quite clear that even if she did kill Eden, I would never marry Alasdair."

"And that's when she decided to shoot the poor fellow?"

"Yes."

"Then how did you get injured instead?"

Donella felt the need to fuss with the sash tied under her bodice. "I suppose I tried to jump in front of Alasdair when Mamma fired the pistol."

The answering silence was so fraught that she couldn't work up the courage to look at him. Instead, she counted the seconds as the mantel clock ticked them off.

"You what?" Logan finally asked.

She peeked up, mentally wincing as she took in the thundercloud that all but roiled over his head.

"I didn't get to Alasdair in time. It was just bad luck that Mamma shot me instead."

His gaze all but scorched her. Grabbing her by the shoulders, he gave her a little shake. "You are never, *never* to put yourself in harm's way like that again. Do you hear me?"

Logan's fury, instead of scaring her, chased away the sadness and shame that always came with remembering that horrible event and her mother's sad fate.

"It wasn't something I planned," she said apologetically. "It was all rather confusing, in the moment."

He muttered something under his breath before snatching her into his arms, all but squeezing the breath from her lungs.

"Daft girl," he growled. "And I should kill Alec Gilbride for putting you in so dangerous a position."

"It truly wasn't his fault," she said in a muffled voice.

"It certainly wasn't *your* fault. I hope you don't think that."

As comforting as it was to be held so securely, it was rather difficult to breathe. She wriggled her hands up between them and tried to push against his rock-hard chest.

"Sir, you're squishing me."

Reluctantly, he eased her back, keeping his hands loosely on her shoulders. In fact, he was now caressing her there, gently sliding his calloused fingertips over her bare skin. The thrilling sensation it evoked made it difficult to focus on anything else.

"I meant it about putting yourself in danger," he sternly said. "You're not to do it again."

"It is not an experience I wish to repeat."

"Where were you hit?"

"It was just a graze on my right arm." She smiled up into his worried gaze. "You can barely see the scar. Alasdair assures me that it's exceedingly paltry compared to all of his."

"He should have done a better job of protecting you."

She tapped his waistcoat. "Alasdair did nothing wrong. If anything, the fault lay with the rest of us for not seeing how disturbed my mother had become."

"Emotions often get twisted about and muddled when it comes to those we love," he said in a somber tone.

Now she placed a gentle hand flat on his chest, knowing he was thinking of his own troubled past. "Yes, they do."

"What happened after she shot you?"

"Mamma became even more hysterical when she saw me fall. Fortunately, I hit my head on the paving stones and knocked myself out, so I missed the rest."

He winced. "That's one way of looking at it, I suppose."

"Then Lady Reese hit Mamma in the jaw and knocked *her* out. That effectively put an end to the immediate crisis."

He choked. "Truly?"

"Her ladyship is a very masterful woman, you must admit."

He grinned. "Bully for her. I'll have to give the old battle-ax a kiss next time I see her."

"Then she'll probably punch you in the jaw, too."

"I'd let her." His smile faded. "But I am so sorry you had to go through that, sweetheart. And I'd like to throttle those two silly chits for rehashing those rumors tonight."

"In a way, that's the worst part. We worked so hard to manage the scandal and protect my mother's privacy. My poor uncle will be devastated that we failed."

"Then there's the impact on you." His hands slipped down to cup her elbows. "We need to figure out why the rumors kicked up again."

She shrugged. "As I said, it's likely because I'm now out in the world. Before, I was out of sight, out of mind."

"There's got to be more to it. I can understand a bit of gossip about why you left the convent, but this is of a different magnitude. And it must be of fairly recent vintage, because otherwise Nick would have heard about it. Very little in this town escapes his notice."

She had a sneaking suspicion about that. Despite the fact that Donella's mother was kept under close watch, her physician encouraged carefully managed walks in his garden and occasionally even carriage rides for a change of scenery.

Under the circumstances, it was conceivable that Mamma had been spotted once or twice, or that bits and pieces of information had somehow reached the ears of those who lived in neighboring parts of Edinburgh.

Jeannie MacArthur had recently arrived from that city. She could certainly have heard or seen something, although Donella would never voice such a suspicion without proof.

"I suppose it doesn't really matter how they started," she said. "All I can do is try to ignore them."

Logan's eyelid twitched, but he refrained from stating the obvious.

"Which I obviously failed to do tonight," she wryly added. "No wonder people think I'm touched in the head."

"Anyone else in the family dicked in the nob?"

"Not that I know of."

"Then leave off with that nonsense. You're the sanest person I know."

Her throat went tight, because it was the perfect thing for him to have said. "Thank you."

"You're welcome."

He let go of her arms and reached for his glass, taking a drink. Then, frowning, he stared out the window, as if searching for something in the darkness beyond the polished glass.

Donella shifted a bit and smoothed her skirts over her knees. Now that he was no longer looking at her, she had to resist the temptation to tug up on her bodice. As she always did when talking about her mother, she felt uncomfortable and exposed.

Despite his sympathetic attention and kisses—three kisses, in fact—he seemed to be subtly drawing away from her. She couldn't blame him. Her life was a mess, and she was now the object of some truly mean-spirited gossip that would reflect poorly on any man who courted her.

Was he regretting his intention to woo her? Between the

debacle with Roddy and this disaster, she could soon become a magnet for all sorts of slander.

Her heart suddenly skipped a few beats.

Joseph.

How would this affect him? If she and Logan continued to be seen together, it could make him a target. That was too horrible to contemplate. The poor boy had already suffered enough.

"What are you thinking?" she asked, too nervous to keep quiet.

He glanced at her, blinking, almost as if he'd forgotten her. "I'm simply trying to figure out what to do about this situation. It won't be good if the gossip continues to spread. I'd best speak to Alec first, and then go from there."

He was no longer looking affectionate, or even remotely like he wanted to kiss her. He seemed distracted and perhaps even annoyed.

It almost killed her to say it, but it was the right thing to do. "I understand your concern. And I also think it's best that I return to Blairgal immediately. I'll explain the situation to Joseph first, though, so he understands. The gossip will then die down, and there will be no repercussions for you, or for Eden and Alasdair."

He scowled. "What the hell are you talking about?"

"Joseph shouldn't be subjected to any more nasty gossip." She managed a wobbly smile. "Nor should you. You've been incredibly kind, Mr. Kendrick, but I do not hold you to any obligations you feel you may have—"

He moved so quickly, she barely had time to gasp. A moment later, she was sprawled inelegantly on his lap, staring up into his glittering gaze.

"What are you doing, sir?" Her voice came out more like a squeak than a demand.

"You *are* daft if you think I give a damn about any of

that," he said. "And Joseph loves you, silly girl. He'd kill me if I let you leave."

She tried to steady herself by bracing her hands on his massive shoulders. "That's . . . that's very kind of you. And I know you believe you made a commitment to me, but you didn't. And . . . and it's silly to think you or any man should wish to marry me. Or want to. I'm not the marrying kind, you see. I'm . . ."

She trailed off when his gaze narrowed to ice-blue slits.

"Are you quite finished?" he asked with heavy sarcasm.

She felt the first stirrings of irritation. "I'm not sure."

"I am."

"I don't see how."

"Because of this."

He swooped down and captured her mouth in a soul-searing kiss that blasted every thought and every reservation straight to oblivion.

Chapter Twenty-Five

Donella tasted like honey and sunshine. Her kiss was like everything Logan had been missing for so long—goodness, laughter, and sweet joy. And despite her obvious trepidation, her innocent fervor set him afire. With Donella in his arms, Logan could believe it was safe to open his heart and love again.

He knew, as well as he knew himself, that once Donella gave *her* heart, she would give it forever. He wanted that more than he could say.

When he gently teased the seam of her mouth, she froze for a moment and Logan's heart skipped a beat. But then she opened for him with an endearing little whimper, as if part of her wanted to resist but a larger part couldn't deny the fire between them.

Still, he had to be sure. She was unused to the ways of men—especially men like him.

He briefly tasted her silky warmth. Her mouth was a luscious invitation to explore other intimate places, where he could drink her in until she shook with passion and cried out in his arms.

The image of her naked before him ravaged him like a storm. It urged him to spread her out on the chaise and strip the clothes from her beautiful body.

With a mighty effort, Logan throttled back. He nuzzled her mouth and gave her lower lip a soft tug. She moaned, which almost demolished his willpower before he retreated.

Donella sucked in a wavering breath, her parted lips moist and raspberry-red from his attentions. Large, black pupils stood in stark contrast to the vibrant green that surrounded them. Her cheeks were flushed, and she looked altogether ready to be stripped naked and kissed from the top of her pretty head right down to her wee, soft toes.

"Why are you stopping?" she whispered.

He adjusted his hold, resisting the temptation to push down the sleeve that was already slipping off her shoulder. "Because I want you to be sure about this."

Her fine, auburn brows pulled together in an eloquent line. "Since I am neither boxing your ears nor shrieking at the top of my lungs, I would seem to be quite sure. And that is an appalling lack of decorum on my part, I must say."

Logan hid a smile against her forehead.

"Are you laughing at me?" she suspiciously asked.

"Never, love. I'm simply enjoying you. Enjoying this."

Donella shyly smiled in return. "I'm rather enjoying it, too."

God, she was lovely, a slender lass with a sweet arse and soft breasts that plumped up over her tight bodice. Her dress had twisted around her body, outlining her long legs and exposing her pretty ankles. Logan could already imagine those legs propped up over his shoulders as he knelt between them, using his mouth and tongue to explore her.

He had to clamp down on the need to flip her over onto the chaise and begin that exploration without further ado. Donella was a virgin, and she was to be his wife. She deserved her first time to be as gentle and as pleasurable as he could make it.

"I'm very glad to hear it," he said, gently rubbing his thumb along her exposed collarbone.

He was a bare inch away from that sagging sleeve, which

tempted him beyond all reason. He had always been attracted to Donella but was discovering that his attraction had stealthily transformed into something very close to obsession.

Or love.

Not yet, he cautioned himself. Not until he was sure of her.

"Do you think we can get back to the kissing?" she asked in a hopeful voice.

"Of course. As I said, I just need to make sure you're comfortable with this."

She wriggled a bit, trying to pull herself up to a sitting position. Logan had to bite back a moan as her round little bottom pressed down on his cock.

"As I already said—" Her eyes popped wide as she finally noticed his erection. "Well, I'm certainly not ready for *that*."

He let out a strangled laugh. "Of course not. But I want to know if you are ready for *this*. For us to be together, starting down this road. And what that will ultimately mean."

She thought about it, and then gave him another tentative smile. "I think so. I'd like to try it, anyway. But nothing more than kissing, for now."

He gently tapped her adorable nose. "Yes, for now. In any case, if we disappear for too long, people will notice."

She winced. "You're right. I cannot imagine what you must think of me for not even realizing that. I'm just awful."

He rested his hand against the back of her neck, playing with her soft curls. "Awful in the best possible way. And that blasted party is so crowded, that I'm sure we can take a few more minutes before anyone notices we're gone."

Eventually, though, someone would come looking for them. If he had any brains, he'd get her back to the party before that happened.

But when she rewarded him with that glimmering smile, he tossed caution out the window.

You're going to marry the lass, anyway.

Donella touched a gentle finger to his lips. "Then I suggest we put those minutes to good use."

As he leaned in to kiss her, she pressed two fingers over his lips.

"But let's be sensible," she teased. "Heaven knows, Mr. Kendrick, we don't want to cause any gossip."

"Cheeky lass," he growled.

When he took her mouth in a devouring kiss, she sank into his embrace. For long delicious moments, Logan pleasured her mouth, as he wanted to pleasure the rest of her body. When she snuggled closer, he wrapped his fingers around the back of her head, dislodging the bandeau. While made of the softest of velvets, it wasn't as soft as Donella's bright curls or the silky texture of the nape of her neck.

Her breath was sweet against his lips, and the sound of her happy sigh whispered through him. Logan planted a searing kiss against her mouth, openmouthed and hungry, before reluctantly beginning to pull back. But the creamy skin of her cheek, the delicate curve of her jawline was so tempting that he had to sample them as well. Then, he promised himself, he'd stop.

When he trailed kisses across her kitten-soft cheek, she moaned and wriggled again, the movement shooting heat through his groin. Swallowing a curse, he pulled back to gaze at the beauty he held fast in his arms.

That was almost his undoing, since her delectable breasts had swelled over her bodice, and her dress was now hiked up over her knees, exposing the tops of her garters and affording a peek at her rounded thighs.

Unable to resist, Logan rested a hand on her knee, playing with her delicate stockings.

Her innocently seductive gaze, soft as moss, met his. "Should we stop?" she whispered.

"Probably," he whispered back.

Just a few minutes more.

He tipped Donella back over his arm and trailed his tongue over the pulse beating just under the delicate skin of her neck.

"Oh, oh," she gasped, arching beneath him.

Something broke free, and all his restraint fell away. As he lavished kisses on her neck, Donella let out a moan. Logan slid a hand under the hem of her gown, trailing up over smooth skin—

A startled feminine gasp from behind them was followed by a string of masculine curses.

Fate, it seemed, was about to catch up with them.

"What the hell is this?" roared an aggrieved voice.

Donella's eyes flew open, wide with panic. When she started to struggle, Logan clamped her firmly in his arms and brought her to a sitting position on his lap. Then he twisted them both around so he could face the impending mayhem.

Alec charged into the room, all but breathing fire from flared nostrils. Right behind him, shaking her head but looking more amused than irritated, was Edie.

"What the hell does it look like?" Logan replied.

"Oh, my God." Donella buried her face into his cravat.

Logan gave her a reassuring squeeze. "It's all right, sweetheart. Everything will be fine."

"Yes, it will," Alec barked. "After I rip your head off, you bastard."

Edie elbowed her better half. "No fighting in the middle of parties." Then she adopted a stern look. "Really, Mr. Kendrick. I expected better of you."

Logan ticked up an eyebrow. "Really?"

Her mouth twitched. "I suppose not. Although you might

want to allow Donella the chance to, er, arrange herself before this discussion goes any further."

Logan glanced down and sighed. Bringing them around to face the room had done a splendid job of twisting the poor girl's dress *well* above her knees and pulled her bodice sadly askew.

When Donella glanced down at her gown, she yelped and started to flail.

Logan ducked to avoid her backhanding him. "Hang on, lass, or you'll knock me out."

"I'll be doing that myself," Alec threatened.

Edie shoved her husband aside. "Get out of my way, you big Scottish oaf." She marched up to the chaise. "Would you please put Donella down so I can help her correct herself?"

"As soon as she stops wriggling about like a hog in a gun-nysack, I will be happy to do so," Logan said.

Donella froze, and both women all but incinerated him with smoldering glares.

"Sorry," he said with a wince.

"You are as big an oaf as my husband," Edie replied as she helped Donella off Logan's lap.

"Are you just going to sit there?" Alec demanded of him.

"I rather think I am."

"It's quite rude to remain sitting while the ladies are standing," Edie said as she brushed Donella's skirts back into some semblance of order.

"Best if I stay seated, lass."

"Get up, you coward," Alec said.

Logan sighed and came to his feet. Everyone's gaze im-mediately went to the unfortunate tenting arrangement underneath his kilt.

"That explains why you wanted to remain seated," Edie dryly said.

"Aye." Fortunately, the situation was quickly self-correcting.

Donella sank back onto the chaise and covered her face. "Someone please kill me now."

"No, I'll just kill Logan," Alec replied. "And then your problem will be solved."

Edie, who was starting to fix Donella's hair, scowled at her husband. "No one is killing anyone. We know what needs to happen, and I'm sure Logan does, too."

"Of course I do. In fact, I was in the middle of proposing to Donella when you interrupted us."

Donella raised her head. "You most certainly were not."

"Now I *am* going to kill him," said Alec.

Logan stared at Donella with disbelief. "What in God's name did you think this was about? Playing skittles? Of course we're going to get married."

She crossed her arms over her chest, which disheveled her bodice anew. "Sir, I do not recall hearing the beginning of any such proposal."

"But I specifically asked if you were sure about what we were doing, and you said yes."

"And *I* said I was sure about this." She waggled a hand between them, as if to explain what had transpired on the chaise. "Not about that."

"Well, *that* is exactly what I took it to mean."

"Then you assumed incorrectly," she said in a haughty voice.

"This is a ridiculous conversation," Alec complained. "You're not making any sense."

"They're making perfect sense." Edie struggled to pull Donella's tight sleeve up over her shoulder. "You're just too thickheaded to understand."

"Edie—"

She rounded on her husband. "Donella is making it clear that she will not be forced into marriage simply because we discovered them in a private moment."

"She'd damn well better marry the bastard, or else."

"Keep your voice down," his wife ordered. "You'll bring the entire house down on us."

"Of course I'm going to marry her," Logan said. "That's what I've been trying to tell you from the moment you stormed into the bloody room."

"You might try *proposing* first," Donella said in a freezing tone.

Logan stopped glaring at Alec long enough to take in her angry flush and the stubborn tilt to her jaw. But behind the irate expression, he saw shame in her eyes and, worst of all, an uncertainty that made her look achingly young.

That almost broke his heart. That she could still be uncertain of him . . .

He crouched down and took her hands. They were trembling, and her fingers were cold.

"I'm sorry that I got it backward, love," he said gently. "But you know how I feel about you, and you know what I want."

She gnawed her lip. "I don't, actually."

He raised his eyebrows.

"Very well. I'm quite certain about the second part," she said in a grumpy voice.

"I want it all, Donella. I want *you*."

She shook her head. "Not like this. Not when neither of us is given a true choice."

Logan mentally frowned. He understood her embarrassment but got the sense that something else was holding her back.

"That's because you don't have a choice," Alec barked.

Donella suddenly batted Logan's hands away and rushed to her feet. "How dare you lecture me, Alasdair Gilbride? I caught you in the *exact* same situation with Eden."

Logan stood. "That was worse, since you were engaged

to the idiot at the time." He flashed his teeth at Alec, who was steaming like a kettle about to boil over.

"You must admit the irony is rather thick on the ground, dearest," Edie said to her husband.

Alec fumed a bit longer before capitulating. "Oh, very well. But this has got to be dealt with. And it has to be tonight, or I will kill Logan."

"I do wish you would stop making outlandish threats," Donella said. "It's annoying. And nobody is forcing me—or Mr. Kendrick—to do anything tonight."

Now it was Logan's turn to feel frustrated. "Donella, your cousin may be an idiot most of the time—"

"That's rich, coming from you," Alec interrupted.

"But he's right about this," Logan continued. "We need to announce our betrothal as soon as possible."

Her chin went up again in that stubborn tilt. "I'm not doing anything until I've had time to consider it fully."

"That's the spirit," Edie said. "Let's just get you moderately presentable, and then we'll sneak you upstairs."

"No one is sneaking anywhere until this is resolved," Alec sternly said.

Edie rolled her eyes. "Would you *please* keep your blasted—"

"Laddie, are ye in there?" Angus called from outside the door. A moment later, he barreled into the room. "Nick is lookin' for ye, and . . . what the bloody hell is goin' on here?"

"Grandda, this is not a good time," Logan said. "Why don't you find Nick and ask him to meet me in the supper room? I'll be there in a few minutes."

Angus stomped across the room and halted in front of the chaise, his gaze flickering between Logan and Donella. His eyes grew wide as he took in her sagging bodice, wrinkled skirt, and messy hair.

"It's not as bad as it looks," she said, blushing so brightly, her freckles disappeared.

"So, this is what ye have been up to." Angus jabbed a finger at Logan's nose. "Shame on ye for goin' it about so shabbily. Yes, ye should be marryin' the good lass, but deflowerin' the Flower—"

Logan clamped a hand over his grandfather's mouth. "Shut up, Grandda."

The old man removed Logan's hand and grimaced an apology at Donella, who looked all but ready to faint.

Logan rather wished *he* could faint, or better yet disappear with Donella. This was probably the most embarrassing night of his life, and he'd had more than a few over the years.

"Sorry, lass," Angus said. "I dinna mean to embarrass ye, but I was that surprised to see ye so . . ."

"Fashed?" Edie suggested.

"Never ye fear, though," he earnestly added. "The lad will do the right thing, or I'll kill him myself."

"You'd have to line up," Logan said. "Of course I'm going to marry the girl. Now, will you please go find Nick and—"

"Uh-oh," Edie said. "Too late."

Logan turned to see his brother standing in the doorway, his expression slowly turning thunderous. Victoria, by his side, simply looked resigned.

"Logan, what is the meaning of this?"

The others could shout and bluster as much as they wanted, and Logan wouldn't give a damn other than how it affected Donella. But his brother's icy tone and stern expression had Logan cringing like a guilty schoolboy.

"It's not what it looks like, Nick."

Victoria crossed the room to join Donella and Edie. "If I had to venture a guess, I'd say it's exactly what it looks like." She shook her head at Logan. "Really, I am most disappointed in you."

"Feel free to join the club."

"I'll thank you to keep a civil tongue in your head, Logan," Nick said as he stalked into the room.

"It's just as much my fault as his," Donella said.

"I very much doubt that, Miss Haddon." Nick took in her state of disrepair and then directed another glare at Logan. *"Really?"*

Logan held up his hands. "She's not wrong, you know. We didn't come in here just to . . ."

"Snog?" Alec sarcastically finished.

"I'll thank *you* to keep a civil tongue in your head, Alasdair," Donella snapped. "Mr. Kendrick was about to say that we came in here to discuss an unfortunate scene that occurred in the supper room."

"It looks like ye got distracted," Angus commented.

"We did," Logan said. "It was my fault."

Donella shook her head. "No, it—"

"Lass, would you please let me explain?" Logan interrupted, exasperated. "We'll be here all night if I don't."

"It's going to take me all night to fix this dress and Donella's hair," Edie said as she once more yanked on the girl's sleeves. "You are a menace, Logan Kendrick. The dress is ruined."

"That's not the only thing that's ruined," Donella said morosely.

Logan briefly closed his eyes, feeling like an utter worm. He'd made a complete cock-up of everything, and his poor, sweet girl would suffer the consequences.

As would his attempts to woo her, if her scrambling retreat was any indication.

"Victoria, perhaps you can assist Eden," Nick said, "while Logan explains why, exactly, he felt the need to lure Miss Haddon into a very ill-advised private conversation."

Logan glared at his brother. "From what I heard, you had

more than a few ill-advised private conversations with your wife. While she was still a spinster, I might add."

"Point taken," Victoria said.

Edie smothered a chuckle. "It would appear that every man in this room is a reprobate. How shocking."

"Not me," said Angus in a pious tone.

"We are straying quite beyond the point," Nick said, looking massively annoyed.

"Aye, we are," Alec agreed. "Start talking, Kendrick, and it had better be good."

Logan glanced at Donella, now sitting on the chaise while Victoria tried to readjust her lopsided bandeau. She nodded her silent approval.

"It was about Donella's mother," Logan said. "About her current unfortunate situation."

Alec immediately went stiff as a plank. "My aunt's situation is no one's business."

"Tell that to the guests who were loudly gossiping that my mother was in a lunatic asylum," Donella countered. "They said I belonged in there with her."

Her stark statement knocked the room into momentary silence.

Predictably, Angus recovered first. "Yer mam's in a lunatic asylum?"

Logan jabbed him in the shoulder. "Of course she's not. And do not repeat that gossip."

His grandfather scowled. "I wouldna do that. I'm not a boob, ye ken."

Edie bent down to give Donella a hug. "I'm so sorry, dearest. It must have been incredibly distressing to hear such ugly talk."

Donella gave her a wan smile.

"Hell and damnation." Alec rubbed a frustrated hand over

his head. "I thought we'd scotched that sort of nonsense years ago."

"Apparently not," Logan said. "I might also add that you've done a piss-poor job of protecting Donella from gossip. You and your uncle have left her dangling in the damn wind, from what I can tell."

"Language, Mr. Kendrick," Donella said.

He smothered a smile. Even in the middle of a crisis, the almost-nun managed to scold him for cursing. It was perverse, but he loved that about her.

"That's bloody nonsense," Alec snapped. "And it's none of your damn business, anyway."

"Language, dear," Edie said in a mocking tone.

Alec shot her a disbelieving glance before switching his attention back to Logan. "May I remind you that Donella has been staying with the Kendrick family, under *their* protection? If you ask me, your family has been making a hash of it, especially after that incident in the sweet shop."

Angus bristled. "Now, see here—"

Nick held up a restraining hand. "While it's true that Miss Haddon is under my protection, I cannot be happy that Victoria and I know so little about her mother's situation. It obviously makes it difficult to manage any resulting gossip."

"Always holdin' it close to the vest, is Riddick." Angus sniffed. "Thinks he's better than the rest of us." Then he pointed at Alec. "As do ye, laddie. But let's not forget whose wife is the daughter of the Prince Regent, ye ken."

That helpful intervention had the expected result. The other men started arguing, with their wives trying to intervene.

For a few moments, Logan almost enjoyed the ridiculous scene. While Victoria was the illegitimate daughter of the Prince Regent, Alec was the illegitimate son of one of the Regent's younger brothers. And since Victoria's mother had been a barmaid and Alec's mother a countess, Logan figured it was debatable when it came to bragging rights.

Then again, Scots tended to take the finer points of family heritage rather seriously.

While the various parties were distracted by the argument, Donella tried to sneak away from the room. She was nearing the door when Logan reeled her back.

"None of that, lass." He dropped a kiss on her messy curls, barely held in place by the still-lopsided bandeau. "By the way, I like your hair."

She gave him a shove. "You're as ridiculous as the rest of them, and this entire episode is making my head ache."

He tipped up her chin and pressed a quick kiss to her lips. "We'll get it sorted, I promise."

"You, Kendrick," Alec barked. "No kissing until you're betrothed. Better yet, not until you're married."

Edie feigned surprise. "I don't believe we waited, dearest. Perhaps you can refresh my memory, if it's faulty."

Alec scowled. "Edie—"

Nick chopped down a hand. "Enough. This discussion has become absurd."

"Don't blame me," Alec retorted. "Angus started the whole damn thing."

"Now see here, laddie," Angus snapped. "Yer not too old—"

"What in heaven's name is happening in here?" interrupted a stern female voice.

Logan sighed at the sight of the woman in the doorway. "Just what we didn't need."

Lady Reese marched into the room. "You must cease this ridiculously loud argument. I could hear you from the other wing."

"Well timed as always, Mamma," Edie said. "Things were getting a bit out of hand."

Her ladyship eyed Donella and Logan. "Good God, not again."

"It's obviously a family trait," Edie said, trying not to laugh.

Lady Reese shook her head. "Really, Miss Haddon, I cannot believe it of you."

"Hang on," Logan protested. "It was my fault, not hers."

"That I can believe," her ladyship replied. "However, I know exactly what to do. We will sneak Donella up the servants' stairs, and tomorrow you will formally announce your betrothal."

"We most certainly will not," Donella said, choosing that moment to go stubborn again.

"Which part?" Victoria asked. "The sneaking upstairs or the betrothal?"

"Both."

"Pet, you look rather messy," Edie said. "You have to sneak upstairs."

"And Mr. Kendrick will certainly be proposing marriage," Lady Reese intoned. "Or Lord Riddick will have something to say about it."

"Dinna be threatenin' my grandson, ye daft *Sassenach*," Angus said. "Of course he'll be marryin' the lass."

Lady Reese bristled like a hedgehog. "Now, see here, Mr. whatever-your-name is, I will abide no Highland nonsense from you or anyone else." She gave a loud sniff. "Deranged, the whole lot of you."

"Mamma, that's not helpful," Edie said, jerking her head toward Donella.

"Miss Haddon knows I am not referring to her. After Lady Arnprior and myself, she is the most sensible person in this room. The men, however, are all idiots."

Angus stomped up to her. "What ye are is a stuck-up *Sassenach*—"

"Enough," Donella yelled.

Logan winced, since she was standing but a few inches away from him. The lass had a healthy pair of lungs.

"Lady Reese is correct," Donella said. "In fact, I'm so sensible that I'm leaving this deranged scene right now."

She stormed out of the room without a second glance at Logan or anyone else.

"Backstairs, dearest," Edie called, rushing after her.

"Oh, dear," Victoria said, following her.

Lady Reese inspected the rest of them with haughty regard. "Highlanders. Morons."

Then she, too, sailed from the room.

"That went well," Nick sardonically commented.

Angus stomped over and clapped Logan on the shoulder. "Best elope with the lassie tonight, ye ken. Dinna want to let her get away from ye."

"No elopements," Alec barked. "I won't have it."

Logan sighed. "I need a drink."

Chapter Twenty-Six

Donella helped Joseph down to the drive, murmuring her thanks to the groom who held open the carriage door.

"It was fun to stay overnight at Breadie Manor," the little boy said. "We had a Christmas party in the nursery."

"I wish I might have joined you. I'm sure it was jollier than our party."

Given the humiliating events of last night, there was little doubt of that.

True, there *had* been that enjoyable interlude with Logan. But having been discovered in the middle of it, probably the most embarrassing moment of her life, diminished any fond remembrance.

She'd put Logan in a terrible position, all but ensuring he'd have to marry her. The fact that he seemed fairly keen on the idea still puzzled and worried her. She suspected it had little to do with love.

And let's not forget the issue of Roddy and your—

"Hurry up, Donella," Joseph said as he tugged her toward the front portico. "Auntie Edie said there'd be leftover cakes and all sorts of good things for lunch today."

Since it was Boxing Day, most of the servants would have the day off. But there was plenty of food left over from the party, including a vast array of sweets.

Despite her personal disaster, the Christmas festivities had gone off without a hitch. That was one thing she could be proud of.

"Thank you for taking me to church today," Joseph added. "Papa and I went yesterday, but he always forgets the words to the carols."

Donella repressed a smile as they climbed the steps. "I was very happy to go with you."

She'd needed church this morning, given her atrocious conduct last night. A month ago, she'd been preparing to take her final vows as a nun. Now she was engaging in scandalous behavior with alarming regularity.

Perhaps you can take up highway robbery in your spare time.

Donella knew exactly who to blame. Logan Kendrick was temptation incarnate. Sadly, she had proven all too willing to be tempted.

"Grandpapa and Meme always used to take me to church in Halifax." He looked down at his feet. "I miss my grandfather."

Donella gave him a quick hug. "And I'm sure he misses you. But he's now with your mother, so you have two people in Heaven to watch over you all the time."

His brave little smile broke her heart. "Papa misses him too, but he says we should be happy that Mama has Grandpapa to keep her company." He paused. "I guess you don't have a mother, either."

Donella frowned. "Did someone tell you that?"

When his gaze slid sideways, she mentally sighed. "It's all right, Joseph. I promise I won't be upset."

He twisted his mouth into a pucker before answering her. "I heard two of the nursemaids talking. They said your mother got sick and had to go away. Did she die?"

Blast.

If even the servants had got wind of it, the gossip about Mamma must be more widespread than she'd realized.

"I'm very lucky that my mother is alive," she said. "But she's quite ill, so she had to go away and live with a special doctor."

He grimaced with childish sympathy. "I bet you miss her."

I miss who she used to be.

"I do."

"So it's like you don't have a mother, either."

"Fortunately, we both have nice families who take care of us. And *you* have a splendid papa who loves you very much."

Joseph rolled his eyes. Apparently, Papa was still in the doghouse. He was rather in Donella's doghouse, too.

After she rapped on the door, it swung open to reveal Angus.

"Er, good afternoon," she said, a bit flummoxed to see him. "Are you playing footman today?"

"Aye. Thought I'd spend the day here, seein' if anyone needed my help, ye ken." He gave her a broad wink.

She thought it best to ignore the implications of that wink.

Angus helped Joseph off with his coat. "Seems like ye were havin' quite the chat out there on the porch."

Donella removed her bonnet and gloves and placed them on a side table. "We were discussing some very deep thoughts."

"That sounds verra important."

"It was, Grandda," Joseph said in a serious voice. "Very important."

"That does sound interesting," rumbled a familiar voice. "Care to share those deep thoughts with me?"

Oh, God.

She was not ready to face Logan again. She might never be ready to face him.

Bracing herself, Donella forced a smile and turned to greet him. But the words died on her lips as he crossed the entrance hall to join them. Logan seemed entirely calm and collected, and very handsome in his dark blue tailcoat, form-fitting breeches, and tall boots.

Logan's eyes were normally a cool blue, like a mountain lake. But now they glittered with a knowing heat that sent blood rushing to her cheeks. Memories of last night flooded her mind, unnerving her.

Joseph came to her rescue.

"No, Papa. It was . . ." He wrinkled his brow as he struggled to find the right word. "Private. About our mothers."

If Logan was startled by that revelation, he didn't show it. "Then you must certainly keep it to yourselves. Private conversations are always to be respected."

Joseph rolled his eyes, his de facto response to his father these days. "I know, Papa. I'm not dumb."

Logan only slightly winced. "You are the opposite of dumb, laddie boy. You're the smartest one in the family."

"Aye, that's true," Angus said. "The rest of us are dummies, especially your da. Just ask Miss Donella."

"Thank you for that, Grandda," Logan said as his son giggled.

"I hope we're not too late for luncheon," Donella said, hoping to divert the discussion to safer channels. "Joseph assured me there would be cakes."

"Indeed there will be," said Eden as she emerged from the back hall. "Nick and Victoria stopped by for a visit, and I was just about to join them and my mother in the family dining room. Would you like to come along?"

Joseph gave a vigorous nod. "Yes, please. I like your mother. She's funny."

Eden grinned and held out her hand. "That's one way to describe her."

Joseph took her hand and started across the hall, before stopping to look over his shoulder. "Are you coming, Donella?"

"Actually, son," Logan said, "I need to have a word with her. We'll join you in a bit."

Donella held up both hands. "That's not necessary, sir. I don't want to keep you from your son. Or from luncheon."

"I'm not hungry."

"I am."

Logan narrowed his gaze. "We need to talk, lass."

"And Alec is waiting for you in the library, remember?"
Eden said.

Logan snorted. "How could I forget?"

Oh, drat and blast.

Now Alasdair was going all *lord-of-the-manor,* no doubt
gearing up for another scold—or dire threats if they didn't
fall into line.

Joseph frowned. "Papa, is something wrong?"

"Not a thing, son. Just go with Auntie Edie."

The boy suddenly brightened. "Are you going to ask
Donella to marry you?"

Donella shot Logan a warning glare that he ignored.

"Yes, Joseph. I am."

"Can you make sure she says yes?"

Donella's heart sank. Both their families were making it
all but impossible to say no—and she was finding she had
no desire to say no in the first place.

"I'll try my best," Logan said, throwing Donella a wry
glance.

"Try very hard, Papa," Joseph called back as Eden led
him from the hall.

Logan raised his eyebrows at Angus. "You can go with
them."

"Nae, lad. Someone has to look out for yer interests. That
Gilbride is a crafty one, ye ken. Not that we don't want ye
gettin' everythin' ye deserve, lass," he hastily said to Donella.
"But these marriage negotiations can be tricky."

"Good God," Logan muttered.

Donella shared the sentiment, but when Angus gallantly
offered his arm, she sighed and took it. Her erstwhile suitor
fell in behind.

As they trooped to the library, she had the unnerving

notion that she was being led to the gallows. But when she glanced over her shoulder at Logan, he gave her a wink and a reassuring smile.

"I won't let anyone pester you," he said.

She couldn't help but return his smile. Whatever else might happen, she knew he would always protect her. It was an incredibly comforting certainty.

"About time," Alasdair said as they entered the library.

Donella took one of the chairs in front of his desk. "Preparing to read us another lecture?"

"I've been working on it all morning."

"Very well, but I'm warning you. I am not in the best of moods."

"We're just going to have a sensible little chat, Donella. There was too much commotion last night for that, you must admit."

"Most of the commotion was caused by you."

Logan flashed her a grin as he took the other chair. "Speaking of that, why isn't my brother here to deliver his best *head-of-the-clan* speech, as he glowers like a bear with a sore paw?"

"Victoria decided we only needed one bear to glower," Alasdair said.

Logan snorted. "I give it ten minutes before he barges in here."

Angus, who'd dragged a padded bench over to join them, shook his head. "I told Nick I'd take care of everythin'."

"You mean you told him you'd *tell* him everything," Logan sarcastically replied.

"He is yer laird, laddie. He deserves to know."

Donella clenched her hands in her lap. "This is *so* embarrassing for me. I hope you all realize that."

Logan reached over and covered her hands. "I'm truly sorry for that, love. I would have spared you this silliness, if possible."

Angus scowled. "And if ye hadn't been dallyin' with her last night, ye would have."

"Can we please not rehash last night's events?" Donella asked. "Once was quite enough."

Alasdair gave her a sympathetic grimace. "I hate to pile on, but we do need a plan. There's already too much gossip making the rounds, and it's damaging your reputation."

"I don't give a hang about my stupid reputation."

"I do," Logan said. "And I won't have you hurt by my actions, Donella."

She yanked her hands out from under his. "So, that's what this marriage proposal is truly about? Your wounded honor?"

Logan recaptured one of her hands. "You know it's not, daft girl. But the honor of both our families is a consideration we can't ignore."

"He's right, Donella," Alasdair said. "There's a general expectation about the two of you, now that Logan has made his intentions quite clear."

"With one notable lapse," she couldn't help adding.

Logan looked a trifle annoyed. "And could we not rehash *that* incident, please?"

She gave him a sweet smile. "Sorry. It just slipped out."

"Ye canna be blamed for being annoyed, lass," Angus said. "Logan was a chowderhead that night."

"Indeed," Alasdair dryly agreed. "Which simply reinforces my point. Donella cannot be subjected to gossip about the sincerity of Logan's intentions."

"And what about *my* intentions?" she asked. "Does that merit any discussion, or am I expected to meekly sit here while you men decide what happens to my life? What happened to not letting anyone pester me?"

Both Logan and Alasdair had the grace to look embarrassed.

Angus, however, gave her an approving grin. "That's the spirit, lass. Dinna let them push ye aboot."

"I didn't mean to cut you out of the discussion," Logan regretfully said, "and I'm sure Alec didn't, either. What *you* want means more to me than anything else."

Her ire subsided a bit. "Thank you." She glanced at her cousin. "And you?"

"I want you to be happy, Cousin," he said gently. "I always have, which I think you know."

"I do know that, but I rather feel like I've lost control of the circumstances." Starting with the day she'd been kicked out of the convent.

"That's because the circumstances are running ahead of us," Alasdair said. "Last night was a perfect example, apart from the gossip about you and your mother. From what Edie tells me, some of the servants caught a glimpse of you after you, er, left the library."

Stormed out, more like it, and she'd promptly run into a footman and then two housemaids. To say she hadn't been looking her best was an understatement.

"Och, that's nae good," Angus said. "Servants love to gossip."

"As do other people whose names I will refrain from mentioning," Logan commented.

Angus curled a lip but didn't deny the accusation.

"Donella, I will support whatever decision you make," Alasdair said. "That includes joining a convent, if that's what you truly want."

"Now, hang on—" Logan indignantly started.

Alasdair held up a hand to interrupt. "But you need to think about the rest of us when making that decision—not just our family, but Logan and the Kendricks, too." He leaned forward, earnestly meeting her gaze. "We all love you, lass, every last one of us. And we *all* want you in our life. You're not an outsider, no matter what you might think. You're one of us."

For so long, the bonds of family obligation had chained

her and Alasdair together—the ones neither had ever asked for, and the ones that had generated friction and resentment. Now, she saw love and loyalty in him, the kind that family gave family, without question.

Logan took her other hand and turned her to face him.

"Donella, if your true desire is to join a convent, *I* will cease pestering you," he said in a somber tone. "But you need to tell me straight out."

She rolled her lips inward, holding back words that longed to burst forth. Words like *I love you, but there are things you should know about me*.

"Love, you can tell me anything, and I will never judge you." Logan shook his head. "As if I have the right to judge anyone, much less the kind, bonny lass you are."

Oh, Lord, he was making her feel like a guilty, miserable coward. She could live with the guilt. But feeling like a coward, afraid to live her own life? No.

"I do not want to enter a convent," she said. "I want to stay here, with all of you."

"Including me, I'm assuming," Logan said.

While he didn't voice it as a question, she caught the uncertainty.

Donella squeezed his hands. "Yes. It just happened so fast, it's rather unnerving."

His smile was lopsided. "Believe me, I understand. This wasn't anything I was looking for or expected to find, either."

"Laddie, yer supposed to be wooin' the lass," Angus said, "not scarin' her off."

Alasdair snorted. "Excellent point."

Logan scowled at them. "We could do without the bloody audience."

Donella glared at her cousin. "And I won't have him forced into marrying me, despite what you lot say."

"Tell that to Riddick," Alasdair replied. "I imagine he won't be too thrilled to hear about any of this."

"Then don't tell him."

"Och," Angus said. "It's bound to get back to Lord Riddick, sooner or later."

"I don't care about that. What I do care about is Logan being forced into something he doesn't want to do."

"He'll do exactly what's expected of him," Alasdair sternly said.

"This is getting ridiculous," Donella said. "Again."

When she started to stand, Logan pulled her back down. "Ignore them, love. They're idiots, and nobody is forcing me to do anything."

Donella stared into his eyes, trying to quell the anxiety swirling inside. "Are you absolutely sure?"

His blue gaze was now as warm as a summer sky. "Of course. Do you honestly think either of our families could force me to do anything I didn't want to do?"

"Well . . ."

"I am absolutely sure I want to marry you, Donella. Word of a Kendrick and a Highlander."

Emotion forced its way up her throat, blocking her words.

Logan pressed a kiss to the back of her hand. "I can think of nothing I'd rather do more than protect you and care for you," he added.

Donella managed a wobbly smile. Though she was quite capable of taking care of herself, she did appreciate the sentiment.

"Well, ye canna get a better promise than that, can ye, lass?" Angus hauled himself up and clapped Logan's shoulder. "Well done, laddie boy. Ye've captured the Flower of Clan Graham, when all those other jinglebrains failed."

"Including me," Alasdair said with a grin.

"My thanks to both of you for ruining the moment," Logan dryly said.

"Och, it's a grand moment, and I'm that happy to share it with ye."

It was so absurd that Donella had to giggle, mostly from relief. Logan's assurance that he did truly want to marry her was . . . amazing.

Angus rubbed his hands. "And now we'll get to the guid part. Ye children can leave the room while the Master of Riddick and I discuss the marriage settlements."

Donella had to repress another laugh at Alasdair's alarmed expression. He rarely referred to himself by his Scottish title and likely didn't relish the idea of negotiating anything with Angus.

"Grandda, I'm several years older than Alec, ye ken," Logan said. "And you won't be negotiating anything for me."

"But—"

"No buts. The only thing we need to decide now is when to announce our betrothal." Logan glanced at Donella, seeking her opinion.

"I'd like a few days to get used to it," she said. "Just keep it among family for now, if you don't mind."

"Of course, sweetheart."

"We could announce it at the Hogmanay Ball," Alasdair suggested. "Half of Glasgow always shows up, so we can get it over with all at once. A bit of fussing and then you're done."

Donella grimaced at the notion of so much public attention, but her cousin's suggestion made sense. "Very well."

Logan gave her an encouraging smile. "It would mean we'd only have to listen to people being idiots for one night, and then we can ignore them."

Alasdair pushed back from his desk. "Excellent, so let's go tell the others. We can work out the details later."

Logan raised a hand. "One more thing, Alec. This situation with the Murray family has to be dealt with. I won't have Donella fearing for her safety."

Startled, she exchanged a glance with her cousin.

"Don't think I didn't catch that," Logan said. "It's time you tell me what's going on."

"We're taking care of it," Alasdair said.

Logan stood and placed a hand on the desk. "It's up to me to protect Donella, and I can't properly do that until I know the reason why the Murrays are acting like such addlepated fools."

"It's clan business," Alasdair said.

"Sorry, but that won't wash."

When the two men commenced a hostile staring contest, Donella knew she had to explain at least some of it.

"Logan, it's because Roddy Murray wished to marry me. Naturally, my uncle refused him. Mungo Murray took that as a great insult, one he has apparently not forgotten."

Logan looked puzzled. "But you were betrothed to Alec at the time. How could Murray possibly be insulted?"

"Because the Murrays are idiots," Alasdair said.

"Aye, Mungo and his kin were always a few cards short of a full deck," Angus added. "Especially poor Roddy."

To forestall Logan arguing, Donella laid a hand on his arm. "Once our betrothal is announced, the Murrays will have to give it up."

He shook his head. "I still don't like it, and it makes no bloody sense."

It would make perfect sense if he knew all the details, which she fervently hoped he never would. "It's simply a bit of old history and means nothing."

"Donella is right," Alasdair said. "Mungo is a bitter old man who hates my grandfather, but the Murrays have been warned off. Besides, even they wouldn't be so foolish as to take on both the Arnprior and Riddick families."

Donella patted Logan's arm. "It'll be fine, I promise."

His mouth twitched. "All right, I'll give it up for now, but at the first sign of trouble . . ."

"You can have at it," Alasdair said.

Donella's stomach curdled at the thought of having to face more trouble from the Murrays, but she did her best to maintain an untroubled expression.

Alasdair stood and came around the desk. "Congratulations, lass." He pulled Donella to her feet and hugged her. "No one deserves happiness more than you do. Edie and I are thrilled for you."

She hugged him back, her emotions too jumbled for a coherent reply.

"And best wishes, old man," he said to Logan. "Make Donella happy, or I'll flay you alive."

"Thank you for so graciously welcoming me into the family," Logan replied.

"Let's join the others," Angus said, "and drink a wee toast to the happy couple."

Logan shot a glance at Donella. "You go ahead. We'll be along shortly."

"You two behave yourselves," Alasdair said as he walked out with Angus. "No repeats of last night."

Donella sank back into her chair. "Well, that was all very embarrassing."

"It's certainly not how I intended to propose." He leaned against the desk, crossing his arms as he regarded her.

"What are you thinking about?" she asked.

"I have to ask what's truly bothering you, lass."

The Murrays, for one. Under the slew of her other problems, she'd let that one slip into the background. Yet trouble from Mungo was not just possible but quite likely.

"It's all just happened so quickly," she said, which had the benefit of being the truth. "It's hard to absorb."

"I wish there was another way, but Alec's correct. We need to get ahead of the gossip. *All* the gossip." He suddenly flashed an extraordinarily wicked grin. "And after what happened between us last night? Lass, I'd haul you off to the nearest blacksmith and marry you right now, if I could."

Donella had to admit that his rather outrageous suggestion held a great deal of appeal—as did the idea of being intimate with him. Clearly, she was a sad case when it came to Logan Kendrick.

"My family would kill you, I'm afraid." She wrinkled her nose. "Uncle Riddick will want a big clan wedding with all the trappings."

Since she'd never enjoyed being the center of attention, that prospect made her even more nervous. Aside from all the unpleasant bother, there were simply too many chances for things to go wrong.

"Part of me truly does wish we could run out and get it over with right now," she blurted out. "Before anything else happens."

He frowned. "What do you think might happen?"

She ducked her head for a moment, wishing she could put her tangled emotions into words. "I . . . oh, nothing. I'm just being silly. I'm sorry."

He continued his nerve-wracking study of her for another long moment before giving a decisive nod. "Are you hungry?"

"Not after this discussion."

"Good, because I think you need some fresh air."

"It's not exactly balmy out, you know."

He pulled her to her feet. "Nonsense. It'll do us both good."

"But everyone's waiting for us," she weakly protested.

"An even better reason to escape, don't you think?"

When she didn't even bother to deny his assertion, Logan grinned. "Come along, my bonny lass. Let's go for a drive."

Chapter Twenty-Seven

Donella paced her bedroom, occasionally stopping to strain her ears. Breadie Manor had fallen silent, everyone safely abed.

She should also be sleeping, given the stresses of the day. If one more family member insisted on discussing wedding plans, or trousseaus, or betrothal parties, she might have to resort to an uncharacteristic bout of hysterics.

Then there was Logan. The prospect of his imminent arrival had twisted her nerves into a bundle of knots.

After the maid had helped her change into her night-clothes and banked the fire, Donella had made a show of crawling into bed. As soon as the girl left the room, she'd leapt up, straightened the bed linens and plumped up the pillows, before stashing away the undergarments hanging over the dressing screen.

God forbid Logan Kendrick should see her stays or stockings. After everything she'd gone through these last several weeks, it was a miracle she could still be embarrassed by something as trivial as that.

She stopped in front of the hob grate, shaking her head in disbelief. Here she was, waiting for a man to sneak into her bedroom. She'd argued against it on the way back to Breadie

Manor this afternoon, but Logan had been gently persuasive and she'd eventually and all-too-easily given in.

Annoyed ever since at her disgraceful lack of self-discipline, she took the poker and jabbed at the banked coals. They sullenly smoldered, like her.

Replacing the poker, she drew her wrapper around her body, fighting a shiver. If Logan didn't appear soon, she would lock the door, crawl into bed, and try to forget that the past month had ever existed.

When she heard a noise in the corridor, she tiptoed to the door and pressed her ear against the oak panels.

Nothing.

How in heaven's name *was* he going to sneak in? Maybe he'd already tried and been stymied in his attempts. If she had any brains, she should hope that meant he'd given up.

She didn't.

Resuming her pacing, she vowed to give Logan five more minutes and then mentally send him straight to Hades.

When she passed by the pier glass, she stopped to check her appearance. In her plain lawn nightrail and thick flannel wrapper, she was hardly a temptress. She'd forgone the nightcap, at least, but her short curls could only be described as boyish. Any man in his right mind would find her lacking in feminine enticements, particularly when compared to a woman like Jeannie MacArthur.

But he picked you, didn't he?

Even more amazing, was that she had picked him. She'd never imagined marriage, and certainly not to a man like Logan. Brawny, arrogant men set her teeth on edge and generally made her nervous.

Logan did make her nervous, but for entirely unexpected reasons. She was madly in love with the blasted man. And she was so eager to be with him that she couldn't wait even a month for a proper wedding night.

When the Sevres clock on the mahogany chest softly chimed out the late hour, Donella decided to give up.

"And you should be happy he didn't come," she muttered to her reflection, "instead of wanting to bash the man over the head for not showing up."

She blew out the candle on her dressing table and crossed to the bed. But as she started to shed her wrapper, a thumping noise froze her to the spot.

Was it coming from the window?

That was ridiculous. Her room was two stories above the ground floor, over the terrace. Even Logan wouldn't be able to—

A firm rap told her it was definitely coming from the window.

Donella rushed over and pulled aside the heavy drapery. Logan was standing on the narrow ledge outside her window, as if it was the most normal thing in the world.

After a short struggle, she managed to shove up the sash.

"Took you long enough," he said.

"What are you doing?" she hissed.

He hunched down and kissed the tip of her nose. "What does it look like, daft girl?"

She grabbed the collar of his coat and began to drag him over the sill. "Are you insane? It's a two-story climb up to this window."

He swung down to the floor with his usual grace, extraordinary in a man his size.

Logan pulled her away from the window and shut it. "You'll catch your death, lass. It's a wee bit nippy out there."

After stripping off his leather gloves, he shrugged out of his greatcoat and tossed it on a nearby chair. He'd forgone a tailcoat—apparently not necessary when climbing large buildings—but wore a fine linen shirt and a bottle-green silk and wool vest. His cravat was impeccably tied, his breeches were perfectly tailored, and his boots showed nary a speck of dirt. He looked like he'd been spending the evening by the fireside, instead of scaling walls in the dead of night.

At the end of December, no less.

She jabbed him in the chest. "You are a lunatic. You could have easily fallen and splattered your brains all over the back terrace, leaving me to explain everything to our families."

Logan captured her face and pressed a lingering kiss to her mouth. Donella had to resist the urge to snuggle closer, because he should *not* be rewarded for his stupidity.

"Och, no chance of that," he murmured. "There were plenty of footholds on the way up."

She managed to insert both hands onto his chest and wriggled some space between them. "You had no way of knowing that until you started climbing. What if there were no footholds, or something came loose?"

"I made a quick check this afternoon before I took Joseph back to Kendrick House." He flashed a grin. "And it wouldn't be the first wall I've had to climb."

She pulled out of his loose embrace. "Ah, so you have done this sort of thing before. How typical."

"I've certainly climbed walls before, but never to reach a lady's bedroom. I can promise you that."

She eyed him suspiciously.

"Word of a Kendrick, love. You're my first." His gaze slowly heated as it tracked over her. "And I'm *your* first."

She battled down nerves that threatened to get the best of her. "I've certainly never had a man climb through my window before. Not that anyone showed such an inclination," she added for clarification.

"The idiots didn't know what they were missing." His gaze lingered on her breasts, and a smile best described as wolfish curved up his mouth.

Donella rolled her eyes. "Logan, I'm wearing a flannel

wrapper. In an altogether hideous print, in case you failed to notice."

Sadly, she didn't have another wrapper. She'd toyed with the notion of borrowing one of Eden's, since she owned several frilly, feminine robes in lovely materials. That, however, would have appeared decidedly suspicious.

"I did fail to notice that. Possibly because you look splendid in everything."

"Even in those dreadful boy's clothes?"

"Especially in them. Your sweet little rump looked altogether delectable in breeches. I think I might buy you a pair to wear in the bedroom."

"And that is an altogether improper thing to say." Better to scold him than to blush and flutter about like a silly schoolgirl.

He waggled his brows. "Under the circumstances, it's exactly the right thing to say."

"You are utterly hopeless."

"And you are shivering." He cast a frowning glance at the hob. "Why is the fire banked? You must be freezing."

"I didn't want to rouse any suspicions."

"Donella, you're not in the convent anymore. You can have the servants pile on as much coal as you like and stay up as late as you like."

She sighed. "I'm being a ninny, aren't I?"

"Not at all. Why don't you hop into bed while I warm the room up?" His smile was so kind and loving that the anxious knot in her belly began to untwist.

As he tended to the fire, she pulled back the bedclothes on the four-poster bed. She started to untie her wrapper but paused. "Do you mind if I keep my wrapper on?"

He shot her a surprised glance over his shoulder. "Sweetheart, you should do whatever makes you feel comfortable."

"It's just that it's all a bit strange."

"I know, but we agreed we simply wanted to spend time together. We won't do anything you don't wish to do, all right?"

She nodded.

"Good lass. Now, get into bed, while I take care of the fire."

Donella resisted the temptation to burrow under the covers, instead plumping the pillows so she could sit upright and watch him.

"Is your door locked?" he asked as he stirred the coals.

"No, because I thought you'd be arriving that way. Like a normal person."

"Nothing normal or mundane about us, love." Logan finished with the fire and went to lock the door.

"You'll have to leave before daylight," Donella warned. "The housemaid will be suspicious if my door is locked. And you're much too big to hide under the bed."

He strolled over and propped a brawny shoulder against the bedpost. "A bit nervous, lass?"

She raised an incredulous eyebrow.

"It's understandable," he said with a lopsided smile. "I confess to feeling the same way."

"I have never once seen you nervous, even when we were attacked on the Perth Bridge."

"Och, that wasn't nearly as nerve-wracking as tonight."

Donella scowled. "You shouldn't tease, you know. I already feel like a henwit."

He came around to her side of the bed. "May I sit?"

She scooted over to make room for him.

Logan took her hand, lacing their fingers together. "On top of everything else, I'm guessing my reputation might be making you apprehensive."

"You mean your reputation as a rake," she softly replied.

He nodded. "I know I've made some blunders in these last weeks that may have . . . reinforced that impression."

He meant his interactions with Jeannie MacArthur, of

course. Since she had no intention of even saying that woman's name, she simply nodded.

"What people say about me might have been true long ago," he said. "But remember I'm now a widower who loved his wife and grieved for a long time after her death. I would never wish to dishonor her memory or act in any way that would embarrass my son or family. My stupid, selfish behavior is in the past, Donella. I promise you that."

Her heart ached for him and all the sorrows he'd suffered. And for how hard he'd tried to make up for his youthful mistakes.

"Anyone who knows you understands that you're a good man." She squeezed his hand. "And I also know how much you loved your wife. And how much you miss her."

It seemed rather selfish of her, but Donella could only hope he would love her as much someday.

"I did miss her, for a very long time," he quietly replied. "But then I met you."

She saw the stark honesty in his gaze, and the breath caught in her throat. "I'm glad, because I want you to be happy."

"I'm happy when I'm with you," he gruffly replied. "But, like you, I'm dealing with a new feeling. Hence, my inclination toward a wee bit of hysterics, myself."

Donella choked out a laugh. "I have some smelling salts in my dressing table. Do you want me to fetch them?"

"I do feel a swoon coming on. But if I lie down for a bit, I will surely recover myself."

"That is a very transparent excuse for getting into my bed, sir," she severely replied.

"Is it working?"

"Better than you know."

He chuckled before starting to yank off his boots.

Donella settled back and watched him. "This reminds

me of that night in the inn, when I was in bed and you were getting undressed. I was mortified by the entire situation."

"There were occasional comical elements, though. I recall a great deal of talk about chamber pots."

She groaned. "Please, I've been trying to forget."

He dropped the first boot to the floor. "And there was Hamish, who thought you needed a wee paddle to get you in line."

"You were a great deal too amused by that suggestion, sir."

He wrestled with his other boot but finally got it off, then stood to unbutton his vest. "You responded by threatening to murder me if I came near you."

She scrunched up her nose. "I suppose I did overreact a bit."

"I was a brute to tease you, but you made an utterly adorable urchin. It was a wonder I was able to keep my hands to myself."

"I believe you didn't keep them to yourself the following night."

He tossed his vest on top of his coat. "You can hardly blame me, since I was asleep at the time. Until I was rudely awakened from that very pleasant slumber."

"I was afraid Alasdair was going to murder you."

"And I was afraid *you* were going to murder him."

She let out a reluctant chuckle. "He can be very irritating, but I shouldn't complain. My family has always been protective of me."

"And rightly so, but now it's my job to protect you."

When he began to unbutton the fall of his breeches, Donella's heart stuttered.

"I'm quite good at protecting myself," she said as pertly as she could manage, trying to compensate for her nervous reaction.

Logan's breeches followed his other clothes onto the chair. Thankfully, he wore linen smalls and his shirt hung down to his thighs, sparing her blushes for the moment.

When he snuffed the candles on her bedside table, shadows drenched the room. Outlined by the uneven light of the flickering fire, he was a large, masculine presence looming over her.

"I've never met a braver woman," he said in a husky tone. "It's a miracle I didn't carry you off myself, when I had the chance."

Donella took his hand and held it to her cheek. "At the time, part of me wished you had."

"I've got ye now, lass, and I'll nae be lettin' ye go."

His low, rough brogue made her shiver. Donella had to resist the impulse to pull him down to the bed and kiss him with a mad passion. She'd never felt like this in her life, and it was both wonderful and terrifying. Life without Logan now seemed utterly inconceivable, and that made her vulnerable in ways she was only starting to realize.

"I'm happy to hear that," she managed.

Logan braced his hands on either side of her, his face inches from hers. "Almost from the moment I met you, I wanted you, Donella."

She wrinkled her nose. "But I was quite awful to you."

"That was part of your charm. And it did take me a wee bit of time to recognize what was happening between us. After all, you were going to hike off to another convent. That would have been a rather formidable obstacle to romance."

"You rather frightened me at the time," she confessed. "You made me feel things. I thought I needed to keep you at a distance."

"It worked," he wryly replied.

"Sorry."

"Don't apologize, love."

He kissed her—a slow, lingering seduction she felt down to her very bones. She clutched at his shoulders, whimpering with pleasure.

By the time he finished demolishing her self-control, Donella was almost flat on her back, and she'd pulled him halfway on top of her.

Logan kissed the tip of her nose. "Do you think I might get in bed with you now?"

She let out a sheepish laugh. "I think you'd better. And you can take off your shirt, if you like," she added shyly as she moved to give him room.

"Are you sure?"

"Yes. I'm ready to take off my wrapper, too. I'm feeling quite warm."

"It is rather toasty, now that the fire's going."

She innocently widened her eyes. "Is that what it is?"

He grinned, then pulled his shirt over his head and tossed it in the general direction of the chair.

Goodness.

After wriggling out of her wrapper, she paused to stare at him. His shoulders were massive, and his chest, covered in dark hair, was nothing short of magnificent. The brawny muscles tapered down to a flat stomach and narrow hips, exposed at the tops of his smalls.

As for what lay beneath those smalls, well, that simply made her mouth as dry as a desert.

He glanced down and winced. "It's not as bad as it looks."

She swallowed. "It looks quite big to me."

"And if you keep looking at me like that, it's going to get even bigger," he replied in a gruff tone.

His absurd response made her laugh. "Then you'd best get in bed immediately."

Logan slipped under the covers and settled her on his chest. Donella sighed and snuggled close, enjoying the tickle of crisp hair under her cheek. Everything about him was so intensely masculine and so different from anything she'd ever wanted from her life.

"All right, lass?"

"A bit anxious, perhaps." Not simply because of him and what they would do together this night, but also because—

Don't think about it.

He gently massaged her shoulder. "No need to rush. We can talk, if you like."

"About what?"

"My family, for one thing. You've made them very happy, especially Joseph." When he chuckled, his pleasure vibrated through her body. "I thought the wee lad would burst. I don't think I've ever seen him so excited."

She briefly turned her face into his chest, smiling at the memory.

After the momentous discussion in the library this afternoon, Logan had whisked her from the house without giving her the chance to see anyone. Their drive had been intended to give her a chance to settle her nerves. In that respect, it had been something of a failure.

When they finally returned to Breadie Manor, their families had rushed out of the house, offering up congratulations and hugs. The men thumped Logan on the back and jested about stealing Donella away like a Highland brigand.

Joseph had initially hung back under the portico, obviously overcome by all the fuss. Only when Donella turned to him, too nervous to do anything but give him a hopeful smile, had he reacted. The lad had then raced across the drive and thrown his arms around her waist, hugging her fiercely. When Logan joined them, bending down to talk to his son, Joseph had flung his arms around his father's neck and promptly burst into tears.

Donella had shed more than a few tears herself, as had Victoria and even Angus. Eden, however, had come to their rescue, herding them inside for a splendid Boxing Day luncheon. Glasses had been raised and toasts exchanged, each more extravagant and ridiculous than the next. Joseph had spent most of the meal on his father's lap, alternately beaming at Donella and stuffing his face with cakes.

Seeing the boy so happy had been one of the best moments of her life.

She rested her chin on Logan's chest so she could study his face. "And what about you, sir? Are you happy?"

"Very, although there's one thing that would make me even happier."

"Which is?"

"The chance to kiss you."

He rolled her onto her back. With one arm cradled beneath her neck, he softly brushed his lips over hers. "In fact, I'd like to kiss you from top to bottom, ending with your wee toes."

She crinkled her forehead. "Why would you want to kiss my toes?"

"I've seen them, remember? They're quite delightful."

Donella couldn't help but laugh as she slid her hands to his shoulders. "That sounds exceedingly interesting, but won't my nightrail get in the way?"

His gaze all but scorched her. "Perhaps you're ready to remove it now?"

She began to think she'd been getting ready for Logan for a long time. Ready to be with a man who wanted her as much as she wanted him. "I believe so."

His eyes glittered like gems. Then he took her lips in a soul-searing kiss she would never forget.

As his mouth caressed her, searching and passionate, his hands began to wander. He shifted to his side, still cradling her but free to explore while melting her with his devastating kisses. She closed her eyes and retreated into the warm, velvet darkness. All that existed was his touch and the feelings it evoked.

His hand skimmed lower, lingering to stroke and tease her nipples into tight points. When Donella moaned, he sucked her tongue into his mouth, drawing deep. Sensation stormed through her, and that most intimate part of her ached for the claiming that would make her forever and only his.

His skillful hands moved lower, stroking over her belly to briefly rest between her legs. When he rubbed her through the linen fabric covering that hidden place, her thoughts scattered like fog in a howling wind. His hands, his touch, his strong body arching over hers—it was all she needed in the moment—and then another moment, and then another, stretching into a lifetime of wonderful moments with him.

"Open your eyes, darling." His voice was a husky rumble.

It was too lovely in the dark, with just his hands and her body. "Don't want to."

He licked her lower lip before giving it a wee nip.

Donella's eyelids snapped open. "Ouch."

"That did not hurt."

"Maybe a little," she grumbled.

"Not even a little."

He was right. In fact, it had been rather . . . stimulating.

"My eyes are open," she said. "Now what?"

"Are you truly ready to take off your clothing?" His smile was lopsided and teasing. "You certainly feel ready."

Her throat went tight. He was always so careful to put her first, even as she felt the rampant press of his desire nudging against her leg. His own need had turned every muscle in his body as hard as stone, and yet he still waited patiently on her.

With Logan, Donella never felt stupid or lacking. She felt cherished, as if her every need was as important to him as it was to her.

She smiled up at him, love making her brave. "I'm ready for everything."

He blew out a sharp breath. "Thank God, because you are absolutely killing me, lass."

As he helped her wriggle her nightrail upward, he followed its path with a trail of leisurely kisses.

"What are you doing?" she asked when he lingered over her hipbone.

"I'm kissing your freckles," he murmured.

She choked out a laugh. "That's ridiculous."

"I love your freckles. It's like a celestial baker sprinkled you with cinnamon."

"Since I have a lot of them, this could take all night."

He glanced up with a grin that was all male and all him. "And is that a bad thing?"

She blinked. The notion of being the object of Logan's amorous attentions for an *entire* night sounded . . . wonderful.

"Carry on, sir."

His soft chuckle vibrated against her skin.

He slowly made his way upward, kissing and licking as he drew the gown up to her shoulders. When he reached her breasts, he stayed for long minutes, gently sucking on her until her nipples were a bright pink, stiff and aching against his tongue.

Then he did something especially wicked with that tongue, and she moaned and arched her back, grabbing fist-fuls of his hair.

Logan raised his head, his eyes gleaming with laughter. "You'll make me bald, love."

"Sorry." She gasped for breath. "But if you keep that up, I might *not* make it through the rest of the night." Donella was beginning to wonder if one could actually die from ecstasy.

"That would indeed be a shocking turn of events."

He eased the garment over her head, and finally she lay naked before him, the bed linens bunched low around her hips. For long, intent moments, Logan studied her body.

Anxiety threaded its tendrils through her sensual daze. "Is everything all right?"

His blue eyes appeared dark as pitch in the dim, flickering firelight. "More right than I can explain, lass."

Logan swooped down and took her lips, his kiss so ravenous it made her dizzy. He pleasured her mouth the way he'd pleasured her body only moments ago. She clung to him, kissing him back with an abandon she'd never thought possible. He'd opened a gate within, and all the love, all the longing for something *more* that she'd repressed for so long came spilling out.

When he pulled back, she blinked open her eyelids, trying to focus through the haze of emotion and sensuality. Like her, he was breathing hard, and a faint sheen of perspiration glistened like polished bronze on his skin.

"I *am* going to kiss ye from head to toe, lassie," he rumbled. "So if ye have any objections, now's the time to say it."

She had to clear her throat before answering with an imitation of his brogue. "Nae, I canna think of a one."

His almost feral grin suggested he might eat her right up. And as he made a sensual tour of her body, he rather did. Logan feasted on her, his lips, tongue, and even his teeth driving her into a quiet frenzy.

When he reached that delicate place between her thighs, he slowed even more, his mouth nudging through the silky nest of hair while his fingers gently opened her. Donella slapped a hand over her lips to muffle a cry, arching up as an astounding, delicious sensation rippled out from her womb.

"Och, that's my beauty," he growled.

When he started to shift down, she grabbed his shoulders. He glanced up and their gazes locked.

"Now, please," she whispered.

"Sure, lass?" he whispered back.

"Entirely sure."

His eyes warmed with tenderness, and he kissed the tops of her thighs before gently spreading her legs wide. Then he moved between them, covering her with his body. He was huge and muscled and somewhat intimidating—but he was hers, and she was about to become his.

She couldn't wait.

Logan took his time, sliding the broad head of his erection back and forth against her delicate sex. All the while, he lavished her mouth with languid kisses. Donella wrapped herself around him, tilting her hips to increase the luxurious pressure.

It was so different from that first and only time, a foolish and awkward encounter in a musty old barn. She'd wanted to tell Logan about it, to confess the secret that had weighed on her for years. Her pent-up anger and defiance, and the feeling that she'd never be worthy of love, had fueled that long-ago night.

But he was proving her wrong. Held in his loving embrace, her shameful secret now belonged to a distant past that no longer even seemed real. *This* was real, what she had with Logan. He made her feel different, as if what they shared was a sacred act.

Let the past stay in the past, where it can do no more harm.

He drew back so he could see her face. "Ready, love?"

The growl made every muscle in her body tremble in response. Donella drew her legs up and wrapped them around his backside, opening herself to him even more. Logan's eyes flared with surprise, then burned with a scorching heat.

She gave him a misty smile, too emotional to speak.

He groaned as he slid into her. His big body shook in her arms as he tried to enter slowly, holding himself in check.

And he *was* big, and it had been years. Donella forced herself to relax against the insistent pressure.

Then he flexed his hips and was all the way in, so close that she could feel the beat of his heart in every part of her body.

And now she let the tears fall. "Oh, Logan."

He tenderly brushed her hair from her face. "Och, lass. Is it all right?"

"It's perfect. You're perfect."

"We're perfect."

He moved inside her, slow and steady, building her desire into a glittering spiral. Donella wanted to make it last, to keep him inside her all night, but soon she was cresting, sensation gathering like a fast, rippling tide.

She cried out as the wave broke.

Logan swallowed the cry with an urgent, devouring kiss. He moved in deep, long thrusts, driving hard. As she shivered through her climax, he slipped a hand under her bottom and tilted her up. Donella gasped as she clenched around his thick erection, sending out a second wave of delicious contractions.

He pressed his face into her shoulder and poured himself into her, his climax intense and beautiful because he had surrendered to her, as she had to him. It was incredible and overwhelming, and Donella knew instantly that she'd tumbled into a life she'd never been able to envision before.

A life that now truly felt like a blessing.

After several moments, Logan breathed out a heavy sigh and carefully pulled out. He rolled onto his back, taking her with him. She sprawled on his chest, which rose and fell like a bellows. They both lay like that for some time, catching their breaths and letting the air dry the perspiration slicking their bodies.

Finally, Logan untangled the rumpled bedclothes and pulled them up to cover them. He craned his neck to plant a kiss on her forehead.

"All right, love?"

She rubbed her cheek against his chest and smiled. Then she daringly licked his nipple—which caused him to twitch—and lifted her head to meet his gaze.

"More than all right. In fact, I think what just happened was rather a miracle."

He let his head drop to the pillow. "I think we were both rather due for one, don't you?"

She did. Donella had been looking for signs of miracles all her life. It would seem she'd finally found one.

They rested for a while, Logan's hand languidly stroking down her spine. She was fine with the silence. Neither of them was the sort to spill out their emotions in speech. For her, their bodies had said all that needed to be said.

At least for now.

She frowned, mentally pushing back against that pestering secret. She wanted no part of it, especially not now.

His hand stilled on the swell of her bottom. "Something wrong?"

Drat.

The man was too perceptive for his own good. "As a matter of fact, there is."

"Tell me, and I'll make it better."

She lifted up to look at him. "You never made it down to my toes."

His grin flashed like a beacon. Before she could catch her breath, he'd flipped her onto her back.

"Then let me correct that unfortunate omission right now."

Donella choked out a laugh, stunned as the large erection nudging her belly made clear how ready he was for more.

She didn't know if she was quite ready yet, but as he worked his way down her body, she realized she was more than willing to try.

Chapter Twenty-Eight

With only a few nights until Hogmanay, it seemed the majority of the city's residents had squeezed into the Glasgow Assembly Rooms to begin early celebrations.

Donella swore that at least half of them had trod on her feet.

After retreating into a window alcove to catch her breath, she went up on her toes to peer over the expanse of pomaded hair, silk turbans, and feathered headdresses. In the confusing mass of people around the edges of the dance floor, she couldn't spot either Eden or Victoria.

Her two friends had been forging ahead of Donella through the crowd, heading for the supper room to meet up with the other members of their party. When a piece of netting on Donella's gown had snagged a woman's bracelet, she'd been forced to stop to untangle it. The wearer of the bracelet in question had glared in rigid disapproval while Donella labored to work herself free. She'd finally resorted to giving the netting a good yank, with unfortunate results for the delicate fabric of her gown.

By the time she looked up, the other ladies had disappeared into the crowd. The Kendrick twins were wandering somewhere close by, and Logan should arrive soon. Still, she couldn't spot anyone she knew, and the mob blocking the path to the supper room remained dauntingly thick.

It would appear she was on her own, for the moment.

Of course, the only risk of danger was from terminal boredom or possibly expiring from the heat. Donella had forgotten how much she hated large parties. She could only hope that in their new life together, Logan wouldn't insist on a steady round of social events. He didn't seem the type for that sort of thing, but it was undeniable that he was a constant surprise to her.

One surprise was how determined a lover he was, and how inventive. He'd climbed up the wall to her bedroom three nights in a row, and each night had been more wonderful and astonishing than the last. With Logan, Donella hardly recognized the woman she'd become, more willing to take risks than she'd ever imagined.

Still, once he departed like a phantom in the night, she was left with all the same worries about her future. Could she be the sort of wife he truly needed? Could she support him outside the cocoon of their families and the quiet existence she longed for? There was a reason she'd been attracted to life in a nunnery. The world Logan moved in was one Donella often found irritating and even overwhelming.

She went up on her toes again. Not a blasted Kendrick or Gilbride in sight. Sighing, she pulled a handkerchief from her beaded reticule and dabbed her neck, then shoved it back and prepared to elbow her way through the crowd.

Suddenly, Jeannie MacArthur glided through a small gap in the throng. She was stunning in her sapphire blue gown, not a golden curl out of place or even a faint sheen of perspiration on her brow. The woman might as well have been a perfectly chiseled statue come to life.

By contrast, Donella felt like a head of lettuce left too long in the sun.

"Ah, Miss Haddon," Jeannie said. "Just the person I was looking for."

Her determined advance had Donella retreating back into the alcove.

Donella pinned a smile to her face. "Mrs. MacArthur, how nice to see you. Are you enjoying the ball?"

"I find Glasgow affairs quite dreary compared to Edinburgh's." Her gaze flickered over Donella's gown, lingering on the torn bit of netting. "And so provincial, don't you think? One can hardly scare up a decent dressmaker worth the effort."

"I haven't spent much time in Glasgow, and none in Edinburgh."

"Yes, it's quite evident you prefer the country, which is so charming of you." Jeannie's smile was mocking. "And of course the convent, which must be positively rustic."

Since she'd always been hopeless at thinly veiled sparring, Donella decided to forgo the attempt. "What is it you wished to speak to me about, ma'am? I was about to rejoin my party."

Something hard flashed through the woman's cornflower blue eyes before she composed her features into another smile. "So delightfully blunt. I'm sure Logan finds you very amusing."

Logan did seem to enjoy Donella's unvarnished manner of speaking, but Jeannie clearly meant it as an insult. "I wouldn't know," she crisply replied.

"Then I suppose I'll have to ask him," Jeannie purred. "When next I see him."

Donella held on to the fraying ends of her temper. "Mrs. MacArthur, is there a point to this conversation?"

The woman's golden eyebrows ticked up in an incredulous lift. "My dear Miss Haddon, I simply wish to offer my congratulations. I do apologize if I've offended you."

Since Jeannie had no doubt sought Donella out with

the express intention of giving offense, she didn't bother to acknowledge the half-hearted apology.

As for accepting congratulations, the formal announcement of her betrothal to Logan would take place at the Gilbrides' Hogmanay party. Until then, it had been agreed to keep the news strictly within the family. That didn't mean, of course, that servants didn't gossip or that rumors hadn't circulated about Logan's marked attentions to her.

Still, it was in bad taste for Jeannie to make such a bold assumption.

"I'm not sure what you're referring to, ma'am," Donella replied. "Now if you'll excuse me—"

Jeannie smoothly blocked her way. "There's no need to be modest, my dear. You've managed to snag the most eligible bachelor in Glasgow, perhaps in all of Scotland. That is quite the feat for a countrified young lady who only recently was residing in a convent."

Despite the coolly ironic smile, Donella saw anger in the woman's gaze and barely contained jealousy.

"I know you and Mr. Kendrick were once close," she replied. "So if you have something to say, I suggest you speak to Mr. Kendrick. Your former relationship is truly none of my business."

Jeannie's smile turned malicious. "It was a great deal more than close, you know. Unfortunately, circumstances prevented us from marrying."

Donella stared at her in disbelief. "The *circumstance* was the tragic death of Logan's nephew."

"I said it was unfortunate, did I not? But it was nevertheless unfair that we were forced to separate."

"From what I understand, when he asked you to marry him, you turned him down. No one *forced* you to do anything."

A sneer lifted the corners of Jeannie's mouth. Suddenly, she didn't look quite so perfect. "You know nothing of—"

"What happened?" Donella interrupted. "I believe I do. Are we finished, Mrs. MacArthur? Because I would like to rejoin my party."

If the blasted woman tried to get in her way again, she'd give her a good shove to make her move.

Jeannie made a visible effort to contain her emotions. Donella had to give the woman credit for impressive self-control.

When that chilling smile again lifted the corners of her mouth, Donella couldn't repress a shiver, despite the hot-house atmosphere.

"Logan was my first," Jeannie said. "One never forgets one's first."

Donella frowned. "First love? Yes, I know that."

"No, my dear. Logan was my first *lover,* and what a lover he was." She regarded Donella with amusement. "Logan, however, will not be *your* first lover. I cannot help but wonder how he'll react to that on your wedding night."

The double blow knocked the air from Donella's lungs, and the second carefully aimed jab went straight to the gut. How in God's name did the bloody woman know about Roddy?

Donella stood frozen as she tried to think past her growing panic. Perhaps it was simply a stab in the dark, fueled by jealousy and old rumors that had resurfaced because of her return to society.

While she struggled to muster a coherent response, Jeannie patted her arm.

"Logan is a very forgiving man, my dear. I'm sure he'll be happy to overlook any former contretemps, particularly since your betrothal will be so helpful in sealing his new business relationship with Lord Riddick." Jeannie laughed. "How charmingly old-fashioned of your family to offer your hand in marriage for financial gain."

Donella's mind went blank for a moment, so she simply stared at Jeannie, unable—unwilling—to reply.

The lovely blonde waved a casual hand. "You know, of course, that Logan has been in trading negotiations with your uncle for some weeks. Apparently, the arrangements will greatly advantage Kendrick Shipping and Trade." Again, her contemptuous gaze flickered over Donella. "No wonder he wished to marry you."

Donella tried to ignore the black spots floating across her vision. It had to be the heat of the room. She had to get away, find someplace to sit and be quiet.

"Mrs. MacArthur, if you do not move, I will be forced—"

"Och, there you are," Logan said, squeezing between two portly gentlemen at the edge of the dance floor. "Edie was in a stew that she'd lost you—"

He broke off when Jeannie turned to smile at him. "Jeannie, er, Mrs. MacArthur, how nice to see you."

The woman all but sparkled. "Mr. Kendrick, I'm so pleased to see you. I've been having quite an interesting chat with Miss Haddon."

Logan's gaze narrowed. "Have you now?"

Jeannie pressed his arm. "Indeed. And allow me to offer my sincere congratulations on your betrothal. What splendid news."

He threw Donella a startled look. She gave a slight shake of the head.

"Thank you, but congratulations are a bit premature," he replied.

Jeannie arched her elegant eyebrows. "Really, because the *on-dits* are quite insistent on the matter. Surely you can verify for one of your oldest friends if the rumors are true."

Donella didn't think she misheard a thread of hope in the woman's voice.

When Logan smiled down at his first love, Donella's

heart almost stopped. Was he going to deny that, despite all his protestations, he still cared for Jeannie MacArthur?

And had Donella been stupid enough to believe that he didn't?

"The *on-dits* have it right for once," Logan said. "But since no formal announcement has yet been made, I would ask that you keep the news to yourself."

Jeannie blinked, but then adopted a charmingly fey smile. "You have my word, dear Logan." She gave Donella a nod. "Miss Haddon, I wish you the best of luck."

When she slipped gracefully into the crowd, Logan frowned after her. "That was odd. I wonder how she found out about it."

"I don't know, and I don't care," Donella said in a tight voice.

His attention swung back to her. "Lass, are you feeling all right?"

"I was, until your former lover decided to accost me."

His eyebrows practically shot up to the ceiling. "What the hell does that mean?"

When two young ladies standing a few feet away turned to stare at them, Donella winced.

"I . . . oh, nothing. Can we please leave? The heat in this room is appalling."

"I take it Jeannie said something unpleasant."

"She said many things. Now, are you going to escort me out of here, or do I have to find my own way home?"

"Of course I'll take you home. Do you want me to fetch Edie or Victoria?"

"No, I just want to leave."

"Let me get you out of this mob, and then I'll rustle up a carriage."

"I'd prefer you not bull through the ballroom, leaving bodies in our wake," she warned as he took her elbow. "There's already enough gossip about us."

He snorted. "You have no idea."

Her stomach did a nasty flip. He'd been looking harassed when he found her, which didn't bode well.

Logan maneuvered her through the ballroom with a minimum of fuss. Many curious stares followed them, including a few disapproving ones in Donella's case.

You should be used to it by now.

It took every bit of her self-control and a heartfelt prayer for patience to maintain even the semblance of a smile.

When they reached the entrance hall, Logan left her to speak to a footman, returning a minute later with her cloak.

"Sure you don't want me to fetch Edie?" he asked as he draped it around her shoulders. "You're rather green around the gills, love."

"I just need to go home."

"I asked one of the footmen to call for Nick's carriage." He briefly cupped her cheek. "Just a few more minutes and we'll be on our way."

"How will your family get back to Kendrick House?"

"The twins won't mind walking, and Nick and Victoria can take a hackney." He steered her to a chair tucked behind a column. "Wait here until I arrange to deliver a message to Nick, all right?"

She sank gratefully down onto the seat, feeling dizzy with distress.

Had Jeannie and Logan been lovers? His reaction suggested otherwise. More upsetting was Jeannie's contention that Logan's marriage proposal had been primarily financial in nature. In a terrible way, it made sense that it would be. Although they'd been discovered in a compromising position, all but sealing their fate, Logan had already been making a show of courting her. As much as she wanted to believe he cared for her, other interests had to be at play—specifically, his desire to gain her uncle's considerable business influence.

Donella pressed a hand to her stomach, sick at the idea that she could have been such a dupe.

A gentle touch on her shoulder brought her out of her grim reverie.

"Lass, we can go," Logan said.

He kept a protective arm around her shoulders as they hurried down the front steps and into the cold night air, where the Kendrick town coach waited at the curb. It took but a moment for Logan to hand her up and give instructions to the coachman before climbing inside.

As the carriage started forward, he sat and took one of her hands. "Tell me what she said to upset you."

Donella sucked in a shaky breath. "I hardly know where to start."

"Och, that woman has always been trouble."

His disgusted tone was a relief, but she still felt battered by emotion.

"Donella," he said, "whatever it is, we'll handle it."

It was difficult to say the words. "Were you and Jeannie . . . did you and Jeannie have . . ."

"Relations?" He shook his head. "Good God, no."

"She said you were her first lover."

"We were never lovers, Donella. Word of a Kendrick *and* a Highlander."

In the flickering light of the carriage lamps, she read sincerity in his expression.

He cracked a rueful smile. "And as Angus would say, 'If ye canna depend on the word of a Kendrick and a Highlander, what can ye depend on?'"

"In any case," she said, "I have no business letting it bother me. You and Mrs. MacArthur loved each other and were to be married. It wouldn't be entirely surprising if you had an intimate relationship."

"I wouldn't have done that. Not to a gently bred lass I hoped to marry."

Donella lifted an ironic brow. "Really?"

Logan winced. "It's different with us, and you know it. And looking back on that time," he hastily added, "we both had a lucky escape."

"Mrs. MacArthur obviously doesn't feel that way now."

"What else did she say?"

Too late, Donella realized she'd wandered into dangerous territory. "Ah, I sensed that she would still be happy to marry you."

"She'd be happy to marry my money," he said dryly.

His words hit her hard, but she bit back a sharp reply.

"Come, lass, what else did she say to upset you?" he quietly asked after a few moments of silence.

She sighed. Better to get *her* worst out of the way before she asked about *his* worst. "She referenced some rather unfortunate rumors circulating about me."

"Having to do with the Murrays?"

She flashed him a startled glance. "You heard?"

"Graeme overheard some talk about you and . . ."

"Roddy Murray."

"Right. It was vague gossip, for the most part. But Graeme said it was enough to draw certain conclusions, if one had a mind to."

It was time to come clean. Logan would hear the details sooner or later, either from Jeannie or from Mungo Murray himself.

"Mrs. MacArthur had a mind to," Donella replied. "She said that although you were *her* first, you would not be *my* first."

Logan spat out a string of curses that were quite shocking in their specificity.

When he finished, he gathered up both her hands. "Sweetheart, I am so sorry you had to bear such an ugly scene with her. I'll be taking it up with both Jeannie MacArthur and Mungo Murray, because I've had just about enough of this."

"No, Logan, you won't."

"Donella, I know you hate conflict, but—"

"I'd prefer to avoid more scenes and gossip."

"Unfortunately, the cat is well out of the bag and must be dealt with. As soon as I drop you off, I'm going to hunt down Mungo Murray and shut him the hell up."

She yanked a hand away and slapped it onto his chest. "You will do no such thing."

He began to look exasperated. "These rumors will not go away, even after our betrothal is formally announced. In fact, they're likely to get worse. I won't have you subjected to insults any longer. You're my—"

"But they're not rumors."

Logan frowned. "Well . . . of course they are. I've been with you, Donella. I remember our first time."

Clearly, she'd done a splendid job of convincing him that she was an inexperienced maiden, and she hadn't even been trying.

"Logan, I was not a . . ." She twirled a hand. "You know."

He looked mystified. "No, I do not know."

"A virgin," she said through clenched teeth.

His features relaxed into a smile. "Of course not, daft girl. You've been with me."

Were all men this dense, or was she supremely unfortunate?

"I was not a virgin when you . . ." Again, her nerve failed and she twirled her other hand.

His jaw sagged for a moment before clamping shut. She wondered if he'd be able to pry it open enough to respond.

"When I came to your bed that first night," he finally said.

"Yes."

He let go of her other hand.

"Say something," she said after several fraught moments of silence.

His reply was soft and yet terrifying. "I am going to kill

Mungo Murray, and then I am going to rip Roddy's stupid head off and shove it down his neck."

"No, you will not."

Logan yanked off his beaver hat and threw it into the corner. "The hell I won't. The bastard took advantage of you. Either that or, he—" He sucked in a harsh breath. "Did he force himself on you?"

She flattened a hand on his chest. "No. It wasn't like that, I promise."

Logan exhaled long and hard, and then he seemed to gather himself. "How old were you?"

"I'd just turned seventeen."

"So he *did* take advantage of you, the bloody bastard. I'm sorry, Donella, but I'll be calling on the Murrays tomorrow and—"

"I said no."

"Why the hell not?"

"Because it was my bloody idea!"

Logan jerked back, startled.

Donella threw her reticule into the corner, where it landed on top of his hat. "That is why you will leave poor Roddy alone. He was the one who was wronged, not me. That silly boy only wished to marry me. He tried to be honorable, and for all his trouble saw *his* name and *his* honor dragged through the mud." She rubbed a hand across her eyes, wiping away angry tears. "So, that's why Mungo Murray and his men tried to kidnap me. Because we truly had insulted his family's honor, and he was determined to set it right."

"By kidnapping you?" Logan asked in an incredulous voice. "That's a bit extreme, even if you did insult his bloody honor."

"Of course it is. I'm not excusing it, or his attempts to embarrass us by spreading gossip ten years later. I'm simply trying to explain it to you—if you'll have the courtesy to actually listen to me."

She snatched up her reticule and struggled to open it.

Logan took it from her. "You'll rip the laces."

She wanted to tell him to bugger off—or burst into hysterics. All that emotion had poured out in a raging tide that made her sick with shame. Telling the truth was supposed to make one feel better, but Uncle Riddick had been right. It just felt awful and dangerous.

She might lose the one thing she wanted, just when she'd finally found it.

Logan handed over her kerchief. "I'm listening now, so tell me whatever you want."

She took a moment to steady herself. "It happened during a clan gathering at Blairgal. Alasdair had been gone for over a year, with no sign of return. Despite that, my father and my uncle had made known our arrangement. That I was . . ."

"Off the marriage mart?"

"It didn't occur to me to object, because I never objected."

"It bothered you, though, having no control over the circumstances."

Donella looked down at her hands, now clenched into fists. "I'd been abandoned, and everyone knew it."

He was quiet for a few moments. "And that's when Roddy Murray entered the scene."

"The Murrays and some of the other local clans attended the gathering. Roddy was very popular with the girls."

"Including you."

She shot him a glance. He gave her a slight smile and nodded, as if encouraging her to continue.

"You have to admit he's very handsome," she said, feeling defensive.

"I'll grant you that, but he doesn't seem your type." Logan tapped his head, indicating Roddy's lack of intellect.

"He was very impressive in the caber toss," she stiffly replied.

Logan smothered a grin with his hand.

"I wasn't looking to fall in love, or throw Alasdair over," she said. "I simply wanted a little . . ."

"Attention?" he gently finished.

She nodded, feeling stupid and humiliated.

"And Roddy was happy to give it to you."

"It sounds awful when you put it that way."

He grimaced. "I didn't mean it to."

Donella waved a hand. "It doesn't matter. I'll just finish, shall I?"

She described how Roddy had quickly become smitten with her, ignoring the other girls to follow her about like a puppy dog. Because she'd been hurt and embarrassed by Alasdair's desertion and the resulting gossip, she'd let him.

"It was the first time in ages that anyone had made me feel special. And it didn't hurt that all the other girls were jealous." She managed a smile. "That had never happened."

It had also led to her downfall. Annoyed that Roddy had singled Donella out, some of the other girls had made her the target of mean-spirited jests. They'd joked that Alasdair would rather run away than marry her, the most boring girl in Scotland. According to them, Roddy simply felt sorry for her.

So when Roddy found her later, crying her eyes out, he'd sworn up and down to take his vengeance on everyone who'd insulted her. He'd pledged his undying love and claimed he'd do anything to win her hand, including facing down the wrath of Lord Riddick and the entire Haddon clan.

"He was ready to go to my uncle right then and there," she said. "Naturally I panicked. So I dragged him off to one of the barns to . . . to calm him down."

"That's one way to describe it," Logan said.

"Well, it worked," she replied, annoyed that he'd gone back to scowling at her.

"Apparently a little too well."

Part of her wanted to whack him with her reticule, but

the other part acknowledged the truth of his words. As she'd lain with Roddy in a scratchy pile of hay, she'd been horrified by her actions. She'd betrayed her family, and she'd betrayed Alasdair. More importantly, she'd betrayed herself by using a sweet young man who'd wanted nothing more than to love her.

"I tried to swear him to secrecy," she said. "I told him I could never renege on my vows to Alasdair. So, when he insisted on going to my uncle to ask for my hand, I said I would deny the whole thing."

"Then he should have kept his bloody mouth shut."

Donella shot him a startled look. "He was only trying to do the right thing."

Logan scoffed. "He wasn't interested in what you wanted, Donella. He was only interested in what he wanted."

"I . . . I never thought about it that way before."

"It's time you did."

She took several moments to do just that. "Thank you," she finally said.

"We all do silly things when we're young, lass. No need to keep punishing yourself."

"I did punish myself for a long time," she confessed. "Especially since it all turned out so horribly."

"Mungo went to Riddick and demanded you marry his poor, dishonored son, I take it."

"Needless to say, it was quite the kick-up." She wrinkled her nose. "I did feel quite awful about Roddy."

"Don't. He should have kept his mouth shut. Does anyone in your family know the truth?"

"Only Uncle Riddick, and he swore me to secrecy. He said it was the only way to prevent a clan feud and preserve the family's honor."

"At your expense," Logan said in a hard voice.

"It was my mistake, and it hurt the entire family, especially Alasdair."

"Donella, what do you imagine Alec was up to all those years he was away? Do you think he was faithful to his vows to you?"

"Uh . . ."

"I'd bet my fortune he was not."

She cut him a sideways glance. "Doesn't it bother you that I gave myself to another man first?"

When he hesitated, her throat constricted. But then he took her hand and gave her a rueful smile.

"Perhaps a wee bit." He shook his head. "And with Roddy Murray, no less."

She grimaced. "Sorry."

"I'm hardly a saint, so no apologies are necessary, love. But you should have trusted me enough to tell me all this when I asked you—which I did, several times."

She pulled her hand away. "I told you, Uncle Riddick swore me to secrecy. He said it was better for all concerned."

"I know how seriously you take vows and such, but your uncle was wrong." He blew out a deep breath. "I'll deal with the Murrays, naturally, but I wish you'd told me when you accepted my proposal. I could have managed it better, before the gossip spun out of control."

Donella couldn't help but bristle at his tone. "Gossip spread by *your* friend, Mrs. MacArthur."

"Jeannie is simply repeating what apparently has already been circulating. This is Mungo Murray's fault. When his ridiculous kidnapping scheme fell apart, he decided to ruin your reputation." He snorted. "And he's done a good job of it, too."

Donella had to struggle to hold on to her temper. It had been horribly embarrassing to tell him everything in the first place, and now she had to endure a lecture.

She stared blindly at the flickering carriage lamp, struggling with an unholy mixture of anger and guilt. The worst part was, he was probably right. But that didn't make it easier to bear.

"Lass, I promise I'll take care of it," Logan said. "I just need to know if there are any other secrets you've kept from me."

His unfortunate word choice triggered a small explosion in her brain. She twisted in her seat to face him. "Like the fact that you're negotiating a business arrangement with my uncle that will be facilitated by our marriage?"

"Who the *hell* told you that?"

"Is it true?"

When he hesitated, her heart plunged through the floor of the carriage.

She faced forward, avoiding his gaze. "It doesn't matter."

"It's not like that," he tersely bit out.

"Really? What is it like, then?"

"I *am* conducting business negotiations with your uncle, but it's got nothing to do with you. We started before I even met you."

Understanding dawned with an unwelcome light. "So that's why you agreed to escort me home. You were hoping to curry favor with my uncle. How clever of you."

"Donella, you've got it all wrong," he ground out.

"Apparently I have a habit of doing that. It would certainly seem I was wrong about why you wanted to marry me."

"Christ Almighty. I wanted to marry you because you're a bonny lass, and because Joseph loves you."

"How splendid for you. You get a complacent wife, a mother for your son, and a business partnership with my uncle. I wonder, however, what I get out of it."

"A family, for one thing, and a rich husband," he retorted. "And that's a hell of a lot better than spending the rest of your life with a bunch of pious spinsters in brown robes and silly hats."

Donella slowly turned and fixed him with her frostiest glare.

"Oh, hell." He rammed a frustrated hand through his hair. "I didn't mean—"

"Not another word, sir, or I will throw myself out of this carriage."

"Donella—"

When she reached for the door handle, Logan clamped his mouth shut and silently fumed for the remainder of the ride.

Chapter Twenty-Nine

Donella sat behind Alasdair's desk cradling her glass of whisky. Normally, she wouldn't touch the stuff, but it was both Hogmanay and the night of her betrothal party. Getting cup-shot seemed almost obligatory, as did hiding out in the library.

Alec and Edie's annual party was already a mad crush. Logan was out there somewhere, no doubt snarling at people and causing delicate maidens to swoon from fright. Donella was hiding from him too, still rattled by their dreadful fight three nights ago.

"You can't keep sending him away, dearest," Eden had said this morning after Logan had come to call, and Donella had refused to see him again. "Sooner or later, you'll have to make a decision about your future."

And therein lay the problem. While she loved the dratted man, she had no idea about his true feelings for her. Love seemed too much to hope for. She could live with warm-hearted affection if it were genuine on his part.

She'd written to Uncle Riddick, asking for clarification of his business dealings with Logan. His terse reply had simply offered his congratulations on their betrothal, along with a thinly veiled threat that Logan best honor his commitments to her or face his wrath.

Sometimes, it all felt like a conspiracy to keep her in the dark.

Even worse, Logan had not made one attempt to scale the wall to her bedroom. That was both depressing and completely ridiculous, since she was supposed to be angry, not longing for secretive trysts.

"You're an idiot." She shot back another mouthful, wincing as it burned down her throat. Then she carefully dried the glass on her sleeve and placed it on Alasdair's pristine desk blotter.

"Don't want to make a mess. You've made more than enough to last a lifetime."

Was it really expecting too much to hope for a marriage between loving, equal partners? Donella didn't know if she could bear life with a man whose primary interest in his wife was one of financial calculation.

Well, there was only one way to find out, she supposed, which was to ask Logan straight out.

She stood and shook out her skirts, then eyed the remaining whisky in the glass.

"Can't hurt," she muttered before swallowing it in one gulp.

It went down easier this time. And, yes, she was starting to feel a wee bit tipsy. Given tonight's impending challenges, she needed the fortification.

She was crossing to the drinks trolley to replace the glass when the library door opened and Alasdair walked in.

"I thought I'd find you in here." He eyed her empty glass. "Needed a bit of liquid courage?"

She shrugged. "It seemed like a sensible response to the situation."

"I take it you're referring to your betrothal announcement. Half of Glasgow's showed up to hear it, by the way."

"Splendid. Alasdair, don't people have anything better to do?"

"Apparently not. The whole blasted house is buzzing with gossip, if you must know."

"Which is an excellent reason to hide in the library."

Alasdair took her hand and led her to one of the leather club chairs in front of his desk. He propped himself against the edge of the desk, arms crossed as he studied her.

"What?" she asked defensively.

"Logan isn't the only person you've been avoiding." His smile took the sting out of the remark.

She wrinkled her nose in silent admission.

"Why, lass? We're good friends, are we not?"

Donella sighed. "I'm embarrassed."

"Because of that nonsense with Roddy Murray?" He shook his head. "It's ancient history, my dear. Besides, I'd abandoned you, like the stupid, selfish prat that I was."

"Your actions were understandable. I don't blame you anymore."

He scrunched up one side of his face in a comical grimace. "Maybe just a wee bit?"

She reluctantly laughed. "All right, maybe just a bit, but that was still no excuse. I'd made a solemn vow, and I broke it." She shook her head. "With Roddy Murray. What in God's name was I thinking?"

"That he was a good-looking and braw fellow who paid attention to you?"

"That's still no excuse."

"Donella, you were lonely and hurt. That was my fault, not yours."

His gray gaze was so warm with sympathy and understanding that it made her chest hurt. "It was wrong, though. And I'm ashamed to have betrayed your trust. Betrayed my entire family's trust."

Alasdair snorted. "You didn't betray me, lass. What do you think I was doing all those years I was away from home?"

"Not living with any great degree of chastity, from what I understand."

He blinked. "Who told you?"

"Logan. He said I shouldn't feel guilty, because you were certainly not faithful to me."

"Bastard," Alasdair muttered. "But he was right. I was a young man away from home for the first time, and I was not very good at resisting temptation."

"I won't tell Edie," she said with a wry smile.

"She already knows, and thankfully doesn't hold it against me." He leaned forward and took her hand. "You've not wronged me in any way, lass, nor the rest of the family. So if any of that convent business was about atoning for sins against us, you must get that out of your head once and for all."

Donella was about to utter an automatic denial before stopping herself. It was time for truth telling, for all of them.

"I truly did think the convent was the right choice for me," she said. "I was never very good in the world, you see, and I thought I would be a happier and better person with the sisters."

"Still, maybe there was just a bit of atoning for all those imaginary sins?"

She held her thumb and forefinger an inch apart.

"Especially after your mother fell ill," he added.

Alasdair meant after Mamma had tried to murder him.

"Yes," she said.

"No one blamed you for wanting to get away from that mess. It was difficult and distressing, especially for you and Fergus."

"But I ran away, leaving the rest of you to deal with it. I've been a coward for much too long, Alasdair. It's time I stopped running."

He let go of her hand and crossed his arms again. "Does that also include running away from Logan?"

"It's . . . it's complicated."

"How so?"

"I'm not sure how he feels about me. I'm not exactly the biggest prize on the marriage mart. I've no dowry to speak of, nor any inheritance. The only thing that makes me remotely attractive is—" She cut herself off, hating how pathetic she sounded.

"Is the fact that you're the beloved niece of wealthy Lord Riddick?"

"I know I sound utterly hen-hearted," she said with a sigh.

"If that's all Logan Kendrick wanted from you, I would throttle him. But you, my dear, are the Flower of Clan Graham. Of course Logan wants you. He'd be a fool not to."

"Alasdair, you know how much I loathe that name."

He grinned. "It fits. You're the prettiest, nicest, smartest girl in all of Scotland. Logan knows that, as does any man with a brain in his head."

She lifted an eyebrow. "Prettier than Eden?"

"She's English. It doesn't count."

Donella laughed. "All right, I'll admit I'm not entirely hopeless, but . . ."

"But you're afraid Logan doesn't want you simply for yourself."

"Yes."

"If you'd seen him these last few days, you'd realize such is not the case. The man has been roaring about like a deranged fool. I thought he was going to toss me out a window yesterday when I told him—again—that you were unavailable."

She rather liked the sound of that but adopted a regretful expression. "How unfortunate."

He snorted. "You can't fool me, lass. Trust me, Logan Kendrick is mad for you. And if you don't come out and let me announce your betrothal, he'll likely tear Breadie Manor apart with his bare hands."

"We certainly cannot have that."

"So, shall we go out and make the poor fellow happy again?"

Donella's heart fluttered with a complicated mix of love, longing, and anxiety. She'd never thought to be a wife or mother, much less married to such a potent man like Logan Kendrick. Was she truly up to it?

"I want to," she whispered. "I really do."

Her cousin took both her hands in a comforting grip.

"Donella, listen to me. You deserve happiness more than anyone I know. You've faced up to every trial with dignity and kindness, and God knows you've borne more of them than any young woman should have to. It's time to stop feeling guilty about your mother, Roddy Murray, me, or any of the rest of us. You deserve to be loved, and you *are* loved. By your entire family, and by Logan and his family, too."

Her cousin's words were a healing balm to her spirit. For so long she'd shouldered a heavy weight of guilt. It now seemed silly and rather selfish, as if she'd worn a hairshirt to make herself feel better, when she'd simply been running away from life.

"Thank you, Alasdair. I think you're the only person who could truly have made me hear that."

"Then there's only one question, isn't there? Do you have the courage to seize what you deserve?"

She mustered a smile. "I'm the Flower of Clan Graham, so I'd better, or I'll have to relinquish the title."

Alasdair gave her hands a final pat before coming to his feet. "Thank God, because everyone's in an uproar. Joseph's mad at his father, which is making Logan act like an even bigger idiot. That's put Nick into a stew, so Victoria is fretting. And when Victoria frets, Edie frets."

"As do you, along with everyone else."

"Everyone except my mother-in-law. She simply gives scolds."

"Yes, I've been on the receiving end of one," Donella said as she also rose. "Lady Reese said that I didn't properly understand the masculine mind. Sadly, she's not wrong."

"If it's any consolation, she whacked Logan with her fan this evening and told him to stop acting like a Scottish nincompoop."

"I rather wish I'd seen that."

"Yes, it was vastly entertaining. I had to separate her and Angus. He wasn't best pleased at the insult to his grandson."

Donella laughed. "I suppose I'd best find Logan and get it sorted before any more disasters occur."

Alasdair swept her into his arms. "Good lass. And if he gives you any guff, tell him that I'll rip his heart out."

Donella hugged him back. "Thank you, dearest, for everything."

"My pleasure. Now, let's go and stop all hell from breaking loose."

She still felt a bit shaky. "Can you give me a minute to compose myself?"

"Absolutely." He started toward the door. "But no more whisky. Can't have you passing out at your own betrothal party."

"I promise I'll be right out."

When he was gone, Donella smoothed her skirts, fluffed her curls, and made sure her bandeau was on straight. Then it was time to go tell the man she loved that she did, in fact, love him.

She closed her eyes for a moment and sent up a silent prayer for courage. Then she said one of thanks—for her family, her friends, and for the chance to start again.

Leaving the quiet shelter of the library, she lingered for a moment in the corridor. The sounds of revelry drifted from the front of the manor—talking, laughter, and the sound of music. She smiled because, astonishingly, she wanted to be part of it, especially with Logan.

Then she heard a quick rush behind her. Turning, she found herself face-to-face with someone she'd never hoped to see again.

The years had taken their toll on Mungo Murray. He was wizened and hunched, barely coming up to her chin. But anger still burned in his rheumy gaze.

The two men with him were neither old nor frail. She recognized them from the attempted abduction on the bridge.

"Well met, lass," Mungo rasped, pulling a pistol from his greatcoat. "It's time we had a wee chat."

"Where the hell is she?" Logan growled as he strode down the corridor. "It's almost midnight. We need to make the blasted announcement."

"How the hell should I know?" Alec retorted. "She said she'd be right out."

That had been well over a half hour ago, and still Donella hadn't appeared. Having reached the end of his patience, Logan had decided to track down his elusive prey once and for all.

"Perhaps she went upstairs to freshen up," Edie said, trying to keep pace with them.

"I sent a footman to check a few minutes ago," Alec said. "She's not there."

"Damn, damn, damn," Logan muttered under his breath. He could only hope she wasn't halfway to some blasted convent by now.

He'd made the usual cock-up. Donella was justifiably angry with him, and he'd tried not to put pressure on her. That was why he'd left her alone these last three nights, even though he'd been crawling out of his skin. He was beginning to think that had been a capital mistake.

Three days and three nights without Donella had made him realize how madly in love he was with the lass. He had every intention of telling her just that—if she didn't murder him first.

"Perhaps she's in the nursery. With Joseph spending the night, she might have wanted to visit him," Edie breathlessly said as she scurried beside them.

Alasdair slowed his pace. "Now that's an idea. Would you mind checking?"

Edie nodded and turned back in the opposite direction.

"Donella obviously still doesn't want to talk to me," Logan said.

He wanted to throw something, preferably a large and breakable item. On top of everything else, his son wouldn't speak to him. As far as Joseph was concerned, Logan had ruined everything, because Donella wouldn't be his mother. He'd tried to reassure the boy that it would be fine, but Joseph hadn't believed him.

What else is new?

They turned into the cross-corridor that led to the library.

"No, she definitely wanted to talk to you," Alasdair said. "In fact—"

He broke off and came to a sudden halt.

Logan stopped, too. "Now, what?"

Grim-faced, Alec charged ahead to the library door. He swiped up a shoe from the floor.

A woman's shoe, the dainty sort one would wear to a ball.

"It's Donella's," Alec said.

Logan shoved past him and threw open the door.

"Donella—"

The room was freezing because the bay windows were

wide open. A stiff breeze flapped the heavy velvet drapes, and papers from Alec's desk had scattered onto the floor.

Logan bent to retrieve a lady's fan from the carpet. He'd seen it before, in Donella's hand the night of the Assembly Rooms ball.

"Goddammit." Alec strode to the window and leaned halfway out. "I can't see a bloody thing."

Fear spiked through Logan, followed by a shimmering haze of fury that seemed to cloud his brain.

"Mungo Murray," he spat out.

When Alec vaulted out the window, Logan strode to the desk and grabbed the Argand lamp. Then he leaned out the window, holding the lamp high to give Alec some light.

His friend was crouched below, inspecting a trampled bush. He took the lamp and did a quick sweep of the surrounding area before returning.

"How many?" Logan asked, taking back the lamp.

Alec climbed up into the room. "Four, I think. Hard to tell because the ground's so wet."

"How the hell did they get in?"

"Not this way. The windows lock from the inside."

Logan had to resist the urge to slam the lamp down on the desk. "Why didn't anyone see them?"

Alec, inspecting the window alcove, glanced impatiently back at him. "Half of Glasgow is here. You could slip the bloody Prince Regent and his court into the house, and no one would notice."

"Well, I'll need to borrow a brace of pistols then I'm off to the Murray house."

"I know you Kendricks love to charge off half-cocked, but can we just think this through for a moment?"

"I have no intention waiting for you to be the great master spy while Donella is in danger."

The very thought was killing him.

"She's my family, Logan," Alec replied, "and I love her, too. I promise we'll get her back, but we need to come up with a plan."

Logan sucked in a breath, forcing himself to think rationally. He'd faced many dangers in his life, and Alec was right. To both survive *and* prevail, one needed a plan.

"What do you suggest?"

"It's highly unlikely they took her to the Murray's town house in the city. Too obvious."

"True, but somebody there might know something." And he would throttle it out of them, if need be.

"We'll get to that. First we need to talk to my servants, in case any of them noticed something off. Then we organize search parties. Ring the bell, would you? I want to speak to the housekeeper."

After Logan did that, he rejoined Alec, who'd gone back to inspecting the window alcove.

"What's so bloody interesting?"

"Bad choice of words, I'm afraid." Alec pointed to a small smear on the frame.

Logan peered at it, then had to close his eyes for a moment. "Fresh blood."

"Not a lot, fortunately."

Edie rushed into the room, followed by Nick and Victoria.

"What's going on?" Nick asked.

"Donella's gone," Logan grimly replied. "The Murrays took her—through the window, it seems."

Victoria pressed a hand to her mouth.

Edie came up and laid a hand on Logan's arm. "My dear, I'm afraid no one has seen Joseph for almost an hour. Angus and the nursemaids are searching the house."

Logan felt like a massive weight had slammed into the back of his head. He pressed a hand to the window frame as a wave of dizziness swept through him.

A steadying hand clamped onto his shoulder.

Logan opened his eyes to meet his brother's concerned gaze.

"It's all right, lad," Nick said. "He's likely hiding somewhere about the house, watching the festivities. No need to worry about him just yet."

In his gut, Logan knew that wasn't true. "I can't lose him. I can't lose either of them," he choked out.

"If Murray has either of them, he has no cause to hurt them."

"Och, Donella's already been hurt," Logan replied. "There's blood on the windowsill."

"Oh, no!" Victoria exclaimed.

"Not much," Alec said. "But there must have been a struggle."

"Of course there was," Edie grimly said. "Donella's a fighter."

That's exactly what Logan was afraid of. The idea of anything happening to the two people he loved most in the world—

Nick gave him a hard shake. "Logan, you're the best man I know in a crisis. We'll find them, but we need to use our brains."

He managed a nod. "Alec wants to talk to the servants, and then we'll send out search parties along all the major roads into and away from the city. The bastards would need one carriage at least, and probably a few riders. That might attract some notice."

"Someone needs to go to the Murray house, just to be sure," Victoria said.

"And someone should rustle up the twins and Braden," Logan added. "If Donella has been injured, we'll need Braden."

Braden was one of Logan's younger half brothers. He

lived in Edinburgh, where he was studying to be a physician, but he'd come home for the Hogmanay party. A brilliant young man, he was already accomplished at his work. If Donella were injured, he would fix her.

If Joseph was hurt . . .

Don't think about it.

"I'll find them," Victoria said, "and check in with Angus, too." She hurried from the room.

Alec strode to the bell pull and all but yanked it out of the wall. "Where's the damn housekeeper?"

"If you rang before, she probably didn't hear it," Edie said. "The service rooms are a madhouse tonight."

"Nick, you and Angus go to the Murray house," Logan said, heading for the door. "Alec and I will talk to the servants and start on the search—"

He broke off when his grandfather hurried into the room carrying Joseph, bundled up in a cloak. Mrs. Webb, the housekeeper, followed them in.

"I've got him," Angus said.

Logan swept Joseph from his grandfather's hold. The boy's arms snaked around Logan's neck, hugging him with a grip that practically choked him.

He didn't care. His son was safe and in his arms.

"Papa, I was afraid," Joseph said in a quavering voice. "I didn't know what to do."

Logan rocked him, swallowing past the boulder in his throat. "It's all right, laddie. I've got you. I won't let anything hurt you." He frowned. "You're shivering, and your hair's wet."

"I fell into a puddle of water."

"Aye, and got covered with mud, too," Angus said.

Logan carried the boy to the fireplace, hooking a chair with his foot and pulling it close. Nick went down on one knee and shoveled more coals into the grate as Logan sat and cuddled Joseph on his lap. He eased the cloak aside to get a better look at his son.

Joseph's face was smudged with dirt, and his hair was clotted with mud. His velvet jacket was missing a few buttons and was soaked in spots. His pants were only a bit damp, but were covered in dirt, as were his shoes and stockings.

"Let's get this jacket off before you catch a chill," Logan said.

The boy's teeth were chattering. "I . . . I think I already caught one."

Logan wrestled the jacket off. Mrs. Webb, who'd brought in some towels, helped Logan dry the boy's face and hair. The wee lad didn't make it easy, clinging to him like a limpet.

"Where did you find him, Angus?"

"In the herb garden, runnin' flat out up the path to the kitchens. We wrapped him in the cloak and brought him here."

"Thank you, Grandda." Logan carefully wiped a clot of mud from Joseph's neck.

"Thank the lad. He got himself back here, ye ken."

Joseph tugged on Logan's cravat. "Papa, the bad men took Donella. I saw it."

Logan's heart jammed against his ribs. "Did they see you?"

The boy shook his head. "I wanted to talk to Donella, and I thought she might be in the library. I saw her coming out when the bad men grabbed her."

"Where were you?"

"At the other end of the hall. They pulled her into the library, so I snuck down to see if I could help." He grimaced. "But there were three of them. I couldn't do anything."

It almost gave Logan a heart attack thinking about what might have happened if the kidnappers had seen Joseph. "It's all right, son."

The little boy rubbed his eye. "They threw a cloak on her and carried her out the window."

Nick crouched down in front of them. "Joseph, could you tell if they hurt Donella?"

"She was kicking like anything until they got her to the window. Then she went all funny and limp."

It took Logan a moment before he could speak. "Then what happened?"

"I climbed out the window and followed them."

Logan and Nick exchanged an incredulous glance.

"And then?" Nick said.

"I followed them through the garden to the carriage." The lad suddenly looked worried. "There was nobody to help, and I wanted to see where they were going. Was that bad of me?"

Logan smoothed the damp hair from his son's forehead. "It was incredibly brave. I'm proud of you, son. I'm only sorry I wasn't there to help you."

Braden hurried into the room, followed by the twins and Victoria.

"Is Joseph all right?" Grant asked in a worried voice.

"I'm fine, Uncle Grant," Joseph said. "I just fell in a big puddle."

"Let yer uncle Braden have a wee look," Angus said. "Just to make sure."

Braden, a tall young man whose spectacles lent him a serious aspect, exchanged places with Nick.

"Can you stand up and let me have a look at you, laddie boy?" he asked with a kind smile.

Logan helped the boy to the floor. He seemed steady on his feet and was no longer shivering.

"Joseph, how did you fall into such a big puddle?" he asked while Braden expertly ran his hands over the boy's arms and legs.

"I fell off the back of the carriage when it went around a corner."

For a few seconds, a stunned silence hung over the room.

"Uh, what carriage?" Nick asked.

Joseph made an exasperated noise. "The carriage they put Donella in. No one else was around, remember? I had to do it."

Everyone but Angus looked appalled.

"Joseph, that was very brave," Victoria said, "but also—"

"Very smart," Logan interrupted.

He'd be damned if he criticized the boy for his brave but foolish act. Not when he and the rest of them had failed to be there when they were needed.

"Aye, smart like yer da," Angus said with pride.

"Son, did you get any sense where they were going?" Logan asked.

"Hang on a moment," Braden murmured as he checked Joseph's eyes and felt his little head for bumps.

"I couldn't tell, Papa," Joseph said a moment later. "It was dark, and when I fell off, the carriage got away from me." He blinked hard. "I'm sorry."

Logan stroked his head. "You did a splendid job, and it was very capable of you to find your way back here."

"But Donella's in trouble, and I couldn't help her."

The boy's anguish almost broke Logan's heart and battered him with fear. It sounded like the lass could have been badly hurt during the abduction.

He lifted Joseph back onto his lap. "Not to worry, lad. We'll find her."

Graeme came to stand beside Logan. "Joseph, do you remember where you fell off the carriage?"

The boy nodded. "Where the road gets wider. When it turns away from Breadie Manor."

"And did you notice if it went in the direction of where there are a lot of lights, or not so many?"

Joseph frowned. "Away from the lights, Uncle Graeme."

"Up a hill, correct?"

The boy nodded.

"You're sure?" Logan asked.

"Yes, Papa. I remember because the horses slowed down."

"It's definitely Balmore Road," Graeme said.

Alec clapped him on the shoulder. "We'll make a spy out of you yet."

"I hope not," Victoria muttered.

"I think I know where they're going," Graeme added. "It must be to Dun Manor."

"That's all but a ruin," Nick said. "And why go there? It belongs to Clan Graham, not to the Murrays."

Alec snapped his fingers. "But it used to belong to the Murrays, a few hundred years back. The Grahams claimed it during one of the clan dust-ups."

"Clan feuds," Edie said in a disgusted voice. "I'm so sick of them."

"Amen," said Victoria.

"Och, *Sassenachs*," Angus said. "Ye canna understand."

"We can argue the idiocy of clan dynamics later," Logan impatiently said. "Graeme, are you sure about this?"

His brother nodded. "Grant and I used to be friends with Roddy when we were younger, and . . ."

"Stupid," Grant said in a sardonic tone.

Graeme flashed him a smile. "Aye. We went there a few times with Roddy to lark about. It is mostly a ruin, but Roddy said the old place would always mean a lot to the Murrays, especially Mungo. He was determined to get it back one day for the family."

"Good luck with that," Alec said.

"Yet another reason to hate Lord Riddick and your family," Nick said to him.

Logan cocked an eyebrow at Braden. "Is Joseph all right?"

His brother nodded. "Yes, but he needs to get into a hot bath, and then to bed with a posset."

"Mrs. Webb and I can take care of that," Victoria said.

Logan stood. When he started to hand the boy over to his aunt, Joseph clung tight.

"Son, you have to go with Aunt Vicky. I have to find Donella."

"They're bad men, Papa. They might hurt you."

"Och, laddie, nothing can hurt me."

"That's true," Nick said. "Your papa is a giant, remember? And giants can do anything."

Reluctantly, Joseph allowed himself to be handed over.

"All right," Logan said. "Braden, you're coming with us, in case Donella . . . needs your help."

Braden's eyes flashed with sympathy. "Understood."

"Graeme knows the layout of the place, so he'll come, along with Nick and Alec. We'll take a few of the grooms, too."

"What about me?" Grant asked.

"I'd like you and Angus to stay here with the women and children. I won't leave them unguarded. Edie, Victoria, and Lady Reese can manage the party and hopefully quell any gossip."

"I'm coming with you," Edie said.

Alec looked stunned. "The hell you are."

She ignored him to stare meaningfully at Logan. "Donella might need me. A woman, I mean."

Logan wanted to deny the implication, but Braden touched his arm. "It's not a bad idea. And I'll fetch my surgery bag, in case we need a few things on the spot."

"All right," Logan gritted out.

"I don't want my wife in the middle of this," Alec objected.

Edie patted his arm. "You don't have a choice, dearest. But I promise not to get in the way."

Alec fumed but obviously knew it was a losing battle.

Logan was now in a fever of impatience. "You all know what to do. If you need to change clothes, do it now. Alec and I will scare up some weapons, and we'll meet at the stables in fifteen minutes."

"You'll bring Donella home?" Joseph anxiously asked from the shelter of Victoria's arms.

He smiled at his son. "I will."

"Promise, Papa," Joseph insisted.

He kissed the lad's forehead. "I promise."

Chapter Thirty

The carriage came to a rocking halt.

"We're here," Mungo Murray announced.

Here was unknown, since Donella still had the hood of the wretched old cloak—which smelled like a horse blanket—pulled over her face.

Thankfully, her head had stopped ringing. When Mungo's men had hoisted her out the window, she'd panicked and started to flail her arms. One of her abductors had lost his grip on her shoulders, and she'd clunked her head on the window frame.

She'd been only dimly aware of her passage through the gardens and into a carriage. By the time her head had started to clear, the carriage was already moving.

Mungo had pitched a fit, berating his men for hurting her. That had prompted defensive protests and claims that it was *her* fault for not meekly submitting to her abduction.

Donella had finally snapped at the whole lot of them, forcefully reminding Mungo that he would face the combined wrath of the Kendrick and Riddick families. The old man had pulled the hood back down over her face and threatened to gag her if she didn't *shut her gob*.

She'd spent the rest of the short ride worrying about Logan and her family. They would be wild with fear and furious at Mungo's audacity. Both Logan and Alasdair would be vowing bloody murder, and Mungo was obviously in no mood to back down, either. It was up to Donella to prevent mayhem, murder, and a clan feud, yet she hadn't a clue how to do so.

Anything she might say to Mungo at this point had the potential to make things even worse.

The carriage door opened. Someone grabbed her arms and hauled her up.

"Have a care, ye chowderhead," Mungo barked. "She's my future daughter-in-law, not an old piece of mutton."

Oh, dear. Things were definitely going to get sticky.

After she heard Mungo climb out, Donella pretended to stumble, slapping a hand down onto the leather cushions.

"It might be easier if I could see where I'm going," she meekly suggested.

"Ye promise not to make a fuss?" asked the man holding her arm.

"Yes. I promise."

A moment later, he gingerly pulled back her hood.

"Thank you, ah . . ."

"Rory, miss," he said with a shy, gape-toothed grin.

Donella recognized him from the Perth Bridge. Fortunately, he wasn't the brute that had tried to drag her from the carriage. Rory seemed quite friendly for a kidnapper.

She'd take allies wherever she could find them.

"That's ever so much better, Rory," she said with a winsome smile.

He blushed.

"What the hell are ye doin'?" barked Mungo from outside. "Get the lass out here."

Carefully, Rory helped her down, holding on as she found her balance. She teetered a bit, since she'd lost a shoe during her abduction and the ground was freezing.

Donella blinked up at the tall structure that loomed over them, lit by the flare of torches. "It's Dun Manor."

Mungo, who'd been conferring with one of his men, stomped over. He gave Rory a shove.

"Why the hell did ye take off her hood, ye ninny?" he snapped.

"You needn't bark," Donella said. "It's not as if I can tell anyone where you've taken me."

"Poor lass canna do a thing about it," Rory said with a sympathetic grimace. "Besides, you said to take care of her. We dinna want her trippin' and hurtin' herself again, do we?"

"Might I point out that you are trespassing on Clan Graham property," she added. "As a member of that clan, I demand you vacate these premises immediately and return me to Breadie Manor."

Mungo sneered at her. "It used to be Murray land, and it'll be ours again. On my word as a Murray and a Highlander, we'll take it back."

He took her arm and marched her through the open door of the keep. For an elderly man, Mungo was surprisingly strong. Donella had counted at least three other men, and there might be more lurking about the premises.

Her only chance for escape was through the use of her wits.

Built well over four hundred years ago, the building was more a keep than a manor—an old tower house with a great hall, and decrepit spiral staircase leading up to probably even more decrepit upper floors. An ancient banquet table stood in the middle of the hall, and some benches and a few old settles were in front of the empty hearth. It had the unfortunate odor of a place now primarily home to wildlife.

Donella couldn't help but wonder why Mungo was so intent on regaining the old place. Estates and holdings had changed hands so many times over the centuries as a result of clan feuds or financial mismanagement. Dun Manor had been abandoned long ago and hardly seemed worth the fuss.

She lifted her skirts to avoid a pile of droppings. "It might more properly be called Dung Manor."

"And that be the fault of the Grahams," Mungo groused. "The Murrays would nae have let it fall into ruin like this."

"Well, you're welcome to it, as far as I'm concerned," she retorted.

In the light of the torches carried by his men, she could see the crafty gleam in the old man's gaze. "Aye, we'll get it back. And ye along with it."

"Over my dead body, you will."

When his wrinkled features pulled tight with malice, she mentally kicked herself. The situation was fraught enough without petty comments. Still, the entire situation was so ridiculous and annoying that she found it almost impossible to hold herself back.

"Rory, get ye out and take care of the horses." Mungo jerked his head at one of his other men. "Charlie, take the lass and follow me."

Rory threw Donella a morose look as Charlie clamped a rough hand on her shoulder and steered her forward in Mungo's wake.

When a cold wind whipped around her legs, she glanced up to see a gaping hole in the timbered roof. It struck her that there would probably be breaches in some of the outer walls, too. It was a miracle the place was still standing.

At the back of the dimly lit hall, Mungo opened a door. He took Donella from Charlie, and ushered her in.

It was a small room, brightly lit compared to the hall. She had to blink to properly focus, and was not presented with a reassuring picture.

Kitted out as a tidy and rather comfortable bedroom, a large bed piled high with blankets and pillows was tucked against the wall. Several branches of candles shed a soft glow over the room. Two wooden chairs were pulled up in front of the hearth, with its cozily burning peat fire. There was even a carpet on the stone floor that looked quite new.

Standing on that carpet was Roddy Murray, a sheepish grin splitting his genial features.

"Hullo, lass," he said tentatively.

Donella turned on Mungo and glared at him.

"No," she said through clenched teeth. "Absolutely not."

Mungo barked out a laugh. "After all these years, ye'll finally be doin' right by my boy. And then in the mornin', we'll be off to the parson to make it formal."

"Logan will kill you for this," she said, "as will my brother and cousin. And you don't even want to *think* about what they'll do to poor Roddy."

Mungo shrugged. "Nay. Ye'll be a Murray, and Riddick will have to go along with it, if he doesna want ye labeled a whore."

"Da!" exclaimed Roddy. "Ye canna be callin' Donella a—"

"Shut it, ye ninny," his father ordered. "Ye only have one job tonight."

"But—"

Donella rounded on Roddy. "Were you actually in on this plan to kidnap me, Roddy?"

His eyes went wide with alarm. "I, uh . . ."

"Tell me the truth, or I'll throttle you." She thought she might be able to kill him with her bare hands, at this point.

Mungo snorted. "He'd nothin' to do with it. Ye know he's a witless fool. Why I had to be saddled with the likes of him as my heir is a sad mystery."

"That's not very nice, Da," Roddy said in a wounded voice.

Argh.

"Your father is *not* a nice man, Roddy. He and his men kidnapped me at gunpoint."

Wrath gathered on Roddy's handsome features. "Ye took Donella against her will?"

"I had to, ye booby. Do ye think she would come otherwise?"

Donella pressed the side of her head and tried to look fragile. "One of his men even hit me. It's a wonder I'm still alive."

Mungo snorted. "Och, ye bumped yer stupid head because ye wouldna come quietly."

"Ye hurt Donella?" Roddy gently led her to one of the chairs. "Here, sit ye down, lass." Then he glared at his father. "Ye shouldna done that, Da."

"She shouldna resisted," he retorted.

"I was so frightened," she said in a quavering voice. "Roddy, I just want to go home."

When Roddy glowered at his father, Mungo stomped up to his son and whacked him in the shoulder. "Yer a Murray, are ye not? So, start actin' like one. Take what's yers and be done with it."

"But—"

"The lass gave herself to ye, did she not?"

"Aye," Roddy said. "She did."

"That's entirely beside the point," Donella indignantly butted in. "Besides, I'm now—"

"Well, ye did, lass," Roddy interrupted. "Ye canna deny it."

"She denied it and called us liars," Mungo said. "I'll have our honor restored if I have to lock ye in here all night."

Donella shot to her feet. "Now, see here, you old goat—"

"Get the job done." Mungo pointed a gnarled finger at his son. "Ye owe it to yer family's honor."

With considerable alacrity, he stormed out. The door slammed, and a key turned in the lock.

"Blast." She sank into the chair and covered her face. She was cold, tired, and her head was pounding again.

She'd gotten herself into this mess by telling lies all those years ago, and now she'd get herself out of it by telling the truth.

Roddy cautiously approached. "Can I do something for ye, lass?"

"Yes, you can get me out of here."

"But my da locked the door, ye ken."

Really, the poor man was hopeless.

Then he brightened. "Can I fetch ye a glass a wine?"

"I suppose it couldn't hurt. And you wouldn't happen to have an extra sock or slipper lying about, would you?" She wriggled her stocking foot at him.

Looking concerned, he hurried to pour a goblet of red wine from a pitcher. Then he dug around in a small pack stowed in a corner, and unearthed a pair of thick woolen socks.

"I won't hurt ye, Donella," he earnestly said as he returned to her. "I promise."

"I know." She thankfully pulled on one of the socks. It was too large and smelled rather musty, but was blessedly warm.

"But my da's right. Ye betrayed me and dishonored my family. Da just wants to make things right, and I want to do right by ye, too. I still have feelin's for ye, Donella. Yer the bonniest lass I ever did meet."

She hated what she had to do. "Please sit, Roddy. We need to talk."

He perched on the edge of the other chair, looking as boyishly eager as he had ten years ago.

"Roddy, I'm truly sorry I lied about us all those years ago. It was very wrong."

He tilted his head. "Why did ye tell such a great fib, lass? I knew ye didn't love Gilbride. Ye loved me."

She winced. "I didn't love Alasdair, but I didn't love you, either. I was mad at Alasdair for running away from me. You were very nice to me, and I appreciated that."

He blinked. "Ye mean, ye didna have feelin's for me?"

"Not in the way that you wanted me to. Besides, I *was* betrothed to Alasdair. For my family's honor, I could not go back on that vow."

"But ye did canoodle with me, so ye must like me a little bit. Ye were happy that night, were ye not?" he finished on a hopeful note.

That night hadn't been terrible. Awkward, yes, and the deed over so quickly it had surprised her. Roddy had been kind, however, and she'd needed that kindness.

But it had been *nothing* like her experience with Logan. Their time together was imprinted on her body and soul.

"Roddy—"

"Donella, ye have to marry me to set it right, or both our families will be dishonored when the truth comes out. I'll nae be responsible for that. We'll get married, just like we should have done all those years ago."

When he beamed at her, so pleased with his solution, she knew only the blunt truth would serve.

"Roddy, I never wanted to dishonor you or your family, and I will speak to my uncle and try to make amends for what I've done to the Murrays. But I *cannot* marry you."

"But why not?"

"Because I'm already married."

Roddy's expression went completely blank. "Uh, what's that ye say?"

"I married Logan Kendrick on Boxing Day."

"Are ye sure?" he asked after an excruciatingly long pause. "Because I heard not a word about any such thing."

She had to resist the impulse to bash him over the head with the pitcher.

"Of course I'm sure. We decided not to tell anyone because it was, well, very sudden. And my family wished to have a formal betrothal party on Hogmanay, and then a big clan wedding at Blairgal Castle. We didn't wish to ruin the fun for them."

He stared at her as if she'd sprouted a writhing pile of snakes from her head. Donella couldn't blame him. Even to her ears it sounded exceedingly lame.

She and Logan hadn't set out that day to get married—at least *she* hadn't. But Logan's curricle had somehow ended up in front of a kirk in a nearby village, and somehow he'd convinced her that getting married immediately would be a grand idea. He'd pointed out that it had been her suggestion in the first place, one that would nicely serve to eliminate the fuss and bother of a large wedding later on.

The idea had made a crazy sort of sense at the time. Before she'd had a chance to truly think about it, he'd rustled up the parson, who'd rustled up a few witnesses, and Donella had found herself transformed into Mrs. Logan Kendrick in short order. It wasn't a wedding across the anvil, but just-barely not.

As soon as they left the kirk, she'd begun to panic. Not about marrying him. The moment when she'd sworn her vows to Logan, she'd felt incandescent with joy. She'd panicked about her family's reaction, especially her uncle's. Their families hadn't even formally announced their betrothal, and yet she and Logan had snuck off like thieves in the night.

Donella had lost her nerve and made Logan promise to keep it a secret until after Hogmanay. Then everything had turned into a complete disaster, which only served her right. If they'd told the truth in the first place, none of this would have happened.

The wages of sin were very unfortunate, indeed.

She braced for Roddy's fury. God knows she deserved it.

Instead, he simply frowned for several long moments before sighing. "Well, ye did seem taken with Kendrick that day I ran into ye. I suppose it's nae surprise."

"You're not angry?" she cautiously asked.

"Donella, I could never be angry with ye. Yer the nicest, prettiest lass in the world."

Now she felt like the vilest person in the world. "I'm truly sorry about this, Roddy. And I meant it when I said I would talk to my uncle to try and set things right by you."

He cut her a lopsided smile. "Dinna fash yerself, lass. To tell ye the truth, it was always my da making the big fuss. I always knew ye were too good for me."

That choked her up. "I'm sure you'll find the perfect girl someday, Roddy. In the meantime, we do need to tell your father I'm married."

Roddy jolted a bit. "Mayhap it would be best if we stayed in here for a while. At least till my da settles down."

"That is *not* a good idea. I know my husband is already searching for me. If I don't get back to Breadie Manor forthwith, there's no accounting for what might occur."

"Er . . ." he started.

"Roddy, if you don't get me home quickly, we *will* have a clan feud on our hands."

He looked morose. "Yer right. I keep forgetting that bit."

She rose. "Then let's go talk to your father."

He followed her to the door. "Ye'll explain it to him, won't ye?"

"Yes, dear. I promise. Now, we need to hurry."

He gave her a relieved grin and then started banging on the door. "Da, we need to talk to ye. It's important."

When they were met by silence, Roddy banged louder. "Da, open the door."

"Mr. Murray, we need to speak with you," Donella shouted.

"Have ye done the deed, lad?" Mungo finally yelled back.

Roddy grimaced. "Da, I canna do it. It would be a sin, ye ken."

"What the hell are ye talkin' about, ye daft fool?"

"He's talking about the fact that I'm already married,"

Donella said. "And if you do not let me out of this room, there will be hell to pay when my husband finds you."

A key rattled and the door flew open.

"What do ye mean yer already married?" Mungo roared.

Roddy winced. "Och, Da. Yer breakin' our ears."

"I'll break yer head, ye moron. Get out here and explain yerselves."

Roddy escorted Donella into the hall, making a wide berth around his father.

Fortunately, someone had lit a fire in the hall's giant hearth and pulled one of the settles in front of it. Roddy silently urged her to sit.

When his father joined them, Roddy hastily retreated into a dark corner.

Donella couldn't truly blame him. Mungo was ready to explode.

"Explain yerself, lass," he snapped.

"As I said, I am already married. My husband will be happy to prove it, once we return to Breadie Manor."

"And who is this mysterious husband?"

"Logan Kendrick."

Mungo's face turned splotchy with rage. "The bastard who shot my men and threw them over the side of the bridge?"

"Sir, please stop shouting," Donella said. "And might I remind *you* that those same men attacked us and tried to kidnap me."

"Because ye shamed my family and my puir lad. I was only trying to put things right."

"Da, she's married," Roddy said. "There's nothin' ye—"

"Shut it," his father snapped. "If ye were half the man ye needed to be, this wouldna happened."

"Your son is a decent, kindhearted man," Donella retorted. "Which is more than I can say for you."

"Then why did ye treat him so badly those years ago, ye stuck-up—"

"Another word, Murray," a harsh voice interrupted, "and I'll put a bullet in your head."

Donella jumped to her feet, overcome with relief. "Logan!"

He stood in the doorway, looking like Zeus in a greatcoat. Instead of thunderbolts, however, he was armed with a pistol, aimed right at Mungo.

.Mungo's men yanked out their pistols and aimed them at Logan.

"Everyone, stop!" Donella shouted. "No guns."

"Best listen to the lass," barked another familiar voice.

She spun around again to see Alasdair advance from a dark corner of the hall, his weapon pointed at Roddy.

"I've got your son in my sights, Murray," her cousin said. "If anyone makes a move, I'll shoot him. So stand your men down."

Mungo snorted with disgust. "Ye may as well shoot him. The lad's useless."

"Da!" Roddy exclaimed.

"Everyone put those blasted weapons down," Donella ordered. "I'm perfectly safe, and you're all just making things worse."

"Get out of the way, love," Logan said.

He'd lowered his weapon but looked enraged enough to kill both Roddy and Mungo with his bare hands. He stalked across the room. Behind him followed Lord Arnprior and Graeme, both pointing their pistols at Mungo's henchmen.

Darting around the table, Donella intercepted her husband. "I'm fine, Logan. Truly."

For a moment, she feared he'd bowl right past her, but he came to a halt. He loomed over her, his breathing fast and harsh as he inspected her face.

"They hurt you," he ground out.

She rested a hand on his chest. "It's nothing, I promise."

Logan swallowed hard, then raised a gloved hand to gently touch her temple. "Your poor head, lass."

"I bumped it when they hauled me out the window. It was an accident, really. No one meant to hurt me."

"When Joseph said you'd been hurt, I—" He pulled her into his arms. "I thought I'd lost ye, lass. That would have killed me."

Donella sank gratefully into his embrace. "Joseph saw that?"

"Aye, that's how we found you. He followed you out the window, and Graeme figured out the rest."

She drew back to search his face. "Please tell me Joseph is all right."

"He's fine." Then Logan directed an irate glare at Mungo. "No thanks to you. My boy fell off the back of your bloody carriage. He could have killed himself."

Donella turned to scowl at Mungo, too. "Really, sir, this nonsense must stop. It's one thing to kidnap me, but to endanger the life of a little boy—"

"I had no bloody idea there was a bairn on the carriage." He waved his arms, which brought his pistol back up. "Ye canna blame me for that."

All the pistols went back up.

"No guns," Donella again ordered.

Everyone ignored her.

Logan moved her aside. "Blame you, Murray? We're just getting started."

"Best stand down, Murray," Arnprior said in a stern voice. "You won't be picking a feud with just the Grahams. This is Kendrick business now, too."

Mungo sneered at the earl but kept his pistol pointed at Logan. "Ask me if I care."

Fed up, Donella shoved Logan out of the way and marched up to Mungo.

"Christ, Donella," barked her husband. "Get back—"

She spun and pointed a finger at him. "Stay right there and put down that stupid pistol."

He gave her a disbelieving look but lowered his weapon.

She turned back to Mungo. "You and the rest of your idiot men will do likewise. If you do not, I'll report you *all* to the Glasgow magistrate for kidnapping me. And I will not tolerate any more ridiculous clan feuding."

When Mungo started to argue, she chopped down a hand. "No, sir. This has to end here."

"It's not up to ye, lass," he barked, "and ye canna just dismiss a matter of honor."

"Give it up, Donella," Alasdair said. "There's no reasoning with the old fool."

"Shut up, Alasdair." Then she turned back to Mungo. "Mr. Murray, I am deeply sorry for the shame I brought to your family, especially to Roddy. That was poorly done of me, and I sincerely apologize. But you know this is about more than that. It's about the bad blood that has been between our families for decades. I will do whatever I can to help resolve your grievance, but the matter is truly between you and my uncle."

Something like grief and shame flashed through Mungo's eyes and, for a moment, he looked very frail.

Then he straightened up. "Ye hurt my boy, ye ken."

"I know, and I truly feel awful about that."

"Hurt your son? That's bloody rich," snorted Alasdair. "You kidnapped my cousin with the clear intention of taking advantage of her and forcing her hand."

"Nae," Roddy said earnestly. "Donella is a married woman. I'd never touch a married woman."

There was yet another fraught pause before Alasdair turned to look at Donella. "Married?"

Lord Arnprior looked at his brother. "Married?"

"Oh, hell," Logan muttered.

"Ye all could have told us, and saved more than a wee bit of trouble," Mungo said in a surly tone.

"You're going to blame this on us?" Alasdair asked with disbelief. "You are a bloody idiot."

Mungo's response was predictable. He jabbed a gnarled forefinger into Alasdair's chest, and the two commenced yelling.

"Stop it right now," Lord Arnprior thundered. Then he glared at Logan. "I'll deal with you later, little brother. For now, I will sit down with Mr. Murray and try to resolve this ridiculous situation. If nothing else, we can agree that this unfortunate set of events could have been avoided if you and Donella had told us the truth."

Donella winced. "I'm sorry. It seemed like a good idea at the time."

Logan wrapped an arm around her from behind, pulling her gently against him. "It's my fault, Nick. I talked her into it."

"I have no doubt," his lordship replied. "Now, please take Donella to Braden so he can check her injuries."

"It's safe to come in, I take it," called a sardonic feminine voice from the doorway.

Donella gaped at Alasdair. "You brought Eden with you?"

"She didn't give me a choice," he replied in a sour tone.

"Come, lass," Logan murmured. "Let Braden have a look at your head."

He steered Donella to one of the wooden settles.

"You're looking a little worse for wear, pet," Eden said as she and Braden joined them. "Are you sure you're all right?"

"It's just a little bump."

Braden put his bag down and gave her a kind smile. "Let's give it a quick check before we leave."

Logan held Donella's hand while Braden examined her, asking a few questions. Then the young man cleaned the small cut with a tincture and a soft cloth.

Eden regarded the other menfolk with a jaundiced eye. "Are they going to argue all night?"

"Apparently," Logan said. "I suggest you ignore them."

"You there," she said in an imperious tone to one of Mungo's men. "Miss Haddon . . . er, Mrs. Kendrick . . . could use a drink. Please bring her a glass of whatever you have there."

Mungo broke off from his discussion with Arnprior. "Dinna be givin' my men orders, ye daft *Sassenach*."

"And don't you be insulting my wife," Alasdair growled.

"Gentlemen, please," Arnprior said in a long-suffering voice. "If you will stick to the point, we might manage to get home before New Year's Day."

"I take it my husband has been causing the usual trouble?" Eden said to Donella in a wry tone.

"What do you think?" Donella replied.

"Is she all right?" Logan anxiously asked Braden.

"She's fine." He smiled at Donella. "But if your head is still aching when we get home, I'll mix up a powder for that."

"Speaking of that," Logan started.

He was interrupted by raised voices. Mungo and Alasdair were going at it again, the old man waving his fist in Alasdair's direction.

Lord Arnprior shook his head in disgust and stalked over to join Logan and Donella's group.

"You'd best get the ladies home," he said. "This probably will take all night."

"Do you want me to knock some sense into my husband's head first?" Eden asked.

"Best not try," Logan replied. "He's gone full Highlander."

"As has Mungo," Donella said.

"Yer cousin dishonored my whole family with her lies," Mungo yelled at Alasdair. "I'll nae be forgettin' that."

"She was just an innocent girl at the time, you barmy old coot," Alasdair exclaimed, "and your son took advantage of her. I should thrash the moron right now."

"Oh, dear," Eden said.

Roddy had been hanging morosely back by the fireplace, but now he stormed up to Alasdair. "I did nae such thing. The lass took advantage of *me,* ye ken."

Alasdair launched himself at Roddy, bringing him down to the floor with him. They started to grapple and exchange blows.

Cursing under his breath, Arnprior stalked toward them, but one of Mungo's henchmen darted up from behind and gave the earl a shove, almost knocking him off his feet.

Arnprior quickly recovered and spun around, drilling a fist to his attacker's jaw. The man staggered but shook it off and charged in for more as Graeme yelled and launched himself at another one of Mungo's men.

Within seconds, the hall was transformed into a melee.

"Well, I'd best go help sort this out," Logan said.

Donella grabbed for him but missed.

"Blast," she muttered.

"Good thing I brought lots of bandages," Braden said.

Eden sat back down. "This might take a while, so you might as well have a seat, old girl."

"I have no intention of spending any more time in this dreadful place," Donella said. "Does either of you have a pistol?"

Braden's brows shot up. "I don't think—"

Eden reached inside her cloak and extracted a small pistol. "Maybe you can get one of them in the backside."

"Don't tempt me."

Donella marched into the middle of the hall. Then she cocked the pistol, pointed it at the ceiling, and fired.

The boom reverberated through the hall, freezing everyone. The flock of pigeons roosting in the timbers instantly took flight, performing the natural function that one might expect from startled birds.

Bird droppings splattered down onto most of the combatants. Mungo and Alasdair took precise hits to the tops of their heads, while Logan—who'd been wrestling with two of Mungo's men—got a generous splattering on his shoulder and the back of his coat.

"What the hell?" Alasdair yelped.

"You will cease acting like Scottish nincompoops," Donella shouted. "I have had *enough*. My head hurts, I'm tired, and I want to go home. So you will all stop fighting right now."

"All right, lass," Logan said, trying not to laugh. "Dinna fash yerself."

"I'll fash you," she threatened.

"God, I'm covered in the stuff," Alasdair said as he tried to wipe his head with his sleeve.

Eden marched up to him. "Leave Roddy alone and go clean up. Braden has some cloths you can use."

Lord Arnprior, who had managed to escape the avian deluge, flashed Donella a grin. "Well done, lass. And welcome to the family. You'll fit right in."

"That's what I'm afraid of."

Logan came over and tried to wrap his arms around her.

Donella pushed him away. "You are covered with pigeon dung. I have no intention of hugging you."

"Och, getting hit with bird dung is a sign of good luck, ye ken," he teased. "Besides, your cloak is smelling none too fresh, love."

"I know. I've been wearing it all night."

Logan shrugged out of his coat while glancing at his brother. "You'll manage the rest?"

Arnprior nodded. "You and Braden get Donella home. We'll join you shortly."

Logan took Donella's arm and started to lead her out.

"Good-bye, Miss Donella," Roddy called forlornly. "I wish ye well."

"Can you wait one moment?" she asked Logan.

She hurried back to Roddy, who was looking rather worse for wear. She went up on her tiptoes and gave him a gingerly hug.

"Thank you for trying to help me, Roddy. I just know you're going to find a nice girl someday who will love you."

He sighed. "Not as nice as ye, Miss Donella."

"Don't give up." Perhaps she could ask Lady Reese to find Roddy a wife. Her ladyship was quite good at matchmaking.

"Are you finished, lass?" Alasdair sardonically asked. "Because Logan's starting to look fashed by your tender leave-taking."

Eden whacked his arm. "You, stop being such an oaf."

Donella flashed her a smile and hurried back to join Logan. "I'm ready now."

His smile was wry. "You're a kind woman, love, but I hope you don't make a habit of hugging former swains."

"Don't be silly. I'm a married woman now."

His gaze flashed with heat. "That you are."

They went out to the Gilbrides' carriage. Logan helped her in, then climbed up and settled beside her on the plush seat. Braden took the opposite bench, and they drove off.

Donella sighed contentedly and snuggled into her husband's arms. "Thank God that's over."

"Don't ever scare me like that again, lass. I don't think I could take it."

"Yes, I'll try not to be kidnapped again," she sardonically replied.

He tipped her chin up. "Donella . . ." He glanced across at his brother.

"Don't mind me," Braden said. "I'm going to take a nap, and I suggest Donella do the same." He wedged himself into the corner and tipped his hat over his eyes.

In the gentle light of the carriage lamps, Logan's gaze

was solemn. "I'm sorry for this, my love. I should have done a better job of protecting you."

"Logan, no one could have predicted this nonsense."

"No, but I should have been with you. I promise I will never keep away from you like that again."

Donella curled a hand into his cravat. "I was the one who kept turning you away, remember?"

"Och, I should have climbed through your window. It worked every other time."

There was a choking sound from Braden's corner.

Donella did her best to ignore her brother-in-law. "Why did you stay away? It's not like you."

"I didn't want to put undue pressure on you. I'd already done too much of that."

"I thought you were having second thoughts," she softly said.

He cupped a hand around her chin and brought his face down to hers. "I *love* you. I started falling in love with you that first night, when we were on the run. I'd never met such a brave, bonny lass. I don't deserve you, Donella, and that's the truth."

"Here, here," came a murmur from the opposite corner.

"Braden, shut up," Logan said, exasperated.

Donella was torn between tears and laughter—grateful tears and joyous laughter. "I love you, too. And thank you for coming to rescue me."

He pressed a sweet, lingering kiss to her lips, then kissed her eyelids where a few tears had gathered. "I will always be there for you, my darling girl. Never doubt it."

"I won't."

Logan gathered her close. "Now try to rest. We'll be home soon."

Donella closed her eyes.

It seemed she'd only dozed a few minutes before the carriage rolled into the stable yard behind Breadie Manor.

Logan assisted her down, steadying her as she found her balance.

"We'd best go through the kitchen gardens," Braden said. "We all look rather a mess."

"Especially me," she said with a huge yawn.

The housekeeper was waiting at the back entrance and ushered them into the blessedly warm kitchen, where a few footmen were putting away the last of the silver. The spacious room was tidy and showed little evidence that a rousing party had been in progress a short time ago.

"All is well?" Logan asked Mrs. Webb.

"Aye, sir. Lady Arnprior is waiting for ye—"

"Here I am." Victoria hurried over to throw her arms around Donella. "Are you all right?"

Donella hugged her back. "I'm fine. Everyone is fine. The others should be returning shortly."

"Nick stayed behind to get everything sorted," Logan said. "He was gearing up for a grand lecture when we left."

Victoria smiled. "Of course he was."

Logan ticked up an eyebrow. "I thought the party would be in full swing until morning, as usual. How did you clear the place out?"

"You can thank Lady Reese. When people began to notice that half the family had gone missing, she announced that the lobster patties had apparently been tainted, so any partakers best return home immediately. As you can imagine, it had the desired effect."

"Brilliant," Logan said with a grin. "Though I have the feeling that Gilbride parties might not be so well attended in the future."

"Eden will be happy to hear that," Donella said.

"How's Joseph?" Logan asked Victoria.

"Waiting up for you with Angus, because none of us could get him to sleep. He's in Donella's room. He insisted on staying there."

Logan took Donella's hand. "We'll go up right away."

As they climbed the stairs, he flashed her a wry smile. "Ready to be a mother, lass?"

"I'm more than ready to be Joseph's mother."

He stopped at the top of the stairs and pressed a heartfelt kiss to her forehead. "Thank you for loving him. And for loving me."

"Joseph is easy to love." She smiled. "Surprisingly, so are you."

He snorted. "Cheeky lass."

When they reached the bedroom, Donella quietly opened the door and stuck her head inside. Joseph was lying down but shot up when he saw her.

"Donella, you're home!"

He was about to throw off the covers, but Angus, who was sitting in a chair next to the bed, gently restrained him. "Ye'll catch a cold, lad. They'll come to ye."

Donella hurried over, briefly hugging Angus before reaching down to fold Joseph into her arms. He burrowed against her with a tight little sob.

"I was so afraid when I saw those bad men take you," he said in a teary voice.

She patted his back. "I'm fine, dearest, and I understand I have you to thank for my rescue. I want to hear all about it in the morning."

After exchanging a few quiet words with Logan, Angus left the room.

Logan joined her and Joseph. "Aye, the brave lad is definitely the hero of the night."

The boy pulled out of her embrace to throw himself into his father's arms. "Thank you for bringing Donella home, Papa."

"Och, laddie, both of us will always come home to ye," Logan gruffly said as he fiercely hugged his son.

"What happened? Are Uncle Nick and Uncle Graeme and Uncle Braden all right?"

"Everyone's fine. I'll tell you the whole story in the morning. Now, though, I want you to lie down and go to sleep. It's very late."

Joseph cracked a huge yawn. "I couldn't go to sleep before you got home." Then his eyes popped wide. "Oh, this is your bed, Donella."

"You stay right there, dearest." She plumped his pillows and helped him slide under the covers.

"Will you lie down with me a bit?" the boy shyly asked.

Donella's eyes stung. "Of course I will."

"You too, Papa."

Logan made a suspicious, throat-clearing noise before sitting on the edge of the bed to yank off his boots.

Donella dispensed with the remains of her footwear, dropped her ghastly cloak on the floor, and climbed onto the bed. Joseph snuggled against her. Logan spooned her from behind, reaching around to hold them both in a strong but tender embrace.

The little boy soon fell asleep. Out in the hall, the long-case clock struck the first notes of the approaching dawn.

Logan kissed the top of Donella's head. "A good New Year to you, Mrs. Kendrick," he whispered.

It was better than good. All things considered, it had been the best Hogmanay of her life. "And to you, Mr. Kendrick."

A few minutes later, she drifted to sleep in her husband's loving arms.

Epilogue

January 1820
Blairgal Castle

The Twelfth Night ball was in full carouse, and the sounds of celebration drifted up from the ballroom. Donella heard the faint skirl of the Highland reels and the echoes of boisterous revelry.

But here on the highest parapet, the music of the spheres held reign. The stars were bright as comets, and the cold breeze snapped the heraldic flags on Blairgal's turrets. In front of her stretched the land of her ancestors, glittering like a sugary confection under a blanket of snow. The Trossachs rose in the distance, rugged in the darkness, like silent, eternal giants.

Leaving for the convent three years ago, Donella had thought she'd never see this vista again. It had been a quiet sorrow, and a sacrifice she'd been determined to make. Now the beauty of her home stretched in front of her like a dream magically come to life.

"Are you warm enough, Mrs. Kendrick?" Logan murmured in her ear.

Donella enjoyed the feel of his brawny body against the

curve of her backside. After two weeks of marriage, she was *very* familiar with her husband's body, as he was with hers.

"Yes, thank you. How could I not be when I am wrapped in such a magnificent cloak?"

The fur-lined, velvet cloak was just one of the wedding presents Logan had showered on her until she'd finally put a stop to it. Gifts were lovely, but she truly didn't care about frilly bonnets or pretty bracelets or any of the other fripperies he wished to bestow upon her. Donella only cared that they were finally together.

"You're the one who should be cold," she added. "You're wearing a kilt."

"Och, it's positively balmy here compared to Canada, love. And I've got you to keep me warm."

When he pulled her even closer, she choked out a laugh. Even through their clothing, she could feel a formidable erection pressing against her bottom.

"If you think I'm doing *that* up here," she said, "you are quite out of your mind. I'm a respectably married woman. I don't engage in reckless behavior anymore."

"You were reckless enough to let me climb into your bedroom even after we were married."

"I suppose I can make an exception on occasion, but only when the weather is better. I don't want you slipping on icy windowsills."

"No fear of that. Speaking of ice, Joseph had fun skating this afternoon. He seems to be much happier, don't you think?"

Donella wriggled around to face him. A loving smile curved up the edges of his mouth, but she sensed his latent worry. "He had a splendid time, as did your brother. However, you and the rest of the family were nervous hens."

When Uncle Riddick had discovered that she and Logan had snuck off to get married, he'd insisted on throwing a formal ball on Twelfth Night to properly celebrate their union. Eden and the castle staff had instantly sprung into action to pull off a grand house party and ball on short notice. Since the Kendrick family's arrival en masse a few days ago, it had been a non-stop series of activities, each more festive than the next.

This afternoon's treat had been a skating party on the small pond behind the castle. Trestle tables had been set up, loaded with cakes, pastries, hot chocolate, and mulled wine, and a raging bonfire had allowed the skaters to get warm.

Joseph had ignored the sweets in his eagerness to don his new skates. Logan, however, had kept him back until he'd tested the ice with time-consuming caution. Since the pond was no more than five feet deep at any given location, some thought his concern a bit excessive. But given the Kendrick family's tragic history, Donella had understood. She'd kept quiet while her husband carefully ensured the ice was solid.

Finally, Lord Arnprior had impatiently ordered Logan to cease stomping about like a lummox, and moments later, uncle and nephew had taken to the ice with exuberance. Alasdair had joined them, his little daughter on his shoulders. She'd slapped her papa's head with glee as he spun in circles and taught Joseph how to skate backward.

Donella had blinked back tears at the sight of her stepson's unrestrained glee.

Every Kendrick male not on the ice had watchfully guarded the skaters, as had Lady Reese. Her ladyship had been on alert for the slightest risk. She'd even delivered a reprimand to Lord Arnprior, commanding him in stern tones to moderate his *excessive* speed. That, naturally, had triggered an argument between her ladyship and Angus, and Eden had been forced to separate the combatants.

All in all, it was a splendid day.

Logan's smile turned wry. "I know I was a bit of a nervous old biddy—"

"A bit?"

He leaned down to kiss the tip of her nose. "Cheeky lass. I still worry that he'll be overwhelmed. He's not used to being around so many people and so much fuss."

"He's not the only one," she said wryly, "but he'll be fine."

The festivities had reached their peak with tonight's huge ball. Various Haddons and members of Clans Graham and Kendrick had turned out in impressive numbers, filling the castle to the rafters.

The most surprising guests were the Murrays. Initially, Uncle Riddick had refused to even consider talking to Mungo. But Donella was determined to bury the claymore and end the stupid feud once and for all. With the support of Alasdair, she'd offered a solution—her uncle would purchase Dun Manor from the Grahams and gift it to the Murrays, specifically to Roddy. Donella had insisted on that part. The poor man deserved something for all the trouble she'd caused him.

They'd finally managed to convince Uncle Riddick to support her plan. The magnanimous gesture had stunned Mungo into a semblance of goodwill, and the truce was still holding.

"Sorry, love," Logan said. "I know you hate these massive affairs. But everyone seems to be having a splendid time, even those blasted Murrays."

"Especially Roddy. I think Lady Reese has introduced him to every eligible girl at the ball. Several seemed quite taken with him, too."

"It's amazing what even a rundown estate can do to improve one's marital prospects," her husband dryly replied.

Donella smothered a laugh. "Roddy is a very nice person, and he deserves a fine wife."

"Just as long as it's not *my* wife."

She went up on tiptoe and brushed a kiss against his lips. Logan murmured his appreciation and deepened the caress.

He left her breathless.

"Poor Roddy. I probably would have murdered him if we'd married," she finally said. "He is just a wee bit boring."

Her husband's husky laugh vibrated through her body. "I promise I'll never bore ye, lass."

"Of course not. One cannot possibly marry a Kendrick and suffer from boredom."

"We do tend to get into a spot of trouble, now and again."

"Like the twins tonight. They're cutting quite a swath through all the impressionable young ladies."

"At least they haven't broken any furniture."

She grinned. "Yet. Kade and Braden always behave themselves, though."

"I think Braden was as happy to escape the party as we were."

Their excuse to escape had been Joseph. After the dancing and the elaborate supper, the boy had begun to doze off in his chair, and Donella had begun to feel rather frazzled by all the commotion. Logan suggested they take Joseph up to bed. Braden had volunteered to read the boy a bedtime story.

Quietly, they'd left the party and snuck up the back staircase to the nursery floor.

After helping Joseph change into his nightshirt, Donella and Logan had tucked him into bed.

"Good night, Mama," the little boy had whispered after she kissed him good night.

It had been the first time he'd ever called her that, and she'd barely avoided bursting into tears.

Logan had glanced at her face and led her to their bedroom to fetch their cloaks. They'd then climbed the highest castle tower to enjoy the beauty of the winter's eve and give Donella time to regain her composure.

Sometimes, she couldn't help but reflect on the miracle that had blessed her life. She'd only met Logan two months ago, and already he seemed to know her better than she knew herself.

"Your family is truly splendid, Logan. I'm so blessed to be a part of it."

"Och, we're the lucky ones. You're the Flower of Clan Graham, after all."

"And you will find yourself sleeping in the dressing room if you insist on calling me that ridiculous name."

He laughed. "What name would you prefer then?"

"Mrs. Kendrick will suffice."

"Duly noted, wife."

She turned again in his arms, content to rest there a bit longer and gaze over the beloved landscape.

"Speaking of family," he added, "Kendrick House is feeling a little crowded these days. It's time we had a place of our own."

She glanced over her shoulder. "But what about Joseph? He loves living with your family."

"I was hoping Angus could join us, since he and the lad are so attached. Plus, it would save Nick from having the old fellow bull his way back into estate business. That is, if you wouldn't mind my grandfather living with us."

"Not at all. I enjoy his company."

"You should. The old curmudgeon is devoted to you. My entire family is devoted to you."

"I love them, too."

After a minute or so, he gave her a little nudge. "Out with it, love. What's troubling you?"

She shook her head. "You could tell?"

"I can hear the wheels turning. No more secrets, remember?"

"I do. It's just that—"

"Yes?" he gently prodded.

"I want to visit my mother in Edinburgh. I think she'd like to see me. And if she's having a lucid day, she'd be happy to know I'm married. That I finally found someone who truly loves me."

He hugged her close. "Of course, sweetheart. Whatever you want."

Donella turned again to face him. "She might not even recognize me, you know. It won't necessarily be pleasant."

He gently cupped her cheek. "Whatever happens, we'll face it. You are not alone anymore, my love. I'll always be at your side."

A quiet, deep joy suffused her soul. "I know, and I promise I will always be there for you."

His eyes glittered like the deepest of sapphires. "I'm counting on it, lass."

"And what about you, Logan?" she softly asked. "Is there anything else you want to do?"

She already had a sense of what he wanted but was reluctant to say it. Silly man, he didn't seem to realize she would go anywhere with him.

"Well . . ."

"Yes?" she prompted.

"I would like to go back to Halifax. Perhaps in a year or so. Royal is doing a splendid job with the Canadian end of things, but I suspect he and Ainsley will wish to return to Scotland soon enough, and especially after their baby is born."

"And of course you want Joseph to see his family again. His grandmother must miss him very much."

"I never want him to lose touch with her or that part of his heritage." He flashed a quick grin. "And I'm sure Marie will be very eager to meet you."

"To make sure I'm a proper mother to Joseph, no doubt," she joked.

His smile turned wry. "You wouldn't mind, then?"

She rested her hands flat on his chest. "Logan Kendrick, I would follow you to the ends of the earth. Where you and Joseph are, there lies my heart."

He blinked several times, as if he had a speck of dust in his eye.

Then he gathered her close. "I don't think I could love you more than I already do. You are my life, sweet Donella. Never forget that."

She relished the strength and comfort of his embrace and sent up a silent prayer of thanks for all the joys that had been gifted to her.

From the nearby village kirk, the bells of midnight began to toll clear and sweet, sending a benediction of beauty through the crisp winter air. The Christmas Season was finally over, and Donella's new life was just beginning.

She couldn't wait.

Connect with Us

Visit us online at
KensingtonBooks.com
to read more from your favorite authors, see books
by series, view reading group guides, and more.

for sneak peeks, chances to win books and prize packs,
and to share your thoughts with other readers.

facebook.com/kensingtonpublishing
twitter.com/kensingtonbooks

Tell us what you think!

To share your thoughts, submit a review,
or sign up for our eNewsletters, please visit:
KensingtonBooks.com/TellUs.